POINTS OF DEPARTURE

Book Three of the Fenaday and Shasti Chronicles

EDWARD MCKEOWN

Ad Astra Books

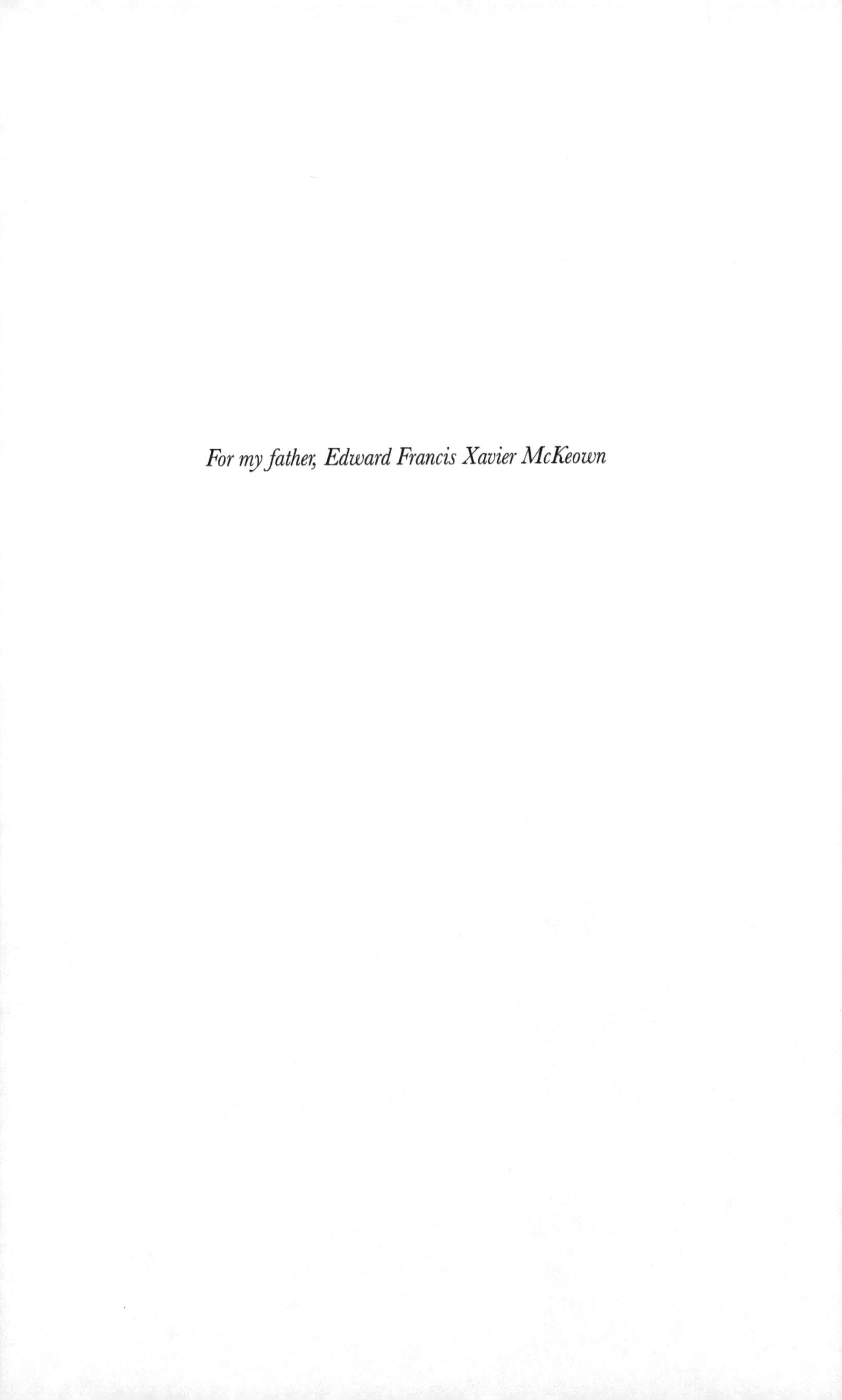

For my father, Edward Francis Xavier McKeown

Prologue

─────────────

Sidhe flung herself outward from Olympus's orbit, clear of the remaining vessels of the Olympian Self-Defense Force. Clear also of her supposed allies in the Confederate Navy. The warship carried the badly injured Robert Fenaday, former privateer and now unwilling agent for Confederate Intelligence. His mission on Olympia had been to bring down the government of Denshi, the genetically engineered assassins dominating the planet and rescue the first Confederate force sent to kill Jalgren Pard, head of Denshi.

Fenaday, weary of war and loss, knew his supply of luck was overdrawn. His wife, Commander Lisa Fenaday, had disappeared years ago in the Conchirri War, along with her scoutship, the *C.S.F.S Blackbird*. Selling off his family's shipping line, he'd taken to the stars, searching for her. All he found was empty revenge on the Conchirri.

Too many close calls later, Fenaday rescued Shasti Rainhell, a genetically engineered Olympian raised as a Denshi assassin. Beautiful, perfect Shasti, as cold as February moonlight, she'd been his right hand until the war ended and the market for privateers dried up. Confederate Intelligence, through an operative calling himself "Mandela" found them on Mars, broke and desperate. Blackmail

1

sent them on a suicide mission to the forbidden planet of Enshar, in the company of ace pilot, Telisan, and Belwin Duna, the Enshari scholar. Against all odds, they survived, destroying their near God-like enemy, the Prekak.

On that dead world, Fenaday first learned Shasti was the escaped wife of Jalgren Pard. Something new and unforeseen grew between him and Shasti as Fenaday finally laid the ghost of his wife to rest. Their friend Telisan had silently feared they were not yet free of their pasts. It proved too true.

Shasti and Fenaday returned to New Eire, wealthy, pardoned, free, and happy. Or so it seemed, until Shasti left unexpectedly. Later, Fenaday learned that "Mandela," alarmed by Olympia's military buildup, had recruited her to kill her former husband, Pard. For Shasti, Fenaday abandoned all he had won back and tried his luck again.

The delicate game of cat and mouse ended in a bloody assault by *Sidhe's* troops. Shasti chanced onto Pard's base at the same time. Fenaday discovered her locked in a losing battle with Pard. Telisan found them both later, nearly dead, in each other's arms.

They were not all he found. In the wreck of the compound, Telisan learned two facts that remade the universe. First was the real reason "Mandela" wanted Pard dead: Olympia's alliance with a new species, the Voit-Veru. The discovery was the nightmare of every politician, general, and admiral in the seven species of the Confederacy. The last contact had been the Conchirri, xenophobic carnivores who dropped out of the night sky, murdering millions.

The second, more personal revelation exploded on them. The Voit-Veru had captured Lisa Fenaday's ship eight years ago. She might still be alive.

As doctors struggled to bring Shasti and Fenaday back from death's brink, Telisan used Mandela's name and General Dominici's power in the chaos of Olympia to repair the *Sidhe* and launch before the Confederate Navy learned what they were up to.

It seemed the past was not through with them yet...

Chapter One

Robert Fenaday lay on his cabin bed, sheets balled in his fists, sanity in shreds. He lifted an agonized face to the crucifix sitting on his locker, a gift from his long-dead mother. As a child, she told him it carried his words to God's ears. Right now, he wanted it to be true.

"Is it funny?" he demanded of the cross. "Is it?"

As always, there was no reply.

"Well," he shouted, "is it funny? It is. Isn't it? A rare joke. You take Lisa from me. I searched. Everyone told me I was mad, searching for what could only be a frozen corpse. The things I did...

"Now that I let her go, tried to start again, you dangle her before me like a taunt. I've betrayed both her and Shasti. Oh, what a fine trap. Either way I turn, I cut a woman I love."

He staggered off the bed and seized the crucifix. His head swam; a buzzing grew in his ears.

"A fine joke," he said thickly and dashed the crucifix against the bulkhead. The seals on his wounds strained, making his breath catch. "Damn you," he muttered, "damn you." He walked away from the sacrilege to the alcove where Lisa's image had hung since the day he bought *Sidhe* from the Confederacy. His lost wife's image looked back at him, dark red hair, startling blue eyes, a nose slightly crooked from a hang-gliding accident as a teen. His heart lurched in his chest looking at the bright eyes and the slight, mysterious smile. He bowed his head in pain.

"I've got to get moving," he muttered, "got to get it together and get in forward motion. Telisan's done well. If he hadn't gotten us away, the Navy would never have let us go, but he can't hold the ship together by himself."

Only days ago, he'd been as close to death as a man might go and yet return. He'd almost taken that journey with Shasti, wounded nearly to death alongside her in their final battle with Jalgren Pard, Master of the Denshi Assassins. Even with the miracles of medical science, he should still be confined to bed. He'd stormed out of sick bay, over Dr. Mourner and Arpen's objections, mere hours after Telisan told him of Lisa's capture by the new aliens, the Voit-Veru. Thoughts of his wife, imprisoned for eight years among non-humans, while he was safe on New Eire with Shasti in his arms, crushed him under a mountain of guilt and rage.

Shasti had learned of Lisa's survival first. Her Engineered body beat death back days earlier than his merely human one could, and Telisan had told her. She too left Sickbay, retreating to her own cabin. He knew he should go to her. There had been so much he planned to tell her when they were finally reunited. Now everything in his heart had frozen. All was pain and confusion.

He took a few more minutes to pull himself together, dashing cold water on his face. Then he opened his weapons locker. His Martini laser hung there on its belt, typical of Telisan's thoughtfulness. His father's old Scottish dirk was missing, lost in the same knife-edged valley into which Pard had plummeted. He belted on the laser and headed for the door. When it cycled open, he found Moshe Karass outside leaning against the bulkhead opposite the door. He looked blankly at the Israeli.

"Hey, Skipper," Karass said, his dark soulful eyes on the taller Irishman. Karass was a survivor of *Sidhe's* many voyages, one of the few reliables from the old privateer crew. Fenaday had hired him when no one else would, refusing to believe Pan-World's cover-up story blaming him for the crash of a moon shuttle. Even after Karass cleared his name using the riches of the Enshar expedition, he stayed with Fenaday.

"Moshe," he said with a small smile, glad to see the man had survived the battles on Olympia.

"You look like hell, Skipper," Karass observed, with typical directness. "You ought to be in Sickbay."

"No time," Fenaday said, weariness pulling at his bones. "Never any damn time."

"Telisan wanted to be here," Moshe said, "but he is trying to keep the lid on. Mmok's in Sickbay; the...visitor...is in quarantine. How long we can keep it quiet is anyone's guess, especially as I have no idea where we are going or why." Moshe paused. "I assume you know?"

"Always, Moshe," Fenaday said. "Straight to hell."

"Ah," returned Moshe after a second, "the usual."

Fenaday found Telisan on the bridge. The Denlenn pilot looked over as his human friend entered. Telisan was younger, tall and elfin, with golden cat-irised eyes set in skin that appeared leathery but was soft to the touch. He was a veteran of the Confed Navy, wing commander, ace fighter pilot, and Fenaday's trusted friend since the Enshar Expedition. He stood next to one of his fiancées, Sharla, a demi-female of his species. The differences were mostly too small for an outworlder to tell. She was lean and flat-chested, only a slight curve to the hip distinguished her gender. She looked up at Fenaday's entrance as well, smiling at the human. Telisan's other fiancée was a full female, Dr. Arpen, empath and surgeon.

"You should be in bed," Telisan said sternly.

Fenaday shook his head. "No time. Sharla," he continued, "I want all flight and control systems put under code restrictions. I will input the codes myself."

"The Enshar protocol?" Telisan asked, unperturbed.

"Just so," he replied. "I am going to move into my cabin off the bridge. How does it stand with the crew?"

"Tense," Telisan grimaced, "particularly with the Marines. Their officer, Lieutenant Gopal, has not yet questioned my authority, but he was very unhappy when we broke orbit. He wanted to call Ambassador Davis and reconfirm his orders. I refused. With Daniel Rigg on his feet and Rask to back him up, the Marines and ASATs are under control. Still he is suspicious, and his men are nervous and unhappy." He hesitated for a second then went on softly. "It would be good if Shasti would resume command of our ground force..."

Fenaday raised a hand. "Let's leave her be for now. I...I need time there."

Telisan nodded, uncertainty in his face. "We may not have that luxury for long."

Fenaday's jaw worked as he bit back a hot reply and just nodded.

"I want to see the visitor," Fenaday continued. "Then we need a council of war. How long till we hit the first warp point for favorable transit?"

"We have eight days," Telisan said, "not a lot of time for you to heal."

"It's okay," Fenaday said. "We've got two more jumps beyond that. It will be over a month before I have to worry about anything too physical.

"Sharla, get me those codes and pipe them into my space cabin. Telisan, come with me, please."

Fenaday retreated to the quiet of the small compartment off the bridge with its terminal and cot. He gestured at his friend to sit on the other end of the cot. "I've got something important to say," he began slowly. "*Sidhe* is going to the world where they are holding my wife. It's dangerous, probably mad, but we are going. I am dragging everyone into hell. Some of them, if we survive, I'll make it up to with money. Some would go anyway. Others are just out of luck. There is only one exception," he said, leaning forward suddenly. "You. Take Sharla and Arpen. I'll give you *Pooka*. Take it. Head for the science station near Atropos; the Navy will pick you up. Do it before I become too selfish to let you go," he finished, his face strained, skin taut over bones.

"Have I given you such reason to doubt me," Telisan demanded, "that you should raise this?"

"No, no, no, no, listen to me," Fenaday whispered. "Forget honor, forget duty, it's all crap, just words. All that's important is the two people you love. I am begging you as a friend, while I still can. Run, please run. You started us on this voyage because you know me better than any other man. You know I must go, but you have everything I am trying to get back. Don't risk it. Don't come with us." Tears slid down Fenaday's cheeks, and he hid his face between his hands.

Telisan looked at his human friend, over a gap of species and culture. They were at that place again, the uncrossable bridge of alienness. Telisan bottled anger and tried to understand. He reached over and pulled Fenaday's hands away. The human's eyes were red with grief. "You want human things for me," he said softly. "I know you mean it well, out of love, but I am Denlenn and Selen, not human. I could not withdraw from this voyage, this quest, and still be me.

"It is no different for Sharla, and I have learned, with some effort, it is no different for Arpen, though I earnestly wish her safely home.

"It is '*Quaren*' in my language," he continued, struggling. "Ah, the word does not translate well. It is the need to go where the universe means for you to be. Understand, it is clear to me, I am meant to be here, in this place, on this voyage. What is to come, must come."

"I'm human," Fenaday said. "How can I want for you what I don't understand? I see you risking too much, for too little reason. To be part of that reason, possibly to see something happen to any of you, weighs as heavily on my soul as Lisa's fate. If something happens, I'll be responsible."

"Yes," Telisan said gravely, "as will I, as will the universe itself. One cannot escape consequences. So, Robert, my friend and you are that, though we barely understand each other at all—you must learn to want Denlenn things for me."

Fenaday sighed deeply. "What did I do to deserve a friend like you?"

"It must have been good," Telisan agreed.

Fenaday did a double-take and a laugh escaped him, then another. In a second he was laughing so hard he had to lean back against the wall, clutching his injured ribs.

Telisan smiled, Denlenn fashion. The human grabbed his arm firmly. "One last time," Fenaday said, "then I will never mention it again. Leave this ship while you can."

"No," Telisan said. "The universe has placed me where I need to be. It is enough, no matter what follows."

"God bless you," Fenaday said. "I was so afraid you would leave, and I have no chance without you."

"You humans are very contradictory creatures," replied an exasperated Telisan. "Do you ever say what you are actually thinking?"

Fenaday smiled sadly at him. "Back to work for you."

The Denlenn nodded, stood, and left.

The next moves, thought Fenaday, lying back on the cot, *are critical. There is so much to do. I need to see Mourner and her regenerators again; thereafter only willpower and exercise can restore me. It will not be lacking this time. I won't fail Lisa again.*

Meanwhile, I'll alter the control codes on the shuttles, fighters, and the subsystems controlling Sidhe's main drive. These I'll keep secret even from Telisan. With Sharla and Arpen aboard, there are keys that might unlock Telisan. Eventually, I may give Shasti the command codes. No one could force them from her, though she might give them up if I become a hostage, one obvious way to scuttle the mission. Already, Telisan is concerned about the Marine commander. Others might also become troublesome.

Unwillingly, his mind kept returning to Shasti. *After the code changes,* he said to himself. *I'll figure out what to do about her then.*

He looked around the small cabin which he often used when they were maneuvering in deep space, or near a combat zone. *Sidhe* had been built by the Conchirri, a race of ruthless carnivores. Her bridge was the captain's den, approachable only by a passage leading to the rear of the bridge. The passage could be gassed or filled with automatic weapon fire as needed. Fenaday had never removed these systems. Once before, he'd faced mutiny in the skies over dead Enshar. Before he'd allow *Sidhe* to be wrested from him again, the starship would die. Those who knew him from his privateer days knew his ruthlessness when it came to the search for Lisa. He hoped to God they were warning the newcomers.

Exhaustion cut him down and he awoke with a start an hour later, dismayed that even minimal efforts drained him so. With a curse, he stumbled to his feet, composed himself as best he could, and reentered the bridge. Telisan was again in the center seat.

"Come with me," Fenaday said.

Telisan nodded. "Mr. Graglia, please take the con."

The senior lieutenant, another loaner from the Confederate Navy, nodded. "Aye, sir."

Telisan followed Fenaday to the turbo, out through the valved doors at the entrance to the bridge. As the doors cycled closed on the turbo, Fenaday punched the button for the sickbay access.

"I want to see it," said Fenaday grimly. "I want to see what took my wife."

Telisan nodded, with a look another Denlenn would have recognized as worry. Fenaday's face was pale and strained. He'd been among humans long enough to see the restrained fury in the man.

They reached the sickbay in half a minute. Dr. Shizuyo Mourner, a tiny, bird-like woman with a predatory look and a sharp tongue to go with it, glanced up as they entered. "Finally come to your senses and decide to readmit yourself?"

"No," Fenaday said shortly. He looked toward the iso-labs. There were guards on each door separated by about ten feet, Murphy and Li, both from Shasti's personal trouble squad.

Mourner followed his look. "Mmok's in the one to the right," she said, her tone rich with disapproval.

"Then I want the one to the left," he growled, pushing aside thoughts of Mandela's cyborg watchdog. "I want to see what they look like." He strode over to the iso-lab door with its small portal. He could have seen the interior by view screen from anywhere in the ship, but for this, only his own eyes would do. Mourner and Telisan followed. Murphy, tall, lanky, and silent as usual, simply stood aside.

Fenaday's eyes bored in at their prisoner. The creature sat on its haunches in the middle of the room. Large brown eyes stared back.

A goddamn kangaroo, was Fenaday's first thought, as his mind tried to resolve strangeness with a known pattern. He'd never seen a live one but remembered the animals from books and tapes. The longer he looked, the less it resembled a kangaroo. This one stood smaller than a man did. It wore some form of short pants and a vest through which its bizarre trio of tentacle-like arms projected.

"So," hissed Fenaday, "at last. At last we meet, you son-of-a-bitch." He began shaking and his right hand cupped the handle of his pistol, half-pulling it. "Bastard!"

Telisan and Mourner exchanged alarmed looks. Mourner reached for Fenaday's gun arm. "Captain," she began, only to be roughly shaken off.

"I ought to kill you," Fenaday spat at the uncomprehending alien. It could not hear him, isolated behind centimeters of metal and ceramic.

"Robert," Telisan said, "you're not recovered enough for this. Leave the alien to me."

Fenaday turned a strained face to him, as if he had not heard him. "Do you know all they took from me?" he said, eyes bright and mad. "I was a rich man. I lived well, with a family, a home of my own. No sins on my head. No deaths. I was in love with a woman. They took it all."

"Yes, yes," said a soft, understanding voice.

Arpen, thought Telisan, *thank the gods.* He turned to see his other fiancée behind them. Short and curvaceous to his and Sharla's tall, angular height, Arpen was a true female of his species. She walked over to the shaking human, holding his eyes with her own. Arpen's eyes expressed the empathetic power of a Denlenn female, the power that made them great healers. Gently, she removed his unresisting hand from his weapon, pushing the pistol back into the holster.

"They have much to answer for," she said, "though this one seems to be merely a functionary, some sort of scholar. Old, I believe, and somewhat helpless."

"I know that he probably had nothing to do with it himself," Fenaday said reluctantly, "but he's of the kind that has her, the ones who wrecked my life."

"Yes," she said. "Telisan is right though. You should leave this to him."

"I ought to…" he began, turning toward the cell.

"Rest," interrupted Arpen, turning him back firmly, with a surprising strength for her small, plump form.

A spasm of rage flashed into Fenaday's face, then faded under her steady gaze. Deprived of the strength of his anger, he suddenly felt weak. Emotions seemed far away. He swayed. Telisan and Arpen supported him.

"Yes," he muttered to Arpen. "You're right as usual. Telisan, I'm going to leave that creature to you. I can't trust myself to think straight around it."

"I believe his name is Henlesch," added Arpen.

Fenaday nodded, "Henlesch."

Telisan watched his fiancée with rueful admiration. There'd been murder in the human's eyes only a minute ago. In that minute, Arpen turned the alien from a faceless monster into a person, someone with a name. Pitiable even: aged, alone, and not a warrior. It was easier to hate and kill the unknown.

"Arpen's right," said a subdued Dr. Mourner. "We should get you back into Sickbay."

"No," Fenaday said more firmly. "I'll be in my cabin off the bridge."

"Well," she said, "rest some, wherever you are."

Fenaday looked over at the little half-Japanese woman. He put a gentle hand on her arm. "Sorry, did I hurt you?"

"No," Mourner replied, "but your good patient discount is revoked. No lollipop for you either."

Fenaday smiled sadly. "Sorry," he repeated. Mourner just waved it off with an airy gesture.

"I'll take you back to your cabin," Telisan said.

"Okay." Fenaday started for the exit. "I'll want to review everything we have on this alien, also the ship's manifest. Have Dobera update it…"

"Already done," Telisan said.

"You're good," Fenaday said. "What do I pay you?"

"Actually," Telisan said, "you don't."

Chapter Two

Shasti Rainhell stretched sore and stiff muscles in a tai-chi exercise. Her long limbs flowed through the form until she finally stretched back up to her full height of six feet-nine inches. Her glossy black hair chose that moment to escape the pins she'd swept it up with and fall in her face. The surgeons who'd worked on her fractured skull had only disturbed the hair around the actual injury. Still, the irregular cutting made it difficult to deal with. Annoyed, she turned to her mirror to recapture it. Her waist-length hair was impractical, despite all the genetic improvements that made it cleaner and stronger than a regular human's. It was also a banner of challenge to Pard, her creator and ex-husband, who had forced her to keep it cut short. Even with him dead, she still refused to return to a more practical style. She finally settled for a ponytail.

She had sufficient vanity to check her face. Her ivory skin had regained its flawless complexion. Her jade-green eyes were no longer blackened. Looking at her reflection now, it was hard to believe she had been nearly beaten to death only days before.

The sensor she always set to cover the area outside her cabin chimed and flicked up a screen. Her heart froze for a moment until she saw it was only Telisan. She composed herself and waited for him to hit her door chime. She opened the door to find him standing there, looking up at her.

"How is he?" she asked softly.

"In pain, both of the body and the soul," the Denlenn said. "In a fury for information and to gain back his strength. Even Arpen's best efforts could not keep him in bed till he is at least minimally healed. I left him in his space cabin." Telisan hesitated a second, then looked her in the eye. "You are the first person he asked of when he awoke in Sickbay. I think he was hurt that you were not there."

"Leave it alone," she warned.

"As you wish."

"Was that what you came to say?" she continued.

"No," he stated. "We are embarked on a rescue mission. For us to have any chance of success, we need information. More than Mr. Vaughn gave us."

"Vaughn?" she asked.

"Yes, he came out on top after Pard died and Dominici took over. He seems to take a special interest in you. He gave me a data crystal for you, as well as one loaded with useful information on Denshi and Voit-Veru operations. The one for you—forgive me, but for reasons of both ship and your security, I scanned it—contains mostly medical records." He handed her two crystals. "I have copied all we need from the one meant for us.

"What I need to know now is, how fast can you learn the language of this new species?" he continued.

Shasti shrugged. "It should be the matter of only a few days, perhaps less. Engineered have eidetic memory; I forget nothing. Sometimes it's a curse. I can learn the sounds and the book meanings easily. Understanding is something else. That will take time."

"We have a prisoner of these Voit-Veru aboard," added Telisan. "He needs to be thoroughly interrogated and that it is not a skill I am trained in. The captain is still too weak, and I fear his temper might overwhelm him. Mmok, with his augmentation could do it, but I do not trust him, especially this side of starjump where he might believe he could still scuttle the mission. Rigg, perhaps. I have similar reservations there. Though he owes us his life, he is a serving Confed officer. Until we pass the point of no return, I judge it safe to rely on only a few."

"I'll handle it," she said easily. "Making people talk is an art in Denshi; I was trained on actual prisoners."

Telisan looked at her and shuddered, thinking of her, then barely a teenager, doing such things. "I would prefer to avoid physical duress, but if it must be, it must be. These people have made themselves our enemies. We must educate them in the error of their ways."

"I'll prepare," she said.

"Good. Thee are well enough to return to duty?"

Shasti almost smiled at his switch to the archaic formal. Denlenn had three forms of speech, reserving the formal for important matters. Even speaking standard, Telisan stuck to the tradition.

"Don't worry. Engineered have two settings, dead and healed."

He turned to leave, then over his shoulder said, "Shasti, find some time to see Robert."

"At the proper time," she said, "not before."

He nodded and left.

———

Henlesch of the Voit-Veru surveyed his surroundings with a mixture of dim despair and terror. It had all gone so wrong on Olympia. His so-called allies were wiped out, and he had no idea of the identity of the faction holding him. Perhaps, if Sommel had survived, there might have been some hope. The agent was one of the best of the Secret Service, but he too was gone, killed in a gun duel with the yellow-eyed leader of these people.

He owed Sommel his life. When their erstwhile allies in Denshi were attacked, the Engineered Humans moved to eliminate evidence of the secret alliance by wiping out the delegation. Assassins shot down poor Gerder and Ambassador Hosh. They had not reckoned on Sommel. The big warrior male bowled over the

Denshi, administering lethal kicks with legs capable of bouncing a full-grown Voit-Veru over two meters in the air. Sommel seized a weapon and shot their way out. Henlesch had followed, numbly obeying orders. He was not a Veru of action, just an old professor, drafted by the military government when the first contact occurred. His intense study of the few surviving tribes of his species' ancient enemy, the Mon-Veru, or sea people, was presumed to give him some edge in the study of true aliens. So he became an aide.

Aide, he thought bitterly, *not much help, too old to fight, never learned how to shoot.* His vaunted studies of the Mon-Veru did not help him puzzle out the nature of the species he was dealing with. Mass murder came as a surprise. He did not even know who was attacking the Denshi headquarters. At first, he imagined it to be the Army, General Dominici or her people. That no longer made sense. He was in the belly of a warship. She had gone through several burns and an extended period of high gravity acceleration that the vessel's artificial gravity system could not quite cancel.

His best guess was that the vessel was from the Confederacy, the allegedly tyrannical government Denshi was so determined to break from. There were no fewer than four species of aliens on the ship, perhaps more. It was impossible to tell if some were different races in the species, or different genders. Yet, the vessel did not have the feel of a standard warship. It was difficult to explain the difference. Still it was there, or perhaps he was just seeing Veru patterns where he should be looking for alien ones.

He had not been mistreated. After a medical exam, administered by an ugly little alien with large, but somehow kind, eyes, they put him in a cell. She adjusted the heat, humidity, and oxygen level for his comfort. Food came at three intervals. It was tolerable, not much more. She gave her name as Arpen, a medical doctor. Beyond that, he could get no answers.

Trembling overcame him: lost, alone, among aliens he could not hope to fully understand. He longed for home, to see his daughter at least once more. Emotions made his ears droop forlornly, and he fought total collapse.

The door to his cell suddenly cycled open. He scrambled up in alarm, facing a leveled weapon.

"Sit," commanded the soldier. Two more aliens entered his cell. The first he recognized as the leader of his captors. Tall as Sommel had been, his skin had the look of tanned animal hide, making the piercing yellow eyes all the more startling and predatory. The other was new to him. A human, he judged, female and possibly Olympian from her size. She towered a head over the other alien. Her fur...hair, he reminded himself, was a shimmered black and cut irregularly.

The yellow-eyed alien gestured for him to sit. None of the furniture was designed with a Veru in mind, so he simply squatted in a three-point stance on the floor.

"I assume you speak Confederate Standard," said yellow-eyes, speaking slowly.

"Yes," he replied. The language was difficult, but not much more so than Mon-Veru. "I speak it."

"I am Acting-Captain Telisan, of the Confederate Private Warship *Sidhe*, sailing under letters of Marque and Reprisal for the Confederacy. Do you understand?"

"No," he said.

"That means this vessel is the private property of a citizen of the Confederacy, Robert Fenaday. It is a warship and operating under military authority."

Henlesch nearly jumped at the name, Fenaday. *No*, he thought, *impossible.*

"Fight/flight reflexes," the female said, in badly accented Veru, "are the same in all species we have met. That was a startle reflex. You have heard the name before."

"Yes," he said, thinking quickly. "An enemy of the Denshi; he had a ship."

"Before that," Telisan said. Henlesch realized the alien's hair concealed a translator.

"No," he said.

"Lie," said the female, baring her teeth. They were not

formidable, but combined with the look in the eyes, betokened slow death.

"Commander Elizabeth Fenaday," continued Telisan, "also known as Lisa. Her vessel was the four-man scout *Blackbird*. Crew: Asa Drok, Caitlin Barrett, and Fontel Ki Teska."

He took out a hand comp and projected a tri-dee holo on the wall. Henlesch studied the figures. *Oh my Gods,* he thought, looking at one face. It had not been so young and confident when he met it, but there could be no doubt. He said nothing.

"That ship and crew fell into your people's hands nearly eight years ago," added the female. "We are on a mission to recover the crew. We are not hostile to your government beyond that, but we will do all that is necessary to recover those people, including use of deadly force. *Blackbird* was a Confed vessel on a scouting mission. Your people's capturing of the ship constitutes an act of war against all seven species of the Confederacy. Perhaps the one truth Pard told you was how we dealt with the last hostile species that warred on us."

"You will tell us all that you know," said the female. "All that is asked, you will answer. You are not listed by anyone as having been found, or your body recovered. No one knows you are here. You depend on us from second to second for light, food, and air. If you wish to survive to be exchanged at some point in the future, you must cooperate now."

Henlesch stared at the aliens, his stomach weak. *I am not a coward or traitor,* he thought. *I can die well, if it comes to it.* But there seemed to be no oxygen in the room.

"My friend Rainhell speaks harshly, as is her wont," Telisan said. "Olympians are a stern people, as you know, given to much cruelty."

"You have no idea," said the one named Rainhell.

"Like as not," continued Telisan, "much of the information is of no military significance. For the most part, we simply need to learn about your people. It is possible your information can save lives while not compromising a military secret. We already know the current codes and IFF signals used by both sides. With Pard dead, Vaughn gave us these freely. So you see, Being Henlesch," said

Telisan, "you harm no one but yourself by not speaking. We already have your military secrets. From what Vaughn said, you were merely a professor and not privy to them anyway."

"He might have learned," growled the female.

"No." Henlesch appealed to the male, who seemed reasonable and less prone to violence. For the female, he suspected violence was an end in itself. "You are correct. I was an academic. I studied the ways of the Mon-Veru, the other intelligent native species of our world. It was felt I could add something to understanding your kind."

"Why don't you leave for a while?" Rainhell said to the other. "We are wasting time."

Telisan leaned back in his chair, shaking his head. "Tell us about these Mon-Verus. Surely there can be no harm in that?"

Henlesch's brain worked feverishly. The alien was right, there could be no harm in giving him such simple information, available in any child's book.

"Yes," he said, "yes, I think that I can answer some of your questions. Perhaps we can come to some sort of arrangement..."

Hours later, they left the Veru's cell. Telisan felt weary and a little unclean; this was not work he had ever faced before. Conchirri were impervious to interrogation. You just killed them. Even that was outside his experience. He was a fighter pilot. All he saw of the enemy was their machines. With a sigh, he looked up at the Olympian. "I used your script and stuck to it as best I could."

"You did well," Shasti said. "Henlesch will not present much of a challenge. Now, he thinks he can reason with us, negotiate, even outwit us by giving information he sees as harmless. At this point he is congratulating himself on how well he handled the situation. Tomorrow, I will destroy all that by hurting him. Nothing major, just enough to destroy his sense of well-being and reason. You will appear and demand I stop. You'll explain that he needs to be more forthcoming, as Captain Fenaday is demanding answers, and if you cannot get them, then I will be given free rein. Continue with subjects that will seem harmless to him. With the stakes raised, he will gradually reveal more information, hoping to control his situation.

"Once someone begins to talk," she continued, "it's hard to find places or reasons to stop. Oh, that was good work getting him to lecture us on the Mon-Veru. Inspired even."

"Not so difficult," Telisan said. "I just remembered how easy it was to get Belwin Duna to talk on his subjects for hours by expressing even a little interest. The professorial mode is almost seductively safe and familiar. Ah," exclaimed Telisan in sudden pain, "what would he think of me now?"

Rainhell looked at him curiously. "Duna was an admirable creature, but he never once hesitated to lie, or put others in danger for a cause he regarded as sacred. Don't forget that."

For a second, Telisan's yellow eyes held a look that gave even her pause. "Well," he said finally, "there is truth to that, bitter though it is to accept."

"Telisan," she said, before he could turn to leave. "I'm sorry. I don't understand tact even with my own species. I never learned how."

"Yes." He put a gentle hand on her arm, a liberty only a handful of people could venture with her. "I do not forget these things. I was only angry for a second and only because it was true. Do not worry. We are friends. For all that we hardly understand each other. No, it is you who are right. We are still on a quest and we must be ruthless in pursuit. Duty demands no less." With another gentle squeeze on her arm, he turned and left.

———

Shasti's next stop was Mmok's isolation cell in Sickbay. She was still in charge of security, and Mmok, commander of the Confed robot force, was a far more dangerous prisoner than Henlesch. The cyborg was still in Sickbay, uninjured, but under psychological care from the empathic Arpen. His strong feelings for Arpen and his unwillingness to kill Telisan's fiancée rendered him their prisoner. Otherwise *Sidhe* would be in his hands, and they would all be under arrest. She slipped into Sickbay, trying to avoid Arpen or Mourner. Li nodded at her, but used to her silences, said nothing. She cycled through the doors to the iso-cell.

Mmok, a tall, slender human, silently watched her enter. His one human eye was a cold gray, set in a face as pale as her own. A metallic headpiece covered half his skull, and a black-green square of ceramic-steel took the place of his other eye. More cosmetically pleasing replacements were available. Mmok disdained them, as he did most other social conventions. Three-quarters of his body had been cybernetically replaced, repairs for the damage done by a Conchirri anti-tank beamgun. Mmok served as Mandela's watchdog, and giving out information was not his business. She guessed him to be in his thirties.

"Come to see the monkey in the cage?" Mmok asked. He sat on his bunk, a book reader face down next to him. His cyborg arm was attached to the wall by a long chain, something Telisan insisted on.

"I was curious," she said evenly. "I thought you died on Enshar."

"Like you give a fuck," he snapped.

"I heard about your capture," she said, ignoring the response. "You surrendered to Arpen when she drew a pistol on you on the bridge. Surrendered, despite having your killer robots with you. Why? Why didn't you shoot Arpen? You could easily have retaken the ship."

"Fuck you," he replied.

"Mmok," she said wearily, "I realize you are a man of few words. Try for something a bit more original."

"Fuck you and the Frokossi speedhound you rode in on."

Shasti suppressed the desire to disassemble the cyborg. "Why, Mmok?"

A long minute passed. Shasti waited easily. It was her game.

Finally, Mmok looked up at her. "She was the first person to treat me as a human being, not a piece of equipment, in years," he said, surprising her. "I just couldn't do it."

"I don't understand," she replied.

He grinned. "Sorry, Assassin. If I have to explain it more, then it's pointless."

Rage lit in her, and she stood, fighting for control. "You," she said finally, "are not the only being to ever be treated as property." She started out of the cell, not trusting herself to remain.

"Rainhell," he called.

She turned, murder in her eyes.

"Sorry," Mmok said, looking away. "I'll call foul on that last one."

She could only stare, confused.

"Talk some sense into him," Mmok continued, still looking away. "He's gotten dozens, maybe hundreds, of people killed looking for his wife. He'll get all of us killed and start a war before we are ready. All for one person, who wouldn't agree to such a mission if you asked her."

She shook her head slowly. "You don't know him. There has never been any reasoning with him when it comes to her. There's even less chance now."

"We all gonna die," Mmok said in resignation.

Shasti shrugged. "Yes, almost certainly."

She left the cyborg to his book, heading back to her cabin. It was time to face Vaughn's message. Once there, she secured the lock and then powered up her own computer. She paused to pet Risky, the K-9 she had adopted on Enshar. The genetically enhanced shepherd had been made by human scientists on Earth, but as he put his head in her lap and wagged his tail, he seemed no different than any dog. It seemed that the Confederacy had fewer problems with the engineering of animals than humans. She placed the data crystal into the comp, settling back into her chair with a sigh. The holo-monitor lit up, projecting the image of Mikhail Vaughn, now leader of the Denshi, under the careful eye of General Dominici. She had seen him only once, when he tried to kill her in the offport of Marathon. He was as she remembered, tall, solid, and handsome, piercing blue eyes under hair as jet black as her own.

She'd learned from Telisan that Vaughn visited *Sidhe* shortly before they fled the madhouse Marathon degenerated into. He'd wanted to see her, comatose as she was from her injuries, simply to look at her face. Telisan had allowed it reluctantly, in return for information, codes, and maps of the Voit-Veru's systems. The Denlenn had ordered two of Mmok's Humanform Combat Robots to hold the powerful Engineered by the arms, with instructions to kill at the least provocation. Vaughn had offered none. He'd merely gazed at her for a few minutes before leaving.

Now those compelling eyes were before her again.

"Hello, Shasti Rainhell," he began. The voice was deep, pleasing, with a hint of a growl. "We have never spoken. I have seen you only twice, during our fight over the rooftops of Marathon and in the sickbay of *Sidhe*. Yet the image of you stays with me vividly. I wish I knew why.

"You have many reasons for your hatred of Denshi. I know only a few, and they are enough. I do not hold your killing of Pard against you. He was a hard man and not always just.

"In some small measure of repayment, I offer you something I am sure you want: information on yourself, your origins, and your capabilities. Things you were never told while you were with us.

"You must wonder if you are good, or simply lucky, to have survived so long against so much. The answer is yes and more. Shasti, you are not Third Generation Engineered, as you were told, nor Fourth like myself, or even Fifth Generation, as some thought Antebei to be. You are Generation Unknown, the sole-surviving product of the special lab run by Pard and the Chief Geneticist Negola. You were created in an attempt to leap multiple generations, short-circuiting engineering evolution. All the safeties were thrown out; everything that could be tried was. Thousands died. You alone survived. The crystal contains every record there is on you.

"You are at the highest end for physical strength for a human. Pound for pound, you may be the strongest Engineered ever created. Ultra-fast healing took with you, as well as resistance to burns. Otherwise that laser hit would have finished you.

"I do not know your reaction speed. I know it exceeds my own and, Shasti, I am fast. I am optimized for it.

"Did you know you cannot drown? The medical records show a filtration system in your lungs. You can process the oxygen out of water.

"Your night vision is as good as a cat's. If the reports are right, you can actually change color. Melanin camouflage they called it. I'm envious.

"I suspect you do not know, or fully understand, the ability called 'situational awareness.' It was difficult enough for me, with proper training. It is the ability to sense, to feel, the location, and to some degree, the intention of people around you. It is not telepathy, but something akin. In a fight, I can feel the location of people, even the ones behind me. I can imagine their weapons, even the position of their limbs.

"Part of it is the superior processing speed of the Engineered brain, recognizing shadows, smells, sounds, patterns of movement, pressure caused by the movement of bodies. All these things integrate in a gestalt.

"There is more. A standard human who is being watched can feel it, without seeing the watcher. You have a heightened sense of this. A person lurking on the other side of a door will present an image to your mind. It varies. Some perceive such a threat as heaviness in the air, or a shadow. I see sparks hanging in the air, angry hot sparks. The more dire the threat or the intent, the hotter the spark.

"You may wonder why I am telling you this. I wonder myself. All I know is that since I first saw you, I have been unable to rid myself of the image of your face. I know what Telisan is doing, the danger he and Fenaday are taking you into. I even know why. I know of your relationship with Fenaday. That may change. If I am to have any hope of seeing you again, you must survive what is to come. So, learn, study, and do not forget me."

Shasti leaned forward eagerly, her hands flying over the computer, her heart pounding. Her eyes devoured the text and images appearing on the screen.

Chapter Three

General Maria Dominici sat in the primary communication center of Army HQ, in the base camp of the First Mountain Infantry, watching the scouts of the Confederate Task Force carefully approach Olympia's orbit. *They have reason to be careful,* she thought. Olympia's naval defense force put up a sporadically fierce, if disjointed battle. With Pard dead, the government fallen, and the Navy minister under arrest, command and control disappeared. She had tried to get the Navy back under control, force them to see the reality of their position. She'd failed. Navy officers would not heed their oldest enemy, even with the iron fist of the Confederacy swinging down on them.

In the end it did not matter. Olympia's nascent fleet consisted of purchases from the reduced navies of the Confederate worlds, a few small carriers guarded by a raft of fleet destroyers and frigates. The OSDFN could not stop a Confed task force of capitol ships. It could, however, cost them. Two of the Confederacy's destroyers were gone. The battle-cruiser *Ganymede* would struggle to make orbit, rammed by a *Spacefire* off the Olympian carrier *Leonidas*. The OSDFN was destroyed or fled; a handful of smaller vessels surrendered.

She waited in growing impatience for her Confederation contact, a man known to her only as Mandela, to finally break radio silence. She made sure every media outlet was back on the air, carefully controlled, broadcasting normalcy and order. An exaggeration, but she had made it abundantly clear that there was no one so quiet as a dead troublemaker. The Confed force wanted no quagmire, and she needed the task force to survive. Pard was dead. A new order would arise. Mandela, she knew, had no concern about who imposed that order, so long as it served the Confederacy's interest. She had to be that person. Not for herself, nor for the Confederacy, but for the sake of Olympia, the great experiment Dr. Alessandro and his eugenicists conceived, home of the superior human. She believed in the dream of human perfection, despite Pard and the Engineered's efforts to hijack and pervert it.

Pard, she mused, *first of the successful Engineered, people born from mechanical wombs, their DNA altered, deliberately mutated.* They had replaced the Selected, people like herself, evolved by the classic and human method of finding the best mate. That would stop now. The lab-born would be brought to heel under her control, the labs destroyed. There would be no more generations of Engineereds. The ones alive now would breed back into the population. Eventually, they would understand the need to cooperate with her to preserve what they could of Olympia.

The days of the laissez-faire Confederacy were drawing to a close, she sensed. History's winds were blowing, and whatever name it bore in the future, the Confederacy of Seven Species would never be the same. The harsh reality of the Xenophobe War and now the Voit-Veru threat would make the Confederacy far more powerful. Planetary governments would wither. The Diaspora of separating humanity would coalesce into something more imperial. It was inevitable.

"Any signal from the fleet?" she asked, regretting it immediately. The tech would have told her. She was nervous and could not afford to be.

"No, ma'am," replied the tech. "No response to our hail."

Her eldest son, Guytano, a huge man wearing paratroop fatigues with suppressed colonel's insignia, looked over at her and smiled. He knew what she was thinking. She smiled back at him. A stranger would not have credited that they were mother and son. She looked scarcely any older than he did. Her olive-complected face was unlined, though some silver shone in her hair. Dominici appeared to be a superbly athletic woman, in her late thirties or early forties. She was more than sixty and still in the prime of life. She had three sons and twelve perfect grandchildren. It was for them she turned to Mandela. For them she destroyed Pard and tamed the Engineered.

Her son walked over. "Ambassador Davis is complaining again. He wants to know when he can return to the embassy."

"When the damn streets are safe," she replied.

"He's been watching the news video and saying the streets look calm enough," Guytano replied, with an ironic smile.

Dominici snorted. She had begun to suspect that, like many of the staff of other worlds sent to Olympia, Davis was chosen more for looks than intelligence. Why couldn't other worlds make the connection the ancient Greeks had, a healthy mind in a healthy body?

"Tell him if he enjoys watching fiction so much, he can tune to channel 23 and watch reruns of *Captain Sword and the Commandos*," she replied.

It was her son's turn to laugh. The show was a notoriously inaccurate video based on the Xenophobe war. Regular soldiers found it highly amusing. "I'll do that," he replied.

"Signal coming in," announced the young tech. "It's on the special frequency you were expecting. Signal identifies Confederate warship *Polaris*, Admiral Xein commanding. Visual denied."

Dominici straightened in her chair. *Showtime.* "Put it on the main board. All non-essential personnel, clear the room." Everyone quickly shuffled out, leaving Dominici, her son, and the one tech.

"The room is clear," Dominici said. "Request visual communications."

The screen lit up, revealing the interior of what she recognized as a *Star* class dreadnought. In the center of the raised dais occupied by the command staff sat an oriental human, Admiral Xein, one of the Confederacy's most ruthless commanders. His presence was a clear warning to her. Next to him stood another flag officer, a Denlenn. His tawny hair was far darker than Telisan's, cropped closer to the skull on a face that was even more angular and inhuman than the Denlenn pilot's.

It was the man next to him that seized her attention: middle-aged, human, once very powerful, and now fighting a spreading midsection. His skin was a dark-chocolate brown, contrasting strongly with the bright, ivory teeth of his broad smile.

"General Dominici," Mandela said in a deep, pleasing voice, "so good to see you looking well, and your son Guytano also."

"Thank you," Dominici replied. "I see you are in good health as well. Despite the OSDFN's best efforts."

"Quite impressive those efforts were too," Mandela said, "as you predicted." Next to him, the impassive face of Xein drew into a frown. She suspected that, despite her warnings, the Confederation forces had not expected a fight.

"How are things on the ground?" Mandela asked.

"Well in hand," Dominici said. "Pard is dead. Vaughn is under my control and with him, most of Denshi. I have control of the capital city. The area around the Confederate Embassy is secure, though there has been occasional sniper fire. Ambassador Davis was taken into my protective custody until the area is completely safe. My casualties have not been light, but my forces are intact."

"Our satellites are picking up heavy fighting around the naval base at Thrace," Mandela said.

Damn, she thought. "Oldark and the Naval Landing Troops are putting up a last-ditch resistance at his combined Navy-Denshi base in the south. They are surrounded by the 69th and 12th armored. Denshi and the Navy have no heavy armor. There is no way they can break out, now that you have cleared space of their ships. I am moving up the mountain infantry and paras to take the base. That will end the last organized resistance."

"Excellent," Mandela said. "Our heavy ships will be in range of the planet in three hours. Call off your ground assault. We will save you casualties and strike the base from orbit."

"No," she said. "Olympian problems can be handled by Olympians. The Naval detector grid is still intact. I left it so they can see you coming. Perhaps the threat will be enough. Vaughn is already trying to get Oldark to surrender. If not, then we will deal with it on the ground. I have no desire to see the surface of my world, even a small section, rendered sterile for the next decade."

"Little hard on the guys on the ground," Mandela said, eyebrow raised.

"When did you develop such a concern for the men on the ground?" she answered scornfully. "You haven't even asked about your operatives."

"Since you mention it," Mandela said, seemingly unaffected by her comment, "I would like a report on developments in that regard."

"The only survivors of the original team were Shasti Rainhell and Daniel Rigg. Denshi killed the rest. They also got most of your on-planet spy network.

"Fenaday came in and raised hell. Faked his death and somehow got down-world to attack Pard's complex in a strike we coordinated. Fenaday and Rainhell killed Pard. He almost killed them in return. For a while we thought they were both history."

"They survived? How badly are they hurt?" Mandela demanded, showing concern for the first time in her experience of him.

"Our doctors are among the best in the galaxy," Dominici said, "and Rainhell is a wonder of the art of the Engineered. Fenaday was closest to death, but he pulled through."

"Good," Mandela said, his face somber. "I would hate to hear of his death."

"Your cyberforce destroyed the Denshi compound and the forces there. A most remarkable engagement. I will spend a great deal of time studying it.

"More importantly, Telisan produced evidence of the Voit-Veru:

documents, data, and best of all, bodies, three bodies, strange creatures, like I have never even imagined. The autopsy records are being uploaded to you." She gestured to the tech.

"We have it," Mandela said triumphantly.

"Yes," she returned. "We do. At long last. Incontrovertible proof of what you suspected. The Denshi are in league with a new alien species."

"More than enough to bring down Denshi and the government that they installed," he said.

"And sweep into power a government more friendly to the Confederacy," she returned.

"Headed by your good self," Mandela added.

"Ah," she said easily, "I do so dislike politics. Annetta Morella will take the presidency. I will merely be an advisor."

Mandela smiled. "I like a modest person."

Behind him Admiral Xein stirred, obviously annoyed by the verbal fencing. Mandela quelled him with the idle motion of one hand, a subtle illustration of his power.

"Do I take it that you will be entering orbit and lending the Confederacy's recognition to the Reform government?" *Here we are,* she thought, *the moment of truth. We stand or we fall.*

"Yes," Mandela said. "Your position seems tenable. You've prepared the way well. You will have Confederate Space Force support as well as Marines and ASATs."

"No need to land troops," she said coolly. "The situation is well in hand."

"You are still protecting my ambassador," Mandela drawled. "There are snipers around the embassy. The troops will land, General Dominici. They will assume control of the embassy, the spaceport, and the offport. All those areas that were Confederate jurisdiction, will be Confederate again. The troops will land, General. Please ensure that there are no incidents. They could have the direst repercussions."

Dominici sat very still. *So it begins,* she thought. "There will be no incidents; I assure you."

"Excellent." Mandela gestured toward the Denlenn officer. "Commodore Adellana will coordinate the landing."

"As you wish."

"Now, if you please, I would like to speak both to Ambassador Davis, and if he is able, Captain Fenaday."

Dominici looked at him curiously. "I don't know Captain Fenaday's status. He and Rainhell were transferred to the *Sidhe* as soon as they were stable under Commander Telisan's care."

"The good commander has not kept you informed?"

Dominici shrugged. "Until he left."

"Left?" Mandela said, his voice suddenly flat and intent. "Left for where?"

"Oh my God," Dominici said, shock numbing her, that Denlenn bastard had fooled her.

"What has transpired?" Mandela asked. "Quickly please."

Dominici took a deep breath and thought. Only the truth seemed to serve her. "Telisan has left in the *Sidhe*. He used your name to gather soldiers, supplies, and repairs. Then he set out, claiming you had work for him. He refused to give details. We thought he was your man. It didn't make sense that he was just working for Fenaday."

"It appears," the Denlenn officer said, "that you misjudged him."

There was a long silence as Mandela stared out of the monitor at her. Her heart pounded in her chest.

"Where did he go?" Mandela asked almost idly. "When did he leave? I assume you have deep-space sensor capability?"

"No," she said, "all such capability lay with Denshi and the Navy. The Army was not allowed that type of installation. *Sidhe* left orbit seven standard solar days ago. I have no idea where or why."

"I suggest that you make every effort to find out that information," he returned. "We will discuss this more completely aboard my flagship."

"Aboard your ship?" Dominici said. "I think it would be better if we met at the capital."

"Please reconsider."

"I do not think so," she replied.

"General," Xein said coldly, "there are several ways of dealing with the present situation on Olympia. One involves fire."

"Admiral," Mandela raised a hand, "please. I am sure there is no need for any such discussion. General, a shuttle will land in the capitol in the morning to convey your party and the Ambassador to *Polaris*. Please accept my invitation for lunch. I will guarantee your safety. We will have much to discuss, especially with the information I hope you will uncover."

"Of course," she replied.

"Then till tomorrow, I bid you adieu."

The image flickered off. She turned to her son and her face was not good to see. "Get me Vaughn," she ordered. *This,* she thought, *will cost me. The bastard will not part easily with the information. Well played, Telisan. You made a fool out of me. Point for you. Now, what are you doing, you cat-eyed devil?*

————

On *Polaris*, Xein and Adellana looked at Mandela, a man they had known only for a few weeks since he appeared at the stardock armed with papers giving him plenipotentiary powers over the Olympian operation and the Task Force. Xein and the Navy had protested the intrusion into their chain of command. The response came down from the Secretary of War's office. Shut up and follow orders. They did, unhappily.

"Admiral," Mandela turned back to face the officer, "have any of our vessels encountered the *Sidhe*?"

"No," Xein shook his head, "we weren't looking for her, but had a Xenophobe *Tokkoro* class frigate leader been detected by anyone, be assured it would have been mentioned. There are only three of them still in existence, none with the OSDFN."

"Any chance we could pick up the trail?"

Xein shrugged. "Effectively, no. They have a week's head start. Could be in jumpspace by now if he was going interstellar. He'd have been accelerating while we've been decelerating for orbit. If you think that they may still be in the system, I could redeploy the fleet in a search pattern, but that risks allowing an OSDFN vessel to make a hit and run on the planet."

"Can't have that," observed Mandela. "Well, we will just have to see what the good general turns up.

"Admiral," he continued, "have *Cheetah* and *Falcon* prepared for fastest possible transit. We may need to call for reinforcements and we ourselves may need to voyage farther than we planned."

"Do you have an idea where this rogue fighter pilot has flown?" Xein asked, disliking the turn the conversation was taking.

"I have a wild idea," Mandela said slowly, "though the why eludes me."

"With respect, Admiral," Commodore Adellana said, surprising both men, "Commander Telisan is no rogue. He is Selen Denlenn, very special, highly honored among us. He is not on Confederation active service, which means his loyalties lie with Captain Fenaday exclusively. Whatever he may be doing, you may rest assured that it comports with his sense of honor and obligation."

"It did not stop him from deceiving Dominici," Xein growled.

"Nor should it," countered Adellana. "One fights the enemy with the enemy's weapons and on his terms. Loyalty and honor are for one's own. I suspect that in this case it was mostly a matter of letting General Dominici and Ambassador Davis deceive themselves.

"No," Adellana repeated. "Telisan has not gone rogue. He is carrying out his captain and friend's orders. He will do this diligently, whatever it costs him."

"A dangerous man," Mandela said.

"Just so," Adellana agreed, yellow eyes flashing.

"Admiral," Mandela headed for the turbovator, "please proceed into orbit and establish an exclusion zone around Olympia. Have all ships refueled and refurbished for extended operations, except *Ganymede* of course, as soon as possible. Land half the planned Marine/ASAT force. I want the other half for contingencies."

Xein looked like he might explode. "Anything else?" he finally managed, seeing weeks of staff work flushed down the toilet and days of contingency planning suddenly ahead.

"Yes." Mandela gave a broad pleasant smile. "Have the cook call on me in my cabin. I'd like to discuss the lunch menu."

Chapter Four

The next morning Fenaday called a council of war in the main briefing room. After the room filled, he triggered the main screen.

"This is our destination." He turned to face the assembled crew. The central table was covered in papers, portable coms, and the usual coffee cups. Most of the command staff was present. Few were as banged up as their leader, but they were a sorry-looking lot. Daniel Rigg was recovering rapidly, but, like Fenaday, still received regeneration treatments. Mmok remained under detention in sickbay. As for the rest—Perez, Karass, Dobera, Fury, Graglia, Hafel, Bernard, Telisan, Mourner, and Arpen—they were suffering from minor wounds, lack of sleep, and the stress of *Sidhe's* escape from Olympia.

Only the Morok, Rask, looked unperturbed, still so relieved over having found his friend Rigg. Rask was busy slurping down another coffee served to him by Leda Jenner. The Olympian refugee was trying to make herself useful aboard ship as commissariat. The new addition was Lieutenant Arun Gopal, the officer in charge of the Marines Telisan had hijacked from the embassy guard.

"NGC 4877," continued Fenaday, "or as the Voit-Veru call it,

Mounus IV, local name, Thorraken. Vaughn's information gives us a fast transit with a favorable current. An express route, if you will, for a trip that would take months if you did not hit the warp line correctly. It will still take us through two other systems, Zealmun and Dralich, before we can jump to Mounus."

"How far?" Gopal asked. The Marine's black eyes fastened mistrustfully on Fenaday.

"Three hundred lights," Fenaday said coolly. "Distance is irrelevant, Marine. It's time in transit and jumpspots. It's three weeks and two system jumps to get there."

Rigg and Rask traded dubious glances. Perez swore something in Spanish under his breath. Even Telisan looked daunted.

"Three weeks, one way into unknown space," Rigg murmured. Fenaday spared him a worried glance. He and the squat Morok were reluctant helpers in Fenaday's plans. They knew Mmok was under arrest in Sickbay. Both also knew what Fenaday had done on Enshar and Olympia. Rigg particularly owed Fenaday, but was clearly uncomfortable in his rogue role. Gopal watched them narrowly. He still deferred to Rigg as nominally in command of the combined Marine ASAT force, as it was clear Rask was behind the tall human with both the ASATs and *Sidhe's* surviving Landing and Expedition Force troops.

Shasti had not taken up her old slot, and Fenaday hadn't figured out what to do about it. She rarely stirred out of her cabin since they reawakened on *Sidhe*. When he did see her, they were never alone, almost as if she'd arranged it that way. He had not found the courage to seek her out, hoping that somehow a moment would arise to make it less painful.

"Do we have the range for this?" Gopal asked. "I was told this was just a frigate."

"Barely," replied Fenaday, nettling some at the disrespectful reference to the ship. "This is a Conchirri Frigate Leader, a type with no counterpart in the Confed Fleet. We have more range and punch than a *Seachange* or a *Swift*. Telisan provisioned us well. We can make it."

"If we aren't blasted by a picket ship," Gopal countered. "We have no support, no resupply, or repair."

"You want to live forever, Marine?" came a familiar, silky, dangerous voice. Heads snapped around. Shasti Rainhell stood, leaning indolently against a bulkhead. She'd somehow entered, unobserved though the door lay in plain view. Gopal turned with the rest, looking up at Rainhell curiously. She was quite a sight. Her build was somewhere between that of a dancer and a bodybuilder. The black ship-pants and severe red top she wore hid little of this. She was human perfection incarnate.

Gopal studied her for a second longer. A retort died on his lips as he met the cold, empty eyes. "Just curious about the threat assessment," he said finally.

Shasti held Gopal's eyes as she slowly, gracefully, walked to stand in her accustomed place behind Fenaday's left shoulder, opposite his gun arm. Fenaday felt his mouth go dry. He looked at her; she didn't quite meet his eyes. He nodded. She didn't react.

I didn't want our first moment together to be like this, he thought. *Damn, I should have sought her out when we would have some privacy.*

"We will have an advantage," Telisan added, also eyeing Rainhell. "We have the current Voit-Veru IFF codes and patrol routes."

"We're not going to take chances, anyway," added Fenaday, forcing himself to concentrate on the task at hand. "This ship is very distinctive and that cuts two ways. First, it will throw them off. We won't look Confed and we have the right codes. Olympia's Navy was growing fast. They may not know every ship profile. We will be new. I want them to hesitate for a few seconds, enough for us to get off the first shot. We've got a single, light-cruiser class, mass accelerator and full spreads of nuke-tipped missiles. We connect, we kill, we run."

"And pray," Rask added. Rainhell's cold eyes tracked over him and Rask subsided.

"What happens when we reach the planet?" asked Rigg.

"We have the latest info on the new base where my wife and her crew are held. Fortunately, the Voit-Veru wanted to keep the prisoners out on the frontier, away from where they might be seen, plausible deniability for the leadership. Thorraken serves as the meet-point in the Denshi-Veru Alliance. Both sides have forces there, and it has been settled for only a few years according to our prisoner. We hit hard, nuke the defenses, snatch the crew, and run like hell," Fenaday concluded.

"Hell of a plan," Perez grunted.

"Don't worry," Fenaday said, with a flash of humor, "if we get whacked, 'La Bitch' still doesn't get your back-pay." The remark drew rueful laughs from the veterans and confused looks from the newcomers. Perez's antipathy for his ex-wife was a shipboard legend.

"So what do we know about our enemy?" Fenaday asked.

"Let's start with their biology," Arpen began. "The Voit-Veru developed on wide savannas, evolving from an omnivorous creature similar to a Terran marsupial. The analogy is not exact. Reproduction is more like you Terrans, or even like Rask's species. The pouch is used for carrying the young. They run about the same size as the rest of the species we've met, one and half to two meters tall, or long in this case. They use their tail for balance and the posture is similar to," she paused and looked at Telisan, "how do you say the word?"

"Kangaroo," the pilot mangled the foreign word slightly.

"They have good hearing, better than Denleni, about as good as a human. Their daylight vision is excellent; night-sight is less so. Henlesch says their homeworld has a very large moon. Sense of smell is good. It was probably useful in the grasslands where they evolved.

"The three upper limbs are a feature we have never seen before. The limbs are not powerful, though they are dexterous. Don't get kicked by one of these people. I suspect they can high jump at least three meters from standing."

"How do you kill them efficiently?" Shasti asked softly.

Arpen looked over at the genetically engineered assassin and shuddered.

It was Mourner who replied. "The information is on a crystal.

You will all get one. It shows vulnerable points for weapon fire and hand strikes."

"The Voit-Veru evolved with another race," Arpen continued, "the Mon-Veru, Veru means people in their language. Mon means sea, and Voit means land. Both species were bitter enemies. Wars raged for millennium. Eventually the Voit-Veru developed technology, explosives, and metal ships. The Mon-Veru couldn't compete. They still exist in small reservations, mostly in inland seas and lakes. This history colors their attitudes toward other life-forms. Enmity will be their reflex reaction to an unrelated species. Unlike us, they have no example of cooperation between species to counterbalance this history.

"Our prisoner is an academic and a specialist in Mon-Veru. His government must have figured that his prior experience with a different species would help."

"Voit-Veru," Mourner added, "are organized in what appears to be loosely a democracy but is in fact a clan-dominated society. I don't know how well any of you know Earth history, but the Veru government reminds me a great deal of the Tokugawa Shogunate that ran Japan for hundreds of years. The current family-clan is the Aporok. They control most of the policy-making apparatus."

"Sounds like the old Irish," Fenaday said.

"From the information obtained from Vaughn and by Commander Rainhell," added Telisan, "we are dealing with a major new power, but one whose technology seems slightly behind ours, at least in terms of ships and weapons. In other areas, they may well be ahead. Our recent experience in the Conchirri War has clearly given us an edge, but it would not do to overestimate it. Our margin of superiority seems slim."

"The Confederacy just finished a war," Gopal said. "I hope you people aren't planning a new one. We lost a lot."

"Don't speak in my presence about losses," Fenaday snapped. "I know the losses."

The room stayed silent for a minute.

Telisan broke the quiet. "Detailed planning on naval engagement strategies begins at 1400 today. That's Sharla, Graglia, Fury,

Wardell, Hafel, and the rest of the 'A' watch staff. We will start combat simulations immediately. Ground Force planning is at Commander Rainhell's option."

"What about Mmok?" Gopal asked.

"At the appropriate time," Fenaday answered. "He's otherwise engaged for now."

"Doing what?" challenged the Marine.

"Can it, Lieutenant," Fenaday said. He looked sidewise at Rainhell. She moved forward. "My team with me. Now," she added with a square look at the Marine. He met her stare, but wisely kept quiet. The four shuffled out, trailing her.

Fenaday couldn't take his eyes off Shasti until she disappeared around the corridor. No time to talk now. Guilt and relief warred in him.

"Meeting dismissed." The others left. Fenaday looked at the Denlenn. "Watch Gopal," said Fenaday. "I want all weapons under lock and key. Only our people are to be on guard duty. Sidearms for you, Perez, Sharla, Moshe, and anyone Shasti says gets one. I think we can trust Rask, and he has influence over Rigg. I know you like him, but he's Mandela's man."

Telisan nodded slowly.

———

Rainhell's planning session was brisk and efficient, like the Olympian herself. They quickly settled on a TOE and operational orders. Shasti named Rigg as second-in-command. Confused and dismayed, Rigg begged off assuming his duties till he was more recovered. More than his injuries troubled him. He suspected Rainhell knew it, and that he had fallen in the measurement of those cool green eyes. Perhaps he even saw a ghost of hurt or disappointment in them? Afterward, Rigg and the others dispersed, heading back for their commands.

Rigg decided to take the radial corridor back, hoping for some time alone, to think. He was not that lucky. A hand grabbed his shoulder, spinning him around. It was Gopal, the Marine officer, the person he hoped most to avoid.

"What the hell is going on here?" the Marine demanded, holding firm to Rigg's jacket. "You know this crap about jumping off the boards is crazy. These people aren't Confed military. Who authorized this mission?"

"Don't ask me," Rigg snapped. "I was in charge of the Alpha mission to Olympia. We got whacked. Captain Fenaday was in charge of the follow-up. Everything is on his authority."

"He's a freaking pirate," spat the Marine.

"Privateer," Rigg growled.

"Same difference, ASAT," Gopal continued more calmly, "and that doesn't answer my question. Whose mission are we on now? Why are my men here? On whose authority are we jumping off the charts? I don't think this is what Davis had in mind when he assigned us to this ship."

"You got questions," Rigg said. "You can put them to Rainhell, rank of full commander in the Confed Reserves. She's in charge of all shipboard security and ground troops. I'm not in command here. I just carry a gun and obey orders."

"Bullshit," Gopal said, his face only inches away from Rigg's. "Fenaday's gone rogue and you are supporting him. Who signs your paycheck, ASAT?"

"Is the gentleman bothering you, sir?"

Rigg and Gopal both turned to see Rask, his red eyes glimmering in the corridor's low light, standing a few feet away.

"This doesn't concern you," Gopal said.

"Question wasn't directed to you, sir. I work for Captain Rigg."

"We were just through." Rigg shook off Gopal's hand.

"Not hardly." Gopal turned on his heel and stalked away.

"You okay?" Rask watched the retreating Marine carefully.

"No," Rigg replied. "I don't know what I'm doing any more."

"Following the captain's orders."

"You know that's bogus." Rigg felt suddenly tired. "Fenaday's authority over us ended with the mission on Olympia. Telisan hijacked that poor bastard and his platoon."

"Skipper knows what he's doing," Rask said. "My orders were to follow his. Nobody has changed that, and nobody could foresee what we ran into on Olympia, or maybe they did and intended for this to happen. Besides, man, you owe him your life."

"Really?" Rigg asked, to Rask's evident astonishment. "He came for his girlfriend, Rainhell. Oh, sure, he kept an eye out for the rest of us, since he was here anyway. Probably even stuck his neck out a little to get us out of a jam, but do you think he'd have started out for Olympia if it had just been me?"

"You humans are a funny bunch." Rask shook his head. "I even grew up among you, on Mars, and I still don't understand you. What does the 'why' matter? Fact is, he came and he got you out. Dan, I couldn't have done it. There was no other backup plan."

"I know. I know," Rigg said. "You're right. Still, I feel so torn up. I know HQ wouldn't approve this. We are off the map here. No orders, no direction. I don't know what's right."

"Then follow the man who saved your life till you figure it out," Rask snapped, rare anger showing in his blue-tinged face. "We're off to rescue some of our own, held by bad guys. We kill some of them, well that's too fucking bad. Frankly, the idea that some REMFs would stop us doesn't sit so well with me anyway. Those guys are people like us. Front-line. Don't they deserve what you got? A rescue mission?"

"Okay," Rigg said, alarmed. He had never seen the usually laconic Morok so angry before. Loyalty was central to Morok culture, he remembered. Right now, he must look pretty bad in Rask's eyes. "We don't have orders not to follow Fenaday. Maybe that will be good enough, for now."

Rask slapped him on the back. "That's the ticket. You're just thinking too much. Wait until we get somewhere you can shoot somebody. It'll all seem clearer then."

"Great," Rigg said sourly. "I can hardly wait."

———

On the fifth day out from Olympia, Shasti entered *Sidhe's* small gym. Li, Rask, and the Morok brothers, Hanshi and Lokashti, followed and surrounded her in menacing attitudes. Fenaday and Telisan lay nearby on the mats, warming up. The human felt his injuries and every one of his thirty-six years. Grim determination to get back into fighting shape kept him going, despite the warnings of Mourner and Arpen. Guilt also drove him, as much as the need to rebuild his body. Only in the empty mindlessness of the Chi could he elude the pangs of guilt and grief. He had given up Lisa for lost. Failed. Faithlessly departed the trail too soon. While he was on New Eire, Shasti in his arms, Lisa was a prisoner all these years, abandoned. The last two nights he'd awakened in a cold sweat.

Nothing would stop him now. No other concern, no friendship, no other duty or promise would hold any weight. He would follow this trail to its end, while there was breath in his body. Only death could release him now.

His eyes strayed to Shasti, the other source of unease in his heart. He'd seen little of her since the meeting, being busy in both Sickbay and the bridge. Seeing her forced him to admit the truth. *I'm being a coward,* he thought, *ducking the inevitable.* It could no longer be delayed. He had started something with her, something neither was willing to define, but both clung to. Now he felt like a traitor to both women, to Lisa, who was alive as of six months ago, and to Shasti, who'd spent so much of her life alone.

"Somebody ought to just shoot me," he muttered.

"What?" Telisan said. Denlenn did not hear as well as humans.

"Nothing," the human said.

Shasti's opponents, all hardened hand-to-hand fighters, suddenly moved in on her all at once. She exploded into motion. Rask's long, ape-like arm swung through suddenly empty space. Li's leg sweep struck where her legs had been. The Tok brothers collided. She went aerial over Rask and snapped a kick into Li. They sorted themselves out, reengaging her. Shasti hit another gear. She blurred, parrying even blows thrown at her from behind. She hit all four of her opponents in nearly the same second. They tumbled to the mats, leaving her standing, alone, with everyone staring at her.

Telisan gave a long atonal whistle of astonishment. "I knew she was good," he said, disbelief in his voice.

Fenaday stood up and walked onto the mat, his grief and concerns shelved by the discipline of a lifetime's study. A practitioner since childhood, he took pride in his fourth-degree status. Until now, he'd held his own in sparring even against Shasti.

He smiled slightly, almost shyly, at her. "You seem to have improved again," he said. "Let's see what you can do."

Shasti stared back at him, the Shasti of old, self-contained, impenetrable. Her eyes reflected light, no warmth or depth, like a mannequin's. They took up stances and engaged. Instantly, Fenaday was on the defense and backing. He switched out of the hard style she was so familiar with to the soft style that had often frustrated her before. She bore in undeterred.

He hit her once, by chance. Suddenly it became a real fight. She broke through his defense, driving him to the mat, stunned. Men shouted and thrust between them. More blows and bodies flew.

Fenaday sucked in an agonized breath. "Stop," he roared.

Everyone froze. Rask and the others again surrounded the Olympian. Telisan picked himself up off the deck. Shasti stood in the middle of them, looking down at her hands as if in shock. Abruptly, she sat on the mat with a blank expression. She wiped a hand across her face, then stared at the moisture on it, as if seeing tears for the first time.

Fenaday got to his feet shakily. Each breath caused shooting pains in his chest. Everyone remained frozen, wary.

"Everyone out," he managed.

"Now," he added forcefully when no one moved. People shuffled out, looking uncertain, even frightened. Telisan started toward him. "Go," he said to the Denlenn. "It'll be okay." With what was probably a doubtful look among Denlenns, he followed the others.

Fenaday walked over to Shasti slowly, holding his side. Bones grated. *Ribs again,* he thought, *damn.* He sat down, carefully, next to her.

She lifted her face to his—shock, pain, dismay—it almost hurt to see her face so unguarded, so vulnerable.

"So," he began, "talk to me."

"Wha...why?" she stammered, something she'd never done before. "I don't understand. I was filled with such rage. I couldn't control it. I've never been so angry in my life, even at Pard. Why?" she cried finally, childlike.

"You're angry with me," he said softly, sadly, not yet daring to touch her. "You feel betrayed. I've failed both you and Lisa. Shasti, poor Shasti, I've caught you in the middle of it all."

She was trembling, also something never seen before. "No," she said. "No. I am sorry. God, I could have killed you." Tears leaked down her face. "After all you have done for me. I have no right."

"You have every right," he said harshly. "I should have come to you sooner."

"No," she insisted, "my fault. You saved my life. No one has been better to me. I just feel so alone, so abandoned. I've been alone my whole life and never felt it before."

She reached across suddenly and hugged him hard. His ribs grated under the pressure and his breath hissed, but he held her tight.

"This is my fault," he whispered.

"Don't be a fool," she said softly. "You couldn't know. It's almost impossible that she could have survived."

"No, not that," he said with a sigh. "I should have come to you and said something, or anything. You're so important to me, important enough to come through hell to find you on Olympia. I should have found the strength to walk a lousy hundred meters to your cabin."

"I knew you couldn't," she said, "and even understanding that, I felt such rage. Why?"

He looked into her eyes, clear green and, for once, accessible. *My God,* he realized, *for all her formidable size and strength, she's really little more than a child emotionally, and an abused one at that. She was raised in a crèche, trained as an assassin, on the run since her teenage years, never able to depend on anyone, with no normal relationships. Why didn't I ever see this before?*

"Shasti," he said, "I don't know what's waiting for me out there, but I have to go to find out. I am all the chance she has, if there is any chance. Until I know...until I know if she's alive and if there is a future for Lisa and me, my life is on hold. Understand, I love my wife. If there is a chance, I'm going to take it.

"I was wrong about one thing. I should have told you that no matter what happens, you are part of my life. You're my friend and much more. You will always have your place here on this ship and in my home in New Eire. I am not going to disappear on you. That is a promise."

She looked down and away for a second, then gently touched his face, sighed, and looked away. They stayed that way for a minute, him stroking her silky black hair, already almost back to full length. When she turned her face back, she was her controlled, calm self. A hint of a sly smile even touched her mouth. "Can't be good for your command image, being beaten up by your ex-girlfriend. Fortunately, there is still some luster left on your legend from killing Pard."

"Yeah," he said ruefully, "some legend. Good thing Pard had already stopped three or four shots, a stab wound, and the odd grenade fragment. Not to mention being beaten half to death by you."

"He'd beaten me ninety-percent to death in response," she said. "I lost. You killed Pard. Don't minimize it. For sheer size and strength, there's never been an equal to Pard. I'll never forget what you did.

"Well," she added after a moment, "is it off to the brig?"

He gave her a mock glare. "You are sentenced to dinner with me. I'll see you in six hours. Go on, hit the shower. Those are orders, Commander."

"Yes sir," she replied, gently touching his face again before walking away.

He waited until she left to try to get off the floor. As he struggled up, he found Telisan at his elbow. The Denlenn looked worried.

"Are you all right?" he asked, helping the human to stand.

"Doesn't anybody ever listen to an order anymore?" Fenaday said.

"I was out of earshot," the Denlenn said. "I saw her leave. What has happened?"

"Just human stuff," Fenaday replied. "Love, betrayal, infidelity, and failure. It's all right," he added, seeing the lack of comprehension on the Denlenn's face. "We're okay. Now."

"You humans have strange ways of showing affection."

"My mother used to tell me it was how you could tell if the little girls liked you." Fenaday smiled.

"It is a wonder you didn't run out of little boys," replied the Denlenn.

"Help me to Sickbay. I need to see Arpen and Mourner again, time for a little more regenerator work before my dinner date."

———

Shasti let the hot water sluice down her taut body, as if it could wash away the fury, the embarrassment, the memory of what had just happened. Control was the secret to her survival and hers lay in tatters. At first, she had been almost grateful that her relationship with Fenaday was over. It had pulled her into unfamiliar, terrifying ground. But her life seemed utterly empty without it. Sex was something she could have any time she wanted. She was young and beautiful and knew it. Her physical needs could easily be met, but this was not about sex. It was a new and frightening dimension.

If I were a normal human, she thought, *I would have faced this over ten years ago. I'd have had parents and friends to talk to, to explain things. I wouldn't have trained to kill since I could hold a weapon. Damn you, Pard. Even now I have to live with your legacy.*

She thought about the future that had begun to open for her. She had slammed the door too soon. Now she regretted her choice. There might be another chance, she thought. Lisa might not be alive. The thought she was hiding from leapt to the front of her mind. Lisa might not still be alive, and if she was, she might not stay that way. *Assassin,* she thought, a sour taste in her mouth, *but that's what I am. What they made me.*

"No." She surprised herself by saying it out loud. She tried to banish the thought, but it would not go away. *"Why should she have him?"* it whispered, silky and dark, to her. *"Does she deserve him? She wanted her career more than her husband. She's had everything you never did. She doesn't deserve to take your chance."*

No, she said to herself again. *Go away,* she bade the voice. *I'm not listening.*

The voice retreated, unvanquished. She knew with a thrill of fear that she would hear it again. Louder.

———

Mmok looked up at the knock on his door. The door cycled open. Leda Jenner walked in with his lunch. He studied the Olympian woman. He suspected she might be older than him, though it was difficult to tell with the Olympians. She could be considerably older and simply better bred to keep age at bay.

"How about lunch?" she asked, with her relentless pleasantry.

He looked sourly at the length of chain on his arm. "Sure."

"I hear you had company a few days ago."

"Yeah, my best pal," he sneered. "Rainhell."

"Most people would be delighted to have as pretty a woman as Shasti visit them."

"Woman." Mmok snorted. "She's not a woman. She's an organic killing-machine that someone shaped like a woman."

"There's something to that," Jenner admitted. "We spent a fair amount of time together, hiding from Denshi. There were times I was more afraid of her than of them."

"I can believe that," grunted Mmok, savaging a sandwich.

"Still," Jenner surprised him by sitting down on the bunk, "she's the reason we survived at all." Mmok suddenly noticed Jenner was an attractive woman, then wondered why he had not noticed before.

"When Dan was shot, I was afraid she might leave us. She

didn't. Even after he urged us to take off and leave him. She told me Robert wouldn't do it."

Mmok looked at her, surprise in his one eye. "Didn't know that," he admitted. "So she hung it out for big Dan? Hard to believe. Maybe there is some humanity in that shell."

"There is," Jenner said softly, but with force. "It's struggling, like a newborn baby."

Mmok just shook his head, reaching for the coffee.

"Then there were other times," she continued, looking him in the eye, "when she was generous and thoughtful. Somewhat naïve at points, almost like a younger sister."

"Hard to believe," grumbled Mmok. "To me she's always been just another killer, looking down her aristocratic nose at a piece of human wreckage." He instantly regretted the slip.

Jenner let him off easy. "I'm sorry about that. Many Olympians hold prejudices against cybernetic replacements. She should know better, having traveled so much."

"Ah, well," Mmok said, "maybe travel isn't broadening to the mind after all. Of course, it might help to have a heart as well as a mind."

"She has a heart," Jenner countered. "I saw it the night that the news announced Fenaday's death. A clever deception, fooled everyone. Us too. I still remember what she looked like when she heard. I don't think I've ever seen a face with such loss on it."

"You like her," Mmok accused.

She smiled easily. "Yes, perhaps you'll forgive me though, since I also like you."

Mmok felt his face go flush. "Well," he mumbled, "you're okay too."

"How about some more coffee?" she asked.

"Yeah," he said. "How's she taking the news about Mrs. Fenaday?"

"It must hurt terribly." Jenner sighed. "Both of them."

"Don't limit it to them," Mmok said harshly. "It's going to hurt a lot more people than just them. All of us are dead if we don't stop them. Maybe thousands more beyond that, if this sparks off a war."

Jenner smiled sadly at the cyborg. "Finish your lunch, Mr. Mmok."

"Dammit, woman, I'm serious."

"Yes, you are," she replied, cocking an eyebrow, "almost grim. Here you are trying to enlist my aid to derail one of the great romance stories of the age, though I don't know yet if it will be a tragic romance or not. I'm afraid my feminine curiosity just won't let me help you."

Mmok glared at her. "You're as nuts as everyone else on this ship."

Jenner laughed and Mmok flushed angrily for a second, finally realizing she was teasing him. Looking at her kind brown eyes, he felt his resentment fade. He barked a laugh. "Well now I guess I'm nuts too. I only hope we all think this is still funny three weeks from now."

Chapter Five

C aptain," Sharon Hafel said from communications. "Mr. Perez wants to see you. He has some concerns about the quantum harmonics on the jump calculations for Zealmun."

Fenaday nodded. It was near the end of watch, and he still found himself wearing down quickly despite everything Mourner and Arpen could do for him. "Okay, clear the turbovator for bridge access." He heard the characteristic hum of the turbovator's operation and then some moments later, the annoying clank of the pressure door.

"Captain," Perez cried. There was a thud and the sound of a body hitting the floor.

"Turn around slowly, Captain," said a voice he recognized as Gopal's. "If anyone else moves, you get it."

Fenaday turned in his chair. The bridge crew sat still. Perez lay on the deck, bleeding from a blow from the Marine's pistol. Fenaday cursed himself. Gopal must have disarmed the engineer, forcing him to call through to the bridge. The only sounds were those of the ventilation blowers and instruments. Shasti stood by her security board, almost crackling with repressed energy.

"This ship is going back to Olympia," Gopal stated. "Your man Telisan sold Davis a bunch of crap. All you Confed crew, this is an unauthorized mission. I expect you to follow my orders. The ship goes back."

"No," Fenaday said softly, his hand resting lightly near his own pistol. "It may go up in flames, or it may go to Thorraken. Nowhere else."

Gopal grimaced. "Okay, we'll do this the hard way. Fenaday, Rainhell, unbuckle your pistol belts with your left hands."

"No." Fenaday stood slowly.

"I'm not bluffing, Fenaday." The Marine's eyes were level and cool.

"Me neither, Jarhead," Fenaday replied, equally cool. "You shoot me and Shasti will hit you before you can retarget."

"Won't do you much good, pirate."

"Killing me won't stop the ship from going where I send it. Telisan will complete the mission. Never doubt it. I'm prepared to die to accomplish my mission," continued Fenaday. "Are you?"

"Figure on it being very slow and artistic," Shasti hissed. "You know Denshi. You know what we do."

For the first time the Marine looked uncertain. He knew Olympians and knew Shasti was special, feared even in Denshi.

"Give it up, Marine," Wardell said. The old gunner slowly turned in his chair. "Nobody has ever made a change in the captain's course when he was on a lead to the missus." He gestured toward Rainhell. "That's Death's own angel right there. You even blink, boy, and she'll kill you before you can open your eyes again."

Fenaday took a step forward. Gopal tracked him with the weapon, sweat beading on his upper lip. At the helm, Graglia stirred; he too was regular Confed, confused now over whom to obey. Without turning, Shasti raised her left arm and pointed a long slender finger at Graglia. Warning, first and only, to the sensible. Graglia stopped moving.

"Put the weapon down," Fenaday said.

"Damn you," snarled Gopal. "Traitor!"

Behind him, Sharla moved a slow finger toward the alarmed

Klaxon, her eyes on Shasti. The Olympian did not look directly at her but gave a barely perceptible nod. Sharla prayed she read Shasti correctly and hit the button. The alarm whooped and the sound made everyone but Shasti jump. She simply blurred into action, her pistol snap-firing in laser mode. The beam lanced into the Marine's left eye, then flicked down, cutting Gopal's weapon free. Gopal didn't even have time to scream. The Marine dropped straight to the deck. Everyone on the bridge stood frozen in shock. Hafel's breath came out in a sob. Graglia jerked to standing, only to find Shasti's cold, empty eyes on him, her weapon held at stomach level pointed at his own.

"I told you, boy," Wardell murmured. "I told you."

Fenaday slumped back in his seat, fighting for control. "Secure the bridge doors," he managed. "Sharla, call Arpen and have Telisan come to the bridge. Mr. Graglia, sit down." The young officer just stared. "Now, Mr. Graglia."

"Shasti, call your trouble team to the bridge. Tell Rigg that I want the Marines confined to quarters. Make sure there are no arms missing."

Shasti walked over to him. Her face reflected nothing, but he sensed concern. He rose, hoping the shaking in his legs was not visible through the loose-fitting ship's uniform.

Ten minutes later, Fenaday was in his space cabin, just off the sealed bridge. Li and his team stood guard at the entrance. Gopal's body lay in the ship's morgue.

Fenaday walked out of the bathroom, hoping that his gut was finally empty. He sat on the bed and put his head in his hands, still trying to get hold of himself. The sting of mouthwash made his mouth tingle, but it had scrubbed out the sour taint.

"Stupid son of a bitch," he said shakily.

"Yes," Shasti said, standing over him, worried and not sure how to help. "A fool not to surrender when checkmated."

"Front of his damn pistol looked like a sewer pipe," Fenaday joked weakly. "What was it, a thousand millimeter or something?"

"No," she replied, "standard issue."

He looked up at her, suddenly serious. "Aren't you ever afraid?

Not just the adrenaline rush, but afraid to be hurt, to die. Afraid to where you don't care about anything but staying alive another minute? Doesn't it ever bother you?"

She sat next to him, looking into his eyes. "No, at least not like that. I was literally made to do these things. I am simply not capable of physical fear at that level."

"God," he said, wiping a hand over his face, "what a blessing."

She shook her head. "You don't want to be me."

"Well," he said, with a small grin, "it would entail a whole new set of underwear."

"What makes you think I'm wearing any?" she replied dryly.

Fenaday did a double take and then started laughing so hard that tears stung his eyes. He stopped before it became hysterical.

"Well, so you've learned how to tell a joke. Admit it, woman."

She smiled enigmatically.

He put an arm around her, and she moved closer. They leaned their heads together. He caught his breath, then kissed her chastely. "Thank you for my life, again."

Shasti's mouth tingled. She wanted to kiss him more thoroughly, but feared to break the intimacy between them. *Damn her,* whispered the voice in her head. *Go,* she snarled at it.

"I should get back out there," he said.

"Are you up to it?" she asked anxiously.

"I have to be," he said, utter weariness in his voice. "For a little while longer, I somehow have to be."

"I am your shadow," she said firmly, alarmed by the fatigue she saw in every line of him, "from this minute on. You go nowhere I do not also go. You are only a few weeks from death's door and only a standard human."

"Smile when you say that," he replied. Shasti looked at him in confusion.

"Just a joke, not as good as yours," he replied. "Okay, let's get out there and look like fearless privateers of the star lanes. It's twelve hours to initial jump point. Catch me if I fall over."

"Always," she replied gravely.

F enaday looked at the screen built into the arm of his command chair. Math and images scrolled before his eyes. The transition point for Zealmun was coming up fast. It would take them to their first alien system, over seventy-eight light-years away. On Confed starcharts it existed merely as a two-line entry: Zealmun, a Class Five black hole discovered by the English astronomer Geoffrey Squibb. No known useful warplines ran to, or from it, according to Confederate records. The system lay so far beyond the Confederacy that not even a robot probe had ever visited it.

The Voit-Veru records added considerable information. Nine planets circled in the frozen hell of the dead star. Four were rocky balls that might have held life eons ago, and five were gas giants. The Voit-Veru maintained a tiny, largely automated base on the fourth world, as did the Olympians, hard duty in an isolated grim corner of the universe. *Sidhe's* computer carried all the necessary navigation information, but the system was far from mapped. The maps for the systems beyond were also rudimentary. The discovery of the route between Olympia and the Voit-Veru frontier was as recent as the Alliance. Good system maps took decades.

"Sound General Quarters," Fenaday called, and the siren began its staccato demand. *Hope there isn't an uncharted rock in our exit cone,* he thought.

"Wardell, arm main gun, lasers, and chain guns. Open outer tubes for all missiles and arm."

"Outer tubes opening and green light on all tubes. Main gun up," Wardell replied. "Chain guns and lasers are online."

"Air Boss," he called to Telisan, "status on *Wildcats*." He knew the Denlenn ace would have rather been in a fighter, but Fenaday needed him to act as Air Boss. He wondered if Telisan had realized the human was protecting him as best he could. *Probably not,* thought Fenaday. *He'd have objected.*

"Green light, engines warm and weapons primed," Telisan replied, his eyes on the screen and instruments that showed the fighters.

"Sharla, ECM and jamming on standby."

"Affirmative."

Fenaday opened the channel to Engineering. "Perez, status."

"Vaya con Dios."

"I'll take that as a ready."

"Sí."

"Wardell, you are weapons free. As soon as we emerge, lock up any target in arc and be ready to fire on the order. All contacts will be hostile."

Fenaday scanned the bridge; all stations were ready. The main engine engage switch glowed by his right hand. He removed the safeties. Hyperspace engagement was the master's call. "All stations and personnel," he announced on the ship's intercom, "hyperspace transit in sixty seconds from my mark. Now, mark."

"Fifty-seven and counting," Graglia called. He sat at the helm, hands poised over the boards in case of an abort. Entry was the most difficult and critical part of the voyage. The wrong angle and the hyperspace could be thicker, the trip longer. Time did not pass for the crew in hyperspace, but it did in the real universe, time that counted for Lisa.

The engines began to moan as they built up, colors around them seemed to change value. Time itself felt strange.

Fenaday watched the clock. "Entry," he called, hitting the button.

Discontinuity, dreams, déjà vu.

Chapter Six

Mikhail Vaughn was in the former Denshi office in downtown Marathon when his security chief, Misa Tanaka, buzzed him to announce that Lieutenant Colonel Guytano Dominici had entered the building. Tanaka managed this despite the fact that internal security arrangements were out of Denshi hands, held now by Army Special Forces, or Military Police. Still, Denshi had built the office tower, and it held secrets the Army had not yet discovered. So Vaughn was prepared when the paratrooper, fully as big as the seven-foot-tall Engineered, strode into his office.

They didn't shake hands, merely nodding respectfully, looking each other over warily. Selected and Engineered, the two paths Eugenics had taken on Olympia. To an untrained observer, the two huge men would have looked like an even match in a fight. In reality, Dominici would have little chance against the new lord of the Denshi. For all that, it was Dominici who seemed the more at ease. He knew he had the high ground. The halls outside were full of his men.

"To what do I owe the honor?" Vaughn asked.

"I would like you to come with me," the big para said. "My mother wished to speak with you on a matter of some urgency."

"Ah," Vaughn said, "a problem has occurred."

"Yes." Dominici nodded. "She seems to think that you may be of some use in regards to it."

"I fear she overestimates the help I can provide."

"We shall see," he replied. "You and your personal guard are to accompany me. Now."

"Of course." Vaughn rose. It galled him to be at the beck and call of a Selected, but this was the new reality. The revelation of the secret alliance with the Voit-Veru had pulled Olympia out of the Engineered's grasp. Vaughn had thrown in his lot with Dominici in the only sensible play. Some Denshi and Navy forces still resisted. *Fanatics and fools*, he thought, *to fight on with the Confederacy moving in. Better to bend than to break.*

Vaughn followed Dominici out. Tanaka, a Selected like Dominici, though raised in Denshi, paced a step behind Vaughn. Six grim-looking paras fell in behind her, all holding full assault weapons to Tanaka's small pistol. *Perhaps I should feel complimented*, Vaughn thought. A gray-green armored aircar sat just outside the doors, its idling motor fitfully kicking up leaves and dust.

Once aboard, the trip to the Army HQ took about a half-hour. No one spoke as the aircar accelerated out over the desert. Army HQ, like the main Denshi complex, lay well outside Marathon, though the Army camp was farther up in the mountains. Those now rose to face him, craggy and stark, harkening to the days before terraforming took the edge off Olympia's inhospitable surface. Dominici's base was over the first range. A sprawling, modern Army base with weapons in hardened sites, it could duel with an orbiting starship. The base didn't look like much from the air, as most of the planetary defense fortress was underground. No matter how weapons evolved, there was no better and cheaper protection than a few meters-worth of packed dirt.

The aircar came down in the main airbase. Vaughn had studied the base plans often but never laid eyes on the place. As the hatches came open, cold mountain air rushed in. It was late winter in this hemisphere, the same winter that had seen Jalgren Pard's death and the fall of Denshi only weeks before. It seemed impossible that it was only such a short span of time. Tanaka turned her collar up against the cold. Vaughn merely adjusted his body temperature by an act of will.

A rumble of jet engines caused him to look over his shoulder. Two stubby *Wildcat* aerospace fighters were rumbling down the runway. Beyond them, two *Hunters*, mere atmospheric craft, awaited their turn.

"This way." Colonel Dominici pointed.

Vaughn followed, shadowed by Tanaka and the paras. They walked into a hardened bunker, past armed soldiers who saluted the colonel. Finally, they faced an ornate door leading to Dominici's office. A dozen alert troopers guarded it.

"You've been scanned, of course," Colonel Dominici said. "Ms. Tanaka and her weapon will remain out here."

Vaughn looked at Tanaka and nodded. The beautiful Asian woman looked unhappy, but she was a realist. Protest would avail nothing.

The doors opened, and Vaughn preceded the colonel and his six guards into a large room. Military flags and unit emblems decorated the walls along with "official" paintings of various military actions. One featured a young Captain Maria Dominici shooting down a pair of dinosaur-like Conchirri troopers who had penetrated her command post during a battle early in the Xenophobe War. She'd earned a medal for that fight.

General Dominici sat at her plain government-issue desk. She glanced up at his entry, then rose, courteous and gracious. "Mr. Vaughn, how good of you to come. Please be seated." She gestured to a collection of overstuffed chairs around a table near a doorway. Vaughn's guards arranged themselves silently around the room. Their mistrustful eyes never left him. Guytano Dominici moved to stand behind his mother.

Dominici smiled briefly at her son, then signaled to an orderly standing nearby. "Coffee and water." The orderly disappeared through another door. Both Domincis walked to the table, but only the general sat.

Vaughn sat in the chair she gestured to. Small talk was not a talent of his, and he knew Dominici to be skilled as a diplomat and tactician. He didn't want to fence verbally with her. The orderly returned with a coffee service that he placed in front of General Dominici.

Small talk didn't seem to be on her mind. She idly poured a cup of coffee for herself, then passed him a cup. Black, as he drank it. He knew it was her way of telling him there was no detail of his existence she did not know.

"I underestimated Telisan," she began. "He seemed an idealistic babe-in-the-woods, like most of the Denlenn. It's sometimes hard to believe they are related to their cousins, the Dua-Denlenn. It should have occurred to me that there was more to him than that. I imagine that Fenaday wore off on him. In any event, he fooled me. The repairs, supplies, and troops he took were not authorized by the Confederacy."

"Ah," Vaughn said.

Dominici smiled at him. "Where is Telisan going?"

"Into Voit-Veru space," Vaughn replied. "I'll grant you that I do not know why. I assume it must have something to do with Fenaday's insane quest."

Dominici stared at him. "Lisa Fenaday is dead. No one comes back from deep space."

"I did not say that it made sense. It merely is, what is."

She looked at her son. "It doesn't make sense. What could they do with a lousy frigate against a whole species? If that's what they were doing, they're dead. Even if they get past the ships Denshi must have assigned to the route, they will never make it past the Voit-Veru. It's their frontier."

He shrugged. "Fenaday has made a career of the impossible: Morokat, Enshar, and now Pard's death. You met him."

"Yeah," she said. "He was something of a disappointment. I expected him to be bigger."

"He was big enough to be the end of Pard."

"What else do you know?" she asked. "You visited the *Sidhe*, the day before she spaced. You spoke to Telisan; I've learned that much."

Now it was Vaughn's turn to smile. "I went to see Rainhell for reasons of my own."

Dominici's pleasant veneer cracked slightly. "Boy, don't play with me."

Vaughn looked back, all bland innocence.

"You know," she said, "I might find a way to allow another Engineered in the new Assembly. That is one, and only one, additional member."

Vaughn looked into her suddenly cool eyes. He had pressed her as far as was safe. "Telisan gave away nothing of his plans. He even deleted the Project Overman files from the Denshi mainframe. Fortunately, I had made certain provisions, copied certain material for my private use. In one of those files was the name *Blackbird*, the ship Fenaday's wife commanded. I assume the Voit-Veru destroyed it. The information is unclear and fragmentary, translated from a language we do not know well. Even computers make assumptions when working in alien languages."

"So Fenaday's off to war on the Veru," Dominici mused. "I don't buy it. The man I met was more practical than that."

"I do not pretend to follow the psychology of standard humans." Vaughn shrugged. "I couldn't understand why he simply did not take up with a new female, especially after he met a superior specimen like Rainhell."

Dominica's lips thinned in distaste. "Are you a friend of my first husband by any chance?"

"No," Vaughn said, puzzled by the non-sequitur.

Dominici sighed. "Buy a book on humor sometime," she said. "It will be a good investment."

"Is that all of it?" she asked.

"Yes," he lied.

"Of course," she replied, not believing him.

Suddenly there was a loud bleep on her desk. "General,"

announced a voice, "there is an incoming message from the *Polaris*. Mr. Mandela says it is urgent he speak with you."

"Follow me," Dominici snapped. Vaughn and Guytano followed her through the rear exit to her office, trailed by the guards. It led, as he suspected, to the command center. Overhead stood a large, segmented video screen. The dreadnought *Polaris* cruised on the center screen. Dominici strode over to the communications center. "Put them through," she ordered.

The screen over them lit. Vaughn saw two humans and a Denlenn in the command center of a warship. The black man in the center did not wear a uniform, yet he seemed to be in command. "General Dominici," he said.

"Mr. Mandela," she replied. "As you can see," she gestured at Vaughn, "I am working on the matter we discussed."

"I have a feeling," said the man she called Mandela, "that the answers may become apparent. We just received a signal from the *Sidhe*. It advised that we would be receiving a message addressed to both of us following the initial signal. It should be coming in seconds."

A junior officer came up to the Denlenn officer and whispered something to him. "The signal is coming in," announced the Denlenn.

"Well," Mandela settled into a seat, "let's hear it."

Robert Fenaday's face appeared on the screen, haggard, thinner than Vaughn remembered. His eyes were sunken, with a bruised look. What little background they could see looked like a ship's cabin.

"Mandela," he husked, "Dominici, I'll assume you're both alive. People like you never seem to end up on the casualty list. I'll also assume that by now you've figured out that Telisan took us out of Olympia on my authority. Doubtless you are curious as to where we're going. I won't hold you in suspense. With our lead, there's nothing you can do to stop me. By the time you hear this, we will be gone in hyperspace.

"These aliens you were so worried about, Mandela, the Voit-Veru? Well I'm going to pay them a visit. You see, eight years ago they took something from me. Something precious…my wife, Lisa. They captured her ship and crew. As of six months ago, three of the *Blackbird's* crew were still alive.

"Did you hear that, you bastard? Still alive!" Fenaday controlled himself with a visible effort. "Our ship will be traveling an express warpline to the frontier world where they are held. We have Voit-Veru and Denshi IFF, along with all the information on patrols, weapons, and ships that Denshi had.

"We are going to get there before the Voit-Veru learn of the destruction of their allies. Never doubt that I will get there. I will. If she lives, I'll find her. Whatever gets in my way will die.

"I suggest you dig in on Olympia, old boy. You might even want to call for reinforcements. If I make it back, there may be a whole lot of company on my heels.

"Yep." Fenaday leaned back in his seat with evident satisfaction. "You might want to think about digging a few bomb shelters, General. As for you, Mandela, maybe you should have taken the job in the Agricultural Department after all.

"Good-bye and go to hell."

The privateer's image disappeared from the screen.

"Oh my God," Dominici said.

"Exactly," Mandela said. If Fenaday's message perturbed him, he gave no sign of it. "It was very resourceful of him to get those IFF codes. Wasn't it, Mr. Vaughn?"

Vaughn looked back at Mandela and Dominici. "He was in the complex and we know that Telisan brought a crack computer tech with him."

Mandela smiled. "Of course."

Vaughn felt Dominici's eyes boring into him. He wondered how much his obsession with Rainhell was going to cost him. He wondered at the madness that impelled him to give Telisan the codes, just to increase the chance that she might survive.

"I thought he'd be destroyed before he penetrated any distance," Dominici said. "With those codes, with that information, he has a chance to do terrible damage."

"His chances," Mandela said, "may be even better than you

think. There's more to *Sidhe* than meets the eye. I can unfortunately attest that the same is true for Fenaday. I had people on that vessel who should have prevented this. He does seem to have the fabled luck of the Irish."

"War," Xein said.

"It could be," the Denlenn agreed.

"With Olympia as the front line," Dominici whispered.   ·

"Surely, you realized that was always that chance," Mandela said, "regardless of what Fenaday does. I will admit that he upset the applecart by months."

"Never mind that. What are you going to do?" Dominici snapped.

"I think," Mandela said, "that I'll take Fenaday's advice and send for those reinforcements."

Chapter Seven

E mergence," Lieutenant Graglia called.

The word hung in Fenaday's brain as he tried to focus. Emergence meant that he and the *Sidhe* were back in the universe. They were real again. They could be killed now.

"Scan," Fenaday demanded, fighting his way out of the stomach-turning disorientation of hyperspace emergence.

"Contact," Sharla called. "No ID, too much distortion. Two contacts, 15 mark 22 range 100,000 kilometers. Switching data to all stations. Main screen coming back online."

"Broadcasting IFF on Olympian Frequency," Hafel said.

"Wardell," Fenaday snapped.

"Locking," the gunner replied. "God, we're on top of them."

"Main gun and half the weapons on the bigger target. All other weapons on the smaller ship. Fire!" Fenaday said. "Telisan, hold *Wildcat* launch. Sharla, full ECM. Now."

Lights dimmed as the ship's energy weapons sucked power and hurled. From the mass-accelerator running most of *Sidhe's* length, a ceramic and metal sabot round of depleted uranium the size of man's leg raced down the ringed tube reaching most of the speed of light in an instant.

Sidhe's main viewer screen lit up, still crackling with the disturbances of emergence. On it, displayed on two panels because of their distance from each other, were two ships. The larger one was lit by the hellish blaze of *Sidhe's* lasers. A flash lit the outer section of the hull and the cruiser's plates buckled, separating like tissue paper as the particle-accelerator's sabot round smashed into her with catastrophic kinetic energy.

Lasers lanced into the smaller ship as well. The frigate was so close, Wardell even fired the chain guns. Collapsed uranium munitions sparkled on the enemy hull.

"Graglia, soon as you have a bearing, see if you can cut us into a blind spot." Fenaday pointed to the screen on his command chair's arm. The computer instantly placed an artifact on both Graglia's board and the main screen, showing the direction.

"The larger vessel is an unknown type, estimating a light cruiser," Hafel said. "Smaller vessel is an Olympian frigate, probably the *Narcissus* or the *Pan*."

The light cruiser emitted a belch of flaming gas and seemed to roll. The frigate's engines lit in a burn as it desperately tried to get up speed from its station-keeping mode.

"The frigate is ranging on us," Sharla said. "ECM in effect. No signal from the light cruiser. She's out of it. No defensive fire coming out against our missiles. Weapons are under local control only."

"Frigate is firing. I've broken his lock."

Sidhe rocked slightly. Everyone looked at the walls.

O'Neill looked up from the damage control board. "A hit amidships, Exterior Compartment A-14 depressurizing. I've got damage control team Bravo on it."

"Missiles three, four, and eight are arriving on the light cruiser," Wardell yelled. "He's shot down number three. Impact!"

On screen, the light cruiser flared in the brilliant globular blast of a one-kiloton nuclear blast, then another. There was only debris.

"I'm cutting us astern of the frigate," Graglia said, sweat beading on his face. *Sidhe* had emerged with tremendous velocity. Relative to her, both enemy ships were standing still. He aimed for a narrow cone behind the frigate's drive engines, a blind-spot starships couldn't use in combat at normal ranges. It was an insane move for an insane battle. "We'll be out of his direct weapon arc for only a second. I can't v-dump enough to make a difference."

"The frigate's counter-measures are penetrated," Sharla said. "One of the lasers must have hit something." On the screen, the frigate flared in silhouette as one of *Sidhe's* conventional warheads went off just short of her. The range was too close for nukes. The small vessel rolled and exploded.

"Enemy missile," Wardell cried. "It's through the chain guns."

The screen overloaded with light and *Sidhe* bucked again.

"Got it," Sharla said. "ECM detonated the warhead one thousand meters out. Conventional warhead, like our Mark VI. Thank God."

Graglia whistled. "Damn, you did it, skipper."

Cheers broke out on the bridge and over the intercom.

Fenaday made a cutting gesture. "Scan."

"Nothing in short scan," Hafel said. "Long scan…is also clear."

"Maintain full passive ECM," Fenaday ordered. "Steady up on the evasive course to the next jump point." He noticed his hands were shaking and surreptitiously pressed them to the seat, trying to breathe regularly.

"Good work," Telisan said.

"We were lucky," the human replied. "They weren't expecting us, and we came out on top of them fast. Their position was lousy, and they were at station keeping. Wouldn't pass muster in the Confed Navy, huh?"

Telisan shrugged. "It would seem to imply that they are on an extended patrol, far from base, conserving fuel. Still, a patrol is always watched by a larger force. There will be others. If not here, then later at the warp point to Dralich."

Inspiration hit him. "Shasti," he demanded, "would another Engineered recognize you as one on a video monitor?"

"Likely," she replied. "We are sensitive to the visual cues: size, look, and design elements, particularly the symmetry of the facial features, something not natural in a born human."

"So what?" Rigg asked.

"There are Olympian as well as Voit-Veru forces in this buffer system. Neither side would allow the other total military domination of the express route to each other's frontier. We have current Denshi codes and IFF, thanks to Vaughn. Let's broadcast a fake report. Pretend to be a courier out of Olympia bringing word of a sneak attack by the Voit-Veru through another route. The Voit-Veru cruiser tried to stop us; the Denshi vessel intervened and was destroyed in the fight."

"Thin," Rigg said, thinking furiously, "but it might work. It depends on how much trust there is in the alliance."

Shasti smiled coldly. "The Engineered trust no one but another Engineered and then only when there is a shared self-interest. We were bred to dominate, not cooperate. I agree; this could work."

"There is no downside to trying," Telisan said. "If there is a vessel in interception range of us, it will start for us as soon as it detects the entry flare and the nuclear detonations. Maybe this will slow them. If not, we will have to fight them anyway."

Fenaday looked up at her. "Can you pull it off?"

She nodded. "Let me try."

Shasti walked over to Sharla's station. "Set up a transmission, narrow the field of focus until it is just my face and torso. We don't need them seeing anyone else. Pull up the Olympian War Book Dominici provided us with. We need to find the closest match for *Sidhe's* silhouette."

Sharla shook her rough mane-like hair. "Almost impossible, this Conchirri frigate leader hull doesn't look like anything the Confederacy built."

"Doesn't have to be that close," Sharon Hafel chimed in. "You're thinking visual. They'll get a radar or microwave image long before they can see us. Back during the Second Sector War, we used to have trouble telling the radar and micro signatures of these Conchirri Frigate Leaders and *Sword* Class destroyers."

Sharla looked dubious. "Let's see them on the screen." She punched up the radar, microwave, and visual silhouettes. "Hmmn, you're right. The radar is very close, at long range anyway. If they don't get to visual range, it might work."

"Remember," Hafel said, "most ships this size don't have sensors as good as what Mandela gave us for the Enshar expedition. This won't fool a heavy cruiser's rig if we're unlucky enough to draw one, but a destroyer or light cruiser, maybe."

"Excellent," Shasti said. "Pick the best match. Look for a *Sword* DD with a female captain between twenty-five and fifty."

Hafel snorted. "You'll never pass for fifty."

Shasti shook her head, the glossy, blue-black hair shimmering like mist. "An Engineered female of my generation will not change appreciably between those ages. We are long-lived and age slowly to the eye."

Hafel, never pretty and whose hair was liberally shot through with gray, simply sighed heavily. Shasti looked at her without understanding.

Hafel worked on her computer for a minute. "Not good. There are five *Swords* in the OSDFN. Best match on ships is the OSDFN *Persephone*, but the captain is Paulo Medeiros. He does have a female second officer, Chell Vanickz. No information on the executive officer. This data is about three months old."

"Do we know where that ship is?" asked Fenaday.

"*Persephone* was the destroyer that tried to catch up to us when we entered Olympia system," Hafel answered.

"Do we have a picture of the second officer?" Shasti asked.

The photo that popped on screen was of a devastatingly beautiful girl, who appeared to be about twenty-five. She was as big, beautiful, and blue-eyed a Nordic blonde as any Viking could want. Even the uniform didn't hide the lines of a full, but athletic body.

"So much for that," Fenaday said. "No hope of passing for her."

"I hope she didn't go up with that ship." Rigg studied her beautiful face. "Got any shots of her in a bikini?"

The women all glared at him. Rigg looked at Fenaday. "Oh, like you were thinking something else?"

Fenaday stared at the bulkhead overhead.

"A more constructive thought," Sharla said. "We're doing this the hard way. We don't have to match you in reality. I can take this image, run it through the computer and overlay your face with it. A virtual mask, I could even do the uniform."

"Won't they detect that?" Hafel wondered.

"I'm hoping that with the proper Denshi codes they won't look too hard. If they do, they should figure it out eventually. We can fake a little battle damage to our com system too. That should help. It won't fool anyone that knows her well, or her voice. I can't fake that without a sample."

"All right," Shasti said, "let's do it."

Sharla and Hafel worked their computer magic for over an hour. "Okay," Sharla said finally. "Sit here and don't shift around."

Shasti sat at the console. "This is Acting-Captain Chell Vanickz, of the OSDFN *Persephone*, DD Nine, authentication code Lima-Lima-Three-Four-Nine-Seven-Epsilon to all Olympian forces in Zealmun system. Voit-Veru forces have attacked Olympia. Our ship has been sent to recall all available forces for planetary defense. A Voit-Veru cruiser attacked us on entry to this system. The patrol frigate aided us when we told them of the Veru's treachery. She's been destroyed along with the enemy cruiser. We are damaged, but operable. Captain Medeiros is unconscious, and the first officer is dead.

"This vessel is proceeding under radio silence to attempt to reach the next system. We will not respond to transmissions and this message will not be repeated. Watch out for yourselves and get back to Olympia. We are badly outnumbered back there and it is not going well. *Persephone* out."

Sharla hit the transmit key.

"With any luck," Shasti said, "that will get them killing each other. If any vessels do head back to Olympia, the Confederacy should get them. It will give us a better chance of an escape route."

"Like we're gonna need it," Rigg muttered.

"Can it, Rigg," Fenaday growled.

"Okay," added Fenaday, ignoring the ASAT's return glare. "We're under stealth protocol, radio and emission silent with the hologenerators going. We should look like a small, iron-ore asteroid. It will take a warship's sensors at close range to tell the difference.

"I want to conserve fuel, so I'm not planning any further burns. We still have our momentum from the high speed run out of Olympia. We'll skirt the outer edge of this system, then cut in for the jump point to Dralich. With any luck, we won't meet anybody.

"Telisan, launch *Wildcat One*. I want her at maximum distance ahead of us. Have *Wildcat Two* relieve her in six hours. It's five days to the next optimum warp point." He stood. "I want to see what the damage looks like. Telisan, you have the bridge. Rigg, you and Shasti are with me."

They met the damage control team by the frame of the depressurized section. Fenaday triggered a computer screen and demanded an interior access shot. The Frokossi ex-princeling, Dobera, led the damage-control team. The custom space suit of the Frokossi had a fishbowl-like helmet, making it easy to spot him. They were working on a small, ragged tear on the interior compartment. Knowing the strength of the armored hull's exterior, Fenaday shuddered. The object that struck them must have been tiny, or the damage would have been far worse.

"Damage report, Mr. Dobera."

"The interior," the Frokossi responded, "can be rendered airtight. Damage to the exterior armor must be significant. It will go ill for us if we are hit on this section again. Fortunately, the frame itself appears in good shape."

"Very good," Fenaday said. "Keep at it. Signal Mr. Perez when you can begin re-pressurization tests." A sudden wave of dizziness struck him. He leaned against the bulkhead.

"When was the last time you slept, sir?" Rigg asked.

"You want me to take a nap after just hitting enemy space?" he replied, feigning shocked outrage.

"Want you to be able to fight the next vessel that we run into," Rigg said.

"Daniel is right," Shasti added. "Space is clear locally, and Telisan is much more able-bodied than you are."

"Fine thing to hear from your girlfriend," Rigg said, "but true."

Fenaday's temper flared, but he let it go. Rigg meant the comment kindly.

"Sorry, sir," Rigg said, sensing the misstep.

"That's all right, Dan," Fenaday replied, his temper vanishing as fast as it came. "We've been through a lot together. When it's just Shasti and me, you can call me Bob, or Robert, if you like."

"You can call him, Bob," Shasti said. "I call him Robert."

Rigg grinned. "Yes, ma'am."

Chapter Eight

Fenaday cycled through the hatch to Mmok's cell. Mmok lay on his bunk, watching a movie on a view-only monitor. Telisan would never have trusted the cyborg with a full-function computer. He looked up as Fenaday entered. They faced each other for a few seconds, then Mmok switched off the set.

"Morning," Fenaday said.

"Somewhere I guess." Mmok fixed his one human eye on Fenaday.

"Before we talk about everything else," Fenaday leaned on the wall, "one question. Did you send Gopal to kill me?"

"What," Mmok snapped, sitting bolt upright. "What's happened?"

"He drew a weapon on me on the bridge," Fenaday said. "He's dead."

"Goddamn Marines," Mmok said, "always with the frontal assault. So, he's dead, huh? Poor bastard. He was a good man."

"I've killed a lot of them," Fenaday replied.

"Ever bother you," Mmok asked, "this price tag you keep piling up on your wife?"

"Every minute of every day."

The answer seemed to disconcert Mmok, who looked away.

"You ever been in love, Mmok?"

The cyborg's jaw dropped in astonishment. "What? Are we supposed to sit and trade girlish confidences now?"

"If you haven't," Fenaday said, "then you don't know what it can make you do. How powerful it is."

"Guess not," Mmok replied, staring at him as if he'd gone mad.

"So back to my first question then. Did you send Gopal against me?"

After a moment, Mmok answered. "I didn't. Not that I wouldn't kill you if I thought it would stop this insanity. It wouldn't. Telisan would follow through."

"Fair enough," Fenaday said. "You felt us go through jump. We are in enemy space now. Irrevocably committed. I could use you and your machines, both for shipboard defense and to rescue my wife.

"Don't get any ideas. All the codes are in my head. You might break the various computer lockouts I came up with, but Sharla did these. You won't get through them."

"What happens to everybody if you get killed in the ground assault?" Mmok asked. "We just get used to our new address?"

"Maybe you should make sure I stay alive."

Mmok shook his head. "You're as overdue as anyone I ever met. You got the mark on you. No, not good enough. I am not asking you to trust me with codes, but at least trust Telisan."

Fenaday shook his head. "Too many keys to him on this ship."

"Keys I won't turn," Mmok said.

Fenaday waved a hand dismissively. "I know you wouldn't. There are others who might."

"No one else needs to know you told him the codes," Mmok said. "You know me well enough to know that no one can extract that information from me."

Fenaday looked at him for a few seconds, hesitant.

"That's my price for helping," Mmok said. "It's my way of protecting Arpen. My way of thanking her for all she's done for me." He held Fenaday's eye, half-demanding, half-pleading.

Fenaday sighed. "I'm taking a chance on you," he said finally, "an unconscionable risk with my wife's future. I don't have the right to take these chances, but maybe this once, for as much peace as this buys between us. In return, Mmok, in return, I want your oath as a man to serve faithfully until we rescue my wife, or learn beyond all doubt there is no hope."

The cyborg gave him a sardonic grin and raised his human arm, rattling the chain. "Cross my heart and hope to die."

Fenaday snorted a small bitter laugh. "That will do as well as any, I suppose. Okay, I'll have an engineer cut that chain. You can get back into your old quarters and start working on your machines. Ship-wise, you report to Rainhell as ground force commander."

"My best girl," Mmok replied.

"Yeah. She loves you too," Fenaday threw over his shoulder as he left.

Fenaday was gone only a minute before Arpen swept in, laser scalpel in hand, her roundish alien frame ablaze with energy. "I told him I wasn't going to wait for Perez," she said. With a few deft strokes of the scalpel, she cut through the chain. "I have waited for this moment," she said, her brown eyes drawing him in. "This has sat poorly with me, and I have regretted it."

"Naw." Mmok stood and stretched. "It was the only thing to do. I'd have told Telisan to do it if he hadn't come up with it himself."

Jenner walked into the ward. "Ah," she exclaimed, "you've been freed. How wonderful."

"Yeah," Mmok said, "free on a tin can, bound for uncharted space, with a nut for a skipper." A chill presence struck him, almost a psychic wave. He turned slowly. Rainhell stood in the doorway, her calm empty eyes on him.

"Acts of insubordination," she said, "will get you rechained to the wall."

Mmok grunted, unimpressed.

Rainhell tossed him a data crystal. He fumbled the catch and had to scoop it off the bed. The cyborg arm was no good for such things. He suspected Rainhell knew it and deliberately threw to his bad side. *Bitch.*

"It contains the unlock codes I placed on your machines. Fenaday ordered them returned to you."

"Which you do not agree with, huh, Rainhell?"

"Captain's orders," she said. "I don't question him. You don't either."

Mmok bit back a reply. He didn't need problems with Rainhell just now.

"Silence is good," she added.

"Ms. Rainhell," Arpen asked quietly, but with some force, "is there anything else?"

"No, doctor," Rainhell answered, with the slightest smile on her lips, as if she were somehow amused by Arpen's defense of Mmok. "Good day."

"Good day." Arpen nodded. Rainhell left without a backward glance. Arpen looked at Mmok.

"She loves me," Mmok said, "really." Leda Jenner started to laugh then stopped at Arpen's reproachful glance.

"You were speaking rudely of someone she cares about," Arpen warned. "She is dangerous when provoked."

"Yeah, I know. I'll cool it," Mmok said. "I want to get out and about. See what those idiot engineers have done with my team." Then, motivated by some sudden impulse, he turned to Leda Jenner. "Care to come along?" The words were out of his mouth before they could be recalled or regretted.

Jenner looked surprised and uncertain. She looked at Arpen, who nodded. "I can spare you for a few hours."

"Well then," Leda said, "shall we go?"

They traveled in an awkward silence to the forward cargo hold. Li and Murphy stood on duty there. Li nodded his scarred face as Mmok walked up. "Rainhell said you'd be along shortly," Li said. "We're to drop the guard after you get the deathbots back online."

"Got it," Mmok said. He inserted the crystal key. The doors cycled open, and they went into the dark and cold storeroom. Moisture beaded on the walls. "Goddammit," Mmok snarled, "is this a warship or a garbage scow?"

Li shrugged. "The evaporators in this section are still being worked on. They were damaged in the explosion. Ain't they weath-erproof?" he said, gesturing at the hold full of machines.

"Yeah," Mmok groused, "when they're turned on. This equip-ment costs more than two starships this size. The HCRs and the airbot are half the cost of the team."

"Techs and their toys," Li said in disgust. "We'll be outside." Murphy silently followed him out.

Jenner and Mmok stood surveying the machines in the dank hold. Some of the crab-robots still showed open panels from when he surrendered to Telisan, salvage and repair operations left incom-plete. Mmok swore again with feeling.

"Um," Jenner said, "could we get a little more light in here?"

"Yeah," Mmok said, "sorry. I forget normal people need light. Got infra-red and imaging in my patented eyeball." He found the panel and brought up the hold lights. Leda gasped, and he spun around.

Leda shook her head. "Nothing…it's just them." She gestured toward the prone forms of the five HCRs. The machines, in their black fatigues and colored sashes, lay sprawled randomly on the floor. "They looked like corpses."

"Not for long," he replied. He went over to his bench, picked up some tools, and walked over to the nearest HCR. Cobalt lay on its back, arms and legs loosely arranged. Its face held only minimal features with doll-like eyes lay open and star-ing. The mouth speaker was sealed; at least no moisture had gotten in that way. He operated several small, boxy tools, hooking them with cables to ports in the machine's head, concealed under the fine pale hair used for antenna and cooling. After opening a Velcro panel in the black coverall, he went back to the bench and returned, lugging a small, very heavy atom battery.

"What does the color mean?" asked Jenner.

"Huh?" Intent on his old friends, he'd forgotten she was there. "Oh. The sashes are for friendly troops to identify them by. Me, I go by telemetry. This one here," he pointed at the prone machine, "is Cobalt. She's the oldest one, the only original from the Conchirri campaign, always served as my personal bodyguard. God knows how many times she's saved my life."

"She?" Jenner said coyly.

"Ah, yeah."

"I never saw such machines before," she added. "We don't have them on Olympia. They were seen as the antithesis of everything Dr. Allessandro stood for. I saw these from a distance when we were docked onworld. They made me nervous, and I guess I kept my distance."

"They scare most people," Mmok said, intent on an adjustment. "Not me though," he said, patting Cobalt's cold cheek. "Nope. In a lot of respects, they are better than people: cleaner, simpler, and straightforward. No false fronts and no snide chatter."

Mmok finished restoring the atom battery in the machine. It was a simple hook up designed for battle conditions. Animation returned to the machine. Cobalt came up smoothly into a sitting position, its eyes focused on Mmok.

"Hello, old gal," Mmok said.

"Greetings, Controller," the machine replied. Its mouth did not move like a human's; it merely opened to uncover a protected speaker. "Sitrep?"

"Sitrep, non-combat situation, no hostile units on board. We will be reactivating the entire cyberforce. Until otherwise advised, we will be under command of Fenaday, Robert F."

"Affirmative," said the machine. It looked over at Jenner, who returned the machine's doll's-eye gaze with evident trepidation. "Note presence of Olympian refugee, Jenner, Leda."

Mmok looked up. "Come on over. She doesn't bite."

The machine turned toward Mmok. "Biting is an ineffective method of fighting," it confirmed. "In addition, this unit is not equipped with teeth."

"Cobalt," Mmok asked, "are you developing a sense of humor?"

"Negative, Controller."

"It's just kidding," he said.

"Was it?" Jenner asked

"Huh?" Mmok said.

"It seems to have a sense of irony."

"No," Mmok said, "the machine brains, complex as they are, simply don't have that capacity. But Cobalt here," he said, tapping the slender, feminine-looking machine on its head, "has been active a long time. Ten years now."

Leda's eyes went round at his casualness with the killing machine.

Mmok continued. "The pathways in her brain multiplied over time and became more complex. She's a supercomputer as good as any running a ship. Her behavior programs are the most evolved of any HCR ever made.

"Like I said, she's always served as my personal bodyguard, since I'm often busy with dealing with coordinating the rest of the force. I've spent a lot of hours working on her, writing new programs to make her more acceptable to people."

"Better table manners," Cobalt added.

Jenner gaped at the machine. "That," she said, "was a joke."

"Answer her, Cobalt," Mmok prompted.

"The comment was the result of a complex program created by Controller Mmok to nuances of human conversation. My program indicated a 90% probability that the comment would be appropriate in human social conversation, producing an improved working relationship with friendly forces."

"So, it was a joke," Jenner ventured, "told for our benefit, but you yourself do not find it funny or understand the purpose of it." Curious, she reached out and stroked the machine's silky, monofilament hair. Mmok overrode the HCR's preprogrammed response to disable anyone touching it, with an instant burst of telemetry.

"I understand the purpose for humans," Cobalt said, giving no hint of how close Leda had come to being struck. "I am programmed to ape human behavior, but as I have no sense of ego or self, humor is an abstraction to me. Even for the purpose of this conversation, my responding to you using personal pronouns is programming for your benefit. As I have no sense of self, I can have no sense of other."

"It's over my head," Jenner said ruefully.

"Simple, really," Mmok said. "She's a tool, like a gun or even a refrigerator. She runs programs. No morals, questions, or inhibitions, she just runs programs. Because she has to work with humans, use human equipment and ships, they made HCRs as humanlike as possible. Without our flaws, but also without that spark of life. Still, even I can't avoid anthropomorphizing them, though I usually communicate with them in their language: telemetry, machine-speak."

"So why the female pronouns?" Jenner asked.

"Back to that again?" Mmok grinned. "You think I have a mechanical harem going?"

"Sounds like a male fantasy to me," she said with mock archness.

Mmok looked at Cobalt; the machine looked back at him. "I dunno," he said finally. "They're small and curvy, to bounce off armor-piercing rounds. Then there is the long filament hair too. We had to use female uniforms and equipment for them because of their size. Add to that the general tendency of men to name anything mechanical, like ship or plane, for the female."

"Well," Jenner said, "Captain Fenaday always refers to the *Sidhe* as female. I suppose it's a guy thing."

"Guess so," he returned.

"Any theories?" he asked, turning to Cobalt.

"Psychologist Bernison suggested that the phenomenon might be due to the intimacy of the relationship of machine mind to human. Controllers preferred to think of their units as belonging to the opposite gender."

"Ah," Mmok said, momentarily nonplussed. "Come to think of it, Andrea Hodgell always referred to her HCRs as 'her boys,' so you may have something there."

"Do you like working for Mr. Mmok?" Leda asked.

"Careful," Mmok said to the robot, "your next lubrication might depend on your answer."

"Controller Mmok has scored in the 99th percentile on all aspects of HCR maintenance," the machine replied. "In addition, he allows this unit many extra hours of operation and access to large supplies of data outside my combat function."

"I give her books," Mmok explained.

"This unit experiences maximum performance with Controller Mmok."

"It doesn't understand the question," Jenner said.

"Like I told you," Mmok said. "It's just a machine, it runs programs. Now, if we're through with all the analysis, I should get them all up and running."

"Tally fucking ho," Cobalt said. Mmok sighed. "As you can see, the program leaves something to be desired. Cobalt, cease use of invective in conversation."

"Does this include all references to Robert Fenaday?"

Mmok coughed as Jenner looked at him with both eyebrows raised.

"Uh, particularly those," he answered.

Chapter Nine

So far," Sharon Hafel said, "we've been lucky. Commander Rainhell's fake message started something between the Olympian and Voit-Veru forces in the Zealmun system. Her message bore all the correct codes and, coming from a ship with the right IFF, could not be ignored." She sat back in her seat, looking exhausted from hours of scanning and enhancing transmissions from her bridge post. Telisan and Lieutenant Graglia stood over her, anxiously awaiting the report.

"Nor could it be confirmed on this side of the starjump," Telisan mused.

"Just so," Hafel replied. "I've picked up bursts of communications traffic following our message. Bernard and I have isolated the signatures of at least five other vessels in the system, Voit-Veru and Olympian. Since we have the Olympian codes, we can listen to half the conversations. We hear questions, threats, orders, and counterorders." She handed him a transcript of the radio traffic. He scanned it quickly.

"Sensors picked up the traces of at least one major nuclear weapon," Graglia added. "Someone opened fire, though we have no idea to what effect."

"Excellent," Telisan said. "It appears from the transmissions that these erstwhile allies have broken ranks and are trying to hide from each other, neither side having a decisive advantage. Captain Fenaday thinks both sides might scurry for home. I believe they will fall back to guard their bases in this system and await orders."

"It would explain why no vessel has come our way heading for the jump for Dralich," Hafel said.

"Which clears the way for the *Sidhe*," Lieutenant Graglia added, "steering an evasive course and running as emission-free as we can, to make the second jump point to Dralich before any returning Voit-Veru vessel catches us."

"Good," Telisan said. "I will report our assessment to the captain. Keep listening and remain alert." He turned and headed down the gangway, preferring to stretch his long legs rather than take the turbo. He passed down the ship's Broadway, then took a short cut and dropped down a hatchway to the medical and supply deck. Telisan ducked under a stanchion as he made the last turn for Sickbay. Arpen had scheduled the human for more regenerator therapy, but Telisan needed to discuss the approach to the second starjump with him.

Emerging from a hatchway, Telisan almost ran into the Ambassador Henlesch and his guard. The Voit-Veru was evidently coming back from his exercise period, with Li trailing him. Shasti had declared the ambassador played out as a source. In a small act of kindness, Telisan made sure the Voit-Veru did not encounter his interrogator again. Shasti had been judicious in her use of pain, but it was done, and it was still torture. The Voit-Veru's body mended; his soul was another matter.

With Shasti finished, Henlesch ceased being a prisoner and became Arpen's responsibility. Now that he was in her jurisdiction, Arpen defended the ambassador's health with a tigerish ferocity that daunted even the troops assigned to guard the Voit-Veru. Arpen was a military doctor and understood the need to gather intelligence. She didn't have to like it. So, she tended Henlesch diligently, as if she could somehow remove the stain of the interrogation from their collective honor. The ambassador remained unconfined, though carefully monitored. Unhappy as Fenaday was over the arrangement, he accepted it out of respect for the Denlenn doctor.

"Ambassador." Telisan inclined his head respectfully.

The alien looked back at him with dead eyes and nodded stiffly. "When do I go home?" Henlesch asked. His muzzle-like face held no expression the Denlenn could read, but the feeling crossed the barrier of species.

Telisan dropped his eyes, sighing in Denlenn fashion, his stomachs suddenly queasy. He too remained haunted by the alien's interrogation. It had been done at his orders. He tried to speak, but his voice failed him.

Arpen came to Telisan's rescue. "Now, Ambassador, you know we don't have the answer to that question. Don't you remember? I did give you my promise that if we make it back alive, I will see to it that you go home."

"I'll add my word of honor to that," came Robert Fenaday's voice. They turned to see him in the hatchway leading to Arpen's infirmary. Telisan had not heard him coming, Denlenn hearing being inferior to human. Fenaday pulled a shirt over a badly scarred chest. His skin showed the characteristic redness of regenerator therapy.

"I go home?" Henlesch asked plaintively, his Confed standard slipping.

"Yes." The human looked at all the alien faces in the room, his voice tight. "If we come through this alive, you get to go home. Somehow, some way. Maybe God will count it in my favor when my day comes."

"Home," Henlesch repeated dully. "My daughter. I'd like to see her again."

"That's enough excitement," Arpen said. "Ambassador, I'd like you to rest now. Everyone else out, please."

The others shuffled out behind Fenaday.

"I'm sorry," Telisan said. "I forgot that he would be there about this time."

Fenaday looked at him. "It doesn't matter. There's no place to hide from the things you do. They follow you. They visit you in your dreams, sometimes even when you're awake. Not seeing him doesn't help. For me, it's just one of many such things. I'm sorry for you, my friend. Sorry for your innocence."

"We are both slaves to our duty," Telisan replied. "You to your wife, me to what it means to be Selen. We both make heavy payments on those duties. Better to be like Shasti," he continued. "These things do not seem to scar her. They are as natural to her as killing is to a kleeyah—you would say tiger, I guess."

"They built her without a conscience," Fenaday said, "and never taught her anything human."

"But you seek to?"

"Me?" Fenaday laughed bitterly. "Who am I to teach her? I destroyed my family when I sold everything for the *Sidhe*. I feel no regret for the Conchirri I've killed. But the others, on Morokat, Winterhaven, other places, that weighs. Then there are all the people who died under my command in the years of privateering. Now all this..."

"Still, you are the only one close enough to reach her," Telisan said.

"I don't know that it's possible to teach such things," Fenaday replied. "I don't know what's innate in her nature and what's a product of the way she was raised. Finally, Telisan, there's a last question: do I do her any favor in this mad, murderous universe by giving her a conscience?"

Telisan could only stand mute.

———

Mmok found himself in *Sidhe's* wardroom, still enjoying the novelty of his recently recovered freedom of the ship. *How ironic*, he said to himself. *Here I am aiding and abetting Fenaday and Rainhell on a raid into unknown space. How the hell did it come to this?* The answer asserted itself at once—Arpen, the Denlenn doctor who had broken the shell in which he'd surrounded himself. It had set her apart from all the others. He could have killed any of them, but not her. It made him as much a prisoner as if he had remained shackled.

His relationship with Fenaday remained uneasy. Fenaday did not trust the cyborg any more than Mmok trusted Fenaday. The Irishman, on his doomed quest for his lost love, had won over the others, at least in part. Even the Confed Navy regulars followed him now, particularly the Morok, Sergeant Rask. Captain Rigg and, to a lesser extent, Graglia and Hafel seemed less bound to the privateer, but they rebuffed Mmok's tentative attempts to find any opposition to Fenaday.

Gopal's Marines resented the death of their officer, but no one in that force had the presence to bring the others to open conflict. According to the book the Marines lived by, Fenaday was in charge, his orders legal and binding. Sergeant Cross, the ranking Marine, told Mmok that Gopal had been an ambitious hothead, unwilling to follow channels and out to make a name for himself. He ended up with a common one, posthumous. The Marines refused to involve themselves in policy. Nor were they prepared to accept Mmok as a leader. *Not much chance there anyway*, Mmok thought. Rainhell had broken the Marines up and mixed them in with the ASATs and the old privateer landing force. Rigg allowed it, though without much enthusiasm.

Who am I kidding? he thought with resignation. *Even if I come up with troops, I'm in the same pickle. Arpen will side with Fenaday, and the privateer had made it clear that, rather than surrender, he'd destroy Sidhe and everyone on aboard.* Mmok knew Fenaday well enough to fear he actually would. *If I was going to stop his madness, I should have done it at the beginning. Too late now.*

Mmok looked up as a familiar face registered on his optic. Leda Jenner walked into the galley. His heart quickened a beat before the cyber implants in it kicked in, dropping the rate back to normal. For the thousandth time he cursed the doctors who'd left him partly alive and partly dead.

The Olympian refugee had been his regular caretaker during his imprisonment. He'd seen as much of her as of Arpen. Friendly and cheerful Leda, so unlike Rainhell they might have come from different worlds. *Of course*, he thought, *Jenner is a real human being, not the synthesis of selected genes from a Petri dish like her deadlier countrywoman.* He hadn't seen Leda since the day of his release, when he reactivated his machines.

Jenner looked about the galley, saw him, and smiled.

Mmok, to his own surprise, gestured with his coffee cup to the seat opposite him. Jenner nodded and went to get some breakfast. She came back and slid into the seat with a full tray. She caught Mmok's surprised glance at her tray.

"I'm blessed with a good appetite," she said.

"Well, it sure doesn't show," Mmok said. *Hey,* he thought, *my mouth came up with something good for once.*

Jenner favored him with a bright smile. "How gallant of you."

Mmok laughed ruefully. "I don't think I've been accused of that before."

"What about you?" she asked. "You just having that mousebite?"

"Doesn't take much to keep me going," he replied. "Just coffee and a nuclear battery, my version of a Mexican breakfast."

Jenner looked slightly confused at the reference.

"Old saying," he explained, "from my home in North America back on Earth, used to mean a cup of coffee and a cigarette. Never heard that one before?"

"No," she said around a mouthful of eggs. After sipping some coffee, she continued. "I've read a lot about Old Earth. North America, does that make you from the United States?"

"No," he said, "not far enough north. I'm Canadian, from Saskatchewan. Ice, snow, moose, and beer, that's my home."

"When were you there last?"

Mmok looked down, his face suddenly tense.

"Did I say something wrong?" she asked.

"No," he managed, then almost visibly struggling. "I went back after I got wounded, damn near killed, in the Red Star campaign. Stumbled about on my new pieces for a few weeks. After I got tired of the sympathy and the clucking, I lit out and never went back. No reason to. Mom's passed. I never got on with my dad or my brothers anyway."

"I'm sorry," she said. "That must have been so hard."

"Your breakfast is getting cold," he said.

They ate in silence for a few minutes.

"It's been interesting since," he added unexpectedly. "I've seen a lot of the Sector. Traveled all over on one mission or another."

"You must be proud of what you accomplished on Enshar."

"Yeah," he said slowly. "I suppose I am. I guess I didn't think much about it. Just another mission."

"Robert told me about it."

"I'll bet," he replied, nettling at the privateer's first name.

"He said they would never have made it without you and your robots."

Mmok grunted in surprise.

"He also said you saved them on Olympia too. He felt it was very strange to owe his life to someone who wanted to kick him out an airlock."

"In his underwear," confirmed Mmok with a grimace.

"So you do hate him?" she asked.

Mmok sighed. "Maybe. Sometimes I feel some sympathy with him, mostly when it comes to his wife. I have to admire his loyalty to her, if not to the rest of us. He's a Separatist. I'm a Federalist. He was born with a silver spoon. Mine was plastic, if I had one at all. He's rich. I'm working class. I don't work; I have no class."

Jenner laughed lightly in appreciation.

"I fought in the war he sat out, at least until he lost something he wanted. He came out with all four limbs. I got one original left."

"Always back to that," she murmured. "Why? Are you any less you?"

"You wouldn't understand," he shot back. "You're damn near perfect—"

"Perfect," she interrupted. "Perfect? No, it's you who have no idea. You were accepted before your injuries. Even afterward you were valued, given important work. Me? I was genetic junk, an unsanctioned natural birth by two parents considered low-order genetic material. I've never been accepted. I've been marked from birth for just the most menial of work. I couldn't even argue the point. I didn't score as high as the others. I wasn't as fast. I can't see in the dark. I had gray in my hair at fifty, for god's sake." Jenner checked herself suddenly, lips pressed together as if to keep any more bitter words from tumbling out.

Mmok looked at her. "I guess," he said finally, "that you just look perfect to me."

Her eyes came up slowly, as if she were afraid to look, to find some joke being made at her expense.

"I mean it," he said, suddenly sure of his words. "I think you're very beautiful."

"Really?" she whispered.

"Yes."

"Thank you," she said, her voice a little shaky.

"Do you want to go for a walk?"

She looked at him, surprised. "Where to?"

"There is a nice view from the shuttle's observation deck. We can go look at the stars."

"Won't the bay doors be closed?"

"I have some influence around here," he replied.

"Oh," she said, miming being impressed.

He drained his coffee and stood. "Ready?" he asked. She nodded and rose. They walked out side by side. As they went, it struck Mmok that he felt better than he could remember feeling since he was wounded. He felt like a man again.

———

Shasti and Fenaday continued to work out in the ship's gym, rebuilding their sorely tried bodies and fractured psyches. After the first few times passed without another explosion, Telisan ceased to hover around them. The Denlenn had seen unexpected flares of temper between them before, on Enshar. It confused the steadfast Telisan, but he attributed it to the peculiar nature of humans.

For Shasti and Fenaday, martial arts became a form of communication, a physical intimacy they could still allow themselves, an outlet for their friendship, a place where a woman who could not talk, and a man who feared to speak, could be with each other.

It was also the place where Fenaday saw the changes in Shasti. Changes wrought by exposure to her own kind on Olympia and by the information she learned from Vaughn. She could parry a blow without seeing it. Her skills expanded daily. Thoughts of the tall, savagely handsome Denshi leader filled Fenaday with unwanted flashes of jealousy, further confusing him.

Today they were working off some of the tension of the run to Dralich, practicing at the highest level. Fenaday went in low, following up on a series of leopard punches to Shasti's body. His right leg flicked out in a sweep, as she backed away, reacting to the weight she placed on her front foot. His foot met only empty air as she shifted her weight back in a liquid move, snapping her trailing foot at his head, stopping an inch off his nose.

Fenaday sighed and put his right fist into his left hand in the traditional Chinese bow. He came up from the half split as she straightened from the cat stance. As usual, the physical effort had given her a glow, with only the slightest hint of perspiration. On her lips was the small quirking that served as her smile. She was at her happiest losing herself in the physicality of exercise.

He was rank with sweat, knees vibrating with fatigue. "Was that a feint?" he asked, breathing heavily and feeling slightly dizzy.

"No," she replied, "a miscalculation."

"You got out of it quickly," he replied. "I thought I had you."

"It seemed—it seemed as if I could sense the energy going into your leg before you started to move."

"You can see *chi* now?" he accused.

"Maybe," she said, her seriousness unsettling him.

"You've changed," he said with a hint of sadness in his voice. "I no longer have anything to teach you. You've grown so far beyond me, Shasti."

"No," she said, walking up to him and gazing into his eyes, "there's much you could show me, if only you would."

So here we are again, he thought in dismay. "I'm sorry," he said. "I don't want to start something I can't finish. I don't want to hurt you all over again."

"Remember what I told you that day on Mars?" Shasti asked, standing close. "When you were going to give me the last of the money so I could escape Mandela?"

He shook his head.

"Not everything is about forever," she said.

"I remember now," he said, touching her cheek, looking into the jade-green eyes, "but some things are."

Shasti sighed. "It would be easier if I didn't feel that you wanted me, but I do. I know that you do."

"I won't deny that," he said.

"Well," she said, feigning lightness, "enough for now. Back to more practical things. Dinner?"

"You gonna cook?" he asked, glad for the change.

"I could," she said. "I think I am making progress. Aren't I?"

He looked at her dolefully. "Maybe it would be better if I cooked."

They laughed together, somehow still friends.

"Eat, drink, and be merry, for tomorrow, we jump," he added.

"Yes," she said, "into Dralich system."

"Beyond that," he said, in a tone gone grim, "Mounus."

Chapter Ten

Sharla stopped by Sickbay on her way to the bridge. She had a few minutes before watch, and she hadn't seen Arpen for a day and a half. As she leaned into the small, blue-painted office, she spotted Dr. Mourner speaking with her fiancée, Arpen, who sensed Sharla at once and smiled her best sun-warm smile.

Dr. Mourner gave them a curious look and then, showing empathy of her own said, "I have a few tests to run. I'll see you later." Arpen waited till Mourner left to embrace the tall demi-female. Sharla savored Arpen's soft roundness against her own slim, more muscular body.

The Denlenn triad was still recovering from the rift between Telisan and Arpen, created when Telisan had asked Arpen to sabotage the cyborg Mmok. Arpen's rage at being asked to violate her physician's oath had clashed with Telisan's Selen oath to Fenaday. It took all Sharla's skills as demi-female, the traditional arbiters of the Denlenn triad, to get them back on track. She loved both the tall pilot and Arpen in the way of her kind, bonding equally to both. Sharla was neither female, male, nor neuter, but an alternative gender in the complex physiology of her kind.

"Good to see you," she said to Arpen. "I've missed you badly."

"And I you," Arpen replied.

"You doing better with Dr. Mourner?"

"Yes," Arpen said. "I am still relearning the adjustments of working with humans. Of course, I shouldn't complain to you. It must be even tougher for you."

Sharla smiled. "At least they have a pronoun for you in their language. They have evidently decided that I look more female than male. So I am ma'am, or miss, to them. You had better watch out. I may replace you as the most desirable Denlenn female on this ship."

"Sharla," Arpen protested, laughing and embarrassed at the off-color joke.

Sharla joined her in a laugh. Denlenn culture was filled with scandalous stories of demi-females passing as either gender.

"Off to the bridge?" Arpen asked.

"Yes." Sharla went suddenly somber. "Back to serving our mad master."

Arpen looked surprised. "Captain Fenaday?"

"Who else?" Sharla replied. "Oh, I understand Telisan's desire to help his friend. We both knew that marrying a Selen would be difficult. Gods, though, I thought it would at least be possible. Here we are outward bound on a voyage that I fear has no return."

"What could we do?" Arpen said. "Telisan would go in any event."

"I know, I know," she replied, "but this wasn't the future that I wanted for us. It may not be any future at all. Sometimes I hate this human, Fenaday."

"I know," Arpen put a hand on Sharla's arm, "but that is not fair to him either. His wife was taken away. Would you expect Telisan do less for us? Fenaday has few options."

"Well, for now, my only option is to report to the bridge," Sharla said, striving for lightness again. She kissed Arpen. "With any luck, we may actually be able to share a bed at the same time tonight."

Arpen smiled. "Ah, something to look forward to."

Sharla, heartened by seeing Arpen, left for the bridge in a better mood. The turbovator quickly deposited her on the bridge. She nodded pleasantly to Fenaday. Her feelings had not changed, but as

Arpen said, the human had not chosen this either. She paused for a touch on Telisan's sleeve. He spared her a smile before turning back to work on hyperjump calculations. She activated her boards, preparing for jump, checking and rechecking her instruments.

———

"Jump point coming up, Captain," Graglia announced. "We are on course for the optimum jump point. Sixty seconds."

"Still appears unguarded," Hafel said. "Nothing, even on long scan."

"Sharla," Fenaday asked, "ready on ECM?"

"Affirmative," Sharla called back.

Fenaday looked around; the bridge was getting crowded. Perez had come out of his self-imposed exile. Sharla and Hafel manned their boards. Leda Jenner had just arrived with the usual post-jump drinks and snacks. Rigg, Rask, and Mmok idled by the turbo doors near Shasti's security station. She endured it with good grace. Telisan stood by the fighter boards. A full house.

"Thirty seconds to entry," Graglia added.

"Same as before, Mr. Wardell," Fenaday said. "Stand ready with the fake message, Ms. Bernard."

"Aye, sir."

Shasti walked down to stand next to him.

"Ten seconds."

The engine began their song and colors went strange.

"I'll see you on the other side," he said to her.

"I'll be there," she replied.

"Jump in five, four, three, two…"

"Jump," announced Fenaday, hitting the button.

———

Am I dreaming? he thought muzzily. It was warm, and he didn't want to wake up. Just five minutes more…

He snapped out of it. "Scan," Fenaday demanded.

He looked right and saw Shasti, looking at him. "Told you I'd be here," she said and started back to her station.

"Ah," said Hafel, looking groggy, "umm, short scan clear. Long scan…no return yet."

"Microwave scanner clear," Sharla called. As always, she seemed unaffected by the jump.

"Dralich system," Graglia said, "with one of the smoothest entries you will ever see."

"If you do say so yourself," Mmok said.

"Long scan remains clear," Hafel said, all efficiency again.

"Two hundred ten light years from home," Rigg murmured.

"Home is where the heart is," Mmok cracked. Rigg ignored him.

"Bernard, pipe it through the ship," Fenaday said. "Secure from battle stations; set Defense Condition Two. Mr. Graglia, evasive course to the Mounus jump point. Ladies and gentlemen, since no one seems to have spotted our entry, we're going to keep quiet. We'll broadcast the fake message if we encounter someone and if it seems necessary. For now, Sharla, how soon can you get the hologenerators up? I want very badly to look like a piece of rock."

"It will take a few minutes longer, Captain," she said.

Fenaday turned to Perez. "Now that we're through jump, get your people out on the hull. Follow the plans Sharla gave you to help with the holo camouflage. We'll look like a rock visually. Let's see what we can do to make the radar and microwave signatures conform to that."

"Yes, sir," replied the engineer. "We'll get right on it."

Carlos Perez's engineers worked steadily with the Mylar and metal frameworks, making the radar signature of the frigate conform to the holographic mask Sharla and her techs made for the *Sidhe*. Mennolly Fitzgerald, one of Sharla's techs, fine-tuned *Sidhe's* electronic warfare suite to aid in the deception. Fenaday and Mmok worked on reducing the electromagnetic signature of the starship, using the stealth computer protocols loaded in *Sidhe* before the Enshar Expedition. They returned to the bridge later to check the results.

"The holo-mask creates a tremendous energy drain on the ship," Sharla said as she brought up the system, "and limits our options. Firing the main gun with the mask operating will require every ounce of auxiliary and battery power the ship has. We can only fire it once, or we will have to drop the holo-mask."

"Of course," Mmok said, "if we need to fire again, there'd be no point to remaining masked."

"True," Sharla conceded. "Ah. Finally the equations have balanced. Engaging holo-mask now."

"Excellent," Fenaday said. He leaned past Sharla and keyed the mike. "Scarlet to Gold," Fenaday said, using their old call signs. Telisan had jetted out in *Wildcat 1* off to maximum range for the fighter scanner to look over the result. "How's the holo-mask?"

"Surprisingly effective," Telisan returned. "With luck, we will be seen as an ore-heavy rock, coasting through a dark, silent universe from time immemorial."

"Very poetic," Fenaday said, with a grin. The smile faded quickly "It's our best hope. If we have to fight, there'll be little chance to reach Mounus."

"True enough," Telisan said.

"Return to the ship, Gold," Fenaday said.

"Aye, aye, sir." With characteristic flair, the fighter jock snapped the fighter in a high-G turn and sped back to the frigate. He docked on *Sidhe's* wing in two minutes, zooming up on the wing in a maneuver that made Fenaday wince.

Sharla smiled noting the gesture. "Don't worry, Telisan is the best."

"In every way," Fenaday replied. He walked back to his center seat and dropped into its brown leather comfort.

Fenaday swiveled at the sound of claws clicking on decking to see Dobera walk into the bridge from the gangway next to the turbovator shaft. The lizard man hated the turbovator for some Frokossi reason Fenaday couldn't fathom. He didn't know what sort of king Dobera would have made in his country, but he was a fine quartermaster. As usual, he wore only a vest and ship shorts, his lizard-like hide being most of the protection he needed. It gleamed iridescently, little prisms of light playing on it.

Dobera stopped to greet Shasti. During a rare squabble shortly after she joined the ship, Shasti threatened to turn the quarter-master into shoes and a handbag. Dobera had shot back that there wasn't enough hide on him to cover her feet. Fenaday managed to stop the Olympian from finding out for certain. While Shasti was built in proportion, she did have big feet and was sensitive about it. Oddly the two became friendly, or what passed for friendly between a solitary assassin and a deposed alien aristocrat.

"Morning, sir." Dobera's voice had none of the sibilant hiss a human expected from his appearance. Despite his species' forked tongue, he spoke standard perfectly in a high, thin voice. "I have the latest consumption manifest."

Fenaday took it with a mental sigh. *Sidhe* came well provisioned, but her crew contained Moroks, Denlenn, Humans, the K-9 Risky, and Dobera himself. Keeping the five species and three sexes clothed and properly nourished was always a trial. The same problem afflicted Drs. Mourner and Arpen.

"Good," Fenaday said, stifling a yawn. He had been on the bridge for six hours. He began to read the report.

"Captain," Sharla said, calmly but urgently, "contact astern. I am detecting an active scanner."

"Damn," he said, sitting bolt upright. "Hafel, call red alert. Sharla activate the mask and initiate EME shutdown and passive ECM. Full stealth mode. Mr. Graglia, stand by for evasive action. Mr. Keogh, bring all defensive systems online." Fenaday knew the contact could not be close. The *Sidhe's* sensors, even on passive mode, searched a sphere of 5,000,000 km. The contact was nearly fifteen light-seconds away when detected. It could be far closer now.

The assistant gunner nodded nervously, hands reaching for the weapons boards. Fenaday didn't concern himself. Wardell would arrive shortly.

"Sharla, have they locked fire control on us?" he demanded.

"No, no firing lock. All I am getting is a broad band search scan.

They see us. So far they aren't interested enough to change scan settings."

"Get me distance and bearing as soon as possible."

Telisan and the rest of the bridge crew poured out of the turbovator or ran up the gangway. Lights dimmed, following the preprogrammed shutdown intended to give everyone enough time to reach their battle stations before power dropped to minimum settings. The Denlenn, still in his flight suit, paused by Sharla's board, taking in the situation at a glance, then came over to Fenaday. "They have not engaged fire control," he said. "They must be fooled by the holographic camouflage."

"Or they see through it," Fenaday said, "and they're going to fire off a passive lock."

"Can they do that?" Mmok demanded.

"Yes," Telisan said, "but it's unlikely. No commander would sacrifice the accuracy of active fire control at relativistic speeds for a passive lock. It's difficult enough hitting anything at long ranges where the tiniest vector change and light-speed delay make firing solutions guesswork at best. You're shooting for a cone of possible locations. He will use the most powerful scan he can."

"Sharla, distance and vector?" Fenaday called.

"Not yet, sir. It will take longer on passive scan. I need to collect enough energy traces for a dopplered baseline."

Wardell looked over at him. "Shall I arm weapons, sir?" The old Navy gunner was clearly unhappy about an enemy warship within light seconds. His eyes looked tight and anxious.

"Sharla?" demanded Fenaday.

"Not yet, sir."

He turned back to Wardell. "Negative on energy weapons and no active fire control. Slave your fire control to Sharla's board and open the outer doors on all missile stations. Telisan, make sure the fighters are ready to drop."

"Yes, sir," replied Telisan, checking the board. "Fighters are manned, ready, and powered down. It will take at least sixty seconds to launch from this condition."

"If he's close…" Wardell warned.

"Still on broadscan," announced Sharla. "No change in amplitude or frequency. No visual. He's too far. Let's hope that all that hull work we did makes us look like a rock to his electronics.

"We do," Telisan assured, "even more so if they close to visual range."

"Ah," Sharla exclaimed, "bearing 270 by 180. Bogey is astern and below. Captain, our relative velocities are nearly matched at .66C, normal cruising speed. His course is roughly parallel, slightly vectored away. He's going to slip under us at 4,000,000 kilometers distance for closest approach, unless he changes course. I think this is just a patrol and we are passing through his area. No obvious signs of reaction to us."

"Any idea on what type vessel?"

"I'm feeding everything into the computer as the passive scanners pick it up. My guess is a warship based on signal strength, clarity, and frequency. That's a military broadscan out there. I think a heavy cruiser-class rig."

"Holy Mary," Wardell said. "We've no chance against a heavy cruiser in a stand-up fight."

"No alteration on course," Fenaday said. "Kind of sloppy. All this emptiness and he doesn't even alter course to come into visual range?"

"Could he be trying to throw us off," Mmok wondered, "and attack later?"

"Unlikely tactics for a cruiser captain," Fenaday answered.

"True," Telisan said. "A cruiser would investigate thoroughly. He has the firepower to handle most problems and the responsibility to keep the area clear. Cruiser captains are aggressive and accustomed to acting alone."

"Any idea if he's alone?" Shasti asked.

"No other scan signals," Sharla replied. "Standard Confed tactics are to have only one vessel do active scanning, so as not to give away the formation's size. With my instruments on passive reception, I cannot tell if he's alone. I don't think so, but a CA's engines throw out enough EME to cover small ships in close formation.

"That's not what I feel, Captain," Sharla continued. "I make this out as one lone vartek, lone wolf, you humans would say."

"How long till he is out of range?" Fenaday asked.

"Best estimate is two hours, sir," Sharla said. She fiddled with her instruments as she spoke. Blue and green lights played across her leathery face. "We are relatively parallel, both of us at cruising speed. It's only a five-degree course shift away. He is essentially passing below us from extreme sensor range to port, and he'll exit our extreme sensor range to starboard. He'll be closest just about when he passes under us at four million kilometers. That's still a good range, but if he goes to active fire-control and fine scans, I don't know how well the ship's disguise will hold up. The longer he looks at us that way, the better he sees us. Captain, we need to get our EME signature as low as possible before he gets close enough to detect changes."

"Okay," Fenaday said. "Initiate the deep freeze protocol. Sharon, relay that on Intership then shut down your board. Mmok—"

"Already done, all cyber units are in sleep mode."

"All that will remain online are minimal life support and passive sensors," Fenaday continued. "Telisan, get the fighter crews inside and out of the cockpits. With all power shut down, the ship is going to get cold."

"They have spacesuits," the Denlenn said, then checked himself. "Ah, of course they can't use the batteries and heaters." He quickly turned to his board, rapping out orders.

Sidhe's bridge went dark. Only a few telltales and an emergency light provided ghostly illumination.

"Shasti, Mmok," Fenaday said, "you two see best in the dark. Go down to the cabins and get everyone's flight jackets. Then meet Dobera in the mess. As part of the cold protocol, he has a shipload of soup and coffee on tap and ready to go. It shouldn't get that bad in two hours or so, but it will be a mite nippy."

"That cruiser spots who we are, it will get hot enough," Graglia muttered.

"Can it, mister," Fenaday said.

"Sorry, sir."

Fenaday relented. "That's all right, Mr. Graglia. You'll feel braver with some coffee in you."

"Don't know if I'm brave enough for the ship's coffee, sir." Graglia grinned. Nervous laughter drifted over the bridge.

Mmok and Rainhell returned up the gangway in a surprisingly short time loaded with the leather jackets Fenaday favored for the starship. Shasti left again to check on her people. Perez headed for Engineering. It had already cooled noticeably in the virtually shut down ship. Occasionally a blower started, refreshing the air. People spoke in whispers, even though there was no danger of the enemy hearing them.

Fenaday realized Mmok was standing at his elbow. "Good thing that was a warship out there," Fenaday said, "not a merchant."

"Why's that?" asked Mmok. Even in the dimness, Fenaday could see him raise his one eyebrow.

"Despite all the high-tech trickery, we still register as a very large hunk of radioactive metal. A merchant would try to plant a mining tag on us. Christ, we look like a mother lode."

"Hah," Mmok said, "the fat would be in the fire then."

"Yep. Katie bar the door, as my mother would say."

Mmok gave a surprised grunt, looking at him curiously.

"Surprised I had a mother?"

Mmok grimaced in return. "Yeah. Kinda. Never heard you mention your past before, leastwise not anything before your wife."

"It's hard to look back sometimes," he replied. "There's stuff looking back at you when you do."

"Yeah," Mmok said, "I know that one."

Unexpectedly Fenaday continued. "My mother died when I was young, fourteen I guess. Transport crash."

"Sorry," Mmok said after a few moments.

"Your parents?" Fenaday asked.

Mmok bit back the "none-of-your-business" that leapt to his lips. He and Fenaday rarely exchanged anything but abuse, but it was no time for quarrel.

"Mom's dead," he said finally, "natural causes. I don't talk much with my father, never got along really."

Fenaday nodded, then looked away. Both men were saved from an awkward silence by the arrival of coffee and soup brought up by Rask who, like the goblin he resembled, had little trouble in the darkness. Mmok took the opportunity to slip away. The food passed the time. For the most part, they were all left alone in the dark with their thoughts.

"Sharla," Fenaday called, "time check."

"One hour, forty-five minutes. He'll be leaving our range in fifteen more minutes."

"Best news today," Telisan added. "You humans keep the ship cool at the best of times."

"Oh, come now," Fenaday teased. "This is merely jacket weather."

"We remain fortunate that the cruiser is lax in his patrolling," Telisan said.

"Perhaps not so," said Sharla, her voice stiff with tension.

Fenaday moved quickly to her panel. "What is it?"

Sharla pointed on screen. The *Sidhe* sat in the center of the screen. A red blip represented the cruiser on the right, almost exiting the right side of the screen. From ahead and to the left side of the screen came two tiny dots.

"What do you make of those?" Sharla asked.

"What you do," Telisan replied. "Fighters, inbound from a patrol."

"On course for us," Fenaday muttered. A sound of dismay raced around the bridge.

"Wait," Telisan added as the screen updated. "Not directly."

"No," Fenaday said in sudden excitement. "It's not direct. A flyby. They'll pass astern about 15,000 kilometers. Well inside of fighter scan range and within visual range."

"So," Telisan said, "we have made the classic mistake of under-estimating the enemy. This was not a sloppy patrol. He had fighters out. Why waste reaction mass and velocity on shifting a 50,000-ton cruiser when you could send fighters to do a pass? If they see something that makes them suspicious, they come in closer. Real trouble and they call the cruiser."

"Damn," Fenaday said. "Those fighters are going to be trouble for us for hours."

"Yes," Telisan said, as grim as his friend had ever seen him. "We are already well into our safety margin. Robert, the ship will grow deadly cold in those hours."

"Mmok, Rainhell," Fenaday called. They were at his side in seconds. "Get to Dobera. Get out every cold suit and space suit we have. Get everyone into them, no power units for now. Get every blanket you can. Use everyone and anyone you need but be sure the word gets to every compartment. We are going to be without power for hours."

"Christ," Mmok said.

"Let's go," Shasti snapped. The two disappeared in the dimness, surefooted as cats with their enhanced vision.

He looked at Telisan. "We have a bad few hours ahead of us."

Chapter Eleven

Moisture that had earlier beaded the bridge's blue and gray walls had long turned to ice. Mmok suffered the most. The metal and plastic of his cyborg body chilled down and transmitted the cold to his remaining human body and organs. That smaller bit of humanity fought a losing battle with entropy. Mmok suffered silently, but visibly. They piled blankets on the cyborg, but he simply didn't generate enough heat to stay warm.

Arpen and Leda Jenner came up the gangway, struggling a little on the slick ice. Fenaday had called the little Denlenn doctor to check on Mmok. She made her way over to the cyborg.

"Did you bring anything more than a warm smile?" Mmok teased her through chattering teeth, trying to be light for her sake.

"How are you, Kyle?" she asked. She and Leda were the only people on the *Sidhe* who used Mmok's first name and the only people he suffered to do so.

"Hey," he replied, "I'm a Canadian. You think this is cold? You should come to Saskatchewan in winter. This is nothing."

Arpen looked him over and used a very short instrument scan. Her huge brown eyes grew concerned at the readings. She quickly covered it with a professional cheer. "I think that I will stick with my beach below the Arcassanot hills. Very sunny on silver sands."

"Sounds wonderful," Mmok replied. Arpen smiled and patted his shoulder. She moved off to check the others, using a flashlight to inspect the pinched faces of the crew.

Leda Jenner brought Mmok the last of the hot coffee. He gratefully slugged it down. "Jeez," he joked, "the cold is even making your coffee taste good."

Leda smiled at him, then reached forward and around him. "Now that we have some warmth in you," she whispered, "we have to keep it there."

"A good idea," murmured Shasti's voice in Fenaday's ear. He turned to see her beautiful luminous face, its pallor heightened by a bluish cast of cold.

"You bet." He made enough room on the luxurious captain's chair for Shasti to slide in.

Fenaday turned his head toward Sharla; it was beginning to hurt to breathe. "How close?" he managed. Sharla and Telisan were also bundled together for warmth. The cold proved particularly tough for the heat-loving Denlenn.

"They remain on course toward us," said Sharla, her voice muffled by a heavy covering. "If Telisan is right and they're doing a flyby on their way to the cruiser, then they will be at closest approach to us in thirteen minutes."

Arpen walked over to Fenaday. "Captain," she said, "Mmok is in very bad shape. Wardell is at least as bad. We can't carry on like this for much longer."

"She's right," Shasti said. "Even if they change course, it will be another half-hour before they are out of scanner range."

Fenaday smiled. "Been boning up on your astrogation?"

Shasti laughed silently. "Always bucking for promotion."

"Break out self-heating blankets, Doctor," Fenaday said. "Use them at your discretion, but only the minimum number, where we are facing a cold casualty. For the rest of us, we have to tough it out for another forty-five minutes."

"Fenaday," Mmok managed, "you can't endanger the ship for a few men. Each blanket has a hell of a battery and raises the EME signature."

"Quiet, Mmok," he responded. "You're no longer under warranty. I gotta pay for anything that breaks now."

Mmok's sulfurous reply should have raised the temperature a few degrees. Arpen shushed him with a self-heating blanket. Mmok's hand was too numb to grasp it, so Leda wrapped it around them. Arpen threw another self-heating blanket over Wardell and Keogh.

"Everyone get as close to these as you can," Arpen ordered. "I'm off to the electronic compartment." She stopped to share an embrace with the irregular bundle that contained Sharla and Telisan. Arpen, shorter and buxom, seemed to take the cold better than her leaner lovers.

"Want me to move?" Fenaday asked Shasti.

"No," she said. "I like it like this." She pressed her face into his neck.

Fenaday stifled a sigh and pulled her closer. *I never figured on this,* he thought miserably. *I never figured how much it would hurt not to love her. Not to give her what she wants and deserves.* He kept his voice light despite the guilt and pain in his soul. "Good thing I am so efficient at turning food into heat."

"That's it," she replied, "need to feed you more pasta." It was a joke between them, from when they were a couple, a reminder of the past he kept hiding from. *I can't do that,* he realized suddenly. *I can't pretend that it didn't happen. We can't go back. We've been friends and lovers, and I want her to know that I treasure it, even if it should not have happened. How do I find words for these things,* he wondered. *How?*

"You're thinking so hard," she whispered, "I can practically hear it."

"I wish that you could," he said. "I wish I could find words."

She surprised him by smiling. "Ah, so I still matter."

"Yes," he said, pain ripping the word out of him. He started to say something more, but she put a hand to his lips, eyes shining.

"I know," she said. "For once I think I know something human."

"Never," he demanded, "never doubt that. No matter what happens, never doubt that."

Shasti smiled her beautiful smile, then put her face back down on his neck. He wasn't sure if he felt tears there.

———

Telisan's breath smoked in the frosty air. He looked at Sharla's face as they huddled as close as possible. Shivers racked her slender body. A thousand things were on his mind to say, but they stuck in his throat. *I did this,* he thought, *for an oath to a friend, for who I am, for my own honor. I brought both my loved ones out here to die. I'm a fool,* he thought. *Fenaday told me, leave the ship. Honor, duty, they were all meaningless, he said, if they cost you those you love.*

Why did I do this? he thought in sudden anguish. *Why were these humans so important to me that I would risk Sharla and Arpen? No friend is worth this. No oath.*

"I'm a fool," he whispered savagely. "I should never have brought either of you into this madness."

"No," she said, "where you go, I go. I love you."

"I should have loved you more and my honor less," he said. "Fenaday told me so. He demanded I leave, take the shuttle and get off the ship. Not once, but several times. Cursed me for a fool when I wouldn't go."

"Did he?" Sharla said. "Well, I like him better for that. You told him it was impossible, of course. No Selen would do such a thing."

"Never again," he swore, "will I be Selen first and your husband second."

"Shush," the demi-female said, lapsing into High Denleni. "Thee are what thee are and I would not have thee be otherwise. I will confess in weak moments I have had such thoughts. I do not now. Put this from your mind."

"I love you," he said. "I would trade everything to have you and Arpen safely home."

"Not without you," Sharla said, pressing her nose against his throat.

He held her close and prayed for the Voit-Veru fighters to turn. They sat together watching the seconds tick by.

"Captain," Sharla called, sounding exhausted. "Enemy fighters are turning, bearing on the cruiser's estimated course."

"Thank God," Mmok said. A weak cheer rang through the bridge.

"Thirty minutes until enemy fighters are out of scanner range," Sharla said. "I think that fifteen minutes will take them far enough so we can start some hotplates and blankets for all the crew."

The fifteen minutes passed slowly, but finally the fighters left effective scanning range.

Shasti and Fenaday stood. "Order Engineering to bring the reactors back up," Fenaday said, his breath smoking in the freezing air.

Gradually, the starship began to thaw. Arpen rushed the cold casualties to the sickbay for better treatment. Sharla's techs worked feverishly with Perez's engineers, racing through the ship, repairing systems damaged by the intense cold. It had been a near run thing. Any longer and *Sidhe* would have had to power up. The fighters would have detected *Sidhe*, and they would have been facing a ship five times their size.

S hasti returned to her cabin hours later. Even her enhanced constitution had limits. She found Risky in her cabin, buried under all the covers of the bed and little the worse for wear. After all, he did have a fur coat. He looked out from the covers mournfully, in severe disapproval of the recent turn of events. Shasti nodded in agreement. She raised the heat in the room and slid under the covers with Risky. He put his heavy head on her shoulder, looking at her with canine devotion.

"Sorry, boy," she said with a sigh, "you aren't the male I want to find in my bed." The depression that stalked her struck in that instant, folding on her like a shroud. Her muscles flexed in shame. No man had ever rejected her before. Many followed her hopelessly, some to their deaths. At times she hated Fenaday, playing out dark fantasies of revenge in her mind. In all of them, he came back to her, repentant. In all of them, Lisa Fenaday was never found.

Only Lisa was not a fantasy, and though it seemed impossible she was still alive, she had been as of six months ago. She was the specter haunting Shasti. Fenaday would not rest till he found her, and death seemed certain to find him first. Worst of all, what if they did find each other? What of her then?

She shivered. The dark voice came back, stronger and stronger. Lately she could not tell that voice from her own.

Risky whimpered. She realized she was gripping his furry ruff too hard. "Sorry, boy," she repeated. He nuzzled her hand and ran a rough tongue over it, trying to reassure her that somehow it would be all right.

"I don't hate him," she whispered to the dog. "Most of the time I don't. It would be easier if I knew he didn't want me," she said, suddenly intense, "but he does. It's her. Damn her. Always her. She may not even be alive, but she's taking him away from me. Damn her." The hate returned full force. She quivered with it. Lisa Fenaday, the woman she knew only as an abstraction, yet her memory alone was enough to keep Shasti from what little happiness she had found in life. It was not fair.

"It's her I hate," Shasti whispered. "She may not be alive. If she is, she may not stay alive."

Risky butted against her, trying to distract her. It worked. She smiled sadly at the K-9, exhausted and wrung out. A rare condition for the Engineered, but her sleep had been difficult, her dreams unpleasant. Her jade-green eyes closed.

———

Sidhe approached the final jump point to Mounus. Other than long-range sensor ghosts, they saw no other vessel, though occasional bursts of code, some decipherable, some not, reached them. Fenaday and Graglia made last-minute calculations on the ship's nav-computer. *Sidhe* could not emerge from the Mounus jump point at the normal emerge point. Denshi information showed sentry satellites and patrols around the area. They were going to have to overjump the exit point to come out beyond the range of those satellites, or risk instant detection.

"This is going to be a bastard," Fenaday observed. "Assuming their sentry satellites are no better than ours, we still have to overshoot the proper exit point by at least 100,000,000 kilometers for the propagation wave to fade. Even then they will likely pick up some residue. The farther we overjump, the more debilitating the effects on the ship and crew. Overjump too far and no one may make it."

"Yeah," Graglia said. "You never did this during the war?"

"No." Fenaday shook his head. "We were privateers going after enemy shipping in contested space, not fleet units. Even the fleet only started running into these sorts of things after the Red Star campaign, when we drove into their space. By the time we privateers followed, all their defenses were swept away. Did you?"

"No, sir." Graglia shrugged.

"I did," said a familiar voice.

Fenaday turned in surprise. Mmok stood behind them.

"Heard you talking about the Red Star." He grimaced. "My favorite campaign."

"You've done this sort of jump?" Fenaday asked.

"Oh, hell yeah," said Mmok. "Not as a skipper or anything, but it was a common attack for us in Special Forces. We went in first, to disrupt planetary and system defenses and facilitate the fleet attack. I still have most of that information in my CPU."

"It isn't hands-on flight experience," Graglia slapped a hand on his knee, "but it's a damn sight better than doing it with no guide."

"You can supply navigation data?" Fenaday asked. Mmok rarely seemed to know what was going on with the operations and movements of ships; he was after all, a ground-pounder.

"Supply it, yes," Mmok said. "I don't understand it, but I was there. I record everything all day long. With the memory built into me and with the storage in the HCRs, I keep all of it. You never know what will be handy. It even allows me to access my pre-cyborg memory at a far greater efficiency rate than a non-cyborg."

"God," Fenaday said in wonder. "I had no idea. Technology took off at such a rate toward the end of the war, I guess it still surprises me."

Mmok shrugged. "There are some benefits to being a cyborg."

Fenaday raised an eyebrow. He'd never heard Mmok say a single positive thing about his life as a cyborg. He often referred to himself as having been mostly killed in action.

"Well, I envy you the memories," he said. "They must be a comfort sometimes."

"Sometimes," Mmok said. "Other times, less so."

"Of course," Fenaday replied quietly. "Can you transfer the memory of those jumps to the nav-computer?"

"Easily," Mmok said. They stepped aside for the cyborg as he took a port connector out of his pocket and wired himself to the ship's computer. Download took a surprisingly long time. Surprising until Fenaday saw the wealth of data flowing out of Mmok. The cyborg unhooked and stood up. "Will it help?"

"Skipper," a broad grin split Graglia's swarthy face, "I think we're in business."

"Thank you," Fenaday said.

"Don't get mushy on me," Mmok returned.

"Don't worry," Fenaday said, "I'll keep my lips to myself."

Mmok snorted and shook his head.

Hours later they gathered on the bridge in what was becoming something of a pre-jump ritual. Fenaday sat in his command chair and checked his readouts. All nominal. He sat back, slowly swiveling his chair around, looking over the bridge with some amusement. Mmok and Jenner were there, as usual. Leda had a tray of drinks and food. The Olympian had almost taken over the ship's commissary. She well understood the need to replenish the body after jump. Fenaday took the additional precaution of having a doctor on the bridge for the overjump they were about to try. Arpen stood silent by Telisan and Sharla, not disturbing her fiancés as they worked their boards.

Wardell and his team calmly and methodically brought the ship's weapons up to power as the ship's techs turned off the holo-cloak. *Sidhe* returned to her blood-red self again, flexing her claws. Graglia and Angelica Fury worked on astrogation, their figures appearing on Fenaday's board as well. Perez stood by his bridge station, monitoring the buildups in the quantum singularity and the Cherr drive.

Shasti finished relaying instructions to Li, Murphy and the Tok brothers, who nodded and left the bridge just as Rigg and Rask entered. They joined Shasti at the security station. Dobera stood next to Rask, watching the main screen, his iridescent scales contrasted with the goblin-like Morok's blue skin.

Despite Gopal's attack, Fenaday still kept the bridge relatively open, though restricted to those he trusted. Occasionally, he even allowed some of the Marines, now under their Sergeant Cross, carefully controlled access in the hope of welding them more into the framework of the ship's company. He could not afford to alienate any more of his crew. Without the support of those on the bridge, he had no chance. For now, the uneasy coalition was holding, for which he thanked Telisan. Many of the crew, especially the Confederate officers and troops, drew comfort from the war hero's support for Fenaday. Through him, he held Sharla and Arpen. With Arpen came Mmok and his robots.

The cyborg and Leda Jenner had become something of an item, even though Fenaday's mind boggled at the very idea, even having dinner with the Denlenn triad. Try as he might, Fenaday could not imagine Mmok making dinner conversation. Fenaday did not understand the bond between Mmok and the Denlenn doctor. He was merely grateful for it. To the others, Mmok had opened up some, seeming more of a human, less a machine. To Fenaday, his enemy, he remained a caustic presence, though even there a newfound moderation was present. He no longer needled Fenaday, trying to create an explosion. A narrow intersection existed across which he and Mmok communicated, a place of shared pain and experience. They were not friends, nor would ever be, but they were no longer strangers.

His mind drifted last and most uneasily to Shasti Rainhell, source of most of his misgivings. She was busy with her board and talking to the two ASATs. She seemed recovered from the pain of their separation, if still confused by it. Without the context of a normal human life, much of what he was doing must be incomprehensible to her. He looked at her sidelong: tall, powerful, and beautiful. Once he thought her invulnerable, almost emotionless. Now, she seemed so fragile. Yet for all the pain he caused her, she still helped him, still believed what he was doing made some sense.

Did it? he wondered in a flash of soul-searing anguish. He looked across the bridge at his busy crew, at people who had become his life. Even the enemies suddenly seemed precious. Could he really put them all at risk? Lose some of them? Suddenly, he felt sick, terrified.

"Jumpspace in two minutes," Graglia announced.

I can call it off, he thought, heart slamming in his chest. *There's still time. It's not too late.* He felt the impulse to scream *Stop!* welling up in him. Suddenly, Lisa's image appeared to his mind's eye. She was not looking at him but down, he realized, at a book. It was the study, the day he had come on her unaware and stood silently, just watching her for minutes. Then it was the cliffside where he proposed, the wind whipping her hair around. She laughed and cried in the same moment and then said the word he waited to hear.

The impulse died. *No,* he thought. *No other concerns, no more doubts. I follow the trail till it ends, or I am dead. There are no alternatives.* He looked around the bridge and quickly, before anyone saw, wiped the tears from his eyes.

"Jump at one minute, Captain," Graglia said.

"All boards are green," Telisan advised. "We are ready for jump."

"Stand by to jump," he said, amazed by the detached calm of his voice, as if someone else was speaking. "Initiate approach protocol. Weapons are free, Mr. Wardell. Just like last time. Any contacts are hostile. Fire first.

"Sharon, sound the jump alert." *I would ask God to forgive me for this sin,* he thought, *if I still believed there was a god.*

"T minus thirty."
In case there is a god, he thought desperately, *just in case. Forgive me.*
"Jump in five, four, three, two, one..."
"Jump," ordered Fenaday.
Déjà vu, disorientation, cold, dead emptiness.

Chapter Twelve

The universe crashed back on Fenaday. *God,* he thought as his stomach tried to rebel. *Worst one yet.* His eyes refused to focus. Sound and color remained distorted. Had they emerged at all? *We must have,* he thought, *or I would feel nothing.* At the back of his mind lay that fear common to every spacer, the legends of lost ships. Ships that did not come all the way back, trapped in a hellish netherworld between jumpspace and real space.

"Status," he croaked.

"Nothing in the immediate area." Sharla's voice was shaky for once. "Active scan is still ranging." With the ship's huge entry flare still propagating, there was no point in using the subtlety of passive scanners.

Fenaday breathed deeply, fighting nausea. His vision began to clear. Distortions faded, shapes became people, colors normalized.

"Weapons and fighters on standby," Telisan added. If the jarring dissonance of this particular emergence bothered the fighter jock, his voice did not reveal it.

"The automatics worked," said Graglia, who at least had the decency to look as ill as Fenaday felt. "We over-jumped the normal entry point by three million kilometers and are off the plane of the ecliptic. If their sentry satellites are no better than ours, we should be safe. If Vaughn's maps are trustworthy, there's a small, Pluto-like ice world eight hours ahead that we can use for a gravity v-dump.

"Sorry for the rough come-down folks," he continued, "but that's what you get when you play with coordinates."

Mmok smiled. "Yep, a real puke-jump. Just like the old days. Boy, when we used to jump into Xenophobe space like this, people would be blowing chunks all over the instruments."

Fenaday looked down, locking his jaw. *If I shoot him now*, he thought, *no jury in the universe will convict me.*

"Then there was the smell," Mmok continued, "days and days of…"

Leda Jenner slapped him on the arm.

He looked at her. "What?"

She glared.

Mmok grumbled but subsided.

"Active scan is negative on all ranges," Sharla said.

"Okay," Fenaday said. "Secure from active scan. Go to passive." He turned slowly trying not to upset his inner ear. "Sharon, relay this to all decks."

"Aye, sir," she said.

"This is Captain Fenaday," he began. "We have arrived in Mounus system. Chances of enemy contact are low for now. If there were anything nearby, we'd have seen it and it would have seen us. The entry flare will fade out shortly. Even if the Voit-Veru detected the flare, it will be almost impossible for them to pick us up unless they chance into detector range. We should be ready to go to Defcon One in three hours unless something comes up.

"Bear this in mind from this moment on," Fenaday continued. "We're here on a rescue mission, but we'll do what we have to. The Voit-Veru attacked and captured the Confederate warship *Blackbird* in an act of war. They've aided and abetted the Denshi in trying to destabilize the Confederacy. We've learned from the Denshi records that they have standing orders to destroy any Confed ship they encounter. They've chosen the sword at every turn. They may live to regret it. Fenaday, out." He turned back to face his bridge crew.

"Well, here we are," Mmok said. "Now what?"

Fenaday had no ready answer. Reaching Mounus had always seemed so impossible that he hadn't planned much beyond this point.

"Shasti has already started planning on a raid using the *Intruder* shuttle," Fenaday said finally. "It seems like the only possibility."

"This isn't dead Enshar," Mmok said, "or Olympia where the Denshi had to let us reach close orbit. In both cases, we got forces down without being attacked. Here we face a hostile frontier world. Approach will be difficult, if not impossible. Even if we succeed in getting down and back, we face the prospect of pursuit through three contested systems."

Perez saved Fenaday from having to respond. The engineer looked even more harried than usual. "Ship systems are nominal after jump," he said. "There are more than the usual number of burnouts, but we can handle it. We've got sufficient power for the holocloak now."

"Sharla, engage holocloak as soon as you're back online," Fenaday said. "How soon?"

"Aye, sir." Sharla turned to her instruments. "It will take some minutes if the system came through jump in order."

"Of course," Fenaday said. "Report when you can." Mandela's gift to them needed to be brought up carefully and calibrated. Pushing Sharla was pointless.

A few minutes later, Sharla turned to him with relief. "System online, engaging now." The image spread over the ship in sections. Gradually, *Sidhe* assumed a rock-like appearance.

Fenaday altered the view on the ship's scanners. Telisan and Mmok walked over to his command chair, as he worked the controls. A huge wall of gas and dust filled almost half of visible space. They were now on the other side of the immense nebula that had shielded the Voit-Veru from the Confederacy. The normal 21cm band hissed and crackled with wild static. Interference from the exploded sun of the nebula and the mind-numbing hugeness of space itself augmented *Sidhe's* artificial defenses. Sensors found such space difficult to search in, full of ghosts and false echoes.

"Man, are we far from home," Mmok said, his eye fixed on the nebula.

Shasti joined them in contemplation of the nebula. The sight of the dead star's torment seemed to grip the bridge in a melancholy mood. "Sharon," Fenaday said, "reduce ambient lighting on the bridge by two-thirds."

The glow from the bridge screen intensified as the lights went down, green, yellows, and gold with hints of angry reds. The nebula stood between them and all they had ever known. A signal would not punch through it in the lifetime of anyone on board. It had hidden the Confederacy and the Voit-Veru from each other for hundreds of years.

He turned to look at Shasti, her ivory skin alive with the colors of the nebula, rapt attention on her face. "Look homeward, Angel," he murmured. She looked at him briefly, and he realized he had spoken aloud. Her attention went back to the awesome spectacle on the screen. *Of course*, he thought, remembering the paintings and sketches that littered her cabin. *She is an artist. I'll pray that she lives long enough to paint it.*

"We must be the first ship to emerge so close to a nebula," Graglia said. "None of the other known jump points are this close to one. The science on hyperspace entry says they shouldn't be."

"First Confed ship," Mmok said.

The reminder that they were furtive warship, not a science vessel, didn't dispel the mood.

"Relay the main view screen to all stations," Fenaday said. It was a gesture, a moment of beauty to share in an uncaring universe. He remembered another such moment, when he, Shasti, and Telisan rode *Wildcat* fighters into Enshar's atmosphere in the early morning hours, dropping toward near certain death on the planet's haunted surface. He remembered the silver contrails cut by the fighters, as if in challenge to the death hidden below. The Japanese had a word for such a moment, for the silent communion of man and nature, *kami*. The word was versatile, meaning anything from god, or spirit, to the inchoate feeling welling up in many of them as they gazed on the remnant of the supernova.

Shasti sighed, a sad, eloquent sound speaking better than words.

Fenaday reluctantly pulled himself back to a here and now in which he had few answers. *There must be a way*, he thought. *I have got to find a way. Somewhere ahead on a world I've never seen, Lisa might still be alive. I've got to find her.*

———

Two days later, the command crew gathered on the bridge. Fenaday had long since dropped the ship down to Defcon One so his crew could be rested and fed. Weapons and essential stations remained manned with some crew sleeping or eating nearby.

Sharla sat at her modified station, commanding her section of techs buried in the bowels of Mandela's high-tech gadgetry. Shasti and Mmok stood at opposite ends of the bridge, joined in morose introspection. Fenaday had taken to brainstorming on the bridge, unwilling to leave it for staff meetings. Despite the crowd on the bridge—Rigg, Rask, Graglia, Wardell, Telisan, and the others— they were no closer to a viable approach to the planet.

"What little we know of the planet's defenses," Telisan began, "makes a direct assault by a lone frigate mere suicide. Our only hope seems to be provoking a fight between the Voit-Veru and any Olympian forces and slipping the *Intruder* in during the fracas."

Mmok shook his head. "That tactic seems chancy given the presence of command and control facilities on Mounus IV."

Fenaday shifted in his command chair, almost mad with impatience. He'd started *Sidhe* on her long fall toward the inner system, shedding velocity by using the gravity drag of a small, icy world followed by a quick, hard burn while hidden on the planet's far side. Fenaday's only concession to the others was the relatively slow speed of the approach. At night, he tossed in fitful, guilty sleep. Visions of Shasti, Telisan, and the others dying plagued his dreams.

"What other choice do we have?" Sharla asked. She leaned against Telisan, who stood next to her boards. Fenaday noted the gesture with silent relief. He knew of the terrible strain his friend had placed on the triad of his engagement by trying to help him on Olympia. Sharla held them together while they worked through the problems.

Curious, Fenaday thought, *how I always think of Sharla as a girl, though she is no more female than male.* Sometimes it seemed she lived in the shadow of Arpen's empathy, or Telisan's easy, fighter-jock manner. Fenaday had come to appreciate the quiet competent computer specialist with her ready, cheerful manner. He knew her and the depth of her love for both Telisan and Arpen. He pinned most of his hopes for his friend's future on Sharla.

"Captain?" Telisan prodded.

"Sorry." Fenaday broke free of his reverie. "My wits are wandering."

"Great," Mmok said.

"Can it," Fenaday replied, without even looking at him.

"The odds of a scan detection are significant as we approach the inner system," Telisan continued, ignoring the spat. He had become used to the two humans' grumblings against each other. They were almost background noise at this point. "If they then go to visual scan to confirm us, we will be attacked."

"True." Fenaday nodded. "You know the standard tactics for a low EM approach as well as I do. The simple problem is that *Sidhe* is a high-speed object. Once we get within a certain range, we draw attention. If they look, we get made."

"Too bad we can't do to the *Sidhe* what we did to Shasti," Rigg said. "Be nice if we could look like an Olympian or Voit-Veru vessel."

"Any chance we could rig up some camouflage, like we did with the *Intruder* over Olympia?" Graglia asked.

Telisan looked dubious. "I've looked at the warbooks Vaughn gave us, as well as our own on Olympian forces. *Sidhe* really does not look like anything in those fleets. I don't think we could do anything with the resources we have. We'd need a dockyard and more spare metal than we have."

"Quit being so literal," Mmok said suddenly. "Think big."

Fenaday controlled his irritation. "An idea, Mr. Mmok?"

"You're forgetting the holographic generators. Sharla had the right idea when she put a holographic mask over Rainhell's face. Take it a step further. Why not throw a new mask over the whole ship? I've been running the math through the supercomputer brains of all the HCRs. I'm not an expert in the field, but it looks hopeful."

"How will looking like a rock help us get near the planet?" Fenaday asked. "In the outer system, sure. In the inner system, even rudimentary planetary defenses would track us coming in from .25 AU. If we're aimed at the planet, they send ships to blast us. If we change course near the planet, they'll know we're a ship."

"Make her look like an Olympian vessel or even a Voit-Veru," Mmok said. "We fake communications damage. Get to close range, attack one side or the other, get a bunch of shots off, and start them killing each other. Meanwhile, we do what we have to do and then bug out."

Everyone looked at Mmok.

"Brilliant," Jenner cried. She had entered unnoticed, except by Shasti, who noticed everything. Mmok preened, buffing the nails of his real hand on his jacket.

"Yes," Moshe Karass said, "like the holographic emitter pods we drop in a dogfight to confuse enemy targeting."

"Those last only for a few seconds," Telisan said. "They suggest the outline of a fighter more than simulate it. Even a quick look and you can tell."

"Damn," Fenaday said, impressed despite himself. He turned to Sharla. "Can you do it?"

The demi-female's face was pensive. "We never had any success achieving a decent projection on anything as large as a warship back during the war. In most tactical situations, it just doesn't make sense to try. The power drain is huge, depleting weapons and systems, leaving you vulnerable in combat.

"An asteroid is an easy projection. It's just one small series of pixels repeated. To do a whole different ship, that is a tall order. Maybe I could fuzz a few of the more incriminating outlines. I doubt it. Give me a few minutes with the equipment and the manuals." She turned to her console and began manipulating the controls, visibly tuning out everyone in the room.

As she worked with no sign of stopping, the others sipped the ubiquitous cups of coffee or wandered about. Fenaday stood and stretched then picked up a protein bar from the tray of foods brought in by Leda. His stomach had finally settled and he knew his body, wracked by hyperspace, needed the fuel.

When was the last time I sat in a restaurant with a real waiter and a wine list, he wondered? *Only months ago, but it seems years.* He leaned back on the table, occasionally looking at Sharla, who showed no signs of letting up.

Shasti leaned back in her chair next to him, her shoulder touching his. The slight touch made his heart race and his breathing irregular. They had reached a fragile equilibrium at last. He still sensed a repressed anger, almost a darkness in her, present but contained, at least for now. The touch felt like fire against his shoulder. His body recalled that heat and its response to her near-perfect body. He didn't want to move, to risk violating the delicate peace between them.

She turned toward him, a slight smile playing on her lips. He wondered how much she saw in his eyes. He smiled back sadly, for things that were not and could not be.

"Jeevah!" Sharla exclaimed, jumping back in her seat. They all turned to the Demi-female.

"What's wrong?" Fenaday demanded.

"Captain," Sharla said, "there's something very odd here. When I started looking through my memory configuration trying to boost the power, new systems began coming online. It's as if all of a sudden the holo-system expanded by an order of magnitude."

"How is that possible?" Fenaday asked.

"I don't know," she said waving a hand at the controls. "This console is just a remote control for all the equipment Mandela placed in that sealed compartment before you went to Enshar. I've never even seen the machinery itself."

"No one has," Fenaday responded. Anytime the spymaster's name came up, butterflies hit his stomach. He put down his coffee.

"Telisan, Sharla, Shasti, Mmok, let's go see what the hell is going on. Graglia, you have the bridge."

The holographic generators occupied the forward part of the ship, under the radome and sensors and partially incorporating them. The room had not been opened since they lifted from Mars en route to Enshar. Even then, the only people allowed in had been Navy techs. Fenaday looked at the security seal, which threatened dire consequences if broken.

Cobalt the HCR appeared at his shoulder and Fenaday felt his mouth go dry. He turned slowly toward Mmok.

"I brought a can opener," said Mmok. "You want it opened or what?"

Fenaday nodded warily. Cobalt stepped forward and casually pulled the seal off, crumpling it in its servo hands. A few quick laser cuts by the machine freed the door.

They entered. Lights went on automatically and they faced the banks of unfamiliar equipment. Sharla made a sound of astonishment looking at it all and practically ran in, running long, spidery fingers over the machinery. She said something in Denlenn, then recollected herself and switched back to standard. "This isn't standard equipment," she said excitedly, "far from it. I've never seen anything like it. There are entire banks of equipment here that aren't on the main board on the bridge." She pulled out a chair and began to study the controls.

Fenaday and Telisan looked at each other in confusion. "Mandela lent us Sue Bernard to operate the system when we went to Enshar," Fenaday mused. "We only used it during the approach to the planet at the basic setting. Since nothing attacked us before we made orbital insertion, we turned off the asteroid camouflage and didn't use it again. The controls for the camouflage are on the bridge. Navy techs sealed this compartment, and we were told to leave it alone or get fitted for prison grays. They kept telling us it would be removed, though they never seemed to be in any hurry to pull it out.

"The crew from the Navy tender that remilitarized us didn't even break the seal for the compartment before we launched for

Olympia. They put more automatics on the bridge and told us we didn't need to go in here to maintain the equipment. Anything we needed to do, we could do from the bridge." He moved forward, leaning on the back of her chair to study the boards.

"It appears that Mr. Mandela did not want you to know the full potential of the system," Sharla replied. "There are several micro-supercomputers in here that aren't tied into the ship's main computer or the board on the bridge. Off-hand I'd guess we were using about a tenth of this system's capacity."

She started the main computer and whistled in astonishment at the displays. "The power and resolution of these additional holographic generators is far beyond anything I've ever seen," she continued. "I'm amazed Mandela let you keep this."

"I've wondered about that myself," said Telisan. "He told us it was an experimental rig. We really did not need it at Enshar. Perhaps he felt it wasn't worth recovering?"

"Equipment like this?" said Sharla, manipulating controls as screens lit with data. "It's worth more than this vessel. Many times so."

"Ah," she said, "fascinating, I was going to download the warbook Vaughn gave us, but the unit is already loaded with an Olympian Warbook. Its file date is older, though. It must have been loaded during the original installation. We'll have to update it."

Fenaday's body jerked upright as if from an electric charge. He stared at the banks of machinery and began cursing, a dark fury in his face. The others looked at him astonished, almost afraid. He rounded on Mmok, face to face with the startled cyborg, who regarded him as if doubting his sanity. Shasti grabbed his arms, fearing he would strike.

"When," Fenaday spat, "when did Mandela plan the assassination of Pard?"

"What?" Mmok said. He held a hand before Cobalt, which had reacted to Fenaday's outburst by trying to interpose itself in front of him.

"When?" he demanded again. "How long has that bastard been manipulating my life? This equipment was installed on Mars before the Enshar expedition. Three years ago. Why does it have a three-year-old Olympian Warbook loaded? How long ago did Mandela plan to send me to Olympia?"

"I don't know, Fenaday," Mmok snapped in return. "You keep confusing me with some confidant of his. I'm just his rusty, trusty cyborg. I go where I'm sent, like a good soldier."

"Bastard," Fenaday said. Mmok bridled, unsure if Fenaday was insulting Mandela or him.

Fearing explosion, Telisan put a hand on his friend's shoulder, edging between them. "Robert, what ails? We don't understand."

"Don't you see?" Fenaday demanded. "The holo-generators—he left them on board, locked down, secured, but operational. Said it was more expensive to remove than it was worth. A damn lie!

"He left this equipment onboard because he knew we'd need it. He knew he wasn't through with us after Enshar. He 'threw together' the Olympian rescue? No, another lie. He planned it from before Enshar. That file proves it."

"I suspected this," Telisan said gently. "The presence of the Navy tender, the priority escort *Cheetah* that brought me to you, Mandela's own presence on New Eire when word of the first failure came. All too convenient."

"Yes," Fenaday said, his equilibrium returning. Shasti released her hold on his arms. "Now we know." He shivered from the intensity of his hatred. "Bastard. I feel like a puppet. How do I know what actions are mine and what he's made me do? How do I know he didn't plan what we are doing now?"

"You're mad," Mmok said. "No one could have foreseen this. For every plan a guy like Mandela has, he has a hundred contingency plans. Maybe two of them actually work. You were the one that worked, the covered long-shot bet."

Fenaday looked away, jaw clenched.

"Fenaday," Mmok said, "not even Mandela could have predicted you would find information on your wife and hare off into unknown space. Mandela, believe it or not, is a cautious man, and what we're doing now is just plain fucking nuts."

"I wish I knew. I wish I knew," Fenaday whispered. "God, I hate being manipulated."

"Welcome to the grown-up world." Mmok shrugged.

"Stop it," Shasti growled. "Warning one and only."

Mmok shut up.

"It's okay," Fenaday said. "Sorry, Mmok. Not your fault. I just hate how he pulls my strings."

"Well," Mmok said, looking away, "he does have that effect on people. Forget it. Let's get back to work. Sharla, can you do it?"

The Denlenn looked back with a grin. "With this rig, I could make us look like a giant lollipop."

Mmok snorted. It broke the tension.

"Seriously, Captain," Sharla said, "I'm going to need every computer tech we've got aboard from now on. We've got good scans of both the vessels we destroyed. Maybe I can use those as templates. Even with this sort of rig, the deception won't hold up close or for long. If they send fighters in for a looksee, or focus precise opticals on us from any range under 1000 kilometers, we will start to look funny. It would help if *Sidhe* were some other color than brilliant crimson."

"Captain Blood," Mmok said, amused.

Fenaday shrugged. "Sorry. It was the cheapest color the dockyard had. Sharla, call for any personnel you need. All our lives may well depend on this. Report to me when you have a working plan."

Chapter Thirteen

Fenaday snapped up in bed with a cry. His eyes focused with difficulty as his heart hammered. He looked around. "My ready-cabin," he murmured to himself. "Damn, another nightmare." Waking didn't seem to help. It was no less a nightmare. *It's insane,* he thought, *totally insane. I've come across over a hundred light years to find Lisa on a planet I've never seen. There were times we missed each other trying to get together for dinner in New Kerry. I can't even pray for luck anymore,* he thought with acid bitterness. *All I can do is keep going forward, following the trail. I can't even allow for hope. I just have to keep moving forward.*

"Captain," called Telisan from outside the door.

"Come."

Telisan slid open the hatch door. "Did you call?" he asked diplomatically.

Fenaday threw off the covers and stood, confused, then realized he'd left the comlink to the bridge open so he could hear the activity. His cry must have penetrated the bridge, particularly if the Denlenn, with his comparatively poor hearing, had picked it up. He quickly switched the comlink off.

"Robert, you're troubled," Telisan said, sealing the hatch before him, "more even than usual."

Fenaday looked at his friend. "The first year, I could feel the weight of her head on my shoulder."

Telisan looked at him, yellow cat-like eyes steady and attentive.

"She liked to nap with her head on my shoulder," Fenaday said. "I always teased her about how innocent she looked when she was asleep. I remembered the scent of her hair that first year, most of the second. I tried to kid myself all the third year that I could still remember, but I couldn't anymore. It was always a fight to retain those little things after that. I still recall how she likes her tea." His voice cracked. "Oh, Telisan," he whispered, "what if she's not there? What if they moved her? God, what if they moved her to the port? We are going to blow a nuke on that port. It's our only chance..."

"I look forward to meeting her," Telisan said.

"What?" Fenaday said.

"I look forward to meeting your wife," Telisan repeated.

Fenaday laughed raggedly. "You know, you may just have enough tact to be married to two women at the same time."

Telisan smiled at him. "See you on the bridge."

———

With the prospect of the new holocloak increasing the ship's chances of reaching Mounus IV, Fenaday stopped their infall toward the planet. They were still far out in the system. After consulting Vaughn's maps, he moved the star-frigate near to the main entry point to Mounus system. From there, powered down in low EME mode, though mercifully with heat and life support still running, they could watch for reinforcements or traffic into Voit-Veru space. What lay beyond the entry point was a mystery. Denshi maps ended there. Mounus was the only meetpoint for the Olympians and the Voit-Veru. Where the Voit-Veru homeworld or colonies lay, remained both a secret and an immense tactical advantage for the aliens.

"Captain," Hafel called. With Sharla devoting every waking hour to the holo-generators, Sharon had retaken her old slot covering all the scanners. Susan Bernard now manned the communications panel. "I'm picking up the wake of a system entry from hyperspace. It's coming from the optimal warp point toward what Vaughn thought was the sector capital, Ansuw."

"Alert," Fenaday ordered. Hafel hit the alarm klaxon. "Bernard, call Telisan to the bridge. Mr. Graglia, stand by for evasive. Mr. Wardell, open outer doors on all missile tubes. No active scans. Stand by for passive weapon lock, but be ready to go active and bring up the energy weapons."

Fenaday jumped from his chair striding over to Hafel's. "How large a propagation wave?" he demanded.

Hafel's hands whipped over instruments. Readouts and screens glowed with information, much of it computerized guesswork. "It's a good size wave. A vessel of at least 25,000 metric tons."

"Double our mass and more to spare," Fenaday murmured.

Telisan entered at a run, followed by Mmok, Rigg, and Shasti.

"*Wildcat* crews to their fighters," Fenaday called to Telisan.

Telisan nodded and moved to his board, rapping out orders to the fighter crews.

"Captain," Graglia called, "we don't know how high a percent of C that ship emerged at. If he came out of that optimal exit point, he's heading in this direction. We could be in his exit cone. He might be right behind that propagation wave."

"I doubt it," Telisan said. "This system has not been held by the Voit-Veru for very long. It's an extremely rocky system, many asteroids and lots of interference from the nebula, especially out this far. Even with most recent star charts, high speed would be risky. Also this is peacetime, in a friendly system. I'd be surprised if he is at more than .10 C."

"If I could risk an active lock, even for a few seconds," Wardell said.

"No," Fenaday said. "That would be the end for us if it is a warship. Stick to passives."

"Captain," Hafel said, "I'm getting a Voit-Veru IFF signal. It's a merchant signal according to the information Mr. Vaughn supplied us with."

They looked at each other. "Of course," Mmok said, "they ain't sneaking around. This is their backyard. No reason for radio silence."

"If their merchants run the way ours do," Fenaday said, "that signal will contain a carrier with all the latest mail and a cargo manifest."

"Course and speed coming up, sir," Hafel said, "on everyone's boards, now."

"Well, Mr. Mmok," Fenaday said, his eyes fixed on the scanner readout, "a freighter. Headed our way and slowly too. A nice juicy freighter. Doubtless a supply ship heading for Mounus IV. He won't see us for hours. Even our passive instruments are likely to be better than his active ones and we're running EME stealthy and camouflaged."

"Kind of takes you back to your pirate days," Mmok returned. "Pity you can't loot it, huh?"

Fenaday didn't rise to the bait. "You may have something there, Mmok."

"What?" returned the cyborg.

"The weak part of the plan has always been how to get a force down to Mounus IV. To avoid detection, we'll have to launch the *Intruder* from so far out she could only take a quarter of her maximum load. That's too small a force. If we take the *Sidhe*, even if we get lucky with the holographics, we'll have to fight our way in. Odds of our doing that and surviving are pitiful.

"What if the Voit-Veru were to deliver us themselves?" Fenaday asked. "What if we came down in that freighter inside their defenses, at the one spaceport on this frontier world? We make a break for the compound, trigger a nuke on the freighter, and blast the port. Confusion reigns." A cold, almost evil expression slid over Fenaday's normally pleasant face. "It might give us a fighting chance."

"Excellent," Shasti said.

"Best I've heard yet." Rigg nodded.

Mmok shrugged. "Guess the Voit-Veru shouldn't have invested in starting a civil war in our back yard. A lot of people got more kilotons for less during the Big One."

"Mr. Mmok," Fenaday said, "congratulations. You are going to get to do a bit of pirating yourself. I want that ship. I want it intact."

Mmok stared at the screen showing the estimated course of their prey, then looked back at Fenaday. "Yo, ho, ho and a bottle of rum."

———

The clanship *Queen of the Night* forged ahead at a steady pace. Her sturdy, inelegant lines belied the grandiose name. She was an out-of-date type, a break-bulk freighter over sixty years old, designed for landings on water or unimproved fields, not a common need anymore.

On the bridge of the old freighter, Clan Mother Adan studied the stars and wondered about the future. With the expansion of bases under the new military government came the opportunity for even politically out-of-favor clans like the Hersi to ship military cargoes to remote outposts. The break came none too soon for the Hersi clan. They'd opposed the Aporok-led government that swept into power after the existence of aliens was proved. Opposition came with a high price tag, near ruin of the clan.

Her ship ran well despite all the skimping and corner cutting in the lean years. They were secure from jump, inbound on an approach to the improved base on Mounus IV, the Voit-Veru's closest base to the massive, parsecs-wide nebula known as the Wall. That nebula separated them from much of the rest of the galactic arm by a maelstrom of interference in the 21CM band caused by the pulsar at the heart of the nebula.

Yet, there were holes in that wall. Those holes had revealed the Voit-Veru were no longer alone. Despite the military's chokehold on all information, rumors spread that life had been found, provoking fear. The Voit-Veru had learned in their infancy as a species that alien meant enemy. The Mon-Veru taught them that in thousands of years of war. The military clans, formerly regarded as anachronisms from the Mon-Veru wars, found a new threat to justify their existence. It allowed them to vault into control and begin converting the economy to a war footing.

One such step was the base that lay ahead. Originally a small scientific outpost studying the nebula, it grew into a major installation requiring so many cargo runs that even the Hersi were able to get a job servicing the military they opposed. So *Queen* found herself with a cargo, inbound to the still barely chartered system of Mounus with its five worlds, and the remnants of possibly two more, destroyed by the system's titanic gas giants. Still, Mounus IV was a green world. If the military ever gave up their stranglehold on it, Mounus IV might prosper as a colony, though it was considerable distance both from Homeworld and the Sector Capitol.

Of course, Adan thought, *they'll have to actually do a decent starmap first*. Until then, everyone without military equipment had to a do a slow cautious approach, lest they make a discovery by the unpleasant method of pranging the ship into it. Not for the first time, she thought enviously of the new technology that seemed to be flowing to the Aporok Clan and their ilk. Their ships received newer and better computers and sensors, making them faster and more efficient. Time was money. Money was the ship's blood.

"How's scan?" she asked abruptly, trying to escape bitter thoughts.

The ship's youngest crewmember, Plik-Alu, seated at Scan 1, jumped slightly at being addressed. He'd only recently graduated out of junior training. Adan preferred to break in the newest crew on her own watch. It was good training for them and safer for the ship.

"Flight Path is all clear, Clan-mother," Plik answered.

"Captain, while on the bridge, youngling," she corrected him.

The young Veru's ears twitched furiously in embarrassment. "Yes, Captain, Flight plan clear. There are two Class Four and one Class Three asteroids within 100,000 km. None pose any threat to our course. There is an unusually high metal content reading on the Class Three."

"Excellent," Adan said. "Are any of them charted?"

"No, Captain."

"Hardly surprising," she said. "This system is damn near unexplored outside of the orbit of the fourth planet. That's why the slow approach, youngling. It wouldn't do to inhale a piece of rock at .05 *C*. That right, Helm?"

Cantel, a grizzled veteran of many years aboard *Queen*, snorted a laugh in reply. "No, ma'am, voids the manufacturer's warranty."

Now it was her turn to snort. "Cantel, there's nothing on this ship that's new enough for a warranty."

Cantel cocked an ear at the young Veru at Scan 1. "What about Plik?"

The bridge crew laughed, much to the youngster's embarrassment.

"Log a claim for that metal-rich asteroid," she said, "money in the bank once they get system mining going. If they do."

Queen shuddered, not a big movement but enough to raise fur on every neck.

"Scan," she snapped.

"Clear," shouted the nervous young Veru.

The ship shuddered again, more violently. Alarms sounded. Blue warning lights flashed on screens. "Hull breach," Metrel called from communications.

"What the hell is going on?" Adan demanded. "Exterior cameras, aft and forward views."

"Scan is breaking up," Plik called, "heavy electronic interference."

"Communications are jammed on all bands," added Metrel.

The viewscreen lit in front of her; the image stunned them. On the main panel they could see the flat rear hull of their ship. On it squatted a large, matte-black shape—a ship.

"How?" Plik stammered. "How did it get past the scan?"

A bulky shape, like a beach crawler, moved from the side of the ship. With a flash, the camera went dead.

On the remaining panel, showing the view ahead, an object moved. Automatics focused on it. An asteroid headed toward them.

"Impossible," Cantel breathed, "it was on a different course."

The image of the asteroid blurred and disappeared. A warship appeared in its place, long, vicious looking, painted an impossible red and completely alien. Then that camera died.

"Bridge," called a panicked voice, "they are on board. Monsters —" The voice changed to a scream, suddenly cut off.

"Get out a mayday somehow," she ordered, cold dread numbing her lips. "Put me on Intership."

"All crew," she announced, "this is the captain. Arm yourselves. Alterday crew, fall back on the nursery. All others, save for Engineering, head for the bridge."

"I'm getting a message in Standard," said Metrel, shock on her face. "It's direct from outside our hull. No interference."

"Put it on," Adan demanded.

A flat metallic voice, obviously computer generated, sounded in their speakers. "This is Captain Robert Fenaday of the Confederate Private Warship *Sidhe* to unknown vessel. You are under our guns and being boarded. Cut engines and make no resistance. Surrender and you will be well treated. Resistance will be met by deadly force."

The message began to cycle.

Adan's brain whirled furiously. None of her training had prepared her for this. No Voit-Veru ship had ever been in such a predicament. Little of the alien's speech meant anything to her, but a quick look at their ship made it clear there was no question of outrunning or outmaneuvering the warship. Using the *Queen's* popgun armaments was clearly suicide. *At least*, she thought grimly, *it will be quick. Maybe the aliens wouldn't fire with their own people on board. If we could get hostages…*

Quickly, she hopped over to the weapons locker traditionally kept on the bridge. It opened with a creak, and she handed out the low-velocity pistols.

"Cantel, stay by the mains in case we run. I have to see what we're facing."

The light suddenly failed and emergency systems cut in. "This is Bolsco in Engineering. They are—" A boom cut the engineer off.

"Never mind, Cantel," she said, her voice sounding old and tired. "Come with us." Backed by the bridge crew, she opened the pressure door to the main corridor. Plik-Alu was by her side. "Captain," he said, tears in his voice, "I'm sorry. This is my fault. I don't know how they got past Scan."

"Later," she snapped.

They were halfway down the hallway when figures appeared at the far end. Horrible, distorted, moving quickly. Metal tore and smashed behind them. Adan whirled. One of the monsters tore straight through a nearby bulkhead. The figures surrounding them were smaller than a Voit-Veru: tailless, two legged, with flat faces that looked identical, longhaired, clad in black with sashes of colored fabric. They pointed deadly-looking, black weapons at *Queen's* crew. It was over.

"Weapons down," Adan ordered.

Plik-Alu suddenly jumped in front of her, bringing up his pistol. "No," she screamed—too late.

One alien blurred into movement, its weapon snapping out a beam. The youngling fell at her feet.

"No one move," she cried. She dropped her own weapon, falling to her haunches by Plik.

His eyes fluttered open for a second. "Clan-mother," he whispered, "I'm sorry." His head rolled back loosely.

"No," she whispered, "no."

"Drop your weapons. Make no resistance. Surrender," one of the aliens said as it advanced, its voice metallic and emotionless.

She looked up at its hideous, flat face, realizing with a distant shock that it was a machine. She looked back down at Plik-Alu and gently put his head on the deck. "We surrender," she said. "No more killing, please."

"That is up to you, Captain," the machine said. "I am the machine's controller, speaking to you through it. We have taken Command, Engineering, and Weapons. A number of your crew are holding a small area near what we assume is your medical section. We haven't gone after them. We want them to disarm, or we take them out. Now."

"That's our nursery; the children are there," she said. "Will you guarantee their safety?"

"Captain," the machine said, "I'll guarantee everyone in there is dead in twenty seconds if they don't surrender."

She stumbled to the nearest wall console. "This is Captain Adan," she said in a voice she did not recognize as her own. "The ship's been taken. Surrender your arms and make no resistance." She rested her furred cheek against the chill bulkhead and hoped to the Gods that it was the right decision.

———

S hip secure," Mmok's image announced on the screen.

"Status?" Fenaday asked.

"No casualties or damage to the assault force," Mmok said. "Rigg's people are handling the prisoners and escorting the prize crew."

"What of the freighter crew's casualties?" Fenaday asked.

"Four dead," Mmok shrugged, "ten wounded, mostly not serious. I've got a total of forty-three prisoners. Some of them might be children. They are much smaller than the others, anyway."

Fenaday sighed. More blood. The trail of it led from his home on New Eire to this new star. "Very good, Mr. Mmok. Have Angelica take the helm of the alien vessel. We'll do all the astrogating from here, but I want someone on that bridge, and Angie has flown freighters. We'll bring *Sidhe* alongside then dock, restart the holographic projectors, and transfer the crew. We'll use the brig and Cargo Hold Delta for the prisoners. Bring the captain to the wardroom when we dock."

"You have the freighter. What are you going to do with it?" Shasti asked. She stood up from the controls from which she had directed the boarding action. Fenaday had refused to give her permission to lead the attack in person. She walked over to his command chair.

"We blocked the distress call," Fenaday replied, "and we have a Voit-Veru freighter with crew, cargo, landing codes, everything necessary to get down on Mounus IV. From what we've learned, that vessel contains a family, not just a crew. The captain is the senior female in the clan. We may be able to persuade her that delivering a small party of us to Mounus IV is in the best interest of her family."

"Threaten a mother with her children," Shasti said softly. "Excellent strategy but not one I ever imagined I would hear from you."

He turned toward her, but the words died on his lips as he looked into her cool eyes. After a minute he could not meet her gaze.

"Let's go," he said avoiding argument, avoiding facing himself. For now.

Adan squatted alone in the corner of a compartment aboard the alien warship, unable to use any of the awkward alien furniture. One of the black-uniformed machines had been detailed as a guard. It stared at her with its unwinking black eyes.

The door at the far end opened and the bipeds stilted into the room. She stared at them dully. They were varied. The largest one had long, night-black hair and eyes like green gemstones. Another seemed as much machine as being. It moved stiffly. Metal covered half its head; one eye seemed to be a black-green square of plastic or glass. Still another was dusky-skinned, with a face like tanned leather and eyes of reflective yellow under a mane of rough-looking hair. All three turned to look at the fourth. A male, she guessed, shorter, stockier, and even uglier than the others. She did not know if they were one species, or several.

They seated themselves at the table, working some instruments set into its top. The shorter creature spoke unintelligibly, but the metallic tones of the translator cut in almost instantly. "I am Captain Fenaday, in charge of the *Sidhe*. I trust you have been made comfortable?"

She stared at the creature, longing to leap across the table and bury her teeth in its throat. Something of her thought seemed to communicate itself to the large female. It shifted, menace in every line. Consciously, Adan relaxed. These people held her family. She could not afford their anger.

"Yes," she stated.

"Captain," said the being Fenaday, "we are from the Confederacy of Seven Species on the other side of the nebula. Have you heard of us?"

"Seven species," she murmured in horror. "No," she said slowly, trying to find time for thought. "We heard a little about aliens being found. There have been rumors of a treaty. My people, the Hersi, are not part of the current government. You picked the wrong ship, Captain. Even this cargo run was grudged to our clan. Our ships are rarely used by the government."

"No matter," said the leader. "Over eight years ago, a ship of ours entered your space. I do not know how or why. All I know is that it was my wife's vessel. She and her crew were attacked and captured by your people. We learned this from the allies you heard rumors of. Olympia, a planet of my people, yet not loyal to their own kind. Your government entered into an illegal alliance with Olympia trying to start a secessionist war in the Confederacy. Doubtless your leaders felt that the easiest way to deal with a new and huge power was to encourage division among us. Olympia has fallen, and the Confederacy now knows of the threat.

"I am here on a mission of my own. My wife and her crew are on the planet ahead. I am going to get her back. That is where you and your ship come in.

"You are going to take me and a team into the base. You will assist us in locating my wife and helping us escape."

Laughter almost escaped her. They were insane. "That would be very difficult," she said. "No, impossible. You ask me to betray my own kind."

"Your own kind are on my ship," said the cold-mechanical voice. It could not menace, but the threat hung clearly.

"Understand," continued the alien, "I mean you no harm. I am driven by desperation. I do what I must. If you and your family clan are to survive, you must help me. If my plan works, there will be minimal loss of life. If I have to attack the planet in a frontal assault, flinging nuclear weapons and mass driver fire about, many more will die, including your crew.

"This is not an invasion. I just want my wife, not your base, your planet, your ship, or your lives. But to get what I want, I'll destroy all of those if I have to. You said you were not in sympathy with the existing government. Why die for them?"

She saw the tightrope ahead of her and edged on to it gradually. "What do you want me to do?"

Chapter Fourteen

Maps and reconnaissance photoprints, some covered with coffee cups, littered the tabletops in the main wardroom. Staff came and went, bringing more reports and analyses. Leda Jenner joined them. To Fenaday's surprise, she wasn't in the standard ship's uniform but wore ASAT battle gear with a Red Cross insignia. He looked at Rigg, the question obvious on his face.

"She makes a damn good medic," Rigg said, "as I can testify. She already knew the basics, and she's been studying for the certification in between working up your commissary. She learns like mad and doesn't seem to forget anything."

"Good," Fenaday said. "I know she's been trying to help any way she can. God knows she's too smart to just be running sandwiches and coffee through the ship. I need her in the ground force anyway. She and Shasti are all the Olympians we have."

"Hey," Rigg said, "don't forget I was able to pass as an ugly-ass Olympian thug for hire."

"Good for you." Fenaday patted him on the shoulder.

Rigg's solemn face split into a grin as he took his seat.

A familiar pang hit Fenaday's heart. *I should never have gotten close to these people. I'm going to lose some of them, maybe all. Maybe myself as well. Damn.*

Fenaday rapped on a tabletop. "As you know," he began, rubbing tired eyes, "we captured the Voit-Veru ship twelve hours ago. We have not altered her speed or course. Sharla here has run through the ship's computers thoroughly. This is what we've learned, and it is not good. Our arrival here has coincided with a visit by some high-level politicians. It has something to do with the Olympians and the treaty with the Voit-Veru. There are extra ships here.

"This freighter belongs to an out-of-favor clan in the Voit-Veru. It was only chartered because they didn't have enough hull space in the regular supply run for all the cargo they needed. The regular supply vessel entered this area a week ago and could have made planetfall two to three days ago. It carried all the high priority cargo.

"So the Voit-Veru are throwing a party up ahead, and the captain of this freighter was told to expect to see three or four Olympian vessels, destroyers and frigates, and five or six of their own, including one heavy and one light cruiser."

A murmur of dismay ran around the table.

"We'll get confirmation," Fenaday continued, "of what's in orbit when the planet replies to the freighter's manifest dump with an updated flight plan. Fortunately, we can read their latest codes, if they haven't changed."

"A direct approach," Fenaday said, "is not indicated."

"The one good thing about all this activity," Telisan said, "is that the arrival of a vessel at an isolated post is a major event. This is a small base of a couple thousand that's been overwhelmed with visitors. More traffic is not a welcome relief from monotony; it's difficult work. All the luxury goods went in with the regular freighter. We are the unwanted and politically unpopular. Nobody will want to bother with us that much. We hope."

"Gentlemen, here is the plan," said Fenaday. "Our entire force of ASATs, Marines, and LFs will be smuggled along with Mmok and his cyberforces onworld in the *Queen*. I think we have her crew sufficiently under control. God forgive me, but I plan to maroon most of their people on an asteroid. A small crew will travel with us. Given that they are on the outs with the current government, one hopes they won't be willing to suicide for them.

"*Queen* will land on the outskirts of the port. We will delay the landing claiming computer fault with the main cargo doors. We can tell the stevedores we'll call them when the problem is fixed. The captain will ask for three cargo carriers for the higher priority stuff, so we can unload the ship ourselves."

"Good thing we ain't on Mars," Li said. "The unions would go ballistic." People laughed briefly.

"The Voit-Veru crew," Fenaday continued, "won't know about the nuclear weapons I've ordered loaded in their cargo hold. I plan to blast the port from inside their defenses after we leave the ship. We'll make our way to the compound where, with more luck than anybody has a right to ask, I'll find my wife and her crew."

"That's it?" said an incredulous Mmok. "How do you propose we get around on their world? You would look awful funny with a tail, Fenaday."

"If we get stopped," Fenaday ignored the jibe, "we pass ourselves off as Olympians."

Mmok gestured at Rainhell. "We've got two. Fenaday, you're too short and homely to pass as an Olympian."

"His obvious genetic inferiority will be lost on the Voit-Veru," Shasti countered, "as will the lack of physical beauty. Height," she conceded, "is a problem."

People looked at the ceiling or walls, some visibly trying to control themselves.

Shasti looked at Fenaday, who had put his head in his hands, then at Mmok. "Why are you smiling?" she asked.

"Because," Mmok's smile widened, "sometimes life is just perfect."

"If you are through," Fenaday growled, "my homely ass, and yours, Mmok, will be out of sight. We have two Olympians aboard as you say, but Rigg and some of the ASATs and Marines are big enough to pass, at least with the Voit-Veru. For the rest, they'll be inside the transports. Not much of a plan, but the deception only needs to last long enough to get us to the iso-lab. We then hit the lab, break into the detention block, get my wife, and withdraw to the pickup point."

"Oh, is that all?" Mmok added.

Fenaday drove on. "Telisan, you and *Wildcat Two* will bring in the *Intruder.* I want Fury at the controls. McLoughlin will fly as your wingman. I'll take Sheehan to help pilot the freighter. I'll leave Mr. Graglia to command the *Sidhe.* He served on a fleet destroyer during the war. He commanded the *Durandel* when her captain died during a ship-to-ship fight. Mr. Graglia knows how to handle a vessel like this in combat. Our best chance is to continue the fiction that we are an Olympian vessel here to warn our forces of a Voit-Veru sneak attack. With the holocloak, proper codes, and IFF, Graglia should be able to approach within firing range of the heavy cruiser. You'll begin broadcasting the message we prepared right after *Sidhe* hits the heavy cruiser with her full throw-weight. If we can take her out and get the Olympian vessels into a fight with the squadron here, we have a chance."

"And if they see through this," Mmok answered, "*Sidhe* is a ball of cosmic dust and we get stranded without a ride. Even if they do buy it, *Sidhe* might be crippled or destroyed. You're turning over our only chance of escape to a lieutenant who's been on this ship only a few months."

"He'll have Perez and Wardell," Fenaday countered.

"You're the best man to con this ship through a fight and you know it," Mmok stated.

"I'm going down for my wife," Fenaday said, his tone and eyes gone chill, even slightly mad. "No argument. No discussion on this point."

"Mmok's right," Shasti said.

"No argument, no discussion," Fenaday said, with a hard look at Shasti, "applies to you too."

Tension flared visibly between them, then Shasti nodded stiffly. People breathed again.

"I have every confidence in Mr. Graglia," Fenaday continued.

"Mandela didn't put him on board without reason. He's young, but he can run this ship in a fight. Right, Mr. Graglia?"

"Done it before, back in the war," Graglia replied. "I've been running simulations against Mr. Telisan since the idea was broached."

"He is good," Telisan said.

"He's not as experienced as you," Mmok countered.

"Not so," replied the Denlenn. "I am a fighter pilot. I have run *Sidhe* and likewise practiced in simulations, but all of my kills during the war were in fighters of one sort or another. Graglia has actual experience fighting large-ship to large-ship."

"He will do," Fenaday said. "If the *Intruder* is interfered with on the way down, we have only two fighters. We need Telisan in one. McLoughlin is a good pilot, but he has only two aerospace kills. One of those was a transport. I need my hot-shot fighter jock."

"Do not fear," Telisan said. "We will cover you."

"What worries me," Mmok said, "are the chances of this holo deception working a second time. It's one thing to cause hesitation and a minute's confusion on a warship using some unknown second officer. Here, we are coming into a defended sector. We could face challenge. Even face a boarding demand. There's a big difference approaching a frontier planet. People are gonna be a lot heavier on the trigger."

Fenaday shrugged fretfully. "What can we do? It's the one image we can make work. We've got the codes and the IFF. All we can do is hope for the best."

"Maybe," said Shasti, "we can do better than that." She stood and quickly exited the wardroom, ignoring everyone's questioning looks. Fenaday grabbed a coffee as the others speculated on what she was up to.

Shasti returned in a few minutes with a data crystal.

"Put this in the playback," she said, handing it to Bernard. The Navy rating looked at it dubiously, shrugged, and put it in the computer. The screen over her station lit. On it appeared the face of a stunningly handsome man, black haired with smoldering blue eyes set in a stern Germanic face.

"Hello, Shasti Rainhell," he began.

"Mute," Shasti ordered hastily. Bernard tapped a button, and the sound faded. Shasti looked at Fenaday. "The message is a personal one."

Fenaday studied the face for a second before he recognized the man as Mikhail Vaughn—one of Pard's inner-circle. He had only seen the Olympian once.

"Who is he?" asked Bernard, looking admiringly at the image.

"Vaughn," Fenaday said in a voice sharper than he intended. It surprised him how much Shasti's description of the message as personal upset him.

"Yes," Shasti said. "Mikhail Vaughn, now the leader of House Denshi."

"Handsome devil," Mmok said drolly, "just the type to turn a girl's head."

Fenaday's vision went dark with the effort not to slam a fist into Mmok's face. "Yes," he managed, "a striking looking man." *I have no right,* Fenaday told himself, *no right whatsoever to feel jealous. None at all.*

"More to the point," Shasti continued, staring at Mmok, "we have his image, his voice print, his security code. He was always one of Pard's closest and most trusted operatives. If we can do the same holographic trickery with this image, then he is too important to be questioned or detained by anyone other than his opposite number."

"Good thinking," Mmok said, gone all professional again. "The high ups, especially the covert ones, don't want their movements noticed, impeded, or challenged. Vaughn is an ideal candidate in that respect."

"And several others," Bernard said, looking frankly at Vaughn's image. The women on the bridge laughed or smiled. The men looked annoyed.

"It will be easier with a body model to project the mask on," Sharla said thoughtfully. "Even with that aid, the message will have to be prerecorded. Before, we just used Shasti's voice. Here we will have to use Vaughn's face and form."

"Who's the best match?" Fenaday asked. "If I remember right, this clown was over seven feet tall."

"Seven feet and two inches, from the ground up, when standing in a one-inch thick boot," Mmok said with that absent look that meant he was consulting his network of computer memories. "Leastwise that was what he looked like when he came to see Rainhell in Sickbay."

Fenaday looked at Telisan in dismay. "Vaughn was on my ship?"

"Only for a few minutes," Telisan said, "guarded by HCRs and monitored by Mmok at all times."

Fenaday knew that Telisan had not forgotten to mention the Denshi assassin's visit. His silence on the subject meant that he regarded it as Shasti's private business. The unwanted jealously flared again. *No right,* he reminded himself.

"I didn't see him either," Shasti said, looking intently at Fenaday. "I was unconscious at the time."

"Yes," Fenaday said, "of course."

"The best match would be you, Daniel," Sharla concluded. While the rest of them were distracted, the demi-female had run a crosscheck on the crew from her computer. "You're a good six inches shorter, but you have a similar physique. I can scale you up a few percent and it should work."

Rigg laughed. "Just what every guy wants to hear."

"Excellent," Fenaday said. "Proceed with a message that Vaughn is on a vital errand at Pard's order. Not to be questioned or impeded. Demand the right to dock with the command vessel. It will get you a good shot at her from close range."

"Communications with the ground force will be a problem," Bernard said. "The portable headsets don't have enough power to reach the ship, especially after we start tossing nukes around. You'll be using radiomen with HR-47As. You'll also be vulnerable to jamming."

"I'll be able to reach the ship using the equipment in my cyberforce, in addition to the five HR47As we have," Mmok said.

"Once the fighters and shuttles are in atmosphere, they can also do the usual relay boost, as we did on Enshar," Fenaday added.

"You know," Mmok observed, "this is actually a lot less crazy than some of the shit we've tried."

Sharla gave a Denlenn smile. "Might even work."

The room emptied quickly. Telisan, planning to attend to some paperwork, stayed. He looked up curiously at Shasti when she did not leave.

"Do you really believe she is there?" Shasti asked. "Or even if she is, that this ridiculous plan can work?"

Telisan sighed. He knew or guessed much of the source of Shasti's anger. Still, she was an alien and there were a thousand cultural nuances that he did not share with the tall Olympian. Putting himself in her place was an exercise beyond any skill he had. Yet Shasti would not consult with Arpen, who was far better equipped to help. It seemed their shared time under fire had built a bridge to Shasti, a narrow bridge, and only he was allowed on it.

"I don't know," he replied. "I don't know that your kind would find what he is doing to be reasonable. It seems most do not. Some would say give up. Some would say that one life is not worth a risk to so many, as if this was mere math and we should ignore the seizure of our ships and people.

"We live in an uncaring universe, Shasti. In our lifetime, over a hundred million have perished in battle with the Conchirri. Billions of Enshari died at the hands of the mad Prekak for no reason but ill luck.

"Our Robert is a very unreasonable person. He insists that the universe treat the people he cares about specially. Entire species may end, but he will not accept that anyone special to him can be so cavalierly dispensed with. You remember when we fled to the surface of Barjan, driven there by the Shellycoats?"

"Yes," she said, in a voice gone soft.

"We were all wounded, exhausted, and without hope when Duna called in from the Prekak's chamber a mile below. Duna was my dearest friend, and I started back for him. It was mad and it was hopeless, but all Robert said was, 'I'm with you.' I will never forget that moment, no matter how long I live."

Shasti nodded, anger draining visibly from her.

"Never doubt that he would do all these things for you," Telisan said, hoping that somehow these were the right words to ease his friend's pain.

"I don't," she said looking him in the eye, "but there are other things that I want from him."

"Ah," Telisan said. There seemed nothing else to say. Carefully, he put a hand on the Olympian's arm, a gesture he had learned among humans. Shasti rarely suffered anyone to touch her, but he was rewarded by a very small smile.

"I'd better catch up to Robert," she said. "He's off to see Henlesch, and I don't trust his temper there."

"Good," Telisan replied.

Chapter Fifteen

Shasti caught up to Fenaday before he made the sickbay, taking a short cut and using the speed of her long legs. He nodded to her at the hatchway, and she fell in behind him. Arpen took them over to see the ambassador in his cell.

"Ambassador Henlesch," Fenaday said. The grizzled professor hopped slowly toward Fenaday, tracked every step by an alert Rainhell. He remembered how Arpen had told him that the ambassador had recovered his focus on reality when the *Queen's* crew came aboard. Knowing others of his kind were near served as a restorative. For Fenaday, thinking of his wife, prisoner among Henlesch's people and suffering far worse isolation, it yielded a bitter picture. Despite Arpen's intervention, Fenaday still had to battle murderous impulses toward the alien.

"Yes, Captain Fenaday," Henlesch said. His Standard had improved considerably, doubtless more of Arpen's work.

Fenaday glared at the alien. "We are taking the command staff of the *Queen* with us. I am leaving the nonessential crew on a nearby Class 6 asteroid with full emergency shelter and rations. As senior officer present, I'm requiring you to take charge of the crew. You'll have some junior officers at your disposal to help you keep order until you're rescued."

"Will we be rescued?" Henlesch asked.

Fenaday looked into the alien's eyes, so much like an animal's to him. He struggled for a civil reply. "We will make every provision for the location of your survivors in accordance with Confederation Interstellar law regarding noncombatants.

"You'll have thirty-six hours to prepare," Fenaday continued. "The shelter from the *Queen's* supplies has been supplemented with equipment from our own stores.

"Li," Fenaday called. The scar-faced Asian walked over, his hand on his pistol butt. "Take the ambassador to meet the crew of the *Queen*."

"Yes, sir. Okay, you, follow me."

"Thank you," Henlesch said carefully.

Fenaday nodded once as Henlesch waddled away. He looked at Shasti. "Make the arrangements. I'll be in the hangar bay if you need me."

Hours later, *Sidhe* and the *Queen of the Night* nestled up to the solitary asteroid, an undistinguished ball of rock and ice over three kilometers long. Fenaday's engineers worked feverishly, setting up the emergency shelter that would hold *Queen's* marooned crew and Ambassador Henlesch. They erected the emergency dome in a hollow on the dark-gray surface of the asteroid. It would be crude at best, but adequate for several months.

From his perch over the shuttle bay, Fenaday watched *Queen's* doleful survivors shuffle toward the umbilical that led to the asteroid, carefully guarded by Marines and HCRs. Crewmen checked the boxes and bales for anything that might be used to set up a com or even a simple radio. Fenaday wanted to take no chances on the survivors broadcasting a warning to either a passing ship or the inner systems. Despite their efforts, Fenaday suspected the Veru would eventually come up with something, but it would be weak, limited in range and unlikely to be heard at any significant distance.

"Any significant distance," he murmured, looking at the

unwinking stars. Distances that light itself crawled through. Cold distances empty of anything bigger than an atom. He shivered.

"Cold?" asked a soft familiar voice. Shasti had padded up on him, silent as usual. He turned to face her, glad for any distraction.

"No," he lied.

"The *Queen's* crew is just about unloaded," she said.

Fenaday looked back toward the rock on which they—on which he—would maroon *Queen's* crew. He remembered the Veru children as they were led over, looking more like small animals than children. *Or am I just rationalizing?* he asked himself. *I want to see them as animals so I can pretend they aren't people? So I can justify this obscenity to myself?*

"God," Fenaday said aloud.

"What?" asked Shasti, recognizing the grim mood.

"Nothing," he replied, tight-lipped. Then abruptly, "The duplicate emergency beacons have been placed?"

"Yes," she said, "just as you ordered."

"They've both been checked?"

"Bernard checked them three times. The odds of even one failing are somewhere around a million to one. Don't worry. They'll go off and call for rescue, as you planned."

He nodded.

"I have a question," said Shasti unexpectedly. She looked around but there was no one else on the deck. She moved closer, joining him in his morose watch out the portal.

"Yes?" he said, preoccupied.

"Do I have a soul?"

He looked at her dumbfounded. "A soul?"

"Yes, a soul, and all that it implies."

"And you ask me?" he said. "Me, who's stranding women and children on a rock registering absolute zero, millions of miles from even the next piece of rock."

"You're a born-human," she persisted. "I've studied about religion. It puts great emphasis on being born. I was made from bits of selected DNA in an engineered egg in an artificial womb."

"You're a person, Shasti." He turned to face her, as usual having to look up into the clear jade-green eyes. "You are as much a human being as any. Better than me. Look at the things I do." He gestured helplessly out the portal.

Shasti's eyes followed the gesture. "You're stranding the crew. Pard would have simply killed them rather than risk leaving them to rig up some means of signaling help, or to bear witness against us. More likely an Olympian would leave a delayed fuse bomb to kill them after we pulled away, so Captain Adan would believe there was still a chance and cooperate. No one I've ever worked for would have considered leaving emergency beacons set to cut in two weeks from now, when we are either dead or gone."

"A decent man," he returned, "the type I once was, wouldn't have done any of it. I wasn't born into this universe to be little better than Pard."

Shasti fell silent, not knowing how to reply, how to find comforting words.

"My parents raised me as a Catholic," he continued. "I prayed to the Virgin, went to Mass, all that. Now I no longer believe, so I may not be the right person to ask about souls."

"It seems to me," said Shasti, finding her voice again, "that all this wouldn't bother you so much if you did not have a soul."

He gave a small, surprised laugh, then reached a hand out and put it on her upper arm. Before he could remove it, she put hers over it. They stood that way for a few moments, then he slowly withdrew his hand and she let it go. "I hope you are right. Come on, let's go. It's time to move onto the *Queen*." He turned and she, as she had always done, followed, protecting his back.

At the other umbilical leading to the *Queen*, stood Telisan, Sharla, and Arpen. Behind them the corridor was full of machines and equipment. Rigg and Rask sorted them out and sent them down the umbilical. Risky sat on the deck watching the humans as if they were a show put on just for the amusement of dogs. Mmok stood farther up the corridor, bossing men and machines equally as they loaded supplies for the mission. Li and the Toks were just disappearing down the passage to the *Queen*.

Fenaday walked over to the three Denlenn, with Shasti in tow. She paused only to pet Risky, who promptly fell in behind her.

Fenaday stopped in front of the somber Denlenn. Fenaday knew that the fate of the *Queen's* crew hung heavy on the three, on Arpen most of all.

Telisan gripped his arms formally. Fenaday hugged the big Denlenn, then turned to kiss Arpen and Sharla on the cheek. Shasti hung back but traded a nod with each of them.

"Good luck to you, my friends," Telisan said. "We will see you at the pickup point."

"I hope so," Fenaday said. "Remember what you promised me. If it seems hopeless, you owe it to me to save yourselves and the ship."

Telisan sighed. "I shall never understand you humans. How can you ask me to run and leave you behind? Still, enough," he said, forestalling Fenaday. "It is enough that you made me swear and that you know I am good for my sworn word."

"No one could ever deny that," Fenaday said. "You will be a legend on that basis alone."

He turned to Sharla. "Look after him, will you? He insists on playing by the rules while everyone else cheats."

"I will," Sharla said.

"Arpen," he said, "thank you for everything."

"Don't go getting all my fine work undone," she said with a warm, human smile. She leaned around him to look at Shasti. "That goes for you too."

"I'll do my best," returned Shasti.

"Let's go," Fenaday said, fighting depression. He could see no chance for them to survive, much less succeed. Sickness bit at the back of his throat. *Just a little while longer,* he promised himself. *I just have to keep moving forward a little longer. Something will end this nightmare.* He kept his despair to himself, putting on a cheerful face. From the sudden concern on Arpen's face, he knew that there was at least one who saw through the facade. Before she could say anything, he turned and strode into the umbilical. Shasti and Risky padded after him, the dog's toenails clicking on the armored floor.

Twenty minutes later, *Sidhe* and *Queen of the Night* decoupled from each other and the asteroid. From here, all three would take separate paths. The *Queen* would continue her planned infall. *Sidhe* would take an evasive course, again camouflaged under the holo-cloak, bringing her to the planet seven hours behind the *Queen*. Time enough for the assault force to reach its objective if they could. If *Sidhe* detected the planetside blast of the nuclear weapons Fenaday had secreted aboard *Queen*, they would try to provoke the orbiting Voit-Veru and Olympian forces to battle each other, using their own codes and IFF against them. The shuttles and fighters would then try to force their way onworld to pick up the landing force. If anything went wrong, it fell to Telisan to judge whether the time had come to abandon the quest and save what could be saved.

The asteroid, with its precious cargo of frightened life, rolled away into the dark as it had for billions of years, away into the deep, lonely dark.

———

First Lieutenant Paulo Graglia watched the *Queen of the Night* disappear into the blackness of space with a sinking stomach. *Well,* he thought, *you wanted your own command.* He looked around. Fenaday left him with Sharla, Hafel, and Wardell and most of the regular crew. Mmok, Rigg, Rask, Jenner, and Rainhell left with the *Queen* along with all Cross's Marines, ASATs, LFs, and Mmok's cyberforce.

Telisan remained aboard, but busied himself with preparing *Sidhe*'s small fleet of shuttles for the assault to come. *He probably also left,* Graglia thought, *to keep the bridge crew from checking every order I give with him.* The Denlenn commander ranked him and had commanded wings of small craft, but never fought a ship-to-ship action. Graglia had. Telisan would be too busy with the orbital insertion and extraction to run *Sidhe* as well. Graglia knew Telisan to be the better officer. It was why Telisan drew the tougher assign-ment, getting their people off world.

All I have to do, he thought, *is close on an enemy fleet, hoping they don't penetrate our jerry-rigged disguise. Get off the first shot. Get the Voit-Veru and*

Olympians shooting at each other and duck the return fire until Telisan makes it back. That's all.

Goddamn Fenaday. How the hell did he bring us all here? Fenaday's single-mindedness had dragged them from star to star, catching up so many people in his insane quest. Some followed him. Some came for Telisan, Rainhell, or Rigg. Others just feared Mmok and his machines. It was a chain, but Fenaday was the anchor. *Without him, none of us would be here.*

It might have been better if Gopal had killed him, Graglia mused. He admired Fenaday's persistence, but too many had already paid the price. *Unfair?* he asked himself. *Maybe.* Fenaday had saved a world and a species, but Graglia knew that Mandela had blackmailed him into it. He had taken out Pard, but only to save Rainhell. Now he was here to rescue Confed officers on a hostile world, but only because one was his wife.

Too late for all these thoughts, Graglia thought. *I could have opposed him, joined the Marine officer. Yeah,* he snorted, *joined him in a body bag. Rainhell would have shot me down in an eyeblink.*

"Planning a grand strategy?" asked a voice.

He looked up. Angelica Fury stood next to his chair, petite and gorgeous with a temper to match her name. They'd hovered on the edge of involvement. A kiss, a smile, nothing more, but his heart sped up when he saw her.

He leaned close. "Wondering how the hell I got here and why."

"Skipper knows what he's doing," she replied. "I've seen it from Enshar to here."

"Does he, Angie?" he whispered. "You think this makes sense?"

"Maybe," she said seriously, "maybe not. Tell you what though, I'd like to think my man wouldn't give up on me. She was alive and here six months ago. She may still be."

"She's one person," he snapped.

"Yes," she shot back. "His one person, but I guess you don't understand that."

His mouth snapped shut. The others on the bridge studiously ignored them. Arguments on the bridge weren't good for either his command image or love life. He shrugged doubts and anger aside.

Angelica still glared at him, nostrils flared, hot with anger and beautiful. He smiled at her in a disarming fashion that had charmed women in a dozen systems. She tried to stay mad, to meet his eyes. She couldn't. A grin spread across her face. "Damn you," she said, "if you weren't so good looking..."

"Ah," he replied, "but I am."

Angelica shook her head ruefully. "I'd better get back to my shuttle. Commander Telisan doesn't tolerate slackers."

———

Fenaday stood on the bridge of the *Queen of the Night*, studying the scans. They'd left *Sidhe* behind three days ago. The star frigate would maneuver so she could approach Mounus IV from the correct vector for an Olympian vessel to use. She'd arrive seven hours after the *Queen* landed. For the hundred and two members of the Confederate attack force aboard the freighter, escape was now impossible. The frigate was gone. *We are committed,* thought Fenaday. *Or maybe it's I who should be committed.* His plan seemed even more lunatic now. *But it's the only one,* he said to himself for the hundredth time. *The only chance. Be there, Lisa, be there.*

Ahead loomed their first real test, a nav-buoy. According to the *Queen's* records, it was a commercial model fulfilling the dual function of sentry and traffic cop. The cost to put out a complete satellite screen was prohibitive to all save the most settled, advanced worlds. Usually, it wasn't necessary anyway. For commercial ships, there were only a few ideal vectors from the system's entry point to an orbit and no reason to take any but the best. For military ships, these were also the express routes for a strike.

"Course and heading," he asked.

Pat Sheehan looked up from the helm. "Course eighty-seven by two-twenty by zero," he replied, "situation nominal. Navigation buoys ten degree to port. Range 5,000 klicks, with an aphelion of 2,000 klicks. More than close enough for them to get a good look at us."

"Hopefully too far for them to see any signs of blast damage," Mmok muttered.

"Not to worry," Fenaday said. "All the damage is on the opposite side. Damage Control got most of it."

He looked around the freighter's cramped bridge. A freighter is a freighter, and he'd spent much of his childhood on such ships. The thought depressed him. *Privateer,* he thought sadly. *Mmok was right about me. I'm just a pirate with better paperwork. How I wish we could have taken this vessel without casualties.*

Fenaday looked sidelong at the two Voit-Veru on the bridge, Captain Adan and her First Officer, Cantel. Despite the vest and other clothing articles, they still looked more like animals to him. Given their fur, they needed little clothing. The vests and odd-looking pants served for purposes of status, modesty, and pockets. Only when the three tentacle-like arms moved did the resemblance to a Terran kangaroo collapse. The Voit-Veru might appear slightly comical, but as a nuclear-armed, space-faring power with tens of systems under their control, they were a formidable power for even the Confederacy to face.

"We're being interrogated by the buoy," Shasti said, serving as their communication officer. "IFF is answering."

Adan looked up. Fenaday caught the alien's eye. "Do not worry, Captain Fenaday. Our IFF has the current codes."

"Would that it didn't," Cantel said.

Cobalt turned suddenly to face Cantel. Cantel flinched, his arm-tentacles stiffened in front of his face as if to ward off a blow.

"Captain," Adan cried in alarm.

"Enough, Mr. Mmok," Fenaday ordered quietly. Mmok did not appear to move or speak, but Cobalt turned away from the Voit-Veru. "Mr. Cantel," Fenaday continued, "confine your speech to matters dealing with the running of the ship."

"With your permission," Adan asked, looking with frightened eyes at the slender killing machines, "I would like to have Cantel begin the final cargo checks before we make orbit. I don't have enough senior crew to do the checks without him."

"Very well, report to Sergeant Cross's team in the main hold."

Adan put a tentacle on Cantel's neck, an oddly intimate gesture, and spoke in a whisper too low for the translators to catch. The exec left, making a wide detour around the motionless Cobalt.

"It appears you were correct, Captain Adan," Shasti said. "We are past the buoy and have given and received standard info-dumps. No unusual reactions, no increase in power or activity level. Scanning of the *Queen* has ceased."

"Lovely," Mmok growled. Fenaday ignored him. Mmok's grumbling had become background noise to the New Eiran.

"The going will be less easy as we gain orbit," Adan said, as if anxious to assert that Fenaday still needed her. "There will be visual and audio communications that will need to be handled."

"Good thing we're not approaching Mars," Sheehan said. "They'd want to send up a pilot in a cutter."

"Then," Shasti added to everyone's surprise, "we would have to listen to Robert complain about unionized ports, idiot bureaucrats, and how he could land the ship himself without interference from fools no longer good enough to fly their own ships, or children still wet behind the ears. Followed by the speech about how impossible the new Confed rules are making it for a ship owner to fly profitably."

Mmok snorted a laugh. This time Fenaday did glare at the cyborg.

Behind him Shasti gave a quick, evil grin.

Captain Adan stared from one to the other, as if wondering if she was the subject of a joke. *What am I to tell her?* Fenaday thought. *Hey, we're just regular guys, not as bad as you think. To her, we are monsters out of deep space, child-killers and thieves.*

"That's enough levity for now, people," Fenaday said. "I'm going to sack out in the space cabin. We don't have enough space-trained officers to have us all on the same watch. Sheehan, you take the next watch, with Rigg on communications and Rask on security. It will be six on and six off for the next five days."

"Captain Adan," he added, turning toward the Voit-Veru. "I'll leave you to arrange your own crew watches, so long as you and your number two are on the bridge for orbital insertion. Keep order,

Captain. Keep people from the stupid ideas that get them killed. I want no more weighing on my soul than needs be."

Fenaday walked over to the space cabin that served as the captain's retreat when he needed to be near the bridge. The furniture had been pulled out when they came on board, as they couldn't use Voit-Veru equipment. He looked forward to a few hours' sleep, even if it was on a cot. In the background, he heard Shasti calling the alter-watch crew to stations. The door slid back to his touch.

A moment later, he returned to the bridge. "Ms. Rainhell," he said. "Your supposedly smarter than average, genetically enhanced, highly trained K-9 has crapped in my space cabin."

"Ah," she said. "Sorry. You know we have prisoners to clean up that sort of thing now."

"Good," he replied, "tell them to bring newspaper."

Chapter Sixteen

Five tense days passed as the *Queen* slowly edged toward the planet. The buoy updated their nav-computer with the information Fenaday feared. Five Olympian vessels orbited ahead, accompanied by nine Voit-Veru ships. The tenth destroyer had left, but both cruisers remained. As the Queen was well beyond simultaneous broadcast range, they easily handled the limited radio traffic, chiefly related to *Queen's* cargo. *Queen's* status as a ship full of political lepers also proved useful. No one at the base particularly needed or wanted to speak with them. Gradually, the freighter closed on the planet until they reached orbital insertion.

Fenaday returned to the bridge in response to Shasti's call. He found Mmok already there, joined by Rigg, Rask, and Sergeant Cross. The Toks stood behind Shasti's improvised chair, watching Captain Adan and Cantel. The Voit-Veru looked more bedraggled than ever.

The Marine turned to Fenaday. "All Voit-Veru, except for Engines and Command Crew, are confined as ordered."

"Thank you, Sergeant," said Fenaday. "Well done."

Now that they'd entered enemy space, with action imminent, Cross and his Marines seemed to have put doubts and resentments aside. They knew their best hope of survival lay with the ship and the mission. Fenaday had left dealing with them to Rigg and Rask. It had worked. Cross and his men cooperated uneasily with the ASATs loyal to Rigg and the regular Army troops who followed the ASATs. Fenaday knew that their lieutenant's death had not been forgotten and the reckoning was only postponed. As for Shasti, she too left the Marines alone, always keeping the Tok brothers nearby when she dealt with them. The Moroks guarded her back with fanatical loyalty.

Cross started to leave, then turned back. "You know," he said, "Marines don't believe in leaving anyone behind either. We always get our people back."

"Thank you," Fenaday whispered.

"Yes, sir." The Marine saluted and left.

Fenaday turned to look at Shasti. She gazed back steadily with a slightly raised eyebrow indicating that she'd heard Cross. *If I can keep the elements of my command from killing each other for one more day*, Fenaday thought, *we might accomplish something.*

"Port coming into visual range," Shasti said. "I detect three vessels ahead, one Olympian destroyer and two Veru, both cruisers are in low orbit. The lesser vessels are higher. Some must be on the other side of the planet. Let me put their orbits on screen," she said. Part of the main screen snapped to life with a schematic.

Fenaday leaned against the back of Adan's bridge chair. "Very interesting."

"What?" Mmok demanded.

"The Voit-Veru don't want the full force of Olympian warships over their base. They assigned them higher geo-synch orbits over undeveloped land and then put a companion warship in the same orbit. Look at the screen." He pointed to the small dots. "Over the base they've allowed one Olympian warship, a destroyer, but keep their two largest vessels nearby. There seems to be little trust in this Alliance."

"There wouldn't be," Shasti said. "Shall I switch to the planet?"

"Please bring it up," said Fenaday, excited in spite of himself. A new world lay ahead, at least new to the crew of the *Sidhe*. Once upon a time, he'd have been thrilled at the prospect of new goods and peoples. He usually found it hard to remember that Robert Fenaday. Here on the bridge of the *Queen,* so like her Shamrock Line sisters, it was a little easier to remember.

Queen's main screen flickered as Shasti made the adjustments, and Mounus IV, local name, Thorraken, appeared. Like most Confederate worlds, it appeared to be mainly ocean covered by a mass of fleecy, white cloud. Thorraken looked far different from their last world, Olympia. He remembered Shasti's home, with its smaller oceans and poles, high mountains, deserts. Olympia had been the color of rock and hard ungiving soil, so different from the lush greens of Fenaday's homeworld. This world seemed more like New Eire, greener, oceanic.

"We are coming up on the landmass with the main colony," Shasti said. "It's got an unpronounceable local name. In the Denshi material, they gave it a human name, Tartarus."

"Great," Mmok said, "land of the dead. Good for tourism."

"Magnify," Fenaday said.

"I'll give you maximum resolution," she said, "but this isn't *Sidhe,* the optics aren't up to much at this range."

They studied the images revealed on the screens. "Only one colony," Fenaday murmured, "a couple of outposts. Good, just as billed."

"Lots more in the way of missile and gun emplacements around the spacefield," Mmok said, pointing to the screen. "They are digging in big time."

"Good thing there isn't a space station," Rigg said.

Beside him, Rask nodded. "Doing customs up here would get us killed."

"Coming up on first approach over the space port," Sheehan announced.

Fenaday gestured at the screen. "There's the regular freighter, another break-bulk like the *Queen,* only a good 10,000 tons bigger. Captain Adan, what's her name?"

"It's the *Imperial Fortune,*" replied Adan. "She's sitting on the main landing pad. There is only one built so far. We're to set down in that improved field beyond."

"Very well," Fenaday said. "Take the center seat, Captain. Shasti, narrow focus the bridge cam to just her face. Mr. Cantel, stand at the back of the bridge on the engineering station. Mmok, have Cobalt watch him. Don't do anything stupid, Mr. Cantel." The kangaroo-like alien looked at its captain with an anguish that communicated across species.

"Do it," Adan said.

"Mmok has all your communications on a delay," Fenaday said to Adan. "Say anything we don't like and he'll cut it off before it transmits."

"For my children," Adan hissed, "I obey you. My own life means nothing to me, and I'd kill you if I could."

"Then think of your children," he snapped back. "It will grow cold on that asteroid in a few weeks." The Voit-Veru made a pained sound and looked down. Fenaday thought about throwing up. *Stay focused,* he said to himself. *The transmitters on the asteroid will scream for help in two weeks. They'll be found. God, please let them be found.*

"Approach vectors coming up," Sheehan announced into the silence. Fenaday turned from Adan and began doing the calculations for landing. Computers at either end handled most of it. Gradually, the ship trimmed up for entry. The outer hull began to heat.

"Visual communication coming in," Shasti advised.

"Damn," Fenaday swore. "How long until blackout?"

"Seventy-five seconds," she replied.

"Captain Adan," Fenaday said.

Adan reached for a control. "This is Captain Adan of the *Queen of the Night* on final approach."

On the main screen, a Voit-Veru's face appeared. He could only see Adan's face on his end, but Fenaday could not help the nauseating feeling that the Veru was looking directly at him, that all his plans and deceptions were for nothing.

"Captain Adan," the Voit-Veru began, "this is Thorraken Ground Control. After landing at the port, confine your crew to the offport area. The main field and outpost are off limits for now. Do not alter course from the vector you are on. Do not, under any circumstances, proceed on any heading that would take you over the science outpost. That is restricted airspace until otherwise advised. Acknowledge."

"Acknowledged," Adan replied.

The screen went blank.

"That restricted airspace, Fenaday," Mmok said, communing with his computers, "is the base where they have your wife according to the information we got from Vaughn."

"God damn it," Fenaday said. "I was hoping to get a better look at it and whatever forces are there. What the hell is going on now?"

Queen came down on her jacks at nightfall, near the port's edge and far from the amenities the clanships in favor with the military government enjoyed. Adan called to the port master's office and got an officious junior officer on the screen.

"Our main cargo doors were damaged on landing," Adan said. "Unloading will have to be delayed. Please have three cargo carriers left nearby in case we can free the doors. I'll use my own crew for the initial transfer to the warehouse."

"Sloppy maintenance, Captain," the officer said. "My crews are assuredly not going to wait for your doors to be repaired. They are going off duty. We'll leave the carriers by your landing pad. Port office, out."

Night fell quickly. From smaller hatchways, the HCRs and ASATs crept out. A single Veru accompanied each team to drive the carriers under the *Queen's* immense bulk, away from the arc lights of the finished section of the port. The assault force piled into the carriers, taking with them, bound and silenced, the remainder of the Queen's crew. The airbot silently floated out and latched itself to the top of a carrier.

From the hatchway above the rushing troops, Fenaday looked out of the airlock into Thorraken's night as if he could see some sign of Lisa. As if the air would hold her scent, the moonlight shine off her hair, or light her blue-gray eyes. *Be here darling,* he thought, *be where I can find you, even if it's only to die with you.*

No despair, he told himself. *Move forward. Don't think. Just take the only chances offered. Move forward.*

Brilliant arc lights shone in the distance, though the field near them remained in darkness. Squat port buildings dotted the horizon beyond the shape of the other cargo vessel. The port, for all its size, was new and crude, roughly hacked out of the soil of a world the Voit-Veru themselves only landed on ten years ago. Fenaday headed back inside to find Mmok in a small hold off the main hold, arming three Mark 1 tactical nuclear weapons, a quarter of *Sidhe's* remaining total. He reached for the timer and looked at Fenaday expectantly. Fenaday nodded. The machine-man sent a telemetric signal to the timer. It began to count down.

"It's done," Mmok said. "The fat's in the fire now."

Fenaday nodded. "Let's go."

They exited the ship, sealing hatches under code, and headed for the carriers. Halfway there, Fenaday stopped, looking at the lights of the base and the nascent city that formed the offport.

Mmok stopped too and followed his gaze. They stood for a few seconds in the night of an alien world.

"Yeah," Mmok said. "All those people, or something kinda like people, drinking, talking, screwing and no idea that it is their last night."

"You're breaking my heart," Fenaday managed.

"I mean," said Mmok, "I mean that it's not like with the Conchirri. They were just fucking animals, teeth with big brains. This, this is tough."

Fenaday looked at him.

"If those were people out there? Real people, humans I mean," Mmok asked. "Could you do it?"

Fenaday turned away from him. "I don't know."

"So it's not just, 'No, I couldn't.'"

"What would you have me say?"

"Christ."

"Who's he? Come on, Mr. Mmok. Time to be happy little murderers."

They quickly reached the lead carrier.

"What the hell were you doing," Shasti snapped from her perch in the cab, "admiring the scenery?" They jumped up into the large, uncomfortable cab, cursing the Voit-Veru seats. An HCR sat behind the nervous, musky-smelling Adan. Fenaday looked at Captain Adan and felt a minute's pity for her. She did not know about the Mark Ones, armed on timers in the *Queen's* holds. In hours, her ship would be a nuclear fireball along with the port and its defenses. A lousy thing to do to a fellow captain, but he had already done worse to her, marooning her crew.

Adan looked at him, and he saw hate across the gap of species. *Kill you. Kill you someday,* the look said. *Join the crowd,* he thought, *but it's a long line.*

Fenaday took the whole crew of the *Queen* with them in another small mercy. One likely to end in tragedy when the ship blew up and the survivors fell back into the hands of their own kind. It was all he could do for them. The trucks required Voit-Veru drivers. No Confed species could manage the design. Fenaday had put one in each vehicle, with the captain up front with him. Troops secured the other Veru in restraints in the last vehicle. An HCR guarded them. Their dread of the machines kept them very still.

They started off on a construction road. Fenaday sat behind Shasti in the cab. He lowered the window, and the smell of vegetation and earth whipped in. He breathed deeply. After weeks of ship air, it filled his lungs like perfume. Gradually, the lights of the port faded as they followed the road. He checked his map for the tenth time. The construction road ran directly away from the port and main base until it intersected another road well in the forest, which led back toward the compound where Lisa and her crew should be.

To their surprise, when they reached it, they found a paved road. The small convoy headed up it.

"Damn," Mmok said, "checkpoint ahead."

"Crap," Fenaday said. "Alert the other vehicles, then get down." Mmok communed with the HCRs in the trailing vehicle.

"Shasti, it's your show," Fenaday whispered.

Shasti looked at Captain Adan. "Play your part well, Captain. You might contrive to give us away, but this outpost cannot stop us, and neither you nor we will be taken alive. The asteroid will never be found in time."

"You need not remind me," Adan replied.

They stopped at the checkpoint, a few curiously shaped Veru vehicles and a barrier across the road. Fenaday's heart hammered, and his guts felt weak. He started to draw his laser pistol, then realized how that would look. He rested a clammy hand on it and tried to slow his breathing to normal. He watched a Veru trooper walking up to their vehicle. More Veru troops lounged on the other side of the barrier.

"Who are you and what are you doing on this road?" the Veru challenged. Fenaday's earpiece rendered the guttural coughing speech of the Veru into Standard.

"Captain Adan of the *Queen of the Night.* I have cargoes to deliver to the science outpost. We came in late and had trouble unloading, so we had to drive the load ourselves."

"You're not on my list," the trooper said.

"These supplies are for the outpost," Adan insisted. "That's all I know. I don't deliver, I don't get paid."

"Let me get the subaltern," the soldier said. He called over his shoulder and another Veru hopped over.

"What?" demanded the newcomer, plainly annoyed.

"Captain of that cargo vessel that landed a few hours ago, sir. She says she has cargo for the science outpost. Three cargo carriers, not on our list."

"Hell," the subaltern said, "everything's screwed up since the fleet pulled in. Now, you people. What's your story?"

Adan repeated what she told the trooper, handing him the cargo manifest.

"Typical Hersi," the officer said scornfully. "Late, sloppy, and inefficient. Don't know why they even let you people run ships." He handed the manifest back. "Who are all these humans?" He gestured toward Fenaday and Rainhell. Mmok lay out of sight beside him. Fortunately the truck cab stood higher than the Veru, but if the Veru elected to bounce up...

"Don't know," Adan said. "They're Olympians. I was told to

give them a lift to the base."

"All right," said the officer. "Get your asses up to the main guard post at the camp. They'll sort you out there."

Fenaday's breath came out in a sigh. He hadn't realized he was holding it.

"Hold it," said a new voice, human. "Olympian? All our people are already at the conference." A tall young man in Olympian battle-dress walked out of the shadows. He held a weapon in his hand. "Who are you?"

Fenaday stiffened and eased the laser out.

Shasti slowly opened the door and stepped out. She dropped to the ground and stood up to her full height. "I am," she said in a cold voice, "Retha Yakima, Lord Vaughn's personal staff. My security code is Callisto 45098-38 star. Check it."

The young man, so sure of himself a second ago, seemed taken aback by Shasti's size and the use of Vaughn's name. There was no question the woman in front of him was high-order Olympian. Genetics were the mark of aristocracy. Hers were obvious.

"At once, my lady," said the officer. He tapped the ID into a code pad.

"It checks," he said, "as his staff, though the entry is for a Selected, Misa Tanaka."

"Killed two months ago by Bremardi," she said. "I'm the replacement."

"Sorry, my lady, but without further proof—"

"Proof?" Shasti said, her green eyes blazing. "Watch." In a second, Shasti's ivory skin went flat black, leaving only her terrifying eyes. Veru and the Olympian stepped back.

"Fifth Generation," the Olympian said in awe. He turned to the others. "All of this Generation of my kind serves Denshi, even if they have a naval commission. There is no doubt.

"Lady," he stammered, "please forgive me. The computer records can only be updated when a new vessel arrives from home. You must have just arrived, and the update has not been relayed. Also I can see that some of the people in the trucks are only

Selected. We have not had such downworld. Only the Engineered are allowed to land."

"Stand close to me," she said. He moved nearer. "Do any of these speak Olympian?"

"No, my lady, I was assigned here as a translator and liaison."

"Name and rank?" she demanded.

"Ensign Laros," he replied, "OSDF Naval Landing Forces."

"Good. I will take you into my confidence, as I must. Mikhail Vaughn is coming within hours. It is the real reason for the conference. The people with me are agents we have used in the Confederacy. I must be passed through and must not be remarked on, either here or over the communications net. Officially, I do not exist. Vaughn will remember you if you serve him in this. Or," she continued, "he will remember you as one who did not."

"Yes, my lady," the officer replied, shaken. He turned to the Veru and spoke in its language. "Pass these vehicles through. Do not log them and do not call the guard house."

"Very well," the subaltern said, evidently glad to cede the problem to the Olympian, "but it is your responsibility."

"Agreed."

Shasti nodded and returned to the vehicle, retaining her flat color. Adan, whose scent had gone rank during the exchange, accelerated the truck away. Fenaday abruptly became aware that he probably didn't smell too good either. Sweat soaked the lining of his clothes.

Shasti looked at him, an ebony goddess.

"Sometimes," he said, "you scare the hell out of me, too."

Twenty minutes brought them to the ravine Fenaday had mapped out as their point of departure. They'd traveled twenty-five klicks from the port, near the science outpost, a base with a small guard, mostly just a lab from Vaughn's information. Fenaday and the assault force had studied this diagram until it appeared in their dreams. Each section knew where they were to go and what to do, though there'd been no opportunity for a full-scale practice. *As usual,* he thought grimly, *make it up as we go.*

They reached the turnoff from the main road to the base.

"Kill the lights," he ordered as they made the turn. Fenaday pointed to the side of the road, to the cutoff into the ravine. Adan pulled over, using the truck's infrared to steer. They went in as far as the clumsy trucks could go, then stopped. He gestured with his pistol, and Adan preceded him out of the transport. People and machines poured out of the vehicles, cursing and shuffling in the darkness as they sorted themselves. Mmok and Rigg's voices could be heard setting up security, posting the troops. The HCRs and the airbot vanished toward the base. Fenaday escorted the Verus to the last vehicle. Rask put restraints on the three Voit-Verus. They trooped into the truck's compartment to join the others.

Adan looked at him. "You will never get away with this," she said. The translator deprived the voice of intonation though the meaning came through clearly.

"Hope that I do," he replied. "Fewer people die if I get away."

"This will mean a war," she added.

"A thought that should have occurred to your species with the capture of my wife's ship and their effort to help start a civil war in the Confederacy."

"Your people would have allowed a Voit-Veru ship to return to unknown space, having located targets in your Confederacy?" she asked.

"Maybe," he said. "Don't know. Don't care. I'm here for my wife and her crew. If nothing else, you declared war on clan Fenaday when you took her. I'm here to prosecute that war."

Adan said nothing more. It occurred to Fenaday that the Voit-Veru and he might be on the same wavelength for once. Clan conflict ran through both their histories.

"Captain Adan," said Fenaday, "these doors will automatically open in twenty-four hours." The Veru stared at him. Suddenly moved by some impulse he couldn't name, he added, "Don't worry about your family, even if we don't make it. There are two emergency beacons with them out on the asteroid surface. They will unseal in two weeks; the batteries have power for months. I give you my word that if we can recover your people we will. If not, your own kind will."

The Veru stiffened as if in shock. "Thank you," she managed.

"No need," he said roughly. "Good luck, Captain. If it means anything at all, I'm sorry for all that has happened." Without waiting for a response, he closed the panel and locked it. He looked about. The draw sat over ten kilometers from the port and on the lee side of the hills. Safe from the blast he hoped. About fallout, he could do nothing.

The dirt crunched under his feet as he moved to rejoin the others. *Be there Lisa,* he whispered to the night. *Be there.*

Chapter Seventeen

They spread out, working patterns they'd used before on Enshar, Olympia, Morokat, and a dozen other worlds. HCRs formed the outer screen, save for Cobalt, who lingered near Mmok. The horrid army of crab-like robots, each more powerful than a light tank, formed the inner screen. Marines, ASATs, and the remaining LFs from Rainhell's Landing Force surrounded Fenaday, Risky, and the command staff. The airbot, a small, saucer-shaped machine armed with light particle weapons, hovered over the force.

Mmok stood next to Fenaday as they forced their way through tall, grassy vegetation. The cyborg's face showed the strain both of the night march and the coordination of forty-five machines of differing types through his augmented, but still merely human brain.

Shasti, up in the lead with Risky, signaled to Fenaday, and he hurried to join her.

"We're on the second hill opposite the compound," she said. "There's just this valley below and then the final hill. No patrols on this side. No guard posts."

"As advertised," Fenaday said.

"Glad this place isn't like Pard's," Mmok whispered, joining them. "It would have taken hours to get through sensor nets, mines, and booby traps even with Vaughn's map."

Fenaday nodded, remembering the torturous approach to the Denshi compound.

"I'd have preferred to stay entirely off the paths around here," Shasti said, "but we don't have the time, and the crab robots are too noisy in the woods."

A crashing fall and curses sounded behind them. They all spun, weapons leveled. Li crawled to his feet. Despite his night-vision goggles, he'd fallen over a root.

"You okay?" Shasti asked.

"Yeah," he called back softly. "Sorry, boss."

Fenaday's pulse hammered in his ears, and he felt faintly sick. Everything slid out of focus for a second. *Take a deep breath,* he thought, pulling himself together with effort. He signaled, and everyone sank into a squat save for Mmok, who found the position difficult. "Mmok, what do you see?"

The machine man froze, hunched over in his "listening" mode. Above them, the airbot slid forward silently. Daniel Rigg appeared out of the small draw behind them, recognizable despite his helmet and low-light visor. He joined them, moving silently for such a big man.

Suddenly Mmok straightened with a curse. Fenaday and the others stood. "We are in deep shit," Mmok said hoarsely.

"What?" demanded Fenaday.

"The airbot's hovering at ridgeline. It's detecting a whole hell of a lot more troops and structures than Vaughn reported."

"Enemy strength?" Shasti asked, unperturbed and practical as ever.

Mmok communed with his machines. "Composite estimate from the airbot, Scarlet, and Cerulean is the equivalent of a regimental combat team, in excess of five hundred troops. There appears to be a company of tracked heavy armor and at least a platoon of hover-cars, maybe more in the distance. The airbot can't tell."

"What's their Defcon?" Rigg asked.

"Unless they are laying for us," Mmok said, "they seem to be on a low security alert, not expecting heavy combat but ready to react to small scale incursions like they have a VIP present."

"Then we still have a chance," Fenaday said. "Mmok, are those hovercars and tanks manned?"

"All three hovercars we can see and one tank show a heat bloom on their engines. They're idling."

"Okay," Fenaday said, thinking furiously. "Concentrate your crab robots on the armor. Destroy the manned ones. Then kill the crews in those barracks as they come out for the others."

"Damn," Rigg swore. "We were going to use them against the pillboxes."

"The HCRs will handle them," Fenaday said.

"Fenaday," Mmok protested, "there's too many. We've got a short company and the cyberforce. It's not enough."

"Too late," he replied, feeling grim and hopeless. "We go with what we got."

"It's suicide," Mmok hissed.

"Stop arguing," Shasti said. "The bomb goes off in two minutes. We don't have time to run. They'll be on us in minutes after the blast. We may as well die in the attack."

"You're fucking crazy!" Mmok spat.

"You have your orders, Mr. Mmok," Fenaday said. "Attack. I will, even if I go by myself."

Mmok looked at him. "Very well, Fenaday, final charges on your bill."

Shasti signaled the advance. Rigg nodded at her and hotfooted it back to his troops.

They moved down the valley, which would protect them from direct exposure to the blast. Reaching the bottom, they spread out and settled into cover, each reviewing in his mind the maps and plans for the attack, updated by the latest download from the airbot.

Fenaday knelt down, pulling up his night-visor for a break from its disorienting green. He grew conscious of the wetness of the ground seeping in through the joints of his plast-armor, the sighing of wind in trees, a man's nervous cough. He could hear men and machines moving in the grass and woods. The air smelled faintly tangy with a strange scent reminiscent of oranges. Suddenly the night felt very cold, despite the black leather over his armor. The tri-auto carbine seemed a tremendous, useless weight. He looked around at the others, wondering if they felt the same. *Seconds,* he thought, *how many more seconds?*

"All squads in position," Shasti whispered.

On impulse, he reached for her. She looked at him startled. He kissed her cheek. "For luck," he said.

The sky flashed an impossible white.

L isa Fenaday heard the shuffling gait of her captors coming down the hall. Wearily, but not without a small thrill of anticipation, she pulled herself to her feet. She brushed back her dark red hair, cut short badly and liberally streaked with gray now. Long years of captivity had aged her, but also honed a sense of resiliency.

The sameness of her days had been interrupted of late. The Voit-Verus were again interested in her and her crew. Feverishly so, it seemed. It had been years since anyone had bothered to interrogate them. Now, she faced more of the same questions the Veru first asked after they learned enough Confed language for a translator program.

They'd segregated her from the two other survivors of the *Black-bird*, Caitlin Barrett and Fontel Ki Teska, despite her protests. The last member of her crew, poor Asa Drok, had gone totally insane in the first and worst year of their imprisonment. Guards shot down the crazed Morok as he attacked his interrogator. Voit-Veru surgeons, with no idea of how a Morok was put together, could not save him.

Sometimes, Lisa thought, *I envy him. Maybe he was lucky. Maybe he found the only way out. I wonder if I'm still remembered back home. What became of Robert? How did he take the news? Did he remarry? Or does he still mourn for me?*

She thought of him on New Eire in the old house above the bluffs. It was hard to imagine him anywhere else. Robert was a bit of a homebody for the scion of a trading family. He loved his home world. After they married, he came off-world more, usually in a Shamrock trading vessel.

Lisa had not planned to fall in love with Robert. Avery Deveraux of Confed Intelligence had sent her to Inkporlin system and New Eire to learn about the Fenadays, rich separatists, whom he mistrusted. He was astonished when she came back with an engagement ring and no report. She didn't regret it, though it cost her a lot in the spymaster's eyes, and her entry into special political operations was postponed, perhaps permanently.

Lisa had returned to combat intelligence in the *Blackbird*. Her burning ambition for promotion and advancement had driven her to impress Deveraux. Driven her to a fateful shadowing of an unknown alien vessel in a star system off the Confederate charts. Only there had been more than one vessel, and a heavy laser hit *Blackbird* before she could flee.

The door to her cell flew open, interrupting her reverie. Her most recent interrogator, a subaltern named Osawa-mu, stood there with two gray-uniformed guards. Lisa was glad she had returned to the old habit of sleeping in pants and shirt. Guards had sometimes grabbed her out of her cell to stand, shivering, under interrogation in her underclothes.

Slowly she stood, reaching for her uniform jacket and cap. The originals had long since fallen apart, but Lisa had demanded replacements as the prisoner-of-war she insisted on being treated as. Solitary confinement and beatings had not changed her demands. Finally a hunger strike had forced the Veru to bend. She got uniforms for herself and her crew.

"You will accompany me to the main hall," announced Osawa-mu. "Someone very important wants to meet you. Be warned to exhibit proper respect and a more cooperative attitude."

She shrugged on the jacket. It hung loose on her five-foot-six-inch frame from a combination of poor diet and bad tailoring.

"Lt. Commander Elizabeth Fenaday," she replied with a resolution she did not feel inside. "Human, Confederate, C.S.F.S. *Blackbird*, Serial number x67389-031158." At times she'd said more under duress, but when she came back to herself, she always returned to the official line, as if there had never been a break or failure. *Just reboot*, she thought, *like they teach you in training.*

The Veru translator snorted in irritation, a sound like a horse blowing. He pointed at the door with all three-tentacled arms, a gesture that meant "now!"

Lisa walked—an act that fascinated the Veru, who varied between a waddle and a hop. She had learned, in a tiny defiance, the pace she could set that would make the Veru move too fast to shuffle and too slow to hop. The officer led, and the two guards took station behind her.

"Who am I going to see?" she ventured.

"One who demands answers," Osawa-mu said, then relenting a little. "A First Minister in the government. Be wary, human, and cooperative. The minister is not a person to trifle with."

This could be a break, Lisa thought. *Someone from the government at last.* She had always been in the custody of the military, with no chance to plead directly with one of the political class. Maybe she could finally persuade them of the need for a friendly overture to the Confederacy. She remembered rumors of the Voit-Veru's contact with Olympia. One guard had let slip the word near her. It had coincided with the arrival of decent food and medicine to the *Blackbird's* survivors. Olympia, Deveraux's greatest fear for the Confederacy. The genetic witch doctors of that obscure world had contributed little to the war against the Conchirri. Each year increased both their strength and isolation from the mainstream of the Confederacy. She wondered what had happened on that dangerous world since her capture.

"Any Olympians at this party?" she suddenly asked of her captors.

Osawa-mu's muzzled face turned over his shoulder. "No concern of yours. Remain silent."

Her heart sped up at the thought of possibly seeing other humans. After eight years, Caitlin Barrett's face was as familiar to her as her own. The older woman had both grayed and aged far more than Lisa herself. Fontel Ki bore up the best emotionally, Dua-Denlenn that he was. His species was far more solitary than humans, and even the Veru had made little impression on the inbred arrogance of the Dua-Denlenn. Allergies and vitamin deficiencies had taken more of a toll on Fontel Ki than anything else, especially on his vision.

"Where are my crewman?" she demanded.

The guard behind her thumped her on the back with a toe, causing Lisa to lose her footing and stumble. The Subaltern turned and began barking in cough-like gutturals. Lisa's hard-won knowledge of Veru wasn't up to a full translation, but the young officer was administering a sound butt-munching, identifiable to military personnel regardless of language. He clearly did not want to deliver a battered Lisa Fenaday to his superiors. The subaltern reached a tentacle down to help Lisa up. She controlled a flinch. There were no slimy suckers on the arms, only ropy muscle and cartilage. Still, she hated to be touched by the Veru.

"Please restrain yourself," continued the officer, seeming nervous. "You will not gain any advantage this way."

Lisa shook off his aid and mounted the very broad, shallow steps the Veru could manage. They led to the main courtyard of the complex, several hundred yards of open grass and gravel pathways bounded by a mixture of Voit-Veru labs and utility buildings. New prefab buildings filled almost a third of the courtyard, and she could see partially built structures beyond white walls of the old science labs.

Lisa's heart leapt. She stood under the stars again, at last, at long last. She stopped. Her arms lifted themselves heavenward as if to embrace the stars she was exiled from. The soldiers, chastened by their officer's rebuke, did not touch her.

Tears filled her eyes as she stared into the night sky. "Someday," she choked out, "someday I go back."

"Lisa," called a voice from ahead. She lowered her eyes. At the end of the courtyard near the prefabs stood Ki Teska and Barrett with their own contingent of guards. The subaltern, realizing that Lisa had stopped, turned back, again blowing in irritation.

Flash. The sky lit up. Lisa dropped out of reflex. *Nuke,* came the stunned thought. *Groundburst.* She had seen it often enough in the Conchirri War.

Cries and shouts sounded. Guards milled in confusion. The lab tower nearest her exploded. Debris came raining down. Small arms and explosives sounded. Ground assault. *My God,* she thought, *the Fleet?*

The Veru moved in on her. It saved her. A blast went off, and steel scythed through the courtyard. The officer and one guard fell dead, the others staggered, blinded. Shrapnel plucked her sleeve and burned across her ribs. More explosions flashed. The courtyard was becoming unhealthy. Lisa got her feet under her and sprinted. There was no way to reach the others. Hysteria built in her. For the first time in eight years, escape might be possible. She had to get away. Lisa ran, ducking as blasts erupted. Over her head, lasers and particle weapons crisscrossed across the sky. She looked heavenward to see the perfect spheres of space-borne nuclear blasts, eye hurting, beautiful, like Hell's Christmas ornaments.

Lisa plunged out of the courtyard, diving into every piece of cover and shadow she could find. Ahead lay the vehicle park, but fire and explosions raged among the machines parked there. Small arms fire filled the night, followed by another blinding flash of a nuclear weapon out in space. Lisa charged into the reed-like underbrush of the marshy area north of the base. She had no more plan than to stay free under the stars. Someone or something had come. It promised an end to the years of captivity. *They don't retake me,* she swore, *not again, not alive.* As quickly as her limbs, weakened by years of imprisonment allowed, she passed northward.

Sidhe, holographically cloaked as the Olympian destroyer *Persephone,* headed for orbit of Mounus IV. Her IFF broadcast the right codes to her interrogators, but she had resisted all contact with the Olympian or Voit-Veru vessels since passing the buoy. Using the image of the Lieutenant Chell Vanickz and Shasti's voice, they broadcast a cryptic message advising that they were an early reinforcement to the Olympian contingent, bearing Lord Mikhail Vaughn. In a code that should still be secure from the Voit-Veru, they broadcast another message. It warned the Olympian commander to slowly raise his defense condition to battle-alert and to prepare for an urgent message. The message concluded with a warning not to reply.

On board the disguised *Sidhe*, Graglia sweated under his collar, looking at the electronic signals representing five Olympian and ten Voit-Veru vessels in orbit. Two of the Voit-Veru ships were cruiser class. The rest of the enemy vessels were a mix of frigates and destroyers. Any one vessel was a match for the privateer. If there were anything amiss in the codes—if the Voit-Veru had cracked the latest Olympian code—they would shortly be atomized gases. At his fingertip was the final loaded message, the one with the Denshi ID. The one that they desperately hoped would trigger the battle. *If it doesn't work*, he thought again, *we are dead*.

"Goddamn Fenaday," he muttered, then realized that he had spoken aloud. He heard a harsh laugh and looked over at Wardell, the old gunner.

"A common sentiment on this ship," Wardell said. "The skipper, he sure can get into a scrap."

Graglia recalled that the over-age, ex-Navy rating had been cashiered for drinking by the regular fleet, yet he seemed calm and steady. Fenaday had told him Wardell kept his problems off the deck of *Sidhe*, but in port he couldn't be trusted near a bottle.

"You want to live forever?" Sharla called from the comp position behind Graglia.

"Yeah, sure," Wardell replied.

"Me too," Sharla said.

Nervous laughter broke out.

"Knock it off," Graglia said, secretly grateful for the break. "Guns, do you have the passive fire control solution on that heavy cruiser?"

"Aye sir, but he's forty klicks away. I've got a better firing solution on the light cruiser."

"Negative," he said, "stay with the heavy. If we don't get him in the first few seconds, then we won't get him. Lock everything but local defense and tubes one through four on him."

"Orbital insertion, now," called Graglia's replacement, the later watch helmsman.

"Sharla," said Graglia, "stand by full ECM."

"Aye, sir."

"Five minutes to planetary detonation," Sharon Hafel added, "if all is going to plan."

"Captain," Bernard said. It took Graglia a second to remember she meant him. "I'm fuzzing with the communications system as best I can, but I think they're getting suspicious. I'm picking up a lot of space to ground traffic from the heavy cruiser ahead. I can't read the Voit-Veru only traffic."

"Any demand that we cease our approach?" he asked.

"No sir."

"Keep with the same reply," Graglia said, sweat trickling down his sides. "Lord Vaughn is under orders from Pard not to discuss anything till we dock." That heavy cruiser could turn them into stripped electrons at this range with one salvo. If they had to abort...

Wardell looked at him. "We've got a nice lock on what should be an ordnance magazine on the heavy," he said reassuringly. "Main gun will cut right through her belt armor at this range. "Good lock on the light cruiser as well with missiles one through four. Hell, Captain, as close as we are, I could lean out the airlock and hit him with a tri-auto."

"Thanks, Guns," Graglia said. "Could come to it."

"OSDFN fleet destroyer *Pindus* is signaling to Voit-Veru ground control that our communications are all in order and that the matter will be explained in due course," Bernard said, relief clear in her voice. "They are asking the heavy cruiser *Alanamu* to be patient about our approach."

"Update?" he asked Hafel. Graglia couldn't escape the feeling he was talking too much. Not doing the strong, silent thing all the captains did on the holo-programs.

"Scan shows the same four Olympian and ten Voit-Veru ships as before. That one Voit-Veru in transpolar may be an armed transport. He's still too low to the horizon to be sure," Hafel replied.

"Good news," he grunted. "One less warship." *Sidhe* could handle any armed merchant, but she was smaller than most of the thirteen full warships circling Mounus IV.

"Best guess on their Defcon?" asked Graglia.

"From the EME and radio traffic, I think that all vessels except for the *Pindus* and the *Alanamu* are at station keeping and Defcon One. They seem to be nearer to Defcon Three or Four," added Hafel. "The others Olympian vessels may be higher if they're following our instructions surreptitiously."

"Sixty seconds," Sharla said. "Mark."

The seconds ticked by with agonizing slowness.

On the darkened world below, a small star quickened, fueled by the spaceport with its thousands of Voit-Veru and hundreds of Olympians. The starships above could only look on in dumbfounded horror. Electromagnetic pulse took all planetary communications offline.

"Fire," Graglia snapped.

Sidhe's first strike proved as good as hoped. The weapon lunged down the ringed tube running the length of the star frigate. Her main particle gun launched a shaped ceramic wedge at near the speed of light. Lasers preceded the giant sabot round. From the four forward tubes, missiles leapt out, bound for the light cruiser. *Sidhe's* depleted uranium chain guns, normally only for defense, cut in, spraying lead particles at the two warships.

The ceramic steel sabot breached *Alanamu's* hull in an instant, shearing through armor and compartments, causing explosive decompression. It struck a magazine, secondary explosions followed in milliseconds. *Alanamu* began to disintegrate.

"Now, Sharla," Graglia said, "the message. Quick."

On the screens of the shocked Olympian destroyers, the

savagely handsome face of Mikhail Vaughn appeared, accompanied by the proper authentication and codes.

"Olympians," Vaughn thundered, "we've been betrayed. The Voit-Veru have attacked our homeworld, virtually destroying it. Strike them down. Strike them down now. Follow my ship. For Olympia and revenge!"

"Helm," Graglia said, "hard over, 28 Mark 180, as fast as she will take it. Retarget all weapons on the light cruiser."

"Missiles one through three have been intercepted," Wardell said. "Come on, number four. No, dammit."

"Intercepted?" Graglia demanded.

"Yes, sir," Wardell said, "but close, I am seeing fragmentation hits on the light cruiser."

"Return fire coming in from the CL," Hafel called.

Everyone's guts clenched as the light cruiser's particle weapons flashed their own deadly sabots at the *Sidhe*.

"We ain't dead," Graglia snapped. "He missed. Stop rotation and hit maximum burn and aim for the other side of the Olympian formation. Are any of them firing yet?"

"Negative," Hafel said, "but EME shows all vessels going to Defcon Four and heat blooms on all engines. "I'm getting complete pandemonium on all channels. *Pindus* is demanding to speak to Vaughn."

The ship shuddered and belled.

"Hit on the port wing by particle accelerator, went right through," Sharon Hafel reported. "Damage control en route."

"ECM has broken enemy firing lock," Sharla said. "They are trying to reacquire. Three missiles just lost tracking and are exploding."

"Olympian destroyer *Pindus* is firing at the light cruiser," Hafel crowed.

"Sharla, cut the holographic drive, all power to weapons," Graglia said. Further concealment was useless, and he needed the power. *Sidhe* returned in a flash to her blood-red self.

"Nuke," Hafel said, alarm in her voice. "Olympian destroyer

Pindus exploding behind us. Hit by an equivalent to a Mark II from the light cruiser."

"Damn," Graglia swore. Whatever else the Olympians were, there were men and women burning behind him. "Riley, alter course, bear on the CL. Wardell, is the damn particle gun up yet?"

"Five seconds," the gunner said, "and she'll be ready to fire a deflection shot as soon as you get her nose up. I have lock."

Sidhe spun on her axis, gravity forces battling her singularity for control of the ship's metal. If the singularity failed, the turn would shred the star-frigate. She held her needle-like bow close enough for the limited deflection of the particle accelerator. Wardell fired. An instant later the light cruiser returned the favor, and *Sidhe's* high tail exploded into fragments. The cruiser took the worst of the trade. Wardell's shot hit below the bridge. The light cruiser's engines lit in a full burn. She clawed and slewed away toward five of the Voit-Veru destroyers, which were finally getting under way.

"I'm getting a visual from the Olympian destroyer *Thessaly*," Hafel said. "They demand to speak to Vaughn."

"No good," Sharla said. "The holographic system is offline. I can't fake Vaughn."

"Okay," Graglia said, "enough damn games anyway. Put them through." The screen lit up, revealing an Olympian.

"Where is Lord Vaughn?" he demanded. "What the hell is going on?"

"Listen up good," Graglia rapped. "Pard's dead. Denshi surrendered to the Army and the Confederacy. Vaughn's in charge in Denshi. He gave us your codes and IFF. You either throw in with us or you'll be arrested as traitors if you return."

The Olympian stared at him, naked shock on his face. The screen fuzzed, and the other vessel's interior shook as something hit the *Thessaly*. Voices in the background reported damage.

"That's your pals, the Voit-Veru," Graglia said, desperation in his voice. "Do you think they'll stop while your ships are in their sky? Over their world?"

"We are just the first," Graglia bluffed. "There's a Confed fleet coming in behind us. You don't think we were crazy enough to do this with one ship? You're between a rock and a hard place. You've got no friends unless you throw in with us and no home to return to."

The Olympian stared for a second longer, then barked an unintelligible order over his shoulder. The screen went dark.

"Main gun still recycling. I have laser power now," Wardell said. "Best target is enemy destroyer number three." Behind him, his assistant Keogh's hands danced over the controls of the chain-guns, sleeting depleted uranium at incoming missiles. Sharla, now free of the hologram controls, turned her complete attention to electronic counter measures.

"Fire all available weapons on destroyer number three," Graglia ordered. "Helmsman, all ahead on 120 by 230. Keep those Olympian DD's between the Voit-Veru and us. It's the only chance we've got. We have to keep close to the planet to drop the rescue force."

"Voit-Veru destroyer number six is exploding," Hafel yelled. "Olympian destroyer *Thermopylae* has hit that transport. General firing breaking out between Voit-Veru and Olympians. The Voit-Veru are backing off, looks like they are afraid of the transport being targeted. We've got an orbital opening."

"Main gun up," Wardell said. "Best target, light cruiser."

"Move toward the planet and fire at the cruiser," Graglia said. "Bernard, get me Telisan."

Commander Telisan," Graglia's voice sounded over the fighter's headset. "I have a window for close approach to Mounus, a trans-polar orbit that will give us an insertion for your force. The Olympian and Voit-Veru forces are moving to higher orbits to open the range. That light cruiser is still operating, but she's not putting out much fire. ETA on drop point is 183 seconds if you say go."

"Affirmative," Telisan said, adjusting his helmet. "Move toward the planet and prepare to drop. Do you have communications with the ground force?"

"No sir," Graglia replied. "No pickup beacon, no call for fire."

"Damn," Telisan said. The nuke had gone off, and the attack must be well underway. He had to make a decision now, drop or flee back for the Confederacy. For him it was no choice at all.

"Mr. Graglia," Telisan said, "you have independent command of *Sidhe* at the moment of our separation. Assume orbit over the pickup point for as long as you can."

"Affirmative, sir. Launch point in 120."

Sidhe surged as her fusion drive brutally changed the frigate's course. Gravity forces strained the Cherr drive's ability to cancel them. In the cockpit of his *Wildcat* fighter, with all decisions made, Telisan sat easily, looking at the amber lights of the launch rail. In a few moments, *Sidhe's* armored sides would open to allow the *Intruder* and both *Dakotas* to launch. Fury would lead in the *Intruder*, followed by Karass and Aidan Findlay.

He and McLoughlin would fly escort in the *Wildcats*. Until then he had nothing to do. He killed time by giving his deck crew a cheerful "thumbs up" as they cleared the last lines from his hull. The top of the *Wildcat* fit snugly into a mechanical linkage bay, allowing space-suited crew to work on the upper part of the fighter in comparative safety, still at least partly inside the hull. The last of the green-suited crew ran for the inner airlock. They returned the "thumbs up" from the plast-steel visor of the airlock.

Telisan continued to work through his checklist as if it was merely another training flight. A brilliant actinic light flashed in the bay. He froze for a second as his canopy polarized the reflected light. Nuke, detonated nearby. *Oh well,* he thought, *what are a few more rads? Just a little more time in detox therapy and chelation after pickup.*

Internal power came online, and he prepared to launch. He thought wistfully of his wartime fighter, a Mark IX *Spacefire*, a fighter pilot's dream, many times more lethal than the stubby obsolescent *Wildcat. Could use a squadron of* Spacefires, he thought ruefully, *might as well wish for the carrier Empress Aran herself.*

"Launch in ten," Susan Bernard announced in his headset.

Telisan braced himself as the amber launch light turned green. Mechanical linkages kicked the *Wildcat* free of *Sidhe's* hull.

Telisan's screens glowed with reads as he locked on to everything in range of the fighter's scanners. Space was full and busy today, according to the instruments. All he could see with the naked eye were flashes of detonating ordnance and the hair-like threads of beamfire between warships separated by thousands of kilometers, trying to open to proper battle ranges from the threatening maw of the gravity well that was Mounus IV. The exploded Voit-Veru heavy cruiser and the Olympian destroyer filled space with thousands of fragments of differing sizes, each a radar target, providing good cover for Telisan's force of small ships.

A beam flashed above Telisan's fighter, scoring on *Sidhe's* part wing, shredding armor and bleeding air. Reacting like a wounded thing, the ship above him thrust sideways and the beam slid off. Return fire lanced out of the frigate.

"It's the *'to whom it may concern'* mail that bothers me," Kyle McLoughlin called over the tacnet.

Telisan laughed. "Quiet on the tacnet," he said. McLoughlin "twooped" a thumb onto his mike in reply as he slid into position off Telisan's wing. *Good wingmen are seen and not heard.*

Above and behind them *Sidhe's* big bays opened, and the transport shuttles launched out both sides as quickly as they dared. It was a moment of horrible vulnerability for the *Sidhe*. Even a glancing hit within the armored doors could wreak havoc inside the hull. As soon as the *Dakotas* and *Intruder* cleared the doors, they cycled shut.

The small fleet quickly lined up behind Telisan as he led them downward.

A blip appeared on Telisan's main screen at the same moment a warning tone sounded in his ear. An ID symbol appeared next to the blip, ground-to-space missile. Telisan snapped his left gimbal-mounted laser around and fired. The chemical warhead ASM blew up twenty kilometers below.

Sidhe disappeared from his view. Telisan did not bother Graglia with questions. *Sidhe* either would or would not be there when they started back up. Fear shot through him at the thought that Arpen and Sharla were both aboard the star-frigate. *Damn,* he thought, *don't drift. Think only mission, only mission. It keeps you alive, gets you back to them.*

His ECM flickered as something somewhere tried to lock on and kill him. *Concentrate on the now.*

Wildcat Two's heat shield snapped up automatically as the ship entered atmosphere. His screens lost information as the sensors shielded themselves from the heat. It reminded him of a similar drop into desperation on Robert Fenaday's wing over Enshar. *Of course,* he thought, *nothing was shooting at me when I flew blind, deaf, and dumb in reentry.*

Long minutes dropped by as the fighter bucked its way down into atmosphere. Suddenly the heat shield snapped down, and his instruments lit up with new signals. He'd reached the ionosphere, nearly the stratosphere, dropping rapidly along the planned glide path.

Another sensor tried to lock on him. It was likely to catch the *Dakota* shuttles' bigger scanner silhouettes. The *Intruder* should still be invisible even at this range. Telisan obtained a passive fire control lock on the sensor and triggered one of his three anti-emission missiles. The missile leapt from the rail and flashed downward. Seconds later, the sensor light went out.

The ground below remained black, though clouds picked up starlight, moonlight, and the flash of detonating weapons above the atmosphere. They continued down. *No enemy fighters,* Telisan thought. *Good.* More sensor lights lit on his screen. He fired another AEM as a laser flashed up at them. He cursed and jigged his fighter. He fired his last AEM. The laser searched around, almost touching him, then cut out.

"Gold to Eight-ball," Telisan called, "assume suppression. Make them last." Telisan flicked on his air-to-air weapons, watching for fighters.

Suddenly the frequency for the landing force lit up. "Open communications on Channel E," he ordered the fighter's small ship-comp.

"Strongbow to Gold, come in," called Daniel Rigg.

"Gold here," Telisan responded, scanning the signal's location and wondering why Fenaday wasn't on the other end of the mike. "ETA of extraction force is ten minutes to your location."

"Thank God, Gold. Things are bad. Very, very many more hostiles than expected. LZ is hot. We are holding on by our fingertips. Hurry."

"Do not fear," Telisan said with a bravado he did not feel. "Sabers are out, and the cavalry are en route." Next to him, McLoughlin fired an AEM. *Down to two missiles now,* thought Telisan grimly, *and still on the way down.*

Chapter Eighteen

Fenaday snap-fired his carbine as he ran. Another Voit-Veru fell. The scene around him looked like Dante's private beach party as crab robots and armored troops scuttled forward. He felt horribly vulnerable amidst all the onrushing metal, despite his body armor. Mmok's airbot raced over him, its light armament chattering, cutting down bouncing Voit-Veru soldiers. The cyborg's control of the machine had reached a point that it was no more difficult to wield than a crab robot. It gave him mastery of the battlefield. Mmok didn't need to be where the machines were; he saw through them wherever they were. HCRs attacked up and down the line semi-autonomously, checking with Mmok by telemetry when they needed further instructions.

The sound of high-pitched Veru screams and the detonations of munitions filled the air. Fortunately the science outpost had not been intended as a fortification like the Denshi camp on Olympia. Their sudden attack carried them into a car park filled with strangely shaped Voit-Veru vehicles. Mmok's machines ranged far ahead, slaughtering Voit-Veru tankers trying to reach their armor.

"Be here, Lisa," Fenaday whispered to himself, "be here."

A blast from a grenade flashed in his face, and fragments stung him even through his body armor. He stumbled to the ground, trying to look in all directions at once, momentarily disoriented by the impacts.

Shasti pulled him to his feet, armor and helmet giving her a gargoyleish appearance in the eerie green of low-light vision. Li dodged around her, his triple-auto flashing fire back in the direction the grenade came from. The Toks joined him, weapons crackling. Fenaday ignored the counterattack and raced forward. Rigg, Rask, and the Confed troops were already ahead of him, dodging in and out of cover. In the distance he saw the lithe form of one of the HCRs make an immense leap up into a guard tower. Fire from the tower stopped instantly. The HCR leapt out again, coming down on some sort of troop-carrier. The carrier careened into a wall. Crab robots stalked the field and the near buildings, killing everything that moved. A rocket came out of nowhere to strike one crab machine. It flopped into an ungainly pile, then struggled forward, firing at a reduced rate.

The Confed troops ran in among the nearer buildings, strange, flute-like structures in whites and grays, almost resembling huge vases. Voices piled on each other as the engagement became close and hot.

Mmok's voice cut in on the tacnet. "Everyone quit the fucking chatter. Call for robot support by squads. I can't read minds. Fenaday, check in."

"Fenaday here," he replied. Shasti and the other members of her Landing Force, including Risky, moved out to secure the area. The dog carried reloads for their weapons under his armored blanket. Fire around them slackened, but it seemed to be picking up ahead.

"We've had good success so far," Mmok reported. "My cyberforce tore up the tank park. It ain't gonna last. We don't have enough force to reach the far areas, and they are rallying out there."

"Mmok, this is Rigg. I'm a hundred meters ahead of you. We need support by the tall tower with the communication array. Heavy resistance. I don't think we can break in there. Best we can do is hold on. Corpsman, get that man," he yelled.

"Support en route," Mmok said.

"Has any one seen Lisa?" Fenaday called into his mike.

"Negative," Mmok said. "Neg—Cross, get that bastard! Negative."

"Command," Rigg broke in again, "I have five down, have to pull back to better cover."

"Hold on," Mmok urged. "Crab robots are coming."

"Dan, we are going around the right flank," Fenaday said, "to do a ground search. We'll try and cut off any reinforcements heading your way. I'll send Murphy and half the Landing Force to support you." He gestured to the lanky Murphy, who swallowed hard and then signaled his men.

"Make it fast, Fenaday," Mmok said. "These guys are quality troops. They're recovering too damn quickly for my liking. We came down on top of what looks more like a reinforced regiment. I've lost a crab robot, and Scarlet is damaged."

"Robert," Shasti said, "this is hopeless. We have to withdraw, head for the alternate pickup point. We still haven't raised the ship. We can't call for fire."

Wordlessly, he shook his head and started forward. Shasti followed; the other dozen spread out and covered them. Overhead another nuclear weapon, or perhaps a ship, flared, lighting the area.

Is this it, he wondered numbly, as a horrible sense of déjà vu overtook him, *all there is to my life, murderous nightmare assaults?* His feet felt leaden as he waded forward, the flashes, distant screams, and weapon fire retreating into a remote background. The weird buildings stood around him, distorted shapes from a drug-hazed dream. *Just have to keep going forward a little while longer,* he thought, *just a little longer. A beam or a bullet will end it soon, release me.*

Reality crashed back in on him. He realized the fugue had only lasted a moment. "What was that?" he snapped.

"Fenaday," Rask yelled, "I've got two, Ki Teska and Barrett! They were in the courtyard."

It hit him in the gut like a sledgehammer; he had to force words out. "My wife, where's my wife?"

"Ki Teska's wounded, can't talk, Barrett says they saw Lisa on the other side of the courtyard fifty meters ahead of you. Fire's too heavy to get there from here, but I can see it. There are no human bodies."

"Mmok!" Fenaday yelled into the net.

"Not so loud," he heard behind him. The cyborg had silently joined them. Cobalt, his personal guard, stood behind him. "I've got the machines looking for her, but they are all committed."

"Get the airbot..." he began.

"Can't," snapped Mmok, "it's supporting the ASATs on the left, keeping a bunch of bastards pinned in a block house."

Fenaday gave an animal growl of frustration then suddenly stood and began dashing forward. He got five paces before Shasti hit him with a flying tackle. A laser flashed over him, just missing. Cobalt raced past, supported by fire from the others. The HCR leaped five meters straight up as the laser licked at her. She gained a vector on the attack and loosed a missile from an arm-mounted launcher. A dull boom sounded, and the laser flicked off.

Shasti pulled him around. Furious, he flipped his visor up. She did the same, rage in her green eyes.

"Idiot," she spat, "to stand and run in the open. Be seen and be dead."

"Sorry," he muttered realizing the truth of it. *I have to get myself under some control.*

Mmok came up and gave him a disgusted look. "I'd suggest moving forward by bounds and low crawl across the open spots. That is," he concluded acidly, "unless you'd like to charge again, Mr. Custer."

"Knock it off," Fenaday growled, wondering who the hell Custer was. "Li, take the Toks and bound forward to that archway."

In proper order and covering each other, they advanced.

"Shit," Mmok said, stopping suddenly. "Someone brought up shoulder-launched anti-air. Damn, that was close. I've got to pull the airbot out. Rigg, get ready to take fire on the left."

"Great," Rigg said into their headsets. "We've got to get out of here."

"Hold five minutes more," Fenaday said, "just five."

"We'll try," Rigg snapped, "but that's all. I'm pulling back after that. Send Risky with those reloads."

Shasti knelt and said something to the K-9. She pointed and the dog raced off.

They closed on the main building, Li's squad in the lead. Suddenly the street ahead of them exploded. Li and the five LFs of his team simply disappeared. Shells began to gouge the street around them, knocking pieces off buildings.

"Artillery," yelled Mmok. "Cobalt, fire to intercept." The machine stood, its heavy triple-auto sputtering as it skeeted artillery shells out of the air.

"Li!" screamed Shasti, looking for her trouble team leader. "Lokashti!"

"They're gone," Fenaday yelled, "gone."

A laser licked between them, and they dodged apart. It fastened on the slower Fenaday for a second. He screamed, dropped, and rolled. Its hot breath lost him, then sought again. He scrambled away. Cobalt switched her fire; the shells had stopped coming as the enemy ground assault began. The laser cut out.

Overhead the shuttles from *Sidhe* were coming in. All three added their armament to the maelstrom below. The fighters flashed by, particle weapons and lasers stabbing down. "Telisan," Fenaday breathed. "Thank God."

Mmok grabbed Fenaday's shoulder. His face distorted. "Call them off. Abort. The flat open ground has enemy armor all over it. No place to land."

"Searcher to Archangel," yelled Fenaday into his headset, "abort, abort. LZ is not secure. LZ is not secure. How is secondary?"

"This is Archangel," came Angelica Fury's voice. "Acknowledged. We are drawing heavy fire, primary and secondary LZs are in enemy hands. Pulling out." Angie in the powerful *Intruder* pulled straight up. The older *Dakotas*, *Pooka* and *Duna*, struggled upward. A shell from somewhere exploded on the underside of the *Duna*.

"No," Fenaday said, horrified. *Duna* spun end for end and crashed into the ground, her blast illuminating huge, moving shapes.

"Tanks," Mmok hissed.

"Telisan," Fenaday called. "Do you read?"

"Yes, I am here," came his friend's calm voice. "One tank destroyed, coming around for another pass."

"Telisan, you'll have to run out west, pancake somewhere out of range till we call for you. Plan B, unless you can make it back to the *Sidhe*."

"The ship is engaged," replied the Denlenn. "Graglia says she is damaged, but he's maneuvering to put the planet between him and the main battle. The Olympians have opened fire on the Voit-Veru. So far one Olympian destroyer is gone, two Voit-Veru DDs and the heavy cruiser are gone, some damage to all ships."

"Then head out and find some place to hide. We will call for you when we disengage. We're being overrun."

"Affirmative, ground fire is getting too heavy. *Wildcat Two* out."

An enemy tank smashed its way around the corner of a building two hundred meters away. The immense ground-crawling fortress had a crushed crab robot stuck on its prow. Enemy infantry bounced out behind it and into the withering fire of the airbot. The tank ignored the small arms fire and turned toward them.

"Run," Shasti screamed into their headsets. She fled to the far side of the street, chased there by beam fire. They scattered as the tank fired. It hit something volatile in one of the buildings; the structure flew apart in a bellowing thunder.

S hasti rolled to her feet in a world suddenly without sound, her ultra-sensitive hearing overloaded by the secondary explosions. *Fuel tanks,* she wondered muzzily, *must have blown up.* Ahead of her lay the mountainous Voit-Veru tank, burning furiously, caught in a river of fire of its own making.

The street to her left also flowed with flaming liquid. Burning wreckage stood between her and the others. She had sprinted right when Robert went left, hoping to draw fire away from him. Now she couldn't see where he was. She started forward, then stopped as the radiant heat began to penetrate her armor. *Damn,* she swore. *They might even be calling me on the net and I can't hear.* For the second time in her life, she began to wonder about the unintended vulnerabilities that genetic engineering had built into her. She could only rely on her eyes for now. She headed down the side street, hoping to back-track and find another way across.

As she passed by a barracks-like building, six Voit-Verus rounded the opposite corner. Shasti did something Voit-Veru could not do. She went down into a forward shoulder roll, coming out prone and firing. The Veru, following surprised instinct, bounded upward and fired where she would have been had she been Veru. She wasn't, and their shots went two meters over her head. Her tri-auto chattered out; laser, minifrags, and particles swept the aliens. They hit the ground in heaps. Fearing a larger force, she ran toward the front of the building, stumbling over odd-shaped furniture, negotiating doorways not meant for humans. She headed for the rooftop, hoping to make her way from roof to roof or at least be spotted by the airbot. As she reached the front of the building, she risked a look out the window. The larger force she feared prowled the street below, light armor and troops. In the distance, a burning aircraft fell. She could only hope it was hostile.

Suddenly, she realized her hearing had returned. The buzzing in her ears stabilized into speech. Voices on the net called out disaster, retreat, and casualties, overloading the battle frequency. She switched to their private channel. All other sound cut out, and she heard Fenaday's voice. A knot of anxiety released in her chest.

"Pull back, pull back," she heard him call, then the stutter of small arms fire. "Rigg, get fire on that armored car. We'll cut our way out east."

"Cancel that," she heard Mmok say in the background. "The HCRs have broken out to the southwest. There's swamp that way. Enemy can't use their armor there. The crab robots will supply the cover fire. The airbot is down. General retreat to the southwest."

"Robert," she called, using their private priority button and ignoring protocol.

"Shasti," he answered frantically. "Where are you? Are you

hurt?"

"No. I am on the other side of the plaza where we separated. I'll have to break out by myself; the area is full of enemy troops."

"The hell you say," he spat back.

"Fenaday," said Mmok, cutting in on their channel. "She's right. We can't hold them. We've got to pull back before we get destroyed."

"Go to hell," Fenaday snarled. "Let go of me or I'll kill you."

"Listen to Mmok," she demanded. "You'll kill me if you try to come this way. They'll just concentrate on this point. I'll have more chance if you create a diversion by fighting your way the way he said. I can get to the swamps the long way around."

"No," he yelled.

"Listen to me," she insisted. "Trust me."

"Goddammit, let go of me." She heard a struggle.

"I love you," she said. The shock of it stopped the unseen fight. "Do this for me."

"Listen to her, spacer," Mmok yelled again. "She knows this work. Do what she says. Shasti, there's a clearing twenty-five klicks in, Alternate Five. Be there."

"Shasti," Fenaday said, his voice breaking, "get out of there please."

"Agreed," she said wryly.

"I love you, too."

She smiled brilliantly, though he could not see it. "I will find you there. Shasti out."

Fenaday looked blankly at Mmok. "I've killed her," he said. "I've killed everyone."

"Not yet," the cyborg said. "On your feet. Now." He hauled Fenaday upward, shoving the distraught man in front of him. "Hi ho, hi ho, into the swamps we go."

The remnants of the Confed Force fled, leaving a slowly compacting line of crab robots holding open the escape.

Chapter Nineteen

Shasti leapt from rooftop to rooftop as she neared the edge of the compound. The Voit-Veru were still trying to pull themselves together. She thought the fuel tank explosions had done more damage to the enemy than to the Confed force. Those troops still under some control were chasing the Confeds. Shasti headed south as the Voit-Veru went southwest. She leapt the largest gap yet, landing on a sloping, flute-shaped roof on the other side and scrabbling desperately for purchase. She grabbed a projection and clung, heart speeding.

Wish they'd followed the more Olympian styles, she thought. She glanced at the buildings surrounding her. They looked like large vases, and the utility of such a design eluded her practical soul. Shasti gathered her feet under her and edged around the cone-shaped roof.

To her intense relief, she could see fields on the other side. *Ah,* she thought, *the compound's edge at last.* She tore open a roof door and headed down. A metal ladder with rungs too far apart led down. She simply dropped down the open hole. It saved her life. A laser sizzled over her head. Two Voit-Verus stood in a side hall. She bounced off the floor in a flat lunge, shooting the nearest Veru, a soldier. He went down. Shasti, with too much impulsion, crashed into a falling Voit-Veru's body and lost her weapon. The other Veru, unarmed and male, leapt at her. They crashed together. The Veru slammed a foot into her with such power that she bounced off the wall, half dazed. It charged over to stomp on her. She rolled under the Veru, reversed, and lunged off the floor onto its back. Before it could react, she wrenched its neck around with explosive savagery. Vertebrae cracked, the Veru squealed piteously, shuddered, and fell.

Shasti grabbed her weapon and raced down the stairs. She threw a weird, V-shaped chair out a second-story window, following it out instantly. She spun three hundred sixty degrees in the air. No targets. Landing on the spongy ground, she rolled to her feet and sprinted into the weeds and trees. A weapon stuttered behind her, shredding the leaves over her head. She cut hard right and put a fold of ground between her and the gunner. The weapon didn't fire again.

I've got a chance now, she thought, moderating her pace. *It'll be a long haul and many hours to go before I sleep.* Weapons and explosives blasted and chattered away to the west. *I'll have to go around the Voit-Veru chasing our people,* she thought grimly, speeding up a little. *No straight line for me. Oh well, when was it ever easy? At least the nights are long in this part of Thorraken.*

She knew that Fenaday and his surviving forces would head for Alternate Five. They were somewhere north and east of her. Unfortunately, the fastest acting Voit-Veru unit was on their southern flank between her and them. Shasti struck westward for a half-hour, hoping to outpace them. In the unfamiliar swampland, too many obstacles existed, and she felt she was behind the leading elements of the Veru force. It might, she reasoned, be just as well. It might be safe to attempt to cut north behind them. Preferring her own enhanced senses, she dropped the night goggles. Guided by starlight and her night-vision, Shasti changed course northward.

A straight line flashed down from the heavens. Before even Shasti could react, a mass-driver slammed into the ground south of her, back toward the encampment. Flash. She dropped to the ground, looking for cover. An outcropping of rock overhung a noisome pool of water. She splashed into it, keeping an eye out for anything like a crocodile. The kinetic energy of the mass-driver's impact sent a tower of rock and earth over a mile into the air. She was too far away for the ground effect to injure her, and there was no radiation to fear, but there would be rocks coming down in a minute. Big ones.

Sidhe, she thought, firing a covering shot onto the pursuit, called down by Mmok or Telisan, a desperate act to fire so close to the Confed force.

A rumbling, like insane thunder, reached her, followed by wind, then the ground began to shake. Debris started to rain down. One chunk splashed into the pool next to her. Water fountained up, drenching her. She waited a full minute after she heard the last crashes and then struck out again, heading north.

As she reached the shore of a narrow lake, Shasti sensed rather than saw movement. She froze. An enemy patrol directly ahead of her, coming her way. She felt them, with her newly developed situational awareness, as a series of hot sparks moving toward her, their anger and fear nearly palpable. She concentrated. Yes, there were more to the east, flanking her. Trapped.

Maybe not, she thought desperately. Vaughn's data crystal had told her that she couldn't drown, that there was a filtration system in her lungs. She hadn't been able to practice such a thing on a warship. *Sidhe* didn't boast a pool or even a bathtub. Now she would have to try it in combat. Silently, she slid out into the weedy water by her side. Shasti searched for a reed that might make a snorkel for her, but if any such existed on this world, they were not to be found here.

Out of time, she thought. Taking a deep breath, she submerged in the dark water. It was damn cold, and the mud at the bottom sucked at her boots. She concentrated on the Voit-Veru. They'd reached the lakeside and weren't moving. Shasti cursed mentally as the sparks stayed in her mind, bright and hot. Her lungs started to burn. She adjusted her metabolism to compensate, but it could only do so much. Her Engineered body actually required more oxygen than a standard human's. *No choice,* she thought grimly, *it either works or I come up firing and die.*

She opened her mouth and let the water in. *No good,* she thought. *I'm drowning.* She struggled to breathe, moving toward the shallows. Suddenly the distress eased. *Damn,* she thought, dazed and for once, fearful. *I'm breathing.* Her heart sped, slamming like a hammer. She willed it to a slower speed, easing the need for oxygen further. Water entered and left by her mouth as some unknown organ cut in, acting as a pump. *Still,* she thought, *stay very still. I'm not getting much oxygen, the organ might be atrophied or barely functional.* Again, she damned herself for not practicing this somehow on the starship. Another lesson learned.

Immediate death seemed averted, but Shasti feared to stay down for long. She might grow faint and pass out or whatever was giving her oxygen might become exhausted. Already she felt unfamiliar pains in her chest. *If I pass out here, I die,* she thought. She bent her mind again to the Voit-Veru, finding the sparks there but fading, heading southward from her. Shasti waited as long as she dared, slowly edging into the shallows. When she felt her mind beginning to grow fuzzy, she used her last energy to crawl ashore. Cold, wet air hit her face, and as if in reaction, her guts heaved, and water shot painfully out of her throat. Her lungs sucked in air, and she lay on the wet grass for several minutes, trying to silence her breathing. Energy and purpose slowly returned to her, along with a pride in her new ability. *I can do it,* she thought triumphantly. *I can breathe underwater. Next time I'll be stronger. Eventually it will become as natural to me as to a fish. But first,* she reminded herself, *I need to get back to Robert and get off this world.*

With the Voit-Veru gone, she again headed north, carefully but quickly. Always in the distance she could see firing or movement. Back toward the port, the sky glowed. Fires left by the atomic blast feasted on whatever fuel remained. Even to her, trained as an assassin from childhood, Fenaday's utter indifference to civilian casualties was chilling.

He's in the same place I was when I fled Pard years ago, she realized, *seeing no distinction among the enemy, seeing all people as the same undistin-*

guished evil. How could he not see the lessons he taught me, she wondered? Women and children had died under that blast, on the orders of a man she had once considered quaintly chivalrous. *Perhaps it was easier because they were not human. Maybe was as simple as that.* She feared it wasn't so. The quest to find Lisa was like a geas, a demonic possession displacing the man she thought she knew.

Thoughts for another time, she chided herself. *I have to get back to the main force or leave my bones on this world.* As she moved, Shasti altered her body, invoking the melanin camouflage. Her night sight was nearly as perfect as a starlight scope. Her hearing, engineered to the level of a hunting animal's, brought her every sound. Unfortunately, on an alien world, the sounds meant nothing. What's the local equivalent of crickets? What's a predator? She tried to tune out anything that didn't sound mechanical in origin. Her new situational awareness sense would be her best chance to detect an ambush before she walked into it.

A pale green moon hovered over the marshy ground. A mixed blessing as Voit-Verus had evolved on a world with a larger, more brilliant moon. Their night sight was significantly poorer than a human's. The moon aided them, but it also threw shadows. Shasti knew shadows. She'd lived most of her life in their comforting embrace. Be one with the dark, be unseen, unfelt and survive.

She spotted and avoided a large animal, feeling it before she saw the creature. It might have been harmless, or it might not. She gave it wide berth. Her weapons would have annihilated the creature, but firing would surely bring enemy forces in her direction.

A series of dull thumps caught her attention, heavy cannon fire, not likely to be friendly. She ducked behind some rocks and looked skyward. There were flashes in the heavens. Sudden lines sprang into existence, and another, larger one pulsed and spat—a mass accelerator. She wondered how the fight was going. Her com unit was damaged. Even if it had been working, it didn't have the range to reach the ships.

It would be comforting to hear the others, she thought, but they were sensibly staying off the air. The Voit-Veru could home in on the signals with either artillery or troops. Mmok and his cyber-force were quite capable of doing spook signals. With any luck, he could even fool the Voit-Veru into calling down fire on their own positions. Because computerized systems were so vulnerable to spooking and hacking, much of modern combat occurred at close range. You simply couldn't believe what you saw on the screen. The HCRs and crab robots were semi-autonomous for that reason. She knew Mmok used a rotating frequency, making it almost impossible for a jammer to synchronize on his telemetry signal.

She picked herself up and started forward, heading toward another swampy ravine. A wooded ridge overlooked it, not much of one, but it stood tall in the surrounding area. Her situational awareness twitched, and she paused, straining eyes and ears on the ridge. Moonlight raised a metallic highlight on some piece of equipment. Enemy troops, a small patrol perhaps left behind by the larger force that passed her earlier. *Amateurs,* she thought, unimpressed, the only real landmark in sight and they made for it. Shasti angled away to the right, finding drier soil and another, far smaller ridge, only barely deserving of the description. It would give her cover. She wormed on her belly for a good piece, only coming upright when she was out of line of sight of the ridge. The Voit-Verus might have night vision equipment as well.

Reaching a piece of exposed, mossy rock, she paused. Engineered did not fatigue easily, but even her strength began to flag. She cautiously peered around the rock, looking at the ridge. From her new vantage, the moon skylined her enemies. She could make out the rounded shapes of helmets. A dozen or more troopers, she estimated.

A sound reached her, a snapped twig, followed by a small splash. Shasti slowly turned back to look into the ravine between the two ridges from which she had just come. The splash could have been any small animal going into the water. The stick breaking implied something bigger. A Voit-Veru on her trail? Shasti loosed her knife in its sheath and shouldered her tri-auto rifle. From the shoulder holster she pulled a heavy, silenced slug thrower. If there was a pursuer, she had to eliminate him before he called the patrol down on her. Minutes stretched on as she waited. On the ridge, the patrol remained oblivious. Snatches of conversation drifted Shasti's way. Special Forces they were not.

Distant firing broke out again behind Shasti, four kilometers by the sound. Mmok and Fenaday must be in contact with the enemy ahead, trying to get past them to the alternate pickup point.

Just as she was about to give up and move on, she saw a figure, following the same track she had, emerge from a pile of weeds, thin, haggard, obviously human. Shasti holstered the pistol and knife. She shrugged the tri-auto into her hands, daring a half-second use of its tele-sight, despite the risk that its tiny, softly glowing screen might give her away.

It was Lisa. There could be no mistake. Fenaday had haunted them all with her image till it was as familiar as their own faces. *We must have been in the same area of the compound,* Shasti thought.

Lisa staggered and splashed again. This time the sound must have carried to the ridge. Lisa stood uncertainly, looking around, unable to see or sense the danger. Shasti's night eyes picked out troopers on the ridge, now silent, moving forward.

I don't have to do anything, Shasti thought wildly. *I don't have to kill her. She's walking right into it. It won't be my fault. All I have to do is be silent a few seconds longer and it will all be over. He can be mine.*

A thousand thoughts and images warred in her mind as she watched the helpless woman struggle further. Fenaday, in Shasti's arms, talking of their life; the holo of Lisa in his cabin; the day he found the book Lisa had dog-eared and the grief that washed over his unguarded face. All that she knew, all that she had so painfully learned, struggled within her. It felt as if her mind were tearing itself apart.

Gestalt, certainty, resolution.

Shasti's hands flashed over the tri-auto's selector, setting it to mini-grenades. Her lungs filled with air. "Lisa, get down," she bellowed. Shasti sighted and fired instantly. Five mini-frags went into the tree-line and boomed. Voit-Veru dropped, injured or seeking cover. Some fired back wildly.

Lisa froze at the yell, then cast herself forward and down. A burst of fire hit the water behind her. Shasti moved quickly, changing position, then using an old assassin's trick, threw her voice, calling out in Standard. "Lisa, get up. Run forty-five degrees to your right. Thirty yards. Now."

With that, she slung the tri-auto and pulled out the auto pistol. Long shots, but she'd been bred for this. The silenced slug gun, firing flashless ammo, was the only thing she could use for now. She snapped five rounds, hitting with four. A being popped up to fire at Lisa. Shasti hit him center of mass, twice. He dropped. *Amateur, that's what you get for skylining yourself,* she thought.

Lisa jumped up, running low and serpentine. Voit-Veru fire began to splash around her, tearing the swampy vegetation. She needed cover. Shasti threw in a new magazine and fired at every flash and beam source on the ridge. Someone started throwing grenades where Lisa had been. The flash and bang drew the Veru's fire.

Lisa plunged past Shasti, breath tearing loudly in her lungs, done in. Shasti leaned out, grabbing the startled woman. "Confed," she said before Lisa could strike. Seizing her under one arm, Shasti lifted Lisa like a small child and ran flat out. She wanted the ridge between them and the enemy. Behind them, fire came down on the position they had just abandoned. Some sergeant was getting things back under control.

After they had gone a half-kilometer, Shasti stopped for a moment, listening for pursuit. She put Lisa down to check their back trail. Sporadic fire continued, feeding on itself. She turned back to grab Lisa.

"Wait, wait," Lisa said in a whispery, exhausted voice, "what..."

"Shut up," Shasti snarled, a thrill of absolute hatred running through her.

No, no, she thought, catching herself. *No going back now.* She looked at the smaller woman. Lisa looked back at her without fear, from a face both thinned and aged from the pictures Robert had treasured. The body Shasti had carried, pressed against her own, was also too thin. A rare feeling of unwanted sympathy stole through Shasti, at the thought of years in alien hands as a prisoner.

"Later," she said more gently. She lowered the tri-auto, reached down, and threw Lisa across her shoulders. "We'll travel faster this way," she whispered. "Hold on."

They sped into the darkness, away from the now sporadic firing, at a rate only an Engineered human could have managed. The firefight had flooded Shasti's system with adrenaline and combat enzymes. Her body had started breaking up fat cells at an accelerated rate. *Unfortunately,* she thought, *it's making me hungrier than hell.*

They ran another two kilometers over broken ground before Shasti felt the chance of pursuit was less than that of running into an ambush ahead of her. She pulled up on some drier ground, in a copse of trees. She leaned the tri-auto against a tree and shrugged Lisa into her arms, gently lowering her to the ground.

———

Lisa Fenaday stared, numb and exhausted, at her rescuer, hard pressed to believe the other in the little hollow was a human. For a second, in the poor light, she had thought her rescuer to be a large black man, but the voice and the body she'd been pulled against was undoubtedly feminine, though incredibly strong. At rest, with a trace of moonlight leaking through the canopy of trees, she could see the symmetrical aquiline features of the woman, somewhere between Caucasian and Asian, stunningly beautiful. She had sprinted with Lisa on her back, as if she weighed nothing, sure as a cat in the night and the treacherous footing of the marshlands. It could mean only one thing.

"Olympian," Lisa whispered, "Engineered Human, right?"

The woman looked at her, green, perfectly clear eyes in a flat black face. Those eyes were calm now, neutral, as if nothing could ever be read in them. Lisa had not forgotten the murderous glare she'd seen in them earlier. For a second, she'd given herself up for dead.

"Yes," replied the woman in a surprisingly musical voice for so large a creature. She looked away from Lisa for a second, as if reluctant to speak, then sighed heavily.

"What do you want with me?" Lisa asked, hope draining from

her. "I know of your alliance with the Voit-Veru, even if they haven't even let me see another human." Suddenly Lisa choked up. Enemy or not, Engineered or not, the woman was another human. After eight years, it was overwhelming.

"The alliance is dead," the big woman said, "along with Jalgren Pard, who created it. The Confederacy is occupying Olympia. My name is Shasti Rainhell, Commander of the Confederate Private Warship *Sidhe's* Landing and Expedition Force, under command of your husband, Robert Fenaday. We came for you."

Lisa sat stunned, her mind unable to process any other shocks. "Robert," she finally whispered, "my Robert, here?" Her husband, in charge of a privateer? She couldn't imagine it.

"Yes," Shasti replied. An undertone of bitterness caught Lisa's scattered wits. She looked into Rainhell's eyes; the other woman looked away.

"Tell me," she demanded, tears close, "is he all right?"

"I don't know," Shasti said. "He was when I last saw him, hours ago. Look, we don't have time. We have to run. Here, eat this." She passed a Confed energy bar to Lisa, who seized it and devoured the bar in a few bites. Shasti did the same. They washed it down with water from Shasti's canteen.

"I think I can run," said Lisa, without conviction. She was frightened Rainhell might run off and leave her. The big woman seemed alternately cold and grudgingly sympathetic.

Shasti shook her head, long glossy hair shimmering slightly. She must have nearly three feet of it, Lisa realized. *Vain, huh,* she thought.

"No," said Shasti. "You don't have night sight and you're half-starved. I'll carry you on my shoulders." She grabbed Lisa's hand, pulling her upright.

Lisa stopped her for a second, face to face. "Thank you," she managed.

Shasti stood very still, her body gone suddenly tense. "You may have less reason to thank me than you realize," she said, "or maybe more. There's much we need to talk of and little of it that I understand. But I am taking you back. He loves you more than anything in the world. I hope you don't learn everything he's done to get here. I hope you're worth it all."

Lisa looked back with a sudden comprehension. "I see," she said softly. "We'll talk later, as you say."

"Yes, but enough for now. Nothing matters if I fail to get you back to him." She lifted Lisa gently to her shoulders, leaving her arms free to manage the tri-auto. "Hold on."

"You got it," replied Lisa.

Chapter Twenty

Fenaday and the fifty-two survivors of the depleted ground force took cover behind a low hill. They were still out of direct communication with the starship. She'd fled to the other side of the planet, fortunately not before Telisan called for fire on the Voit-Veru trailing them. A particle slug from her main gun had wiped out the lead elements of the Voit-Veru armor. Telisan and the surviving shuttles fled westward to hide in the unexplored hinterland until Fenaday's force could disengage enough to be retrieved. Somewhere to the westward, the shuttles lay, saving their fuel and avoiding contact.

Mmok worked with their remaining communication equipment and his HCRs, boosting a signal they hoped Telisan would catch. The Denlenn had gone beyond line of sight, but Fenaday knew that Telisan would pop up periodically, looking for the signal and anticipating their difficulty.

"Got him," Mmok yelled, in a rare show of excitement. The nearby survivors, about half of the force, cheered. "Telisan says he's coming in."

"Good," said Fenaday wearily but with a great sense of calm.

"When he gets here, Mr. Mmok, you will take command of the expedition force and get offworld."

"Where the hell will you be?" Mmok demanded.

"Skipper," said Rigg, "you're not thinking of…"

"Staying," Fenaday finished for him. "Yes, I am."

"The hell you say," Mmok began.

"Don't argue with me, Mr. Mmok," Fenaday said. "There's no point. I'm staying behind. I'm going to look for Lisa and Shasti."

"Shasti's chances don't get any better with you around," Mmok said, "standard human. Or have you forgotten that's what they call us?"

"And you think your prejudices are any better?" Fenaday asked.

"I didn't mean it that way," Mmok said, exasperated.

"Skipper," Rask said, "listen to Kyle. You know him. He's frontline, just like us. He wouldn't say run if he thought there was a chance to recover any of our people."

"I didn't say he would," Fenaday replied, checking the equipment he'd assembled. "Never questioned your courage, Mmok. Never questioned your commitment after you swore it to me. There's only one difference. For you, there has to be a chance. It has to make sense. Me, I just have to go, and it doesn't matter if there is one or not."

"That's suicide," Mmok said. "You're a lousy Catholic, Fenaday."

Fenaday paused and looked at him. "I wouldn't be any more alive if I went with you."

Mmok opened his mouth, then shut it, unable to make a reply.

"Captain," Rigg said formally, "you can't believe either Shasti or Lisa would want you to throw your life away like this."

"I'll ask them when I see them," he replied, closing the flap on his pack.

"Dammit," Mmok said, playing his last card. "What will I tell Telisan?"

"Tell him," Fenaday replied, smiling sadly, "that it was a human thing and he has to want human things for me. He'll understand."

The three stared at Fenaday as if he was already dead.

"He should be here shortly," Fenaday said. "The fighters won't land. I'll pretend to be going up until you leave. Don't say anything to him about my staying until you reach the ship, or he'll come back, and you'll cost both those women a husband. Don't let that happen, Mmok."

Mmok's head snapped up. "Maybe nobody's going anywhere," he said grimly. "The Cobalt picked up fighters inbound, a full squadron. The crab robots and HCRs are preparing to repel. It ain't looking good. Planes are the worst problem for my force. I'm uploading to Telisan. He's coming in on Channel D."

"Damn," Fenaday swore, grabbing his headset. "Telisan, do you copy? Abort. Abort."

"Negative," Telisan replied. "Bandits are too close. The *Intruder* and *Pooka* will never be able to outrun or outclimb them. Turning to engage. McLoughlin, follow me. Fury, land as soon as you can. Mmok will cover you."

"Telisan," Fenaday pled, "there are too many."

"Well," came his friend's unconcerned voice, "let's thin them out a bit."

———

Telisan put his *Wildcat* in a tight bank to stay near the *Intruder*, but just circling the shuttle would get them killed in short order. He turned head-on toward the incoming Veru, afterburners on maximum, heading for the earth. His ECM jammers radiating on full, he held onto his holo-emitter pods. The larger Veru ships were not dog-fighters like the *Wildcats* but interceptors. Lots of climb, good for going after ships and bombers, but would turn like battleships. He needed to get close.

"Lead to wing," said Telisan easily, "launch all fire-and-forget missiles. Roll ninety degrees and head for the ground as soon as they counter. Pop a holo." He thumbed the fire control, and the homing missiles rippled out of their pods. It might cover them as they closed. His screen suddenly blossomed with targets. He'd drawn the instinctive counter fire he hoped for.

"Roll out," said Telisan. He hit the emitter release, and the little pod sprang away. Immediately, it broadcast a crude image of a *Wildcat* fighter to anyone looking at it. Without ECM it should attract the missiles destined for its mother. Telisan roared into a small valley, *Wildcat Two* on his wing. He heard McLoughlin curse as enemy missiles slammed into the ground and trees just behind them, lost in the ground clutter. As they entered a zoom climb, loaded with the inertia of the dive, he saw the black and red Voit-Veru interceptors. Their own missiles tangled with the Veru's. *No holo-emitters,* Telisan thought, *but they have anti-missiles aplenty.* One after another, the Confed missiles flared. One penetrated, striking the middle Veru interceptor. It exploded with a flash, causing its mates to widen their formation.

Telisan and McLoughlin came up as the Veru interceptors banked into a dive. Telisan set his particle accelerator and pulse laser to fire offside to port and headed for the center of the enemy formation. The ships on the wings would have minimal firing windows at him, or had to risk hitting their own ships. In an instant they passed. The Veru's weapons strobed an eerie green light. Telisan's own flashed out silent and deadly. He juked the fighter, sliding into the space between two interceptors that he knew would be there. Satisfaction lit in him as an interceptor shattered. A quick glance showed him McLoughlin also connecting, though his target flew on. Telisan rolled out, inverted. The interceptors fanned out. Several headed for the shuttles. They drew the rest.

"I think these boys are too used to ground control," Telisan observed. "Follow me, Wing."

"Roger that, Lead," McLoughlin said. "I think they're virgins air-to-air."

The Voit-Veru closed again. It became a wild tangle, but the bigger, heavier interceptors couldn't lock onto the agile dog-fighters. Missiles ripped out of interceptors. Some the Confed fighters dodged, others they hit with their guns. Finally, both Confed fighters resorted to the last holo emitters. In the close dogfight, the sudden appearance of additional fighters panicked the Veru. They had never trained for such a fight. Telisan slipped behind a black and red Veru interceptor. It was firing at a holo. He slammed laser fire into it. The interceptor shuddered and the pilot's escape capsule tore loose. Telisan pulled up in a bank and connected with particle beams into the belly of another interceptor. "Five away."

"Lead," McLoughlin called, "I'm in trouble."

Telisan's head snapped around. McLoughlin was caught between two interceptors. Their fire bracketed his *Wildcat*. Telisan pulled into a tighter turn than any human could have, his double hearts keeping blood in his eyes despite the gray-out. As he locked onto the enemy wingman, McLoughlin's ship took a hit and tumbled.

"No one takes my wingman," Telisan snarled. His weapons struck the trailing enemy ship right in the large cockpit. It rolled over and headed down. The other turned, stupidly, away from him. Before its big engine could open the distance, he fired right into the tailpipe. The Veru blew up in a gout of red and yellow.

"Telisan, it's Fury. Get these guys off me. They can't get missile lock, but I'm taking gun fire."

Another tight pull and he headed for the shuttle. Fury had slowed to give the last *Dakota* a chance to escape, but the remaining interceptors circled her now. One limped away, trailing smoke from the wingtip. Missiles winked up from the ground below. Mmok. The damaged interceptor shuddered, returned fire groundward, and then staggered away burning, after a few seconds, another ejection.

"Telisan," Fury called, as they closed in.

"Coming," he called, firing the long-distance lasers. The range was too great, but if he could distract the interceptors…

Fury's gunners blazed away as the last two interceptors came in wingtip to wingtip, firing. They ignored Telisan's fire and connected on the shuttle.

"Help," Fury screamed, then her voice suddenly cut off as the *Intruder* exploded.

"No!" Telisan's weapons slashed out in rage. The lead enemy ship lost a wing. The other turned head-on toward him. "Die!" roared the Denlenn. Fire leapt from both ships and connected. Telisan fought his craft as it bucked and slewed. The interceptor staggered almost sidewise. Again, from the forest below, Mmok's forces struck. The interceptor staggered again.

Out of altitude, airspeed, and ideas, thought Telisan. *Time to die.* He hit the trigger. Suddenly the Veru hit his burner. The interceptor loomed in Telisan's windscreen as it raced to ram. Telisan could not turn; he squeezed the triggers on all three weapons. *Arpen, Sharla, I love you.*

Everything exploded.

———

"No, no," Fenaday screamed, his eyes locked on the air battle. He sprang up, racing from cover, heedless of any enemy, ignoring the cries of Mmok and Rigg. Telisan's fighter emerged from the fireball, still spitting weapon fire, battered, smoking, heading for the ground.

"Eject," Fenaday yelled. "Eject, for the love of God. Eject." Somehow he kept his feet under him as he raced headlong. The fighter headed down. Its VTOL engines kicked in, Telisan or automatics. Fenaday hit a root, went sprawling, but never took his eyes from the falling fighter. He scrambled up, crashing through the vegetation like a madman.

The *Wildcat* tore into the forest canopy a hundred yards ahead of him, falling to one side as a tree snagged the ship. It hit the spongy, swampy ground and vegetation with a bone-jarring crash. The fighter began to burn.

Fenaday raced on, breath tearing in his throat, stitch in his side, eyes locked on the crazed, clear-ceramic armor of the cockpit. The *Wildcat* lay on her side, facing him. With a last desperate effort, he flung himself across the gap between the ship's nose and the swamp edge. The armored hull scorched him through his clothes. He yelped, crawling toward the emergency releases. Smoke billowed up as he fought his way to the release, throwing his weight against the canopy. Its track was damaged. He threw his weight against it again as fire licked around him. The canopy moved another foot then jammed solid. Fenaday crawled in. Telisan lay there, whether dead or alive, Fenaday couldn't tell. He hit the quick releases on his friend's harness.

"Don't worry. Don't worry, my friend, I'll get you out." Fire bit at his left hand on the canopy. He screamed as his flesh burned. Fenaday beat the flames on his hand out, then pulled the Denlenn to him, backing out as best he could. Telisan's left arm flopped loose, what was left of it. The forearm was mangled and bloody. The fighter lurched, and the canopy came down with a thud, slamming into the middle of Fenaday's back. His arm was partly caught outside, and the flames again bit Fenaday's hand. Suddenly he found it hard to breathe. "Sorry, my friend," he whispered. "I told you to leave while you could." It began to get dark.

With a tremendous crack, the weight of the canopy disappeared. Fenaday felt himself lifted up and saw slim hands extend beyond him to pull the motionless Denlenn out of the shuttle. He realized he was up on Cobalt's shoulders. The machine leapt to the shore. The pain of the landing drove sense out of him.

Chapter Twenty-One

After a few minutes rest, Shasti and Lisa started off at their best speed. They traveled on in silence for another mile or so. Then the sky to their right opened up. A particle beam weapon raved out of the clouds as the two women hit the ground. Dirt erupted, fountaining into the sky. Ground rolled like a sea. Shasti sat up first, savage satisfaction on her face. "Particle-beam, fired by Olympians, or *Sidhe*. Either way, less company for us."

Shasti helped Lisa to her feet and they pressed forward. They stayed silent and intent. Shasti kept them to cover, though the heavier going proved tough on the smaller woman. They kept at it, hour after hour, kilometer after kilometer. Shasti's chronometer had been smashed by something, she estimated it had been nine hours since the attack on the compound and four hours since she'd found Lisa. Thorraken's long night had served Shasti and Lisa well.

Lisa, fortified by the stimulants and the emergency ration bar, walked beside Shasti. Shasti had put Lisa down to leave her hands free for weapons and given the silenced pistol to Lisa. The older woman seized on the weapon. The look in her eyes boded ill for any Voit-Veru they came across. *At least we have that much in common,* thought Shasti. They moved forward side by side, weapons covering the marshland and eyes alert.

With dawn growing near, Shasti let her melanin camouflage slip and returned to her normal ivory-toned self.

"Good God," Lisa said, looking at the suddenly changed Olympian. "What else can you do?"

Shasti shrugged and looked back at the smaller woman struggling to keep pace with her. Even the early light showed the effects of years of captivity. Lisa was seven years older than Shasti, but looked older still, a far cry from the young and pretty face in the photo that hung in Robert's cabin.

As if divining her thoughts, Lisa said, "I look like hell and an old shoe. Huh?"

Unexpectedly chagrined, Shasti searched for something to say. "Not bad for the circumstances."

Lisa laughed. "Forget it. Prison takes the pretensions out of you."

Shasti hesitated for a second then asked, "Were you mistreated?"

"At first," Lisa replied, "it was very bad. It seemed that from second to second they couldn't make up their mind between killing us and studying us. Interrogations were tough. I did what I could for my crew. It was never enough. One of them, a Morok, went mad, and they killed him." She sighed.

"I think some of the abuse was a mistake. They didn't know what to feed us, how to care for us. It got better three years ago. We started getting better food and some medicine. That's when your people made contact, I assume."

"Yes," Shasti said, "but remember I'm not with the Olympian forces. I work for Robert."

Lisa struggled up over a tussock of stems. "I'm going to have to talk to my husband about hiring Amazons with video-star looks. You don't even have the decency to look grungy. What's with your hair anyway? The damn mud doesn't seem to cling to it."

Shasti shrugged again. "It's just that way."

"So who are you?" Lisa asked. "You and Robert came looking for us? How? With what?"

"We should be silent," Shasti said. "We have hours to go to catch up with Robert, if we can."

"Have a heart, Amazon. I haven't spoken to another human besides my crew in seven years, and we talked ourselves out long ago."

This time, Shasti sighed; it was obvious the other woman wouldn't let it go. The wind blew in her face with no sound or smell of an enemy. She judged it safe to speak quietly for a little while.

"As I told you, my name is Shasti Rainhell, ground force commander of the Confed private warship *Sidhe* under Robert. Robert bought the starship, a Conchirri Frigate Leader, after you disappeared. It's heavily armed, even has two fighters.

"You saw it last night when it struck this area. Where it is now, I don't know. We have the current Olympian IFF and codes. We used them to start a battle between the Olympians and the Veru. Before my talker went out of commission, I heard enough to know my people," said Shasti, making an unconscious slip, "have been kicking some serious Voit-Veru ass, even though we're outnumbered."

"We came in on a Voit-Veru freighter we captured in-system, with a company of troops and a cyberforce. Robert set up a nuke in the freighter that took out the port and its defenses just before we hit the compound you were in. Then things started to go wrong. There were more ground forces here than we expected. They drove us from the pickup point. Good thing for you, or we would never have hooked up."

"I hope my crew made it," Lisa said.

"I don't know," Shasti replied, eyes searching the way ahead. "*Sidhe* fired down here last night, which means Robert must have been in contact with the starship. It's the only thing that kept the ground forces off us. Robert could have arranged for another pick up and left, but he won't. He's out there waiting for us. Unreasonable man, your husband."

"You're very tactful for an Olympian," Lisa huffed, beginning to flag again. "He's waiting for you. He doesn't know I've escaped, or that I'm even still alive. You must be very important to him."

Shasti looked away. "Talk to him if you have questions."

"Oh, I don't have any questions," Lisa said, looking at her narrowly. "It's pretty obvious to me that you were involved. I can't blame him. Even I thought I was dead."

"Unless you want to ruin my hard work in not allowing you to be killed, let's shut up so I can get you back to him."

They struggled on for another hour before the roar of engines overhead caused them to drop into cover. A flight of strange black and red aircraft passed high overhead. Minutes later there were flashes in the sky.

Lisa pointed. "Dog-fight. It's too far to see anything."

"Telisan," Shasti whispered, "good luck."

The women moved as fast as they could. Both felt that every passing second made escape less likely. Shasti dared a game trail, something she would not normally do. "Get up on my back," Shasti demanded. Shasti managed a running pace over the firmer ground for twenty minutes.

They entered a less swampy section, and the going grew easier. Shasti set Lisa on her own feet. They jogged on wary and alert. After another ten kilometers, Shasti sank down to one knee, motioning Lisa for silence. Lisa froze, weapon cocked. Shasti's delicate nose, with its engineered sense of smell, detected plastic and metal ahead. She breathed deeply, and a familiar scent filled her nose. Motioning Lisa to remain where she was, Shasti slipped forward silently. When she was three meters from Lisa, she threw her voice and called, "Cobalt, this is Shasti Rainhell. Request extraction and cover."

From behind a small hillock, what looked to be a slim girl with long pale hair stood. Its hands held a laser, hooked to direct feed from the HCR's nuclear battery and a 10MM triple-auto. Shasti was not worried about being shot by the machine accidentally. Her profile was in the IFF computer in every weapon, but she was too careful to rely on such protections. The machine wore a black body suit with a thin strip of cobalt blue stitched in like a sash. It quickly located her.

But not first, Shasti thought, *one for us biologicals.*

Cobalt advanced, staying to the firmer ground where its weight, many times that of the small girl it resembled, would not cause it to sink. The machine came up to her.

"Rainhell," it said in the voice of its controller, Mmok. "Damn, you're hard to kill."

"I'll try to take that as a compliment," she said wearily. "Is Robert all right?"

"Yeah," Mmok said, "outside of driving everybody fucking nuts about you going missing."

"I have someone with me," Shasti said. "Keep it to yourself. This is my surprise and it cost me plenty." She waved to Lisa Fenaday. The other woman came out with her weapon carefully pointed up. She looked warily at the HCR, and it occurred to Shasti that there'd been no such machines in existence when Lisa was captured. "It's a robot connected to a man who is a cyborg. It's on our side."

The machine looked at Lisa and did a double take that was pure Mmok. From the machine's pseudo lips came a piercing whistle.

"You did it," he said through the machine. "Damn, you pulled it off. Hell of a job, Rainhell, hell of a job. I am going to take Cobalt off the line. I'll move another HCR to cover. Cobalt will walk you in. I'll get everyone to safe their weapons."

Shasti reached a supporting arm under Lisa as the other woman staggered forward in fatigue. She shouldered her weapon and moved to pick up the smaller woman. "No," said Lisa. "I'm an officer in the Confederate Space Forces. I'm going to walk in on my own. I want Robert to see me on my own two feet."

"Yes, of course," Shasti said, feeling a sneaking admiration.

The tireless but heavy machine turned around and strode back. They emerged from the reeds onto a grassy sward. Shasti extended a hand behind her so that Lisa slowed, giving her a questioning look. Shasti stared back at Lisa with a mix of strange emotions. She had anticipated bitterness and jealously at this moment, but something else filled her now. Something she didn't understand, a bittersweet feeling welled in her chest, a mix of pride and loss.

"Shasti," cried a familiar voice. She turned. Robert, one hand swathed in bandages, ran frantically down the hill. Behind him, trying to catch up, she saw Rask, Rigg, and Mmok. "You're alive,"

Robert yelled. "Thank God. Are you all right?" he demanded, running up and throwing his arms around her.

"Yes," she said, gently disentangling from the embrace. "I'm okay. I have a present for you." Shasti moved to one side.

Lisa stood there, Robert's view of her blocked before by Shasti's towering frame. His eyes flicked from Shasti's and he saw his wife. His arm dropped nervelessly from Shasti's. For a second she thought he might faint. "Lisa," he whispered. He extended a hand toward her, moving slowly as if afraid to dispel a mirage.

"Robert," she said, her voice shaking. They rushed together, calling each other's names, trying to talk, to laugh, and to cry. They knelt together on the ground, him holding her as if she were made of china. His lips found hers. Tears rolled down his face to mix with hers.

The others stared, transfixed by the sight of the lovers, separated beyond any hope and now reunited at last.

Shasti stood to one side, looking at what she had made possible. She had not lost Fenaday. She had given him up of her own free will, to make his dreams come true. Elation like she had never known stole through her, holding at bay the bitterness of loneliness, rejection, and loss. Those emotions lurked still, waiting to be dealt with, but not now. For now, she was the hero.

She gestured toward the others to give the Fenadays some privacy. They nodded and retreated up the hill. As they passed her, Rigg and Rask smiled, touching her arm and shoulder as if they were proud of her. She nodded to each.

Mmok did not touch her, but he walked close. "I'll leave Cobalt by them," he said, his one human eye meeting hers. "It's not safe and we don't have time, but God, there's got to be a few minutes for this." He hesitated, then added, "The machine will tune them out and stay still. I don't want to eavesdrop."

Shasti looked at him as they started up the low rise. "It didn't occur to me that you would."

"It's a far, far better thing I do, than I have ever done before," Mmok said. "Is that it, Rainhell?" For once there seemed no trace of bitterness or mockery in him.

"That sounds like a quote," Shasti said. "Is it from a book?"

"Yeah," he said, "an old one. Mostly about self-sacrifice."

She looked at the cyborg, suspecting he could make uncomfortably close guesses about the darker thoughts she had struggled with. "Something like that."

He nodded. To her surprise, he added, "Good for you, Rainhell. Well done."

"Thank you." Then surprising herself, she added, "I don't feel as awful as I thought I would, having lost."

Mmok shook his head. "You're not a loser," he said, then turned away and headed for two of the HCRs that appeared on the far side of the hill.

Chapter Twenty-Two

When he could trust himself to talk, Robert Fenaday tilted his wife's face up so he could see her eyes. The wind gusted over them, lifting her hair, now shot with threads of gray. "Looked for you," he managed. "Looked everywhere for you." His voice shook and his vision threatened to dissolve. He would not allow it. He had to see his wife's face.

"Robert," she said. "I only dreamed this. Only dreamed I would ever see you again. It's been so long. I've been so far from home."

"I'm here," he said fiercely, "and I'm going to take you back."

"Home," she murmured. "I can't even see it anymore."

He pulled her close with his one good hand, his face buried in her hair as he had longed to do on so many lonely nights. Her body felt thin and frail. Thoughts of what she had endured lit a wild rage in him. *I am not through with the Voit-Veru*, he thought, wishing for the power to exterminate them. *Later for them*, he forced himself to think. *Now there is only her.* He pulled back and lifted her face, kissing her on both eyes.

She smiled slightly. "I look like hell."

"Not to me," he said. "I love you."

"I love you too," she said, lips trembling. "I'm so afraid this is a dream. I'm going to wake up in that cell again. No stars, no air."

"No," he replied with a lopsided smile. "In a dream I would be much handsomer, and not so cut up."

Lisa looked him over. "God, Robert, you're hurt."

"Not so bad," he said, "just burns."

"Robert, Robert," she said, shaking her head in wonder. "How did you ever get here? How did you find me?"

"By destroying everything and anything that ever got in my way," he replied. He thought of the toll in death and destruction from his quest. *Everything and everyone*, he thought, including some who didn't deserve it, but that was his own burden to shoulder.

"The others," she said, looking around the grassy knoll, "my crew…"

"We have two of them," he replied. "They're in rough shape but alive. They're on the other side of the hill with the others."

"Thank God," she said, sagging from relief. "That's all of them. They murdered poor Drok years ago."

"Maybe he'll sleep better in his grave tonight," Fenaday said. "I arranged for a lot of company for him."

"Shasti said you brought only one ship?"

Fenaday was bemused to hear Shasti's name on Lisa's lips. "If it's even still there," he added wearily. "We lost contact early this morning after somebody finally caught on to our frequency and started jamming. All we can do is head for the last pickup point and hope someone's coming."

"No fleet," she said in wonder. "All this way alone. God, Robert, you should have gone into the Navy and I should have stayed home."

"I never liked to travel," he replied.

The irony of it started them laughing. A little raggedly, too near hysterical.

"I don't care what happens now," she said. "I'm free. You're here. They'll never take me alive, again. Promise me that, promise me."

"Yes," he swore. "I promise it for us both." He pulled her close and kissed her again.

"Not bad, spaceman," she said, breathlessly. "You always were a good kisser."

"Just a good kisser?" he teased.

"I dimly remember something about the rest. It's been a while. We'll have to find some time for that again."

"Yes," he said. "First, I am going to get us off this hellhole."

"You said it," she said. "I want a long, hot bath and a soft bed."

"Coming up, my love." They both laughed.

"Back to reality," she said. "What's our sitrep?"

"Not good," he said, looking skyward as if fearing to see beams and missiles lancing down. "We've had fifty-percent casualties on the ground. Fifty-two left with about twenty-five in any condition to fight. We have two-thirds of our cyberforce left. All the fighters and all but one shuttle are history. We're low on ammo and nearly out of food and clean water.

"On the plus side we seem to have cleared out the enemy's aerospace assets. From what we can hear, it sounds like the battle above is ending with both sides shot to hell. We can't tell where the *Sidhe* is yet. We've got to get moving toward the last LZ. Are you up for it?"

"Watch my dust," she replied. "I want off this rock and into that cushy bed and bathtub, spaceman. Sound like fun to you?"

"I'll bring the champagne," he promised.

They struggled to their feet, looking at each other ruefully over the effort it took to even rise. Arm in arm, they started up the low hill. Cobalt moved to join them. The machine had been a short distance off and facing away from them. *Nice of Mmok,* thought Fenaday.

Shasti patted Risky carefully. The battered K-9 seemed overjoyed despite his scorches. *I'm a lousy owner,* she thought. Others greeted her with joy as well. Leda stopped tending Telisan long enough to surprise her with a hug. Shasti brushed the

Denlenn's unresponsive face with a kiss before the others surrounded her, including an older woman she recognized as Lisa's engineer, demanding to know of the amazing rescue. She gave an abbreviated version, to be rewarded by awestruck stares.

She stood, turning to look for the Fenadays, who were finally coming up the hill, arm-in-arm. She moved up from behind the cover where the few LFs, ASATs, and Marines huddled. They spotted Shasti and headed over. Rigg and Rask stood next to her.

"This lady," Rigg said, "I have to meet."

Shasti felt a flash of jealousy. *No*, she said to herself. *I'm better than that*.

Before they could even greet the Fenadays, a cry from Mmok seized everyone's attention. He came running in his fastest stiff-legged gait.

"Christ," Mmok swore. "Enemy armor approaching the perimeter: hovercraft with infantry support, armored cavalry. Goddamn."

"We've only got the one shuttle left," Fenaday began.

"I know," Mmok said. "I've got all remaining HCRs and crab robots moving out to an ambush point. I can't hold them long. Get everyone to the LZ."

"Right," Fenaday said. "Everyone up." He looked to Lisa.

"I'm all right," she said.

He grabbed the makeshift stretcher holding Telisan with his one good hand. Shasti grabbed the back of the stretcher. Murphy, who also had only one good hand, picked up the other pole. Leda Jenner put Lisa's arm over her shoulder, ignoring the exhausted woman's protest. The remaining ASATs, Marines, and LFs staggered to their feet, taking the wounded with them.

"Rigg, Rask," Fenaday called, "find some able-bodied troopers and put out security. *Pooka* will be coming down on the other side of the hill about a klick." The two grabbed up men and began sorting them out.

Fenaday noticed Mmok disappearing back to the east toward the armored cavalry. "Mmok," he called, "where are you going?"

"Can't get out of line of sight with the machines," he called back. "It cuts their effectiveness in half. Get Leda to that shuttle."

"Okay."

"Make that a promise," Mmok called unexpectedly.

"Done," Fenaday shouted. "Don't stay too long." He gripped Telisan's stretcher and struggled forward.

"Yeah," Mmok said, disappearing into the reeds. "I'll just kiss them hello."

Once out of sight of the others, he gestured to Cobalt. The machine bent over as he hopped on its back. "Undignified," he said to the surrounding combat machines, "but we'll go faster this way." Riding his unlikely mount and sticking to the firmer ground, he sped off toward the perimeter held by the other crab robots. As they reached the area facing the deeper swamp from which they'd emerged earlier, Mmok got down. He eyed the ground with a practiced eye and made his dispositions.

Mmok patted Cobalt on the shoulder. "Let's go earn our pay—we got customers coming." He ordered the remaining crab robots to submerge in the bogs. The HCRs, save for the damaged Scarlet, were similarly disguised. Cobalt stood personal guard for him, as usual. "We're in trouble," Mmok said.

"Yes, controller," Cobalt said. "Enemy forces greatly exceed our power. You should set us to independent function and retreat. There is no room for the cyberforce in the Dakota shuttle in any event. You might make it to the LZ."

"No good," Mmok replied. "No insult intended, but the crab robots don't have the systems for that."

"That is true, controller, but you are essential," Cobalt said. "Your survival is one of our highest priorities."

"Mission before men or machines," Mmok said. "Just like the REMFs say. Sorry about getting you destroyed."

"To sleep, perchance to dream," Cobalt said, as the wind lifted her monofilament hair.

Mmok's mouth dropped in shock, then he barked out a laugh. "Guess I programmed you pretty well."

"Yes," Cobalt said, "and I did enjoy the books. I did not understand them, but it generated a sensation I registered as pleasurable."

The machine cocked a head in a curiously human gesture. "They are five seconds from optimum firing range."

"Well," Mmok said, "let's give it to them in five."

"Yes, sir."

The lead hovercraft, a gray-green camouflaged machine over twenty meters long, came up over a fen and erupted in flames, hit from below by a submerged crab robot. Mmok ordered the machines to fire most of their remaining rockets and missiles to maximize damage and confusion. Two more hovercars exploded. Another slammed into a tussock, one engine out. Its turret began stuttering out explosive shells. A crab robot surged onto the hovercraft and smashed the barrel.

"Good outfit," grunted Mmok. The last element of the lead company was reacting well. Anti-missiles sleeted out of the hovercraft; reactive armor blew out flechettes to detonate warheads before they could penetrate. Sabot rounds penetrated anyway, and another hovercraft slammed into the ground. The crabs emerged from their hiding places, weapons stuttering. Voit-Veru hit one crab almost immediately with the combined fire of the two leading hovercars. Mmok winced with feedback as it blew up. On the remaining hovercraft, ramps dropped and armored infantry began to pour out, taking the machines under immediate fire. Another crab succumbed, a leg blown off. Its weapons continued to fire.

"Let's invite your sisters to the party." Mmok subvocalized the vibe that controlled the HCRs. Cobalt's sisters erupted in flashes of speeding steel, tri-autos firing. The machines were too close and too fast for the turrets of the hovercars. Infantry fired wildly from slots and hatches in the armored sides of the hovers at the dashing machines.

"More armor coming up," Cobalt said, "another company at least."

"Yeah, I expected them."

"It is a pity the airbot is gone," Cobalt added. "It would have been useful now."

Slipping and sliding, Fenaday and the others climbed around the hillside heading toward the flat area Mmok had designated LZ 5. Above them in the sky came the distant thunder of *Pooka's* engines.

Fenaday pointed. "There they are! Come on, everyone. The train is leaving."

Pooka grounded in the clearing, immediately catching some of the nearby reeds on fire. From the edge of the cleared zone, the remaining spacers staggered forward with their stretchers and wounded. *Pooka's* turrets searched for targets. With Telisan's stretcher in the lead, they tramped up the ramps. Fenaday gave the Denlenn's stretcher to a Marine crewman who latched it to the wall in the stretcher clamps. He ran back to the ramp, grabbing a carbine he could manage one-handed from the door locker. He joined Shasti and Lisa, who stood on the ramp, weapons in hand.

"Security screen is coming in," Shasti said, her enhanced vision picking up Rigg, Rask, and their fire team pushing through the grass. Risky bounded ahead of them, as intent on bugging out as any. They broke into the clear and raced for the shuttle. The others pounded past, but the two ASATs stopped on the broad ramp, Rask dropping to one knee to cover the grassland they just emerged from.

"Heavy firing from about five clicks east," Rigg huffed, eyes searching the reeds. "Mmok's holding them, but it sounds like a battalion action."

"Captain Fenaday," the pilot's voice came over the intercom. "*Sidhe* is still down over the horizon, out of support range. Graglia says he has broken contact with Olympian and Voit-Veru shipping and is maneuvering for an orbital entry and pickup. We need to take off within ten minutes for orbital window."

"Goddammit," Fenaday snapped. "No chance for ground support fire. Shasti, any sign of Mmok?"

"No," the Olympian said. "He's been gone a half hour. For all that he moves stiffly, he gets around fast enough."

"Shasti, Lisa, come with me," he demanded. "Let's see if we can recall Mmok from the flight-deck." Holding his wife's arm, he pushed through the spacers who were locking down for evac.

Moshe Karass greeted him, a barely concealed look of fear on his face. "Sir, we don't have much margin—"

"Prepare for lift off," Fenaday said. "Have the troops ready to dump all the weapons and armor outside to save weight. We're overloaded. Comm, raise Mmok's command freq."

"Where is Kyle?" asked a frightened Leda.

"We're trying to find out," Shasti said.

"You can't take off without him," Leda shrilled.

"I won't," Fenaday assured her.

"Yes, you will," came Mmok's voice. The screen facing Fenaday lit with Mmok's dirty, sweat-soaked face. Fenaday's brain whirled till he realized he was seeing Mmok through Cobalt's eyes.

"Don't be a fool," Fenaday demanded, "disengage and fall back."

"Can't," Mmok said. "Surrounded and pinned down."

"Kyle," Leda said, tears in her eyes. Lisa put her shoulder against the bigger woman, who looked like she might faint.

"Okay, okay," Fenaday said, despair striking him. "We'll get a team together."

"Negative. Don't be an idiot. I've got a battalion plus engaged. You don't have the troops. The ship still out of support range?"

"Yes," he answered. "Mmok, listen, we'll make a low pass, try for a skyhook."

Dirt and water fountained behind Mmok. A loud bang came in over the speakers. Curiously, Mmok smiled. "Hey, you'd really do that? Nice, Fenaday, very nice. You try it, though, and I'll shoot you down myself."

"Mmok," Fenaday cried.

"You promised me, Fenaday. Remember your promise. Get Leda out of there. There's no way you can reach me. So take Leda, your wife, and everyone else and run like hell."

"We've got to try," Fenaday managed. "I'm not going to leave you behind. Not again, not another like Duna."

"No," Mmok said. "No. Shasti, make him listen. It's suicide."

Shasti looked down and didn't speak.

"Dammit, Shasti, don't go soft on me now. Follow your training," Mmok snarled. "Fenaday, are you good for your word to me or what?"

"Kyle," Fenaday said, voice breaking.

"Are you!"

"Yes," he answered, condemning yet another man to death. *Our Father*, he thought, *who art in Heaven, forgive me my sins.*

"Leda," Mmok said.

"I'm here, Kyle."

"Wish I could see you," Mmok said. "Wish there was more time. You gave me a lot. You mean a lot. Don't forget me."

"I won't," she promised. "Do you hear me? I won't."

"I heard you. You live, that's what I want, that's why I did this. You live, that's what you owe me, love."

"Robert," Mmok said, "get going. Mmok out."

Fenaday bent over the command mike, clutching his chest, his mouth open as if trying to scream. No sound came out. Alarmed, Lisa and Shasti both grabbed him as he buckled, easing him to a sitting position on the deck then stopping to stare at each other.

"Raise the ship," Lisa said, holding her husband's shoulder. "It's what Mr. Mmok wanted." Shasti nodded and ran to the pilot, rapping out orders. The hatches rolled upward.

Leda Jenner sobbed softly, also sinking to the deck. "Medic," Lisa called, frightened by Fenaday's congested face, his difficult breathing. The shuttle shifted under them as *Pooka* struggled into the air.

Fenaday slumped against his wife, looking up at her, his face blank, eyes hollow, exhaustion written in every line. "I killed another one," he said. "I did it again." His eyes fluttered closed.

"Not your fault," she soothed, glancing around. Jenner was still down on the deck crying. "Where's a damn medic?" she rapped out.

A harassed medic ran up onto the flight deck, popped open a scanner, and ran it over the slumped human. "Exhaustion, shock, and fatigue," he diagnosed, shooting a hypo into Fenaday's arm. "Mild sedative, vitamins, and minerals. Get some fluids into him. It's nothing serious. Excuse me, Captain, ma'am, I've got bad casualties."

"Go," she replied.

"Let me help," said a shaky voice. Lisa turned to see Leda Jenner, red-eyed but calm. "We can get him into a bunk."

The older woman was surprisingly strong, taking most of Fenaday's weight easily. Another Olympian, Lisa realized. They put her husband in the bunk, strapping him in. Leda, seemingly recovered, checked his signs.

Lisa straightened. Even with Leda's help, her husband's weight strained her weak muscles. When she turned, she found herself face to face with Shasti. *Goddammit, thought Lisa, does she ever stop looking like a damn centerfold?*

"Is he all right?" asked the big woman.

"Yes," she said, "just at the end of his rope."

"It was a long rope," Shasti said, a touch defensively.

"I know that," Lisa said. "I can see it all around, this ship, the one in orbit, the robots, you. It speaks volumes."

Chagrined, Shasti nodded, biting her lip.

"Thanks," Lisa said.

"You're welcome. Can you go to the bridge? Orbital rendezvous are tricky, and you're a captain."

Lisa straightened, "Yes, I am." She looked back at Robert, reluctant to leave, then mounted the short ladder to the flight deck, coming up behind the pilot's chair on *Pooka*. She remembered Shasti called him Karass. Lisa quickly surveyed the instruments with an expert eye. In space above them, the battle was indeed ending. Olympian forces, those few that survived, were fleeing for deep space, where their jump engines could operate. The Voit-Veru ships, in no better shape, were also pulling away.

Lisa ordered a change of course to take the old *Dakota* shuttle farther away from the path of a damaged Voit-Veru light cruiser. The warship might detect the tiny shuttle, but Lisa hoped the residual ionization from all the near atmospheric nukes would foul their scan. There was little chance they could identify them as Confed; the shuttle was still broadcasting Voit-Veru IFF. Even if they did, chances of a hit at this range and angle were poor. The bigger ships couldn't alter course easily so far into gravity well.

"*Sidhe* had better be there," Karass muttered over and over. "They had just better be there."

———

"**C**ontroller," Cobalt warned, "ammunition is running low. We will be reduced to energy weapons shortly."

Mmok nodded. Sweat ran down his pale face, and he was glad Cobalt had used its voice. Controlling all the machines, some now damaged and erratic, taxed even his mental skills. In his mind he perceived the robots as glowing telltale gauges, with the damaged ones dimmed by the degree of injury.

"I'm ordering the units that are out of ammo to the front," Mmok said. "They can use their cutters and lasers. Hopefully they'll draw fire from the units that still have missile and rocket munitions."

"Logical," Cobalt replied.

"Here they come again," Mmok said. The machines fed the images directly into his brain. He saw a dozen green-camouflaged, armored hovercraft racing over the swamp toward the waiting cyberforce and the wrecks of the first wave. Flame and beams sprang from the speeding machines, tearing at the tussocked, drier ground Mmok chose for the cyberforce's stand. The crab-robots and HCRs held their fire until the hovers came closer, then opened up on the charging Verus with a roar.

Mmok sent a mental command to concentrate fire on two unwisely clustered hovers. The first vehicle took most of the fire. It erupted, damaging the second hover, which began to circle out of control. Mmok ordered the out-of-ammo crabs to attack it.

The hovers spotted the moving crabs and took them under fire. Crab 9 fell immediately. Feedback jarred Mmok.

Midnight and Indigo moved in on another hover, trading fire at close range. It began to burn and turned to flee, but not before blowing off Indigo's leg. Another hovercraft raced toward Midnight, determined to run over the HCR. Midnight's laser flashed as Mmok redirected fire to support her.

The hover smashed Midnight under. In the millisecond before the HCR ceased to function, Mmok sent a self-destruct to Midnight. She detonated her nuclear battery sending the hover and twenty-five yards of the swamp fountaining into the air.

"Ah, well," Mmok said, "never could keep a girlfriend anyway."

The remaining hovers slowed, trying to concentrate fire. One, armed with multiple turrets, slewed around a hillock and blasted Crab 12 into slag. Its telltale winked out of Mmok's mind. The Veru machine abruptly changed course, heading toward the rise that Mmok and Cobalt hid behind.

"Damn. Bad luck or someone has finally traced my telemetry signals."

MGs stuttered, tearing up vegetation and flinging up dirt. With his location compromised, Mmok let Cobalt cut loose. The black-clad machine stood, firing a shoulder-held rocket with one arm and the heavy tri-auto with the other, aiming at the cockpit.

"Fuck you," Mmok yelled, adding his own laser carbine. The armored plastic of the cockpit gave under the fire, and it nosed into the wet ground just short of the rise, half-sinking into the swamp. Voit-Veru troopers spilled out like fire ants. Cobalt, joined by the damaged Indigo and Crab 3, cut them down. Mmok hit one Veru struggling out of a turret. The Veru screamed and fell back into the burning machine.

The rear turret of the hover stitched Crab 3, which collapsed into the swamp. Another hovercraft drew Indigo's fire as it maneuvered for a shot. The nearby hover's rear turret traversed again, and AP rounds danced on Cobalt's titanium surface. The HCR fell over.

Mmok opened a light anti-tank rocket and aimed with his human eye. The rocket slammed into the turret, leaving a small hole that poured smoke.

Cobalt staggered back to her feet.

"Are you okay?" Mmok shouted. *Of course,* he thought, *idiot. Read the telltale.* Only seven telltales still glowed in his mind—all were dimmed by damage. Cobalt's was the strongest.

"Operational, Controller," Cobalt answered. The mechanical voice hissed and crackled from damage to the speaker.

Mmok turned back to face the broad fen of the swamp. In the distance he saw three hovercraft fleeing. Some dismounted Veru troopers fled, hopping through the swamp. Small arms fire crackled as they fought to disengage from the remnants of the cyberforce. Many more floated loose-limbed in the swamp or lay contorted on or around burning hovercraft.

"Controller," Cobalt said.

"Yeah," Mmok replied. "If they're pulling back, that means artillery. Let's fall back with—"

"Too late. Incoming." Cobalt's tri-auto snapped as it fired at the artillery shells. Mmok ordered the others to fire, knowing it wouldn't be enough.

The shells preceded the sound of their arrival, exploding in an airburst thirty meters up.

Mmok found himself face down on the ground, the metallic taste of blood and dirt in his mouth. All he could hear was dull buzzing. *I'm hit*, he thought. Hit bad. Numbness spread through him, just as it had the first time, when the Conchirri laser sliced into his tank and his body. Overhead, more shells burst silently. The ground puckered around Mmok, and he realized that Cobalt was kneeling over him, trying to shield his body.

Thanks, he thought. Mmok could feel himself going. He initiated a fast save of his memory to the black box buried in his cyborg parts. *Somebody will find it someday*, he thought.

Mmok tried to speak, to say goodbye to Cobalt and curse the Veru, but it seemed too great an effort. The cyborg readouts in his mind began to wink out as he lost touch. *Who reads mine*, he wondered, *when it winks out?*

Chapter Twenty-Three

Shasti appeared at Lisa's elbow. Lisa jumped slightly. *How does someone so big move so silently?*

"How is he?" Lisa asked, eyes roaming over the instruments and the erratic scan of the enemy cruiser.

"Leda checked again. She says stable," Shasti replied. "His color has returned. The seizure, or whatever it was, has passed."

"Poor Robert," Lisa whispered. "Was Mmok a close friend?"

Shasti looked at her with remote, brilliant green eyes. "I don't know," she said finally. "I'm not sure I understand enough about human friendships to tell."

"Coming up on line-of-sight with *Sidhe's* estimated position," Karass said. "Still haven't spotted her on scanner."

"I don't understand what happened to Robert," Shasti said unexpectedly.

Lisa spared the Olympian another glance. "Combat Stress Fatigue, I saw enough of it among our ground force people during the war. Too much killing for too long."

"Yes," said Shasti. "Yes, there has been too much killing and for too long. He was not made for this."

"Robert was always gentle," Lisa agreed. "I can't imagine him killing anyone."

"He has faced many terrible foes," said Shasti, a touch of something, perhaps pride, in her voice.

Lisa controlled a flash of jealous irritation at the reminder of the Amazon's history with Robert, part of a whole life he lived in the interregnum of her imprisonment, all unknown to her. A change in the scanner riveted her attention, jealousies and confusions temporarily shelved. A new target lit in the scan, just clearing the planet's disk, yellow for unidentified. Before she could speak, it changed to green, friendly.

"*Sidhe*," crowed Karass. "Switching to Confed IFF."

Lisa reached over his shoulder and narrowed the scan focus. "Huh? *Tokkoro* class Conchirri frigate-leader. Never thought I'd see one of those again. Damaged," she continued. "Doesn't look too severe. The port wing is gone, starboard is shot up, as is the vertical stabilizer. Looks like the rear chain guns are slagged."

"Shuttle bays?" Shasti asked.

Bernard, on communications, answered from the position behind Shasti. "Moshe, I'm getting the ALS beacon. Switching to your board. Shuttle bays must be okay for landing."

"Not like it will be crowded in the shuttle bay," muttered the pilot.

"Enough," Shasti warned with a sidelong glance at Lisa. "Just fly the ship."

Karass didn't look up, but the muscles in his jaw knotted.

"I have Lieutenant Graglia on Com 1," Bernard said. "No visual due to damage, switching to speaker."

"Graglia to *Pooka*, acknowledge."

Lisa realized that everyone was staring expectantly at her. "Lieutenant Commander Lisa Fenaday on *Pooka* to *Sidhe*, acknowledging. We're lining up for ALS landing. Request all available medical teams on standby."

"Holy shit," the speaker exploded, there was a babble of excited voices in the background. "Quiet, dammit. Mrs. Fenaday, is that you?"

"Yep. Confed radio protocols gotten a little less formal these days?"

"No, ma'am. Sorry. Just hard to believe, Commander."

"Yeah, for me too."

"Please tell me you have everyone on aboard."

"Everyone that made it," Lisa said softly, her chest suddenly tight. She looked at Shasti.

The bigger woman picked up the cue. "*Sidhe*, this is Rainhell. Fifty-one survivors on board. Both Fenadays, Telisan is aboard but wounded, Rigg, Rask, Jenner..." Shasti rolled down the list of survivors.

"No one from the *Intruder*?" Graglia asked.

"No." Shasti grimaced. "Lost with all hands. Missile hit, it was very quick."

"Angie," came the anguished voice of the young man on the starship. Lisa looked down at the deck.

"We're lining up for docking run," Karass said into the quiet.

"*Sidhe*, ship status?" Lisa asked, fighting weariness and grief.

After a long pause, the answer came back. The young man's voice was now firm, devoid of emotion. "Operable on hyperdrive and reaction drive, main gun intact, fifty percent damage to secondary armament, minor damage to communications and life support. We are spacetight now, but fragments holed several compartments. We can't fly in atmosphere. Anti-radiation protocol is in effect. Casualties are minor, mostly radiation related.

"Trauma teams are en route to the shuttle bay. You're two minutes from ALS landing."

"Do we have an escape vector?" asked a male voice behind them. Both women turned to see a pale Robert Fenaday climb unsteadily onto the flight deck.

"Affirmative, Captain," Graglia said. "We'll have to evade away from the planet, taking the same route the Olympians have. My bet is that they'll hit jump as soon as field density allows. As long as we stay far enough behind, we should be safe."

"The sooner we get out of here, the better," Fenaday said. "I don't want to pick up an operable Voit-Veru vessel, or any reinforcements."

"Not too much danger there, sir," Graglia said. "The damn Olympians fought like tigers and got in the first shots. I don't think that there's a Voit-Veru ship left without any damage, but it wouldn't take much to finish us off either."

"Maximum burn as soon as we're aboard," Fenaday said wearily. "Head for the asteroid where we marooned the *Queen's* survivors. I want to pick them up if possible."

"Aye, sir. ALS final approach being initialized now. We'll land you."

Fenaday turned to his wife, placing a hand on her shoulder. "Thanks." Then turning to Shasti, "How many did we lose?"

"Later," she suggested.

He shook his head with a stubbornness she knew all too well. She sighed, then began. "*Duna* and her flight crew, Fury and the *Intruder* crew, McLoughlin, both *Wildcats*, Mmok and the entire cyberforce, all the LFs save Murphy and Hanshi, half the Marines, and nine of the ASAT team. Most of the survivors have some wound or other."

"I would say Jesus Christ," Fenaday replied, "but I no longer believe. All gone, all gone." He looked as if he might fall, and both women reached for an arm. He squeezed Shasti's shoulder weakly and took his wife's hand. "I want to see Telisan," he said.

Karass looked up at Lisa. "I have it, ma'am, and we're on automatic, landing in thirty seconds."

Lisa nodded. Screw procedure. "Take her in, Mr. Karass." She started back to the main cabin, she and Robert leaning on each other.

———

As soon as *Pooka's* jacks hit the deck, Graglia fired the main engine.

"The Voit-Veru ships," Graglia called over the intercom, "are engaged in SAR in orbital space, as well as on the planet. Evidently they don't want to risk leaving its surface open for a high-speed attack. No ships are pursuing us."

"I don't know if we can count on that," Fenaday whispered. He sat in a chair in *Pooka's* cockpit, waiting for the chamber to pressurize and the deck crew to secure the shuttle. Rising seemed like an impossible task.

"With the VIPs on the surface," Lisa said, "I guess their commander is more concerned about recovering them and unwilling to chase *Sidhe* into what might become an ambush."

Karass turned to them. "Bay pressurized. It's safe to disembark."

"Telisan," Fenaday murmured, "got to get him to Sickbay." He struggled to his feet.

The shuttle ramps slid down, and the exhausted survivors staggered off. Arpen met Telisan at the ramp, anguish in her eyes for his destroyed hand. Fenaday, still mostly in shock, walked alongside the stretcher, holding his friend's good hand. A crushing guilt waited at the edge of the cottony grayness that enveloped him. Everything seemed muted—sound, emotion, even fear. He knew the guilt lay there and embraced the grayness. Occasionally he smiled at his wife, who left his side only to check on her two crewmen.

Shasti, with her almost limitless store of energy and more shockproof psyche, was everywhere, helping the medics, lifting even the largest of the wounded as if they were children. She ordered Graglia to retain command, realizing neither Fenaday was in a state to handle the damaged ship. With the ground force almost wiped out, and no useful knowledge of how to repair or run a ship, she served as a stretcher-bearer.

———

Fenaday sat on the deck near his friend Telisan. Abruptly, he realized they must be in Sickbay, though he didn't remember how they got there. Looking up he saw Telisan's mutilated hand covered by a med-plast regenerator. The machine would seal the wound, amputating the unsavable and preparing it for prosthesis. Fenaday's own burnt hand was covered with burn spray that someone had applied until regenerators could be spared. He felt eyes on him and looked up to see Arpen.

"I'm sorry," he said to her, unconscious of the tears rolling down his face.

"I know," she said and pressed an injector tab against his arm. "Sleep."

The grayness went black.

———

Shasti came over at Arpen's gesture, just as Lisa returned from seeing Fontel and Barrett bedded down. "Can you take him to his cabin?" Arpen asked. "I have no beds available."

"Yes." She bent and lifted him easily. She looked at Lisa, who nodded, tired and clearly near the end of her last reserves. "It's not far."

It turned out to be a little longer than usual as they detoured around damaged sections of the ship. Shasti's arms grew sorer than she wanted to admit by the time they finally reached the cabin. *Pride goeth*, she thought.

Once there, Lisa pulled back the sheets. They managed to get the unconscious man in without banging his burned hand. Lisa began to murmur something even Shasti's ears couldn't discern, then Lisa's eyes shut and she fell face forward onto the bed next to him.

Shasti sighed and pulled the couple out of boots, armor, torn and burnt clothes, dealing with revealed cuts and abrasions with a first aid-kit in the room. *Never had a mother*, she thought, *now I'm playing one. Worse, I even have to tuck her into what used to be my place.*

After a last check on the unconscious couple, Shasti retreated to her own cabin, refused to think of anything else, and slammed herself into REM sleep for four hours.

When she awoke, she was starving. Stopping only to look in on the unconscious Fenadays, she went to the galley, devouring a breakfast of epic proportions with a ferocity that seemed to disturb the cook. She looked at him. "You're next." He fled to the safety of the kitchen.

Rigg walked in as she was finishing a third cup of coffee,

savoring the flavor of the bitter brew. The ASAT was a veritable quilt of bandages. He walked over to her and sat. "We need to put together a security force," he said launching straight into it. "We'll be coming up on that rock where we dropped the *Queen's* crew in about eighteen hours. Means prisoners coming on board soon."

"What do we have standing?" she asked.

"Damn little," he replied bitterly. "Three Marines fit for duty, six of my people, and Rask are okay. That's it for a few days until the lightly wounded are better. You've got Murphy and Hanshi left from your team, and there's Risky, I suppose."

"Yes," she said slowly. "I'll miss Li and Lokashti."

"Good men." Rigg nodded. "We lost a lot of them. Hope it was worth it."

"You can ask Robert and Lisa when they wake," Shasti shot back. "Barnett and Ki Teska and their families too."

"No," Rigg said after a second. "I don't guess that I'll do that. Besides," he added, "you'd probably kill me if I did."

"Probably would."

Rigg snorted. "I like you, Rainhell. You never change."

To his surprise, she gave him a wide smile. "Oh, but I do. Now back to business," she added. "We need some crewmen. I'll get Dobera, he's good with a gun..."

———

Robert Fenaday awakened with a start. *Where am I?* he wondered. Then the events of the last day crashed in on him. He turned his head, and there she was, lying on his left shoulder as she used to years ago. His sudden awakening had roused her too, and her eyes fluttered open. Husband and wife looked into each other's eyes for several minutes without speaking, as if fearing to dissolve the spell that had rejoined them.

"Somehow," Lisa finally whispered, "when I tried to envision this moment, I never could quite see it."

"Why?" he asked, gently stroking her hair with his good hand.

"Because I'm not the Lisa who left you on New Eire. Each year in prison is a long time. You lose some of yourself."

He hugged her closer. "I love you. That will never change."

She gave him a sad smile. "It's easier to believe after hearing you say it."

"Then I'll say it every day."

She reached up to hold the hand he placed against her cheek. "I'm not the only one changed—my sweet Robert. There are scars on you, and not all of them have been cut into the flesh."

He nodded. "The man who married you couldn't walk where I had to walk. So I'm changed and not all for the better."

Tears slowly tracked down her face. "I am so glad to see you. So glad."

They clung to each other.

"God," he said finally. "I think I hurt everywhere."

"Is there a shower in here?" Lisa asked.

"Well," he replied, "rank—"

"—hath its privileges." She grinned.

They helped each other to rise—exchanging rueful looks at the effort and their injuries. Filthy clothes dropped to the floor, and they squeezed into the small shower, Fenaday being careful with his burned hand. The water, perfectly set to the right temperature, washed soot and blood from them both. Lisa soaped her hair with a vengeance, then his. The hot water melted pain and soreness away. Warm airjets removed most of the moisture, and they grabbed the few inadequate towels and went back to the bed.

Robert and Lisa kissed. Gently at first, with no intention other than for comfort, but the scent and touch of his wife stirred him, and her hands reached and touched him in once-familiar ways. He stroked her, careful to be gentle and slow. His hands and lips pleased her until she was ready, and then they came together. There was nothing in the universe but them and their entwined bodies. Finally she cried out, and he joined her in climax. They held each other, laughing for joy. He rolled over so Lisa could lie on his chest. She pulled a sheet over them, and exhaustion reclaimed them both. They dropped off into sleep again.

Chapter Twenty-Four

Sidhe limped outward at her best speed after recovering the *Queen's* survivors from the asteroid. There was still no sign of pursuit, but Fenaday, recovered sufficiently to resume command, wanted desperately to get into jumpspace. His physical injuries were healing. With Lisa at his side, the pain in his soul over the loss of so many was at least bearable. They sat side by side on the bridge, Lisa on a chair that Perez improvised for her. Fenaday could not believe in her return unless the proof of it stood constantly before his eyes.

Both of them tried to find some time to spend with Shasti, but the big Olympian kept everything light, accepting their thanks, but refusing to discuss anything beyond that.

"There'll be time," Shasti told them both. "Right now we're all still in pieces, and I guess I don't mean just the ship. I'm happy with what I did and the choices I made." Still for all of that, she did not stray far from the bridge and the Fenadays, as if she was determined that the universe not cheat her out of what she had paid so much for.

The three of them were together on the bridge for the first quiet minutes they'd had since fleeing the planet. Lisa sat on one side of

Fenaday, Shasti stood on the other. They all held hot drinks: coffee for him, chocolate for both women. Fenaday felt a crack in the grayness that had enveloped him since Mmok's loss.

He looked over his shoulder. Telisan was seated by Arpen, his missing hand covered with wound seal. His friend's face was gaunt, but a smile graced it as he spoke in low tones with Sharla.

If I had lost that man, Fenaday thought, *I would not deserve to live. Assuming I do deserve to live. Ah, that so many paid so much. How can I possibly repay all I owe, even if I live a thousand years? For now, it's enough that the six of us came through the fire.* He sat still, afraid to disturb the companionable silence around him.

Hafel's head came up with a jerk as she responded to a computerized shriek of alarm. "Damn," she swore. "Massive EM surge ahead. Scan is overloading. Many, many ships coming out of jumpspace, estimating two AU distance. This information is twenty light-minutes out of date. We could be looking at bogies or bandits dropping in range any time now."

"Christ," Fenaday said. "IFF? Are they Voit-Veru or Olympian?"

"IFF is coming through now," Hafel said. "Confed."

"It's the fleet!" Lisa cried, standing. She looked around expecting to see joy, but saw only confusion, fear, and grimness on the faces of her companions. "Robert," she repeated, "it's the fleet. Our fleet."

"Your fleet," he said gently, "not necessarily mine. They will be less than pleased to find me alive here."

Lisa stared at him in shock.

"Orders," Telisan asked, looking as tired as a being could. By rights he should still be in Sickbay.

"You can't fight," Graglia blurted. "Those are our people out there."

"We're too badly damaged to run," Perez said, "and where could we go?"

"No," Fenaday said. He looked beyond them all at Shasti Rainhell. "No," he repeated, "I can't fight anymore." Shasti looked back at him enigmatically for a few seconds, then nodded.

"Mr. Graglia, reduce speed to ten percent. Wardell, secure all weapons under full safeties and cease active fire control. Maintain all defensive systems on standby in case we are fired on. Sharla, stand by on defensive ECM and get me a channel to the command ship out there."

Fenaday stood and turned to his wife. "Lieutenant Commander Fenaday, as the only Confederation citizen not likely to face immediate arrest upon our being boarded, I am surrendering myself and the *Sidhe* into your custody."

"My God," she murmured, "what have you done?"

"Anything and everything I had to," he replied. "Will you take the center seat?"

As if in a dream, Lisa moved to seat herself in the command chair.

Robert watched her, seeing a light come back into her eyes, a firmness return to her jaw.

"Vessel, no, vessels ahead," Hafel said. "Confederation Battlecruiser *Armageddon*, destroyers *Murgleys* and *Mjolnir*. More beyond them, but scan is not clear."

"Confederate vessels have locked active fire control on us," Sharla said. "Our IFF is broadcasting. Shall I attempt to break their lock?"

"Negative," Lisa said.

Sharla looked over at Fenaday uncertainly. He made a gesture toward his wife with one hand. Sharla relaxed at her controls.

"I'm getting a hail from farther back in the formation," Bernard said. "No video, just voice."

"On speaker," Lisa ordered.

"This is Confed Task Force 58 to *Sidhe*, surrender your vessel or be destroyed."

"This is Lieutenant Commander Lisa Hayes, of the *C.S.F Blackbird*, authentication 13-theta-XL5. I am in temporary command of the Confederate private warship *Sidhe* at the request of Captain Robert Fenaday. We will heave to for boarding, though I am unaware why the rescuers of Confederate officers should be treated in such a fashion. Please explain why you are demanding surrender. What charges lie against this warship?"

The speaker remained silent, light speed delay and confusion. The bridge crew stared at each other, anxious for the reply that would determine their fate.

"If Mmok were here," Shasti said unexpectedly, "he'd say that someone is debating blowing us to hell."

The speaker crackled to life. "This is TF 58 command ship, no explanation. Cut drive and stand by for boarding. Resist and you will be fired on."

Suddenly another voice broke into the circuit. "This is the Enshari vessel *Vigilant*, under Captain Moof, to Battleship *Polaris*. Do not fire on the *Sidhe*. We witness all that you do. Robert Fenaday is aboard that vessel. Fire on him, and all Enshari will condemn your actions."

"Enshari vessel," came an angry human voice, "maintain tacnet silence. You are not authorized to broadcast. Return to formation and remember what fleet you're in."

"Negative," came the reply, "or will you destroy us as well? You'll have to kill many to keep such a secret. We will die to shield the *Sidhe* and Fenaday."

More silence.

Lisa bit her lip in concentration. "Avery Deveraux, this is Lisa. I know you are there, and I know you're listening. Call everyone to heel and stop this nonsense."

Everyone stared at Lisa in confusion. "Who the hell is Avery Deveraux?" Robert asked.

Then a familiar voice came over the speakers. "Hello, Lisa," Mandela said, his rich, sepia baritone unmistakable. "Good to hear your voice again."

The screen in front of them lit, showing the immense combat information center of a *Star* class warship. Standing near the main CIC panel was the man who'd dragged them through one terrifying adventure after another.

"Hello, Avery," Lisa said. "You're looking well."

"So he did it," Mandela/Deveraux said. "He found you. Unbelievable."

"Yes. As I found the source of those unknown alien signals you asked about," Lisa said, bitterness alive in her voice. "Then the Voit-Veru found me. Drok's dead. Ki and Barrett are aboard alive. So is my husband. I plan that he stays that way."

It hit Fenaday, he stared at Deveraux, the man he'd only known as Mandela. "You knew," he snarled at the screen. "You bastard, you knew what happened. Where she went. All these years. God's blood, Mandela, I'll kill you."

"No," Lisa cried, alarmed at the insanity she saw filling Fenaday's eyes. His face had distorted into that of a man she did not know. "Robert," she demanded. He seemed to tear his eyes from Mandela only by an act of will. "He didn't know. I brought him the reports and told him of my suspicions of the unknown transmissions. We needed to know if they were Conchirri or some new threat.

"Avery sent me to scout, just to get a vector on where the signals came from, but no, I had to be the one that found the new race, assessed the threat. I pushed it, went in further, found a ship, tried to shadow it, and got caught. I pushed my luck and that of my ship. Robert, I exceeded my orders."

"I wondered how it happened," Mandela said. "We knew you found something, but the Conchirri destroyed the base you set out from. We didn't have enough clues to follow. Why? Why didn't you follow orders?"

"Well," she said. "I wasn't your protégé for nothing. How could I ever hope to replace Avery Deveraux if I didn't take the big chances, just as you had?

"I paid for my ambition. Worse is that I wasn't the only one who was billed." She looked at Robert. "My poor husband," she whispered in a voice suddenly full of tears, "you paid too. Didn't you?"

Fenaday, stunned, his mind whirling, could only stare.

"My fault, this," said Mandela, adding a further shock. "I brought you along too far, too fast. You were the best I ever saw, but overconfident, reckless, always getting away with it. I knew it and I sent you anyway. That was a mistake. If it means anything to either of you, I'm sorry."

"Robert," she said, "it isn't his fault."

"Don't be hard on him, Lisa," Mandela said. "I owe him a couple."

"One day," Fenaday managed, "I'll collect it all, along with your hide."

"Maybe," Mandela said. "You're harder to kill than cockroaches, and you were right, back on New Eire, you're getting bigger all the time. Now, I can't even get rid of you, the hero who brought down Pard, discovered the Voit-Veru alliance and their base, and then rescued the crew of the *Blackbird*. The Enshari and my own fleet are watching. If I repudiate you, I risk undermining my own policy. No, you're going to live. Worse, now you know my real name. That was unkind, Elizabeth."

"He's my husband," she said.

"You must realize that there is no way back now."

"Wasn't looking for one," she said. "I've decided I don't want to be a protégé anymore. It's too expensive."

Mandela looked at her pensively for a few seconds. Then a genuine smile seemed to light his face. "Good for you. Well, Commodore Adellana will see to your reprovisioning. I'll send along the usual pardons for everything your husband has been up to. It's a goddamn form letter by now. We won't be in touch. Good-bye, Elizabeth." He looked at Fenaday. "Good-bye, Fenaday."

"Die slowly," Fenaday wished, fists clenched.

"You're consistent," Mandela sighed, his image fading.

———

Lisa Fenaday squared her shoulders and walked up to the door. Before she could change her mind, she hit the enunciator. After a few seconds delay, she hit it again. "Shasti, please open the door. I'd like to talk to you," she said.

The door whooshed open, and the Amazon stood on the other side. Her face was expressionless, remote.

"Can I come in?" Lisa asked. "I'd prefer not to talk in the hallway."

Without a sound, Shasti faded back into the room. Lisa followed. Shasti walked over to a surprising object, an artist's easel. A painting of a horse sat on it, partially done and well rendered. Shasti seated herself on a stool and picked up a brush, idly turning it in her hands.

Lisa looked around the room. The place was surprisingly feminine. Draperies hung on the walls, along with several other paintings.

"Did you expect something else?" Shasti asked, following her gaze. "Human heads on the walls?"

"Something like that," Lisa replied. "I don't know much about Olympians."

"Robert had the same expression," Shasti added, "when he first saw it."

"Did he?" Lisa said. "Well, that brings me to what I wanted to talk to you about."

"Robert," Shasti said, putting the brush down.

"Was mine, was yours and now? Mine again?"

"You ask the wrong person," Shasti said. "He's not mine to hold or give away, but his own."

"Of course," said Lisa. "You have a claim on him too."

"On his friendship, his help, yes, I do."

"It's been more than that," Lisa said.

"Yes," Shasti said, "he thought you were dead. It took him a long time to believe it. Far longer than was reasonable—"

"I know," Lisa said, pacing slowly through the room. "You come back with your ship or not at all," she quoted. "A motto in the space service, came out of the old submersible services. Either the ship survived, or no one survived. I had a lot of time to think about it, to think of my ambition to be the discoverer of the new race. I pushed my crew's luck, and it ran out. That was the worst of it, down on an alien world, knowing that we'd be given up as lost. 'Missing in action' the report would read, lost to a Conchirri ship or a mechanical failure."

"And then you came back to life," Shasti added. "Odds so high it doesn't make sense to calculate them."

"That must have hurt you," Lisa said, a touch of genuine sympathy in her voice.

Shasti shrugged. "I've been hurt before."

"Not like this," Lisa said. "I remember how you looked at me when we met. How you sounded."

"Do you blame me?" Shasti snapped, throwing down her brush. "As soon as there was any hint you were alive, everything was thrown to the winds."

"No, I don't blame you. I do wonder why you took such risks to save me?" Lisa asked. "I could have died there, when you found me. No one could have blamed you for not taking such a suicidal risk for a woman you didn't know."

For the first time, Shasti looked uncomfortable, glancing away.

"So you thought about it."

There was a long silence.

"Yes," Shasti admitted.

"But you did take the risk. Why?"

Shasti's mouth drew into a hard line. She stood up from the easel and walked toward Lisa.

Be damned if she'll intimidate me, thought Lisa, holding her ground, *but God, she's big.*

Shasti stopped at arm's length away, bending down, her jade-green eyes boring into Lisa's stormy blue-gray ones. "I did it, because I was afraid, and I have seldom been afraid, that if I returned with your lifeless body, he'd die right in front of me. Just simply fall stone dead. If I didn't come back with you, then he wouldn't leave, and he'd have died back on Mounus. Either way, saving your life seemed essential to saving his."

Lisa searched the big woman's eyes for signs of guile or deception and saw none. She sighed. "You do love him."

Shasti straightened slowly, shaking her head, the luxurious black hair shimmering in the light. "Born-Woman, what do I know about love? I came out of a tube, no mother, no father, no brother or sister. I'm made from the DNA of thousands of people, yet I have no relation to any person that ever lived. Scientists and doctors created me as a biological weapon.

"Robert's important to me in ways I don't understand. All I know is that he deserves happiness. You're the key to that happiness. I decided that I cared more about what was good for him than what I wanted."

"Shasti, that is love."

Shasti shrugged. "Is it? He and I have depended on each other for our survival in a universe hostile to us both. Is that what love is?

"This is my life," she said, gesturing at the warship that surrounded them. "They put weapons in my hands when I was a child. I killed for the first time when I was fourteen. I'm literally made to do these things. I don't know anything else.

"Robert only came to this life to find you. He isn't suited for it, doesn't want it. It's changed him. If you're smart, you won't ask him about the things he did to find you. It comes down to this. He still loves you, and you would be a fool not to know it."

Lisa bridled at the words but let the moment pass. She owed Shasti her life, and she suspected, from even the little she had learned, Robert's as well. "Where does that leave us? Are we supposed to go on to be best friends?"

"I realize," Shasti said, "that everything is against our being friends, but I want to be. I don't lie, not to Robert, not to you."

"You know," Lisa began, leaning against a dresser, "I used to daydream about being rescued by the Navy and going home. When I imagined returning to New Eire, Robert was there, unchanged. That was only a daydream. I half-expected if I ever returned, it would be to find Robert remarried, settled, maybe even with a few children."

"I never imagined that I'd owe my life to my husband's lover, a genetically engineered Amazon. It would be easier to bear, if you weren't so damn perfect," Lisa growled.

Shasti smiled slightly. "So far, perfection is hell."

———

Fenaday walked toward the shuttle bay, his mind busy with a thousand plans, now that it seemed he would live to have a future. The last Confederate shuttle had just departed, leaving behind the final supplies necessary for the trip back, as well as the promised pardons. As owner of a civilian vessel, he'd demanded that the Navy stay off *Sidhe*, testing whether Mandela's forbearance was real. Fenaday left everything else in Lisa's hands. Though he wasn't under arrest, he knew the task force was happier with her in charge.

Polaris and the rest of the squadron left, heading for Mounus IV and what reception, Fenaday had no idea. *Sidhe* was bound for the Confederacy and New Eire. They were not to leave on their own. A Confederate Heavy Cruiser, *Tin-tern*, paced them a light minute behind, despite Fenaday's furious protest. Mandela insisted on it.

"*Sidhe* faces a long voyage," Mandela said in his last call. "There might be Voit-Veru or even Olympian vessels on the path back. I am taking no chance that the *Sidhe* might disappear yet again and that I might be blamed for it."

The Enshari scoutship *Vigilant* also followed, keeping herself between *Sidhe* and the cruiser at all times.

His musings were interrupted by a voice calling his name. He looked up to see Telisan walking toward him. The Denlenn pilot wore his favorite battered flight jacket.

"How are you?" Fenaday asked.

The Denlenn shrugged, looking at his partially empty left sleeve. "It aches, though I do not know why. Arpen tells me that with prosthesis and some training, I will fly again."

The Denlenn's loss and the terrible costs paid by so many for his quest rose to choke Fenaday again. "God," he said, his voice breaking, "God, I am sorry."

Telisan looked at him curiously. "Why? You didn't shoot me down."

"It's my fault you were there," he said.

"No more than it was the Voit-Veru's or Lisa's fault," replied the confused alien. "Remember," he said. "I told you when we first set out, *Quaren*. The universe expressed its need that I be here. It is no one's fault. Not even the being who shot me down is at fault."

"I wish I could believe that," the human said. "I truly wish that I could. You are a remarkable person, my friend."

"Well," Telisan said, "I'm getting a bit old to be flying first-line combat anyway. With as many missions as I have, I'm near my statistical limit. My mates will be happy that I will not fly combat again."

The two walked on, side by side, in silence, heading for the hanger deck.

"How does it go with your wife?" Telisan asked. "If the question does not offend?"

"It's all right," Fenaday replied. "If anyone has a right to ask, it's you. It goes as well as could be hoped. In a way, it's like when we were dating. All the mistakes, all the fumbles, yet there is the bond from before. I hope it's enough for us to build again. She seems different, in some ways. She has a lot of regrets. Like me. We're not the people we were. Hopefully, we will be the people that we each need.

"I worry a little about how she feels about Shasti," he continued. "I was honest. I told Lisa what happened with Shasti and me."

"You worry too much," the Denlenn said. "There is no reason for them to resent each other, any more than there is for Arpen to resent Sharla. You should take a page from our book. Three are stronger than two, my friend. A triangle is the strongest of all forms. You should seek to create a bonding for you three."

Fenaday broke into laughter, surprising the alien. "Uh, I don't think so, old friend," he said when he could catch his breath. "Humans are very different from Denlenn."

"I don't see you as so different," the Denlenn replied. "Oh, you have some strange notions, but you are not so unlike."

"Do you remember poor Li?" asked Fenaday. Telisan nodded. "His people used pictographs in their written language, pictures that mean words. The pictograph for disaster is two of the symbol for female, under one roof symbol. The reason for that is because it takes too long to paint a symbol with two females stabbing a male to death in his sleep and setting the house on fire."

"Oh, surely you exaggerate," Telisan said. "Besides, Shasti does not seem much like the other human females I've met. She is far more like a demi-female."

"Oh," Fenaday said. "Oh. Never say that out loud again. Only bad things can follow."

Telisan did the Denlenn equivalent of rolling his eyes. "You need to think seriously about these things."

They reached the gallery over the hanger deck. Fenaday looked bemused at his earnest friend, shook his head with a sigh, and gazed over the deck. Below, the surviving shuttle's crew was working on the damage. Suddenly Fenaday's head came up. "Uh-oh," burst from his lips.

"What?" demanded the Denlenn. "What ails?"

The human pointed. Lisa Fenaday stood by *Pooka's* wing, her hand on its leading edge, speaking to Shasti Rainhell, who towered over her. The deadly Olympian listened intently, but as if sensing his gaze, Shasti looked up. Lisa followed her gaze. The two women waved. Then Lisa said something that made Shasti laugh.

"See," Telisan said, "there is nothing to worry over."

Fenaday turned to face the Denlenn. "Telisan, there is no more terrifying prospect for a human male than to have his wife and his ex-girlfriend in the same place laughing about the chief thing they have in common."

"Humans are unfathomable," Telisan sighed.

Commander Rainhell, report to the bridge."

Shasti looked up curiously at the intercom. *Now what?* she thought. She reached a finger and flicked the responder. "Rainhell here, acknowledged."

A few steps took her to the turbovator for the short trip to the bridge. The doors to the *Sidhe's* bridge slid open. Lisa sat there in the center seat. She stood as Shasti entered, a crisp white Confederate uniform loose on her still too lean form. Robert stood next to her, wearing his normal shipboard slacks and shirt, devoid of insignia. Telisan said something to Lisa, then walked toward the turbovator. As he passed Shasti, he stopped long enough to put a hand on her shoulder and smile. She covered his hand with her own for a brief second. She didn't smile, but the gesture was enough.

To Shasti's surprise, the bridge crew rose, secured their stations to automatic, and followed the Denlenn out. The bridge doors sealed. Shasti was alone with the Fenadays. She walked forward, looking a question at both of them.

"I wanted some privacy," Fenaday said.

"Is something wrong?" she asked.

"No," Lisa said, "nothing's wrong."

"Lisa and I," Fenaday continued, "are going home to New Eire, to put our lives back together. We have a lot of catching up to do." He smiled at his wife. Something silent and electric passed between husband and wife. Shasti looked on, a bittersweet feeling of sadness and loss stealing through her.

"I've negotiated a leave of absence from the Navy," Lisa said. "I'm through in Naval Intelligence and Special Ops anyway. I may not go back at all."

"Which brings us to why we called for you," said Fenaday, idly spinning the command chair. "Once you told me that *Sidhe* was the closest thing you had to a home."

"I remember."

"Then you remember how I told you that you would always have your place here and a place in my home."

"I don't hold you to that," she replied without expression, careful not to look at the other woman.

"My husband always keeps his word," Lisa said, pulling Shasti's eyes unwillingly to her. "You should know that."

"*Sidhe* has been good to me," Fenaday continued. "It was the only thing that kept me sane, kept me going. It carried my hopes and my dreams. I'm coming to the end of my dreaming now. I've accomplished all that I wanted, against all hope. But I'm tired, Shasti, sick at heart over the deaths and wounds of so many. I'm going back to New Eire to use whatever time I have to try and make up for all that I've done. To try and help everyone I've hurt. My trail is ended.

"Yours," he said, suddenly intense, "has not. *Sidhe* carried me to my dream. I want her to do the same for you. There's a whole universe out there, and I want you to have it."

"What are you saying?" she murmured, lost.

"*Sidhe* is yours." A smile stole over his face. "Oh, I'll pay the bills and such, but her course, Captain, her course is yours to chart."

"What?" she said. She looked at each of them. Lisa smiled and nodded.

"I don't have a master's ticket," Shasti said. "I've never been trained—"

"You'll master it easily," Fenaday said. "No one has seen any limit to your ability, Shasti. Until then, I'll supply a sailing master to fly you where you want to go. Think of it: exploration, trade, maybe even a bit of privateering."

"It's too much," she protested. "Robert, this ship is worth hundreds of millions of credits."

He shrugged. "Too much for the woman who kept me alive from Morokat to Voit-Veru space? Too much for the woman who rescued my wife? No."

Shasti looked around at the ship's control center, seeing it in a new light. She walked over to the center seat.

"Try it on for size," Lisa suggested.

Shasti sat in it and leaned back. The chair felt solid against her back.

"My part in this ship's story is over," Fenaday said, eyes on a level with her own. "You must write her story now."

"Thank you," she said, tears glimmering.

"You are welcome, dearest friend," he said, tears appearing in his own eyes. "Lisa and I owe you our lives and the happiness we have now. Never, ever, doubt that we will always be there for you. In any need, against anyone, or anything."

Thoughts crowded close in her mind, piling on each other in a kaleidoscope of images. Places she had been, people she had known, the severe face of a young man, his blue eyes blazing under a shock of black hair. *Someday,* she thought, *not now.* The universe opened before her mind. She had spent her whole life on the run, mostly near poverty, fighting to stay alive. Her enemies were all gone now. There were no more limits.

"Call your crew to stations, Captain," Lisa said with a sly smile. "It's against regulations to leave a ship on automatic for more than ten minutes."

Shasti slowly keyed the intercom, as she had watched him do so often. "This is Rainhell. Bridge crew, resume stations."

The bridge doors cycled open in seconds. The crew came back, with many extras: Rigg, Rask, Jenner, Perez, Dobera, Mourner, Karass, and finally Telisan and his fiancées, Arpen and Sharla.

"Captain Rainhell is in command," Fenaday announced. Applause and cheers broke out.

"Captain," Fenaday said.

"Yes, Robert?"

"Will you take us home please?"

"Yes," she replied, with a smile like March in spring. "I'd be happy to."

The End

Regrets and Requiems

Robert Fenaday eased *Sidhe's* 10,000 tons down on the open field that served as Morokat colony's main spaceport. Her scarlet hull settled on the huge jacks under her winged dart-like body. "Done with engines," he said with relief.

"Aye, sir," Carlos Perez said. The mustachioed and balding engineer leaned over his board and began shutting down the reactor.

Dropping the frigate into a gravity well was a tricky operation. *Sidhe* was overdue for a refit, one of the reasons Fenaday flew her in, though he was master onboard. He also didn't trust the recently hired helmsman to handle his precious ship in a port with so few automatics. The young man stood behind his seat watching Fenaday's every move. *On the job training,* Fenaday thought. *He ought to be paying me.*

Fenaday stood and turned to look at his crew as they locked down their boards. It was the usual motley assortment. He had a hard core of regulars, but a good percentage of his crew turned over in every port. The ship's quartermaster, Dobera, a lizard-like Frokossi, stood at the back of the spade-shaped bridge. His jeweled eyes blinked independently of each other as he awaited orders.

Dobera was doing double-duty as first mate. Fenaday's last mate lay on a mortuary slab on Dimerus, dead from an overdose.

"Prep the cargo bays for off-loading," Fenaday told him, stretching. "General liberty for the crew. Bring me word when our contact calls. It will be after sunset, local time."

Dobera nodded and turned back to his board.

"Security measures?" came a cool voice. *Damn,* Fenaday thought, *how did she get behind me again?* He turned to look up at his new Chief of Security.

Shasti Rainhell gazed down at him, a head taller than his solid six feet. She combined the athletic body of a powerlifter with the grace of a dancer and the face of a goddess. Raven hair cascaded over her broad shoulders to her narrow waist. Jade green eyes looked calmly out of her pale face.

Fenaday had known her for only a few weeks, having rescued the Olympian colonist from a slave ship taken in one of *Sidhe's* privateering patrols. She'd taken quick vengeance on the slavers and looked as if she might try to take over *Sidhe* as well. Instead, Fenaday had hired her. Discipline on his rough and unruly crew was instant and effective. Shasti was far stronger and faster than any human, the result of generations of genetic selection on her home colony. She actively discouraged any discussion of her past, so Fenaday had learned little about her.

Of course, he thought, *with the sort of crews I get, that's often a good thing. All the real spacers are in the Navy or Merchant Marine, fighting the Conchirri.*

"Recommendation?" he said.

"I'd go with Class A," she replied in a surprisingly high and musical voice for so large a creature. "This is a lawless port. I'll put Gunnar and the trouble team in close. I want the Tok brothers wandering about the near port area in local clothes. They're Moroks, after all. Let's see if they can pick up any hint of trouble."

"Expecting something?"

She gave him a look he had come to think of as saying: how in God's name did you survive before I came along? *It's a fair question,* he thought. *Little more than a year ago I was a spoiled rich merchant's son, running a boardroom.* But that was another life. Before Lisa disappeared.

"I always expect trouble," Shasti said. "Would that I were disappointed more often."

"Make your arrangements," he said. "I'll want you to accompany me for the delivery of our refrigeration parts."

"Of course," she said, knowing as well as he that the "refrigeration parts" were twenty crates of Conchirri power weapons from a scavenged base. With the Conchirri driven out of this sector, the Moroks were returning to their first love...civil war. Gunrunning didn't sit well with Fenaday, but *Sidhe* was expensive, and the syndicate backing him was bitching about declining revenues.

Fenaday watched Shasti as she walked to the communications board and keyed a mike, all smooth muscle and curves. Shasti seemed indifferent to male attention. He didn't know if her preferences lay with her own gender, or if she just regarded all the humans on board as beneath her.

What does it matter? he thought bitterly. *Only one woman for me and she's lost in a million light years of space. Lisa, how I miss you. Are you a frozen corpse tumbling in the darkness or stripped atoms moving at light speed? Or do you live under some alien sky and wonder if I have forgotten you?*

Lisa's small scoutship, the CSS *Blackbird*, had disappeared during a clandestine mission. Fenaday had sold off the family shipping business to buy *Sidhe*, a captured Conchirri frigate-leader, and search for her. It was hopeless and foolish, and he'd been at it for over a year now.

Shasti returned. "All security arrangements set."

Fenaday headed for his cabin to change and perhaps catch a few hours' sleep. He assumed Shasti was off to check her guard posts. He opted for the gangway as opposed to the turbovator. To his surprise, she followed him.

"You're still going to see that salvage merchant?" she asked.

"Yes," he replied. "The parts he sent me holos of were clearly from a Confed scout of *Blackbird's* class."

"There've been many such lost during the war," she said, easily keeping pace with him as they walked down the ship's main corridor. Around them crewman were busily shutting down the ship's systems, doubtless anticipating the less savory pleasures of the off port.

"Yes," he said, "it's hopeless and futile. Did you have something on for tonight that I'm keeping you from?"

Her eyes narrowed. "I go where you pay me to go."

"Glad we understand each other, Commander. Meet me at the mule just before sunset." He turned off the corridor toward his quarters. *Wonder if she's drawing a bead on my back,* he thought. *If I were worried about my life, I might look. There is a certain freedom in being totally screwed.*

After nightfall, Fenaday walked down the gangway built into the mid-ship's landing jack. At the foot of the gangway, he paused to zip the black leather ship's jacket and loosen the tie-down on the Martini laser that rode on his right hip. A cool breeze dispelled the smell of burnt rock and vegetation from the afternoon's landing.

Stevedores had off-loaded his legitimate cargo onto carriers. One of the huge flatbeds was disappearing toward the gray warehouses at the end of the field carrying some of his crew as well. A few pallets remained, and behind them sat a small, six-wheeled cargo-carrier mule, painted the same blood red as *Sidhe*. It contained a single crate of "refrigerator parts" to show their prospective clients.

"Looking for me?" Shasti said from behind him.

"Damn," he said. *She's making a point with this.* He turned to see her, also dressed in black leather, but over black fatigue pants as opposed to the olive drab ones he wore.

"You need to be more alert," she said. "I could have slit your throat."

"But you wouldn't," he said.

"No one is paying me to." She nodded.

"That the only reason?"

Shasti gave him an enigmatic look, her face luminous in the reflection of the ship's undercarriage lights.

"Never mind," he said, a chill stealing through him. "I'll drive. You keep an eye out for trouble."

"Always."

They bounced over the grassy, rutted field, through the warehouse district and into the narrow streets of the true off port, watching for the randomly placed street signs, as there was no computer map of the city of Foosha. The town around them was a riot of color and canopies along with the usual hive-like Morok buildings. A mélange of strange scents came from the mule's vents: alien food, alien smoke, alien farting. *You used to be a merchant*, he reminded himself. *Could eat almost anything and never noticed how anyone smelled.*

There were no traffic controls, and Fenaday drove around or honked through the throng. A few drunken Morok spacers made obscene gestures as the mule splashed through one of the frequent puddles.

Shasti peered about, watching the shifting crowds of apish blue-skinned Moroks, the occasional human, Okaran, Frokossi, or other Confederate species. As usual there was no trace of expression on Shasti's cold, perfect face, but Fenaday got the impression she was enjoying the sights. *Maybe she'll hang her head out the window*, he thought.

"Why are you smiling?" she asked.

He shook his head.

They pulled over in front of a dilapidated warehouse made of local woods and concrete. A sign in neon gave names in Standard and Morok. Reliable Salvage, it said. *Hopefully true*, Fenaday thought.

They walked into the building, Shasti trailing, her eyes alert. Black-haired Moroks in drab coveralls paused in their work to look at the pair. A particularly simian specimen with indigo skin came up to them. "Captain Fenaday," it coughed out in badly accented Confed Standard.

He nodded, then realized the gesture might not mean anything to the alien. "Yes, Captain Fenaday and Commander Rainhell."

"Schul is expecting you. Follow me." It rolled away from them. As they came up to a small room, Fenaday saw a number of Moroks seated around a desk covered with papers, holopads, and machine parts. The skinniest Morok greeted Fenaday, its canines bared in a scary imitation of a human smile. "Welcome, Fenaday." Schul's Confed Standard was far better than his assistant's efforts.

"Greetings, Schul," he replied. "I've got a load for your inspection."

"My buyer will be very interested in seeing them. The rest of the load is somewhere safe?"

"Yeah, I moved them to Warehouse Five." Behind him, Shasti stirred, possibly irritated by his frank reply. "What about those ship parts? When can I see them? Where are they?"

"Now if you like." The Morok stood and gestured for Fenaday to follow them down a narrow corridor leading to the back of the ramshackle building.

"Have him bring them out here," Shasti said.

"They are too large and heavy," Schul said. "Come."

Fenaday stood, the familiar eagerness welling in him. *No, no. I can't let my hopes be raised again.*

They followed the Morok.

"I don't like this," Shasti whispered.

Fenaday shrugged in irritation. He had to see the material. There might be some clue to Lisa's fate.

They ducked under a rolled plastic curtain into a large open space. Tackle of various types hung from the ceiling. A huge tarpaulin covered something in the center of the space.

As they walked forward toward the tarp, Shasti cursed under her breath. "Fenaday," she whispered, "there are a dozen men above us in the catwalks. Don't do anything stupid."

He looked up but could see nothing. *Damn you, Schul*, he thought. *What are you up to?*

Schul reached forward and threw back the tarp. Beneath it sat a wizened old Morok and two younger ones armed with rifles. Warned by Shasti, Fenaday did not twitch. Schul pulled a pistol from atop a crate.

"Please do not move, humans," the old Morok said. "My men are all around."

"We know," Fenaday replied, a cold rage shooting through him. "Why?"

"God moves in mysterious ways. He also uses the instruments of the Enemy against the Dark One," the wizened Morok said, his red eyes fastened on Fenaday's. "Relieve them of their weapons." More Moroks appeared. They seized Shasti's and Fenaday's weapons and hand coms, roughly patting them down and finding a knife and small slug pistol on Shasti. She endured the probing without expression.

It may be an open question whether she'd rather kill them—or me, Fenaday thought. *I walked right into it.*

"The weapons are in Warehouse Five," Schul said.

"Good." The old Morok thumped his ornate white staff. "It is owned by a believer. Send the men to move the weapons, then tell the owner that God needs his sacrifice. He must have a fire."

"All things will be as you wish, Venerated One."

"Who are you?" Fenaday demanded.

One of the young Moroks cursed and raised his rifle. Fenaday thought about dying.

"Wait, Disciple," the old Morok said. "Even creatures of the Enemy are entitled to some respect. We are not barbarians."

"Yes, Venerated One." The other ducked his head.

The old Morok rested his hands on the white staff. "I am the right honorable Volka, Senior Mage of the People on this world."

"What do you want with us?" Fenaday asked.

"Nothing more than has been done. You have brought us weapons we will use in God's work."

"Funny way to treat your supplier," Fenaday said, "bad for return business and spare parts."

"There will be no more business," Volka said. "The devout will drive all foreign influences off our world. We will regain control of our destiny under God's guidance. You have brought us the means, hoping for profit, as have others. But now we have no further need of commerce with the Enemy."

"We're not your enemy," Fenaday said.

"God created my kind in his own image," Volka said. "You are creations of the Anti-God."

"So sorry for existing," Fenaday muttered.

The cleric took the comment seriously. "No need to apologize. It is not your individual fault that you are a creature of the Enemy. I do not hate you, as I do not believe that you have free will. After all, you cannot choose to be one of us."

"Attractive though that might be," Fenaday said.

"To each his own, as you humans say. Are you not from a separatist colony of your own ethnic group, Captain Fenaday? Was not New Eire settled only by your tribe, the Irish? Did you fight no religious wars?

"But enough, I bore your kind no malice so long as you kept your contamination from our worlds, but that is no longer the case."

"What's to be done with them?" their guard asked.

"Hold them till after we secure the weapons in case there are complications. After that, their deaths must be painless and quick in accord with the Taborokassa. Dispose of their bodies near the spaceport. Make it seem the work of robbers." Volka looked at them one last time, his red eyes devoid of any expression Fenaday could read. "I shall pray for your peaceful rest." He stood and turned away.

"I will pray for your soul," Fenaday said. "You'll need it, Holy Man. Satan himself awaits you at the gates of Hell."

Volka paused, hesitated as if he might say something, then walked on.

The guards locked the cell door and held a brief debate about how many of their number were needed. They settled on two, the other four wanting to join the crew heading for the warehouse.

Fenaday leaned against the wall. "You would be entitled to an 'I told you so' at this point."

Shasti was conducting a quick inspection of their room. "No cameras and no sensors."

"Just a three-inch door and two armed guards, with God knows how many more armed Moroks in the compound."

She walked over to him. "We need to get them into the cell. Do you think they would come in if you were pretending to rape me?"

"If they even believed there was any chance I could overpower you, they might either just watch or turn away in disgust. God knows I don't want to see any of them having sex."

"Good," Shasti said. "I will mostly pretend to be beating you to death for getting us into this mess. When they intervene, we turn on them."

"Mostly?" he asked.

"You stupid motherfucker," Shasti screamed, seizing him by the jacket. "I told you it was a trap." She flung Fenaday the length of the cell to crash into the door. In a second she was on him again, hauling him upright and thrusting him into a wall, and he wondered if she was really trying to kill him. "You dumb bastard. We are going to die, and it's your fault." She began swinging wildly, her hand slapping the wall and him alternately. It stung and made a lot of noise. "I hate you," she shrieked. "You stupid Irish piece of shit."

"Help, help," Fenaday yelled. "The crazy bitch is out of her fucking mind." They rolled to the ground. He could see the Moroks looking through a panel in the door. "Help, Volka wanted me alive."

"I'll kill you, you ignorant fuck," Shasti shrieked, wild-eyed. "I hate your guts." She rose and pulled Fenaday up to a standing position, her back to the door.

The Moroks charged in. One came forward, his rifle raised to club the berserk Shasti.

"Die, Fenaday, die," Shasti bellowed, then put a foot in Fenaday's sternum, dropped over backward, and flung him like a two-hundred-pound shot at the door guard. Fenaday slammed into the Morok, and they both crashed into the hallway, dazed. Fenaday struggled to a sitting position in time to see the other guard swing and miss Shasti, who pulled him in and snapped his neck. Suddenly she turned to face Fenaday, raising the rifle and pointing at him.

"Shasti, wait—"

The shot cracked past Fenaday's ear and smacked wetly into the Morok behind Fenaday. The red-eyed alien made no sound as he dropped, his weapon clattering on the ground.

She ran over to him. "Grab his weapon and follow me."

Fenaday scrabbled for the slug-thrower and raced after her.

They burst into the main room where they'd come in. Schul had time for a moment's panic before Shasti shot him. Fenaday hit the guard beyond Schul as Shasti leapt over Schul's body and gunned down the others. She was halfway through the room with Fenaday running flat out to catch up with her when he saw a Morok jump atop the crates at the back of the room.

Fenaday shoved Shasti to one side and fired. He missed. The Morok's return beam didn't. It lanced through his jacket, and he fell, his right arm and chest suddenly numb and unresponsive. *I'm hit,* he thought, *I'm hit.* He barely felt the floor as he tumbled onto it. He heard Shasti curse and fire, followed by a choked, guttural cry. *Of course, she wouldn't miss, would she?*

Her beautiful face slipped into his field of view, and he concentrated on it. The numb was beginning to fade to be replaced by burning pain. He realized she was tearing open his jacket and the shirt beneath. "Fool," she said. "I'm faster than you. I'd have spotted him."

"You know," he coughed out, "you really are an ungrateful bitch."

To his surprise, she smiled for the first time that he could recall. "Yes, I suppose I am. That's twice you've tried to save me."

"Tried my ass," he said in feigned outrage. "I plucked you off a slaver and that gunman was behind you."

"I guess I am not used to saying thank you," she said, spraying wound seal and anesthetic into his burn. She produced a small flask from under her vest. "Burn fluid," she said. "Drink it all and it will help with the shock."

"What, no scotch to wash it down with?"

"It wouldn't be—"

"Joking, Shasti, joking." He downed the fluid, full of electrolytes and healing agents. "It tastes god-awful."

"Can you walk?"

Fenaday tried to sit up, and the universe swam. He collapsed back. Shasti caught his head before it smacked on the floor. He drew a deep breath. "You'd better get going."

"That would be practical," she said. "My chances of escaping with a wounded man are very poor."

"Very," he said.

"Very," she repeated. "Perhaps as bad as your chances of ever finding your wife."

"About that lousy."

"Just so you know." She reached forward and with little effort pulled him to his feet and then onto her shoulders. He gasped as his weight came onto the burn and he felt the wound leak despite the air-seal. He grayed out for a second but managed to hang onto his laser.

"Don't shoot me in the leg," Shasti said.

"Nice that you have such confidence in me," he said.

Shasti started forward. If Fenaday's two hundred pounds troubled her, she didn't show it. He gripped his laser tightly and tried hard not to pass out.

Shasti set the dead Morok's laser to narrow beam and cut through a door lock, heading for the loading dock. She saw the mule there. *They must have moved it here to keep it out of sight,* she thought. *Good, that's what I would have done.* Checking the dock area quickly, she sprinted over and almost threw Fenaday in the side door, then raced around to the other side and leapt in. A harsh guttural voice yelled, and a shot cracked. Shasti fired through the mule's windscreen. The plastiglass scattered some of the laser, but enough ripped through to set a Morok guard on fire. Shasti gunned the small mule, charging for the rolled metal doorway. Fenaday rolled down his window to peg shots at Morok fanatics. Return fire spidered the bulletproof plastiglass and blew chunks of metal off the mule.

"Brace," Shasti shouted as the mule hit the garage door. It came off its roller and smacked down into the street beyond, scattering bewildered civilians. Gunfire pursued them, hitting several pedestrians. The soldiers of God seemed indifferent to collateral damage. Shasti cut up onto sidewalks and sped around traffic, heading for the port. A fanatic on a hoverbike started after them, only to be broadsided by a car dodging Shasti.

"The gauge," Fenaday rasped.

"What?" she snapped, focused on dodging a neon-lit hovertruck.

"Heat gauge," he said. "It's peaking. They must have damaged something."

"Damn." As if to confirm his statement, the mule began emitting horrible grinding noises. Shasti kept the machine floored for another three kilometers before smoke billowed out from the small hood and she ditched it in a small alley. She helped Fenaday stagger out from his side of the machine.

"Go on," he said, leaning against the wall. "Get back to the ship. I'll make my own way. I'm the one who screwed up and got us into this."

Shasti briefly debated it. Alone, she might draw off pursuit. Abruptly she realized what he was doing. "You'll never make it alone. You know that. You persist in being concerned about my life. Why? What am I to you?"

He looked at her. "What do you have to be?"

She shook her head. "Standard human, you're a mystery to me. No one from my people would sacrifice themselves. To lose is to be proven unworthy."

"We all lose some time." His eyes fluttered, and he sank against the wall. Shasti caught him and tucked his weapon into her belt, then hoisted him onto her shoulders. "If we're not killed, there may be something you can teach me, Fenaday."

Holding her laser in one hand, Shasti started out for the port. She followed her training from her earliest days on Olympia, cleaving to shadows, waiting for distractions in order to move through open spaces. She kept her weapon out of sight, hoping to be taken for a spacer helping a drunken friend back to the port. She debated whether to seek help from a passing patrol craft but couldn't bring herself to trust them. They might be infiltrated by the fanatics or they might be curious about *Sidhe* and her cargo. Either could be equally lethal.

Gradually Shasti made her way to the field. *Sidhe* sat at the far end. A dozen other ships dotted the grass and hard-packed earth of the spacefield. Most were insystem Morok vessels, two were legitimate freighters from the Kenowa line. No help there.

She opted for an indirect approach in the grasslands, hoping the waist-high orange and gold foliage would supply cover. The jungle beyond the grasslands would supply better concealment, but Fenaday's weight was beginning to wear her down.

Shasti shifted Fenaday a little higher on her shoulders; he groaned in response. She started out, slipping between the two farthest warehouses, then into the grassy fields beyond. As she moved around a low hill, something slammed into her arm. An instant later, the sound of the shot caught up to the bullet. She spun, dropping them both into the grass. Fenaday sprawled, unconscious or dead. She checked her arm. The sleeve of the body armor she wore under her clothes had stopped the bullet, but her arm hung numb. Her genetically enhanced body was already shrugging off the pain. In a few minutes, the arm would function again. Meanwhile her enemies would find she shot equally well off either hand.

Shasti crawled forward, reluctant to leave Fenaday but needing to deal with these new enemies. She moved slowly through the tall grass, reaching with all her senses. Her hypersensitive nose and ears brought her clues—three, possibly four Moroks. Not city folk from the way they moved through the grasses. Hunters, spreading out and heading for where she'd dropped Fenaday. She needed to reduce the odds, quickly.

Shasti holstered the laser and slid forward on all fours, her arm already recovering from the blow. She selected the noisiest of her attackers for a target. A minute's stalk brought her near the Morok. Shasti froze as the stocky blue figure slipped through the grass. She gathered herself panther-like, staring at his weapon, not his face, hoping to avoid triggering his senses. He stepped forward and stumbled on the uneven ground.

Shasti leapt. His startled shot went wide. Then she was on him, carrying them both to the ground. As he snatched for his knife, she drove stiffened fingers deep into his eyes. The Morok shrieked. She put a kagi hold on his knife hand, wrenched the blade away, and slammed it into his brain. Seizing his weapon, she ducked behind the corpse and fired bursts into the grass at waist height toward the sounds made by his charging companions. She heard one cry, then return fire thudded into the corpse she lay behind. Shasti pulled the knife out and scrambled away. She came up for a quick look only to confront a Morok ten meters away. His laser crisped the grass between them. Shasti's shot hit his weapon, breaking off the stock. The Morok dropped before she could fire again.

Shasti backed away from the spreading flames ignited by the laser. She looked westward, where she could see the tall tail fin of *Sidhe* and safety. *I can make it if I leave Fenaday*, she thought, even as she made her way back toward him. She wondered if his stubborn posturing had worn off on her. *Standard human*, she thought, *you owe me big time.*

She jumped up and took another shot at her pursuers and again a laser licked out at her. Suddenly she heard a flurry of shots and a scream, then silence. Shasti waited.

"Thor," a voice called out. "Thor."

"Mjolnir." She shouted the counter password back, slowly coming out of her crouch. The Tok brothers, Hanshi and Lokashti, rose out of the grass. "There were three more. Did you get them all?"

Hanshi, the bigger of the Morok brothers, nodded. "We were patrolling near the warehouses and heard the shots. I spotted you and we came running."

"Good. Get over here and help me with the captain. He's been shot."

———

Fenaday awoke in the familiar cool grays and blues of his cabin on the *Sidhe*. A quick look out the armored viewpoint of his cabin told him they were still on Morokat.

"How are you feeling?" The ship's physician, a nervous old man named Rinaldi, blinked at him.

"Like shit on a stick," Fenaday answered. "Is Shasti all right?"

"Yes," she said, walking into sight.

Rinaldi looked up at her and backed away. "See, I told you, a little surgery and three hours under a regenerator and he's almost as good as new."

"Excellent," she said. "Then you get to live."

He gulped. "You should have left him in the sickbay."

"Go back to the sickbay," she replied. "Wipe all records of this. Officially Fenaday never left the ship. Mention this to anyone, and I will feed you into the main reactor."

Rinaldi left hastily.

"Making friends and influencing people?" he asked.

"You are faring better than some of his former patients. Considering his record, I wanted to be sure he was motivated to stay focused."

"Shasti."

"Yes?"

"Thank you."

She looked uncomfortable for a moment, then leaned forward, gazing into his eyes. "Obstinate man, you interest me. Searching for your wife against all logic. Urging me to abandon you and look out for myself. How many more times do you think you can offer up your life before the universe takes it?"

"Maybe the universe is entitled to it for some of what I've done."

"I don't understand."

"If I don't stop him," Fenaday said, wincing as he sat up, "Volka will start a religious uprising against off-worlders and the Morok government, using weapons I sold him."

"But," Shasti said as she sat back to gaze out the rain-splattered viewport, "he'll pray for our souls afterward."

"Somebody should."

Shasti turned to face him. "You believe that you have one?"

He sat quietly, looking beyond her at the rain. The port was far too dense for the sound of the storm to penetrate, but lightning flickered, illuminating half of Shasti's face. "I hope so," he whispered. "I sure hope so.

"And you," he asked. "What do you believe?"

She looked away, then shrugged. "What do you plan to do? Go to the authorities?"

"And end up in a dank Morok cell? The local government is inept and corrupt and probably riddled with Volka's followers. No, I have to stop Volka, and I have to do it tonight."

"By yourself?" she asked.

"There are so few in the crew I can trust. I can only think of one."

"Yes," she said leaning against the bulkhead. "Sounds like you could use the services of a trained assassin. Fortunately, I just happen to be one."

"If you're in?" He tried to see her half-shadowed face.

"No you, no *Sidhe*, no job for me."

"Sound logic," he said.

"I anticipated you could not leave well enough alone," Shasti said. "While you were in surgery, I sent the Toks to find the owner of Warehouse Five. He is perhaps less devout than Volka imagined. He seemed unenthusiastic about fanatics burning down his warehouse or having his limbs sawed off by Hanshi. I have coordinates for the gathering place of the faithful. They will meet there for evening prayer."

"I feel like a little religion myself tonight, Old Testament style."

"Certainly," she replied, standing. "I'll prepare the flyer and two jetbelts."

———

Johan Gunnar, from Shasti's trouble team, flew *Sidhe's* four-seat aircar to within two kilometers of Volka's jungle compound. Shasti and Fenaday stepped out of the flyer in their short-range flying belts and zipped along at tree-top height. Maps extracted from their reluctant informant glowed green on the inner screens of their helmets. An evening storm strobed around them, and the rumble of thunder covered the small sound of the jetpacks.

They came upon the walled compound of the faithful with its scores of poor shacks and tents.

"These guys can always get the have-nots ready to kill the haves," Fenaday muttered.

Shasti signaled him, and they split, heading for their separate targets.

Fenaday continued on to where the warehouse owner said the armaments were stored. With typical Morok disregard for rules, the ordnance lay piled in one wing of what had been an old church. Fenaday flew up to the window. Just as he neared it, a Morok in priestly robes looked out. His mouth opened in astonishment, but no sound came out. Fenaday gave the belt all its remaining power and cannoned into him. The priest and Fenaday tumbled into the silent church with a crash.

———

Shasti landed on a minaret-like tower and slipped out of her jetbelt and into her old role as an assassin. *This is almost literally what I was made for,* she thought bitterly. *Not that anyone offered me any choices.* She tied the exhausted jetbelt to the roof eaves and set its timer to eliminate the evidence. Her fingers found purchase in the roof's rain slick surface, and she froze every time lightning flickered. Using small hooks in her gloves and boots, she maneuvered her way to a window and slid into the building.

Out of the rain, she threw back her hood, struggling slightly with her overly long hair. *Not too practical,* she thought. But the hair was a private defiance of hers. Free of the rain, she adjusted her equipment then strained her senses, picking up faint rhythmic noises and the scent of incense.

Excellent, she thought. *They are still talking to their God. Tonight they will get answers.* She padded along the hallway heading to the balcony above the main chapel. According to their contact, Volka always conducted a last prayer service with his faithful inner seven.

Prayers and incense both grew stronger, and Shasti found herself in a dark wooden hallway, over a chapel, which featured a fountain of pulsing lights and rushing water. Volka sat on a cushion. His seven sat on ornate rugs.

Shasti pulled both lasers from their holsters and sighted. The laser's red beams danced and hissed among Volka's inner circle. In seconds they fell, only barely aware of what was killing them.

Only Volka remained seated. He stared up at Shasti as she dropped from the balcony to the chapel floor. "So it seems the Almighty has other plans for me." His red eyes focused on her green ones.

"Ah." Shasti smiled over her laser. "Am I now an instrument of the Almighty?"

"We all are. Even the Enemy bows to the will of God and serves him indirectly."

"One cannot argue with logic like that," Shasti said.

"Still," the cleric mused. "I did not believe that I could be stopped by any creature born in our universe. A demon perhaps—"

"Let me ease your mind as you step into the infinite. I'll share my little secret with you."

"What?" Volka asked.

"I wasn't born," Shasti said and pulled the trigger.

———

Fenaday huffed, his wound leaking from hitting the priest, who lay with his neck canted at an odd angle. He pulled his laser and scanned for other enemies, then placed charges on the crates of weapons. Hitting the timer, he hobbled away as fast as he could, virtually falling out the second-story window. Fenaday barely cleared the window before the explosives went off. He scrambled into a nearby runoff ditch, partly filled with water, as the air filled with metal and wood splinters from secondary blasts among the ammunition.

Fenaday could feel the heat of a fireball sweep over him as he started crawling toward the pickup point, the pain of his wound forgotten. Shouts and screams sounded as Moroks ran hysterically to and fro. Another blast cut down the running figures. More screams and panic.

A vehicle whined to a stop near Fenaday. He whipped up his laser, then paused as he spotted Shasti and Gunnar in the aircar. Gunnar's auto pistol stuttered as he laid down fire with one hand still on the controls.

"Come on," Shasti yelled. He gathered himself and dove through the door, landing face down in her lap as she fired over his back. Gunnar cursed and spun the wheel as the compound shuddered and belched flame from every window and door. The small flyer sprang up to tree-top level to flee back to *Sidhe*.

Fenaday rolled over in Shasti's lap, looking up at her beautiful, remote expression.

"Comfortable?" she asked.

"Very," he said. "I could get used to this."

She didn't smile, but something told him she was amused. Or maybe it was just having the chance to blow things up.

"Home, Johan," Shasti said. "I think we've worn out our welcome on Morokat."

———

Ambassador Caroline Degas walked into a small office in the basement of the Confederate Embassy on Morokat. The office was far less impressive than her own, but there was absolutely no question of relative power between her and the occupant of this temporary space.

"Ambassador," said the sturdy, genial dark-skinned man seated behind the plain desk. Two ASAT troopers, his personal guards, stood behind him.

"Mr. Mandela." Degas nodded. She suspected it was not the spymaster's real name. "Things have gone rather differently than you planned."

"They so often do," Mandela said. "Please proceed with your report."

"The privateer you were hoping to put out of business seems to have been more formidable than you expected. He and that Amazon shadow of his have killed Volka and his inner circle. They've also destroyed the weapons."

"Well, the glass is half full," Mandela replied. "I had hoped Volka's rebellion would be prematurely triggered with the weapons Fenaday brought. Then we would quickly crush it with the ASAT teams and Mariner raider battalions I have in nearspace, cementing the Morok Conglomerate into the Confederacy. The Conchirri War will be ending soon. We have to plan ahead to the peace."

"The boys won't be sorry," the Morok behind Mandela said. "Fewer casualties for the 71st and the job's done anyway."

"Quiet, Rask," the human trooper said.

Mandela shrugged. "That's all right, Sergeant Rigg. Rask is right. The job's done. We shall have to keep an eye on Mr. Fenaday and his lethal associate. It may be that Robert is destined for greater things."

Degas raised an eyebrow. "You sound as if you know him."

Mandela grimaced. "His wife. Lisa Fenaday worked for me."

"Past tense?"

"Her ship went missing in action," Rigg said.

"A loss to the Confederacy," Mandela said. "She was one of the most promising agents I ever had until I lost her to him. One must admire his single-minded tenacity in searching for her. It's one reason I haven't had his ship blown out from under him for his many violations of Confederate law.

"Yes, I must keep an eye on her husband. He could be very, very useful…"

The End

Follow Shasti's solo adventure in Hidden Stars
And
Her appearances in the Maauro series set in Confed Space decades later.

Also by Edward McKeown

The Maauro Chronicles

My Outcast State

Against That Time

The Lost

All The Difference

When Fighting Monsters

The Shasti and Fenaday Chronicles

Was Once A Hero

Fearful Symmetry

Points of Departure

Hidden Stars

Sha'Daa Series

Tales of the Apocalypse

Toys

Inked

Pawns

Last Call

Facets

The Lair of the Lesbian Love Goddess Files

On the Case

Other Works

Knight in Charlotte